Livin' in High Cotton

Livin' in High Cotton

Jennifer Leigh Youngblood
& Sandra Poole

Mapletree Publishing Company
Denver, Colorado

Printed in the United States of America
08 07 06 05 04   1 2 3 4 5

Cover design by Tamara Deaver, www.tlcgraphics.com

Library of Congress Cataloging-in-Publication Data

Youngblood, Jennifer Leigh,
  Livin' in high cotton / by Jennifer Leigh Youngblood and Sandra
Poole.
    p. cm.
  ISBN 0-9728071-4-4 (softcover)
  1. Georgia—Fiction. 2. Alabama—Fiction. I. Poole, Sandra,
II. Title.
  PS3625.O974L585 2004
  813'.6—dc22
                          2003027762   CIP

Printed on acid-free paper.

Mapletree Publishing Company
Denver, Colorado 80130
800-537-0414
e-mail: mail@mapletreepublishing.com
www.mapletreepublishing.com
The Mapletree logo is a trademark of Mapletree Publishing Company

Acknowledgments

We would like to express our appreciation to the following: First and foremost, our families, and especially our husbands, for their continued patience and support during the writing of *Livin' in High Cotton*. Robert L. Farmer, Sandra's father and Jennifer's grandfather, for sharing his memories and experiences with us. Our publisher, Dave Hall, for his encouragement and guidance. Our editor, Kenya Transtrum, who recognized the novel's potential from the very beginning and worked tirelessly to help make it better. And all those at Mapletree Publishing, whose combined efforts have brought this project to fruition. Shelby and Christy Edwards, Page Hopkins, and Karen Milan, who read the manuscript and offered their advice.

Livin' in High Cotton

Chapter One

Cartersville, Georgia
1923

Down South, things don't ever change all that much and that suits most Southerners just fine. Every year, cotton seeds are planted deep in the red, fertile clay in the hope that come harvest time, the stalks will be loaded with lush, white blooms. And why shouldn't the cotton grow abundantly? It has done so every fall for centuries, providing the life-sustaining bread and butter of the South. Life travels comfortably down a smooth road, and just when the complacent traveler is convinced of the outcome, a bend in the road changes everything.

It's strange, how the day that forever changed Shelby's life began the same as any other day. Had she known what lay ahead, she wouldn't have wasted the better part of her morning listening to the petty rambling of Mrs. Joyce Clements. Shelby had barely gotten Homer and Sarah fed and dressed when she heard a knock at the door. Homer had eagerly run to open it.

"I'll get it."

Before she could stop him, he swung it wide, and the whiny voice of Mrs. Clements filled the hall.

Wiping her hands on her apron, Shelby looked around the kitchen; it was in total disarray. Why did she have to come by today? Shelby had promised to take Homer and Sarah swimming at the creek later on in the day, and she had a long list of chores to do first. She could get everything done in plenty of time if she hurried, but the last thing she needed was to have to entertain Mrs. Clements for several hours. She had already been by twice this week and it was only Thursday. Tuesday, her excuse had been to inquire if Shelby had heard any news from Ellen yet, but Shelby knew the real reason she dropped by unexpectedly. She wanted to find something wrong with the way Shelby was handling things while her mama was away. Shelby glanced at the mess in the kitchen. The sink was piled high with dirty pans and dishes. Sarah had decided that it would be more fun to smear her grits and eggs all over the table rather than eat them. Biscuit crumbs were scattered over the wooden floor.

"I'm going to give that ol' biddy a mouthful to talk about today," Shelby muttered under her breath. "Why couldn't she have waited about thirty minutes to come? I would've had this mess cleaned up by then."

Mrs. Clements followed Homer and Sarah impatiently down the hall toward the kitchen. "Where is your sister? Well, good morning, Shelby." Her arched eyebrows gazed around the kitchen, taking in every detail. "It looks as if you're getting off to a late start."

Shelby felt her face flush and her temperature rise. How dare this woman come barging in and then have the nerve to criticize her? Two things Shelby detested were nosy people and gossips. Joyce Clements, with her constant babbling and haughty air, was both. Once Shelby had candidly told Mama this and had gotten a reproving glance followed by a gentle reminder that one should not judge others. "Joyce has had a difficult time since Henry passed away last fall. She can be a little overbearing at times, but we might be the same if we had to walk in her shoes."

Remembering how Mrs. Clements' pudgy feet always seemed to be stuffed into her shoes, causing fleshy ripples across the top, Shelby had retorted, "Hopefully, I'll never be big enough to walk in her shoes." As soon as she uttered the words, she saw the color drain from Mama's face and quickly apologized for the remark. Since that day, she had tried to be kinder in her thoughts toward Mrs. Clements. Most of the time her persistence paid off, and she was able to view the woman's offensive and intrusive behavior in a comical light. Today, however, she was in no mood to be tolerant. *I must at least try to be civil out of respect for Mama*, she told herself. I'm probably just being overly sensitive because I want to do a good job of taking care of things while Mama is gone.

She took a deep breath and smiled. "Mrs. Clements, I can take care of these dirty dishes later. Why don't you go and have a seat in the parlor? I'll make us some lemonade."

Mrs. Clements nodded, but her feet stayed rooted to the floor. She had something to say first. "Look at my feet. They're so swollen. I just come from Mabel Whitaker's place. It's awful the way Mabel carries on 'bout Linda Joyce, always fussin' over her while her boys run around like wild Indians. She'll fill the washtub and set it out in the sun and let the water get just right for Linda Joyce. She'll wash her from head to toe and then she'll holler for Junior." Mrs. Clements' voice became shrill as she mimicked Mabel. "Come here, Junior. Let me wash your face." Mrs. Clements laughed. "Of course Junior runs up the nearest tree and hides. Cain't say as I blame 'im. I wouldn't want my face washed with the same rag that just washed Linda Joyce's rear end."

Shelby chuckled despite herself. Mrs. Clements' face puckered up like she'd bitten into a sour pickle. She shook her head. "Shame—such a shame. Them children runnin' wild."

Homer tugged on Shelby. "Sarah hit me on the arm."

Instead of reprimanding Sarah, Shelby decided to divert Homer's attention. "Would you take Sarah outside to play for a little bit?"

"But Shelby," he protested, "you said you would let us go swimming at the creek."

"I will, but you have to mind me," she said, giving him a look of warning that dared him to protest any further.

Mrs. Clements glared disapprovingly at Homer. "Children should spend more time workin'. Reverend Dobbs says that idle hands are tools of the devil."

Homer's eyes widened. "I ain't no devil."

"Hush now," Shelby interjected. "Mind your manners. Go on outside."

Firmly, she guided Homer out the back door with Sarah in tow. "Make sure you keep a good eye on Sarah," she yelled after them.

When Shelby brought the lemonade into the parlor, she wasn't surprised to find Mrs. Clements next to the china cabinet, scrutinizing each piece of silver. Seeing Shelby enter the room, she sat down on the couch directly across from Shelby and reached for a glass of lemonade, shaking her head in dismay. "Every time I come into this room, I wonder why in the world Ellen chose to paint it such a peculiar color."

"Mama loves flowers. We chose the rose color in here because this is where we do most of our entertaining and we wanted it warm and vibrant."

"Yes, it certainly is that," Mrs. Clements smirked.

Shelby ignored the comment. "We even dyed our curtains a hint of rose to match. White walls are so boring. Don't you think?" With a hint of mischief in her eyes, she continued. "After all, what fun is it trying to be just like everyone else?" She looked steadily at her visitor and waited for a reply.

Mrs. Clements shifted uncomfortably in her seat. "Well, it is different," she replied, her face slightly reddening. She quickly changed the subject. "Shelby, this lemonade tastes a bit too tart. How many lemons did you use?"

"Three."

"Yes, that explains it. Next time use only two and add an extra fourth cup of sugar."

Shelby politely smiled and nodded at her plump, middle-aged guest and tried to seem interested in their conversation. *Had Mrs. Clements been attractive in her younger years?* She doubted it. Her straight, mousy-brown hair was now streaked with gray and her squinty eyes framed by tiny wrinkles. The plaid dress she was wearing looked stylish and expensive. It had probably looked beautiful in the Sears and Roebuck Catalog, but on Mrs. Clements it looked all wrong. The waistband was too tight and only emphasized her expansive waist. Gold buttons accented the top of the dress, and Shelby had the distinct impression that any sudden or jerky movement would cause them to pop off. She stifled a grin.

"Have you heard any news from your mother yet?"

"No, ma'am."

"Land sakes, it's been two whole weeks since she left. One would think she would be wanting to make sure you young 'uns are doing all right."

The comment struck a nerve. "I'm sure Mama has been extremely busy trying to take care of Gramma. She would not have gone all the way to Alabama on such short notice if Gramma hadn't been so sick."

"Oh, of course, dear," cooed Mrs. Clements. "I didn't mean to imply otherwise. I was only suggesting that this situation must be very difficult for you children and your papa. How is he managing in Ellen's absence?"

"Fine," Shelby answered curtly. *As long as he's not drunk or angry*, she wanted to add.

"Good. I just hope we can receive word soon of when she'll be returning."

Shelby nodded in agreement and smiled politely, saying nothing. *Yes, Mama could not return soon enough.*

*   *   *   *   *

The afternoon sun streamed through the kitchen window and down onto the brightly scrubbed kitchen floor. Shelby wiped her hair from her forehead and leaned against the wall to rest. Mrs. Clement had talked incessantly for two straight hours. After she had repeated every last scrap of the latest town gossip she could think of, she gave Shelby advice.

"Now, Shelby, you had better watch yourself. A pretty, young lady such as yourself should be extra careful not to get too friendly with the men folk. They might get the wrong idea. Take it from me. I know."

With a sigh of relief, Shelby wrung out the mop and put it away. The kitchen was clean. Now all she had to do was dust the parlor before they could go swimming. Mrs. Clements' warning was still running through her mind. Shelby found it interesting that Mrs. Clements would describe her as pretty. At sixteen, Shelby was barely five feet tall and very slender. Her dark, chestnut hair was caught at the nape of her neck, making her almond-shaped eyes even more prominent. She picked up the feather duster and walked into the parlor and over to the fireplace. Shelby stood on her toes and peered into the mirror hanging over the mantle. Critically, she studied her reflection as she wrinkled her nose. She had never given her physical appearance much thought, only making sure she was properly dressed and well kept. Lately, though, more people were paying attention to her looks. When had the change occurred? Even Mama had noticed. She had pulled Shelby aside and told her that while it was a blessing to have good looks on the outside, it was more important to be beautiful on the inside. "Just remember that pretty is as pretty does," she had said.

Her heart clutched. The intrusive questions Mrs. Clements had asked about her mother's absence had left Shelby unsettled. She wondered why they hadn't heard from her. *Has something bad happened to Gramma?* With each passing day of Mama's absence, things seemed to get a little worse. Papa had been okay the first couple of days after she left, and then his disposition turned sour. He seemed nervous and irritable. Homer and Sarah seemed to get on his nerves by just being there. Last night, Shelby had seen him staring at her in that weird way again, the way he had since she was thirteen. It made her skin crawl. Mama, with her genteel manner and quiet way, had always been the rock that held everything in place. And Shelby's protection. *What would happen now that she was gone?*

"Shelby!" Homer yelled impatiently. "Are we ever going to go swimming?"

"Yes, get Sarah and come and help me finish up so we will have time before Papa gets home."

*　　*　　*　　*　　*

After carefully placing her stockings aside, Shelby raised her skirt to her knees and lay back on the grassy creek-side and breathed deeply. The air felt moist against her skin, and a slight breeze was blowing. She closed her eyes and let the warmth of the sun envelop her. It was a perfect afternoon. A bird was chirping somewhere in the distance, and the playful laughter of Homer and Sarah mingled pleasantly with the soothing sound of flowing water.

She sat up and watched the two of them. Homer, not quite seven, was quickly becoming a little man. More than occasionally, neighbors and acquaintances remarked how he resembled Papa with his chestnut brown hair and hazel eyes. Smiling, Shelby remembered how Homer always straightened himself a little taller and jutted out his prominent chin when he heard these comments. Sarah was three and a half and sharp as a tack. Little blonde ringlets framed her chubby cheeks. Despite her stocky frame, she was always running behind her trim, older brother mimicking his every movement. "I can do it!" seemed her favorite expression.

Homer glanced over and realized that Shelby was watching him and Sarah. "Shelby, why don't you get in the water with us?" he asked.

"Please," Sarah chimed in.

"Okay, but you two had better not get my hair wet." Shelby looked sternly at the two surprised expressions and then winked. Jumping up, she ran to the edge and began splashing them both.

"This is war!" shouted Homer.

Some time later, three drenched siblings gathered their things and headed for home. Impulsively, Homer leaned over and hugged Shelby. "I love you. You're the greatest big sister in the whole world."

Touched by his sudden display of affection, Shelby hugged him back as she tousled his wavy hair. "You're not so bad yourself, little man."

*　　*　　*　　*　　*

Glad to finally have some time for herself, Shelby sighed and sank deeper into the thick cushion of the wooden swing on the front porch. The air felt cool and fresh and tasted like the honeysuckles growing along the fence. She swung back and forth, listening to the creaking sound of the swing and the rhythmical chirping of crickets.

The swim had sufficiently tired Homer and Sarah, and after supper they went to bed without complaint. Homer had wanted to kiss Papa good night first, but Shelby insisted that he could see him tomorrow. She had thought about going to bed early herself but feared Papa's wrath too much. No, he would expect her to serve his supper just like Mama always did. She swallowed the dread that crept into her throat. Feeling a sudden chill, she shuddered and wrapped her arms around herself as she gazed across the yard.

Even in the semi-darkness, Ellen's talent for gardening was apparent. Rhododendron and azalea bushes were planted near the house and were bordered by colorful, daisies, tulips, and marigolds. The grass was a lush blanket of green; dogwood, persimmon, oak, and sycamore trees filled the spacious yard. The sycamores grew so tall she used to pretend they touched the sky. Shelby looked up at the huge, leafy branches in wonder and up to the black, velvety sky beyond. It seemed as though the trees were stretching out their long branches in a protective gesture over the home.

For as long as she could remember, she had lived in this house. Some Sundays, she had accompanied her mama and a few of the other ladies from church to deliver food to needy members of the community. She had been shocked by the run-down and battered-looking homes. One even had a dirt floor. Before these visits, she had assumed everyone else lived the same way she did. Running her finger over the grainy, wooden swing, she looked at the massive porch, wrapping around the two-story home with its large, picture windows and white, picket fence. Mama's words flashed through her mind. "Children, we should be ever thankful for the tremendous bounty the good Lord has bestowed on us."

Emotion welled in her breast. "I'm trying to be, Mama," she said aloud. Homer's voice rang out, disturbing the stillness of the evening. Suppressing a flash of irritation, Shelby quickly got up from the swing and ran up the stairs into Homer's room. Homer was crying and tossing back and forth in his bed.

"What's wrong? Homer, are you okay?" Shelby leaned over and nudged him. He was still half asleep.

"I want my mama. Please come back," he wailed.

Shelby sat down on the bed and gathered Homer in her arms. She pulled him close and gently stroked his hair as he sobbed. Then becoming somewhat embarrassed, he pulled away and wiped his tear-stained face. "When is Mama coming home?" he sniffed.

"Soon, Homer."

"I was having a bad dream."

"It's okay. We all have them sometimes."

Homer nodded. "But this one seemed so real I—"

"You can tell me. It's nothing to be afraid of."

"I dreamed that Mama disappeared."

Tucking him in and pulling his sheet up around him, Shelby sat on the edge of the bed and patted his arm. "Mama just went away for a little while to take care of Gramma."

"I know. I know that," said Homer emphatically. "It's just that..."

"What?"

Homer tilted his face upward and looked pleadingly into Shelby's eyes. "I dreamed that you disappeared, too. I looked everywhere for you, but you were gone."

A sudden fear seized Shelby and then quickly faded. "Don't be silly," she answered flippantly. "Wherever would I go without you?"

Shelby's answer gave Homer the reassurance he needed. He snuggled under his covers and grinned sheepishly. "I guess it was just a silly old dream."

Shelby winked. "That's right. Now you'd better get some sleep."

Both Homer and Shelby jumped when they heard a booming voice from downstairs. "Shelby! Girl! Where are you?"

His eyes widening, Homer exclaimed, "Papa's home! Shelby you won't tell Papa I've been crying, will you?"

Was that fear she saw in Homer's eyes? Did he sense the change in Papa too? She wished that she could crawl in bed with Homer and hide. "It will be our little secret," she whispered as she blew him a kiss and turned off the lamp.

She rushed down the stairs and into the kitchen, trying to ignore the sudden pounding in her chest. The disheveled appearance of Papa staggering around the kitchen with his sweaty forehead and shirt untucked caused her to stop dead in her tracks. He looked so haggard she barely recognized him.

"Whur've ya been, Girl!"

"I—"

"Answer me!" He grabbed her by the collar and pulled her roughly to him. Then suddenly he let her go and turned and slammed his fist down on the table. Wearily, he slumped into the chair and clumsily attempted to remove his shoes.

Never before had Shelby seen her papa in such a state. He always took great pride in his appearance. Realization dawned. He was drunk. Mama was always pestering him about his drinking and had forbid him to ever come home drunk. Only on one other occasion had Shelby ever seen Papa drunk, and that had been like witnessing hell's fury. Swallowing hard, Shelby attempted to compose herself. She smoothed her rumpled skirt and went over to the stove.

"Papa, I made some ham, pinto beans, and cornbread. I left yours in the skillet. I'll fix you a plate." With a shaky hand, she placed his supper and milk in front of him and quickly turned to leave.

"Good night, Papa." Before she could walk away, he grabbed her arm and spun her around. "What's your hurry?"

"It's been a long day, and I'm tired. Besides, Mama always says"

He slammed his hand down on the table, causing her to flinch. "Durn you! Your mama ain't here, is she?"

"No. I—"

He reached out and pushed a strand of hair from her face. The look in his eyes made her shrink back. "But you are." Gruffly he placed his arm around her waist and pulled her onto his lap. "Why don't you sit in my lap?"

Shelby felt a surge of panic. "Don't you think I'm a little old for that?"

He held her hands behind her back and placed his mouth next to her ear. His lips felt moist and repulsive. "Not fer what I have in mind."

She could smell the stale odor of liquor on his breath, mingled with sweat. Struggling to free herself, she tried to keep her voice even as she spoke. "Please, Papa. Please let me go."

Throwing back his head, he let out a loud cackle that echoed through the room. He loosened his grip, and Shelby managed to break away from him. She ran for the back door, but he was faster. He pushed her into the stove and began rubbing his hands over her shoulders. Shelby felt revulsion rise and fought the urge to retch. Now his lips were grazing her neck. On the brink of utter despair, Shelby experienced an instant of clarity and felt a sudden burst of anger. Reaching out over the stove, she grasped the handle of the cast-iron skillet, her knuckles white, and hit him over the head with all of her might.

His eyes registered surprise and then narrowed into small slits of molten lava, threatening to explode. "You little hussy. You'll pay dearly for that," he said as he staggered backward, trying to regain his balance.

Shelby hit him again with the skillet, this time using both hands, the sound making a sickening thud as it struck. He fell to the floor, and she hit him again and again. Silence filled the room as Shelby looked at the still figure on the floor. Dropping the skillet, Shelby put her hand over her mouth and backed away, her body shaking violently. A scream tore through the room, and Shelby realized it had come from her. She turned and ran blindly out the kitchen door into the darkness.

Chapter Two

The kitchen chair looked too small for Joshua's bulky frame. He leaned back, causing it to creak in protest as he contentedly patted his round belly and stretched his long legs underneath the table. He smiled broadly. "Sister, if you keep making those fried apple pies of yours, I ain't gonna be able to fit in none o' my britches," he drawled.

"Oh Joshua, you've been the same size for years," she replied reproachfully, but a smile played at her lips.

At six-foot-three, Joshua easily stood several inches above most people. He had always been proud of his big, strong frame. And his size had served him well over the years. He was a farmer—accustomed to rigorous, back-breaking work. Farming was not for the weak, and even Joshua, despite his expertise and knowledge of his work, had experienced his own share of poor harvests, resulting in long, lean winters fraught with worry over the bills. Even though it was still too early in the summer to tell for certain, he felt in his bones that this fall harvest would be abundant. If so, maybe there would be enough money to buy some new tools and a heavy coat for Sister.

"You are grinning like a possum. What are you mulling through that big head of yours?"

Smiling, Joshua looked at his wife of twenty years with unabashed affection. Throughout the hardships of farm life, she had been by his side, supporting him and urging him on without complaint. He shook his head in amazement as he always did when he thought about the life he and Sister shared. Lucille Ann Collins was her real name, but everyone in town knew her as Sister. She had been given the nickname by her older brother, and it had stuck. Barely five-foot-four-inches tall, she was petite and had been slender in her younger years but was starting to collect a little weight around her middle section.

"Look at me, Joshua," she complained on occasion. "I look like a pumpkin."

"You look beautiful," he would answer reassuringly, and he meant it. Although it was true she did not have the flashy good looks many considered attractive, Sister possessed an inner goodness that softened and enhanced her otherwise plain features. She wore her hair, now streaked with silver, high on her head and often jokingly remarked that she chose this particular fashion to add extra height to match her husband.

"When do you think you'll be done with all of the plantin'?" Sister asked.

"Hopefully in a couple of days. I'd like to get everything done so the plants will have time to root before the next rain."

"I noticed today that something's been nibbling on my bean and tomato plants," Sister said.

Joshua shook his head in disgust. "I'll bet it's them deer I saw scampering off this morning when I went out to milk the cow." Reluctantly, he got up from the table. "I'd better have a look," he said, grabbing his lantern on the way out the door. Joshua fumbled around in the dark, trying to light his lantern. A few stars were out but no moon. On his second try, he finally succeeded, the soft ember glow illuminating a circle around him as he walked. One of the first things a city dweller usually noticed when visiting the country was the pitch-black darkness at night. Electric power seemed to be catching on in most towns, and Cartersville, Georgia, was no exception. Joshua figured the time would soon come when even the rural areas would have electricity. That might not be too bad, but he really didn't mind keeping things the way they were. He headed away from the house. "It is dark tonight." He made his way over to the dog pen, where his coon dogs were still barking wildly. "Hey, rascals. Whatcha see out there?"

Recognizing their owner, the dogs began whimpering and standing on their hind legs with their paws on the fence. Joshua affectionately rubbed their heads. "If there were any deer out here tonight, you certainly scared them away." He left the dog pen and walked over to check the vegetable garden where he knelt down by the rows and looked for deer tracks. Finding none, he turned to go. On impulse, he cast his lantern around once more. This time he looked over to the edge of the garden. Something on the ground caught his attention. What was it? A piece of cloth? He moved closer and gasped in surprise at what he saw. "What in the world?" he exclaimed.

It was a person—a girl crumpled in a heap, lying face down. He bent down and turned her over and shone the light in her face. Joshua felt his heart drop. "Shelby!" She was barefoot, and her feet were bleeding. Her gingham dress was torn and dirty. Was she alive? "Shelby, can you hear me?" He yelled as he shook her. He placed his finger on her neck and detected a faint pulse. Scooping her up in his arms, he ran to the house yelling. "Sister! Sister!"

Quickly throwing on her housecoat, Sister ran out the door and nearly collided with her breathless husband. "What's wrong? Who is that?"

"It's Shelby."

Sister's eyes widened in surprise as she followed him inside. "What happened to her?"

Joshua carefully laid Shelby on the couch and placed a pillow under her head. "I found her out by the garden."

"Is she—?" Her voice faltered, and she couldn't bring herself to say the word.

"She's alive. She's fainted.

Sister let out an audible sigh of relief. "I'll get the smellin' salts." She returned and placed the bottle directly beneath Shelby's nose.

Slowly, Shelby opened her eyes as the pungent odor invaded her nostrils. Her head ached, and the world seemed to be spinning out of control. For a second, she tried to make a concentrated effort to figure out what was happening to her. Then, finding it too difficult, she shrugged nonchalantly and closed her eyes again, welcoming the enveloping darkness.

Sister shot a concerned look at Joshua and leaned over and shook Shelby vigorously. "Shelby, look at me."

"Where am I?" Shelby muttered to herself.

"At Sister's...you're here with us."

"Sister?" Shelby opened her eyes and looked around the room

confused. "How did I get...?" Shelby looked down and noticed her scratched legs and bleeding feet. "What happened to me?"

"We were wondering the same thing," answered Joshua. He paused, his voice husky with emotion as he searched for the right words to say. "You gave me quite a scare. For a moment there, I thought...well, um...I thought you weren't gonna make it."

"Child, what on earth were you doing out at this time of the night by yourself? You're lucky Joshua found you. If those dogs of his hadn't been making such a racket, there's no telling what could've happened to you."

Shelby looked at Sister in confusion. "I'm sorry if I've caused any trouble. I didn't mean..."

Joshua placed his hand on Sister's shoulder. When she turned to look at him, he motioned for her to go into the kitchen. "She's had a rough night," he whispered. "Why don't you go and get her some water? I'll try and find out what's going on."

"Okay, I'm going," Sister huffed.

Shelby was still lying down. Joshua sat on the edge of the couch and reached down and patted her arm. He and Sister had never been able to have any children of their own, and he'd always had a special place in his heart for Shelby. Looking now at her confused and ragged state, this feeling intensified.

"This is the first time since you were a young'un that I've seen you running around barefooted with your hair all a mess. You almost look twelve."

Her eyes widening in surprise, Shelby's hand quickly came up to her hair as she attempted to smooth out the tangles. She was about to apologize again until she saw his mischievous grin. Most of the townsfolk were intimidated by her uncle's massive size and brusque manner. He had a reputation for driving a hard bargain, especially during harvest time at the cotton office when he dickered over the price of his crop. Yes indeed, her uncle could be tough as nails when he had to be, but underneath that gruff exterior beat a tender heart. She used to pretend he was a giant. *He is*, she thought. *He's my gentle giant.*

"Shelby, what happened tonight?"

She leaned back on the couch and tried to think. "The last thing I remember was tucking Homer and Sarah into bed and then going outside to sit on the porch."

"Did you go for a walk?"

"I'm not sure. No, I don't think so."

"Is your papa at home?"

"Papa?" Even as she mouthed the word, Shelby's mouth went dry, and her body began to tremble. Like a bolt of lightning, everything came rushing back. She shuttered as she remembered his sweaty hands, the smell of alcohol on his breath, her terror. An image of Papa lying motionless on the floor flashed through her mind and seared its way into her soul as she gasped and then struggled to catch her breath. *Is he...dead?*

Joshua felt his hair stand on ends as he watched the color drain from Shelby's face. Her body was shaking violently. Was this terrified, wild-eyed creature the self-assured niece he knew and loved? She reminded him of a cornered deer, pacing to and fro, ready to bolt. "Is your Papa home with Homer and Sarah? Did anything happen to them?"

Tears welled in Shelby's eyes. She tried to speak, but the sound wouldn't come.

Grabbing her by the arms, Joshua shook her. "Shelby, you've got to tell me!"

"It's Papa. He's dead!" Shelby sank back on the couch, glad to have gotten the words out of her mouth.

Joshua felt as if the wind had been knocked out of him. "Dead? Are you sure?"

Confusion clouded Shelby's eyes. "Yes...no. I don't know."

"What do you mean? What happened?"

Shelby's face contorted in fear. "I killed him." The words came out in a ragged whisper.

Joshua swallowed hard and tried to absorb what he'd just heard. "You *what?*" he asked incredulously.

Instead of answering, she shook her head and stared unseeingly into the distance. Then she buried her head in her hands and sobbed uncontrollably.

Too stunned to speak, he placed his hand on her back and let her cry. After a while, she lifted her head and looked imploring into his eyes. He had always thought that Shelby's eyes were full of expression. As he looked into them now, he had the distinct impression they were windows to a soul racked with anguish. She was so young and tender; he wanted to somehow erase the pain like he did once when she had fallen and scraped her knee.

"What am I going to do?"

"Why don't you tell me what happened?"

She nodded and then began. "I fixed supper for Homer and Sarah and then put them to bed. I went out to sit on the front porch for a while. Homer had a bad dream and started to cry, so I went upstairs to check on him. I had just gotten him settled down when Papa came home. He called me downstairs to heat up his supper, and he was—"

"Whatever it is; you can tell me," Joshua prodded gently.

"He was drunk. He wanted me to sit on his lap, and when I wouldn't, he got angry. Please, Uncle Joshua. I don't want to say any more!"

Joshua's eyes narrowed, and his blood ran cold. He shook his head in disgust. Once again he looked at Shelby's bare feet and disheveled appearance. He didn't need to hear the rest. He could guess what happened next. Right then and there, he made a decision. Whatever the cost, he would stand by her. Shelby wasn't the sort of girl to go flying off her rocker for no reason. If she did do anything to her papa, it was only out of self-preservation. "Did he hurt your or force you?"

"No!" Shelby answered quickly. "I got scared and hit him over the head with a skillet, and then I ran. I don't remember anything else." She paused. "Except waking up here."

"Everything will be all right."

Shelby's eyes filled with uncertainty.

Joshua reached out and placed his rough hand over her dainty one and squeezed it gently. "You have my word."

"Thank you," Shelby whispered, her eyes filling with grateful tears.

Sister returned from the kitchen and paused as she witnessed the tearful exchange between Shelby and Joshua. "Is everything all right?"

Shelby nodded and Joshua answered, "She's had a little scare, but she'll be okay. I suspect Frank is probably wondering where Shelby's gotten off to. I'd better go over and tell him where she is."

Sister watched Shelby's face grow pale, and she shot Joshua a questioning glance. He only shook his head and headed out the door, leaving Shelby and Sister, lost in their own thoughts, staring after him.

* * * * *

His body crouched low; Joshua urged his horse forward as fast as he dared go. Fog was setting in, and it was difficult to see more than two feet in front of him. What would he find? *Was Frank dead?* He shuddered involuntarily as the thought sent chills racing down his spine. What would this mean for Shelby, for Ellen, for Sister? Images of Shelby, tearful and battered, filled his mind, and his fury mounted. *What sort of a man would try to do such a thing to his own daughter?* He shook his head in disgust.

Like Sister, Frank was small-boned and had dark features, but that's where the similarity ended. In fact, Frank and Sister were so completely different, he had often wondered how they had come from the same family. Frank had been bitterly opposed to Joshua and Sister's courtship from the very beginning. He'd tried every possible way to convince Sister not to marry him.

Joshua had a younger sister himself and wanted only the best for her, so he could understand how Frank could have wanted a better life for his sister. If this had been his only offense, Joshua could've overlooked it. But his dislike of Frank Collins ran much deeper than that. Joshua had always relied on his instincts, and the feelings he got around Frank screamed foul. On the surface, Frank was an ideal husband, father, and pillar of the community, and—Joshua begrudgingly admitted—had a keen sense for business. But Joshua had always suspected that behind the carefully constructed facade lurked a cruel and selfish individual. Sister dearly loved her brother and always looked for the good in him. For her sake, Josh tried to keep his feelings in check. Frank was, after all, his wife's brother.

Sometimes Joshua caught glimpses of the real Frank. Last January, he had walked into the store and caught the tail-end of an argument between Frank and Gus Brown.

Farmers purchased goods on credit until after harvest. Frank had allowed Gus to charge an enormous amount and then got mad at him over something petty. Joshua couldn't even remember the cause of the squabble, but he would never forget the outcome. Frank insisted that Gus's account with him be paid in full right there on the spot. Gus, who couldn't possibly pay for his account during the wintertime, apologized right then and there and begged Frank's forgiveness. His pleadings fell on deaf ears. Gus couldn't make it through the winter without essential goods from the store, so he and his family left their farm and moved in with relatives near Atlanta. Eventually, Frank auctioned off the farm to pay Gus' debt.

Frank and Ellen got married about a year after his and Sister's wedding. When Joshua first met Ellen, he was struck by her unusual beauty and assumed she would be snooty. Nothing was further from the truth. Over the years, he'd developed a deep admiration and respect for her. He had often wondered what type of relationship she and Frank had. Ellen was too much of a lady to let on that things weren't right between her and Frank, but Joshua had noticed the lonely, wistful expression she sometimes wore. How often was Frank coming home drunk? On occasion, Joshua enjoyed his share of corn whiskey, but he drank it sparingly. He'd seen enough heartache caused from excessive drinking to last him a lifetime. If a man's gonna drink, he oughta be able to hold his liquor.

When he finally reached the house, Joshua was immediately struck by the calmness of it. Everything looked normal. He opened the gate and walked up on the porch and tried the front door. It was locked. Surely Shelby wouldn't have taken the time to lock the door before she ran out. Then he realized that the events she described took place in the kitchen. She must have left through the back door. He cupped his hands to the window and peered into the front room and saw nothing but darkness.

He walked around the back of the house and tried the kitchen door. It also was locked. "How strange," he said aloud. "Homer, Sarah, open the door!" he yelled as he banged on the door. He knocked and shouted for another couple of minutes, but no one came to the door, so he decided to try the front door again. He went to the front door and banged and then waited to see if he could hear any movement. Just as he was debating whether or not he should break into the house, the handle turned, and the door opened. Frank stood in the doorway.

For a second, Joshua could only gape at the live, standing figure in front of him. "Frank?" he finally managed to say.

"What're you doing here this time uv the night?" Frank demanded as he leaned against the doorway. His speech was blurred and an angry, purple bruise was spreading across his forehead.

"I could ask you the same question," Joshua fired back. His chest tightened, and his eyes squinted into angry slits.

"What're you talking about?" Frank demanded.

"Where's Shelby?"

The question took Frank by surprise, and Joshua caught the flicker of fear in his eyes, which quickly faded. "How should I know whur she is?" Frank stammered. "Since Ellen's been gone, that girl comes and goes as she pleases. She wurnt here when I got home this evenin'."

"What happened to your head?"

Frank gingerly touched his forehead and laughed nervously. "Oh, that. I had a little accident at the store today. A crate fell..."

"You liar!" Joshua hissed through clenched teeth as he knotted his fists. "How could you do such a thing...to your own daughter?"

"I don't know what yer talking about," Frank smirked as he straightened himself up and stared defiantly at Joshua.

Suddenly, all the tension and frustration he'd been feeling reached a boiling point, and he could no longer contain it. He raised his fist and socked Frank in the nose. The blow sent Frank sprawling backwards, holding his nose as blood spurted over his white shirt. This time, the fear in Frank's eyes was unmistakable, and he scurried back against the door to protect himself from another onslaught. Joshua took a step toward him and then suddenly became aware of his own large frame and strength compared to Frank's slighter build. He looked down at his clenched fist in disgust. Wearily, he relaxed his hands and let them fall down by his side.

Frank let out an audible sigh of relief and then flashed Joshua a look of triumph, rekindling Joshua's anger. He bent down and grabbed Frank by the collar and pulled him up so their faces were only inches apart. "I know you think you run this town. But you mark my words, if you every again try to harm as much as a hair on Shelby's head..." He paused and enunciated every word. "I—will—kill—you." His voice, quiet and menacing, sent chills down Frank's spine, and he knew Joshua meant it.

Joshua suddenly felt very tired. He thrust Frank away and turned to leave. He took a few steps and then turned back toward Frank. "I'll send Sister over tomorrow to get Shelby's things...and Homer and Sarah." He paused long enough to note the surprised expression on Frank's face and then continued. "They will stay with us until Ellen returns, and then we'll decide what to do after that." Without another word, he turned on his heel and walked briskly down the steps, leaving Frank staring after him with smoldering eyes.

*   *   *   *   *

Shelby awoke the next morning to the tantalizing aroma of sizzling bacon and the cheerful clanging of pots and pans. For a moment, right after she first opened her eyes, she had thought she was at home and Mama was in the kitchen making breakfast. She leisurely stretched, her legs rubbing over the cool sheets, and was about to roll over and sleep a little longer when the quilt on her bed caught her eye—Sister's quilt. She glanced around the room, taking in her surroundings. Mama had once remarked that Sister was a very practical person who didn't go in for a lot of fancy frills. That was an understatement. All of the furniture was arranged in a box-like fashion with everything pushed against the walls. The bed, dresser, and rocking chair were all made out of sturdy oak. No pictures hung on the bare, off-white walls.

The only accent in the room was the colorful, patchwork quilt on the bed. Shelby lovingly ran her hand across the quilt, tracing its intricate pattern with her finger. She had always loved it. One of her favorite Bible stories was of Joseph and his coat of many colors. Over the years, she had spent many nights snuggled up in the old quilt, pretending it was her own coat of many colors. She raised it to her face and buried her nose into the quilt, inhaling deeply. It smelled like Sister. Somehow, that was comforting.

The morning sun was streaming in through the window, dancing off the wooden floor. She glanced down at the floor, puzzled. Sister had laid out some of her own shoes for Shelby to wear. *What happened to my shoes?* she wondered. *Did I have them on last night?* The intrusive thoughts were an unpleasant reminder, and she quickly brushed them aside. In the sunny light of the morning, the events of the night before seemed less frightful. She threw back the quilt and hopped out of bed. Her stomach growled, and she was suddenly very hungry.

"Good morning, Shelby," said Sister as she turned from the stove, giving Shelby a brief smile.

"Good morning."

"Come and sit down. I'll fix you a plate. How did you sleep?"

"Well. Thank you."

Sister gave Shelby an appraising glance. "You certainly seem to be feelin' better today."

Shelby's cheeks reddened slightly. "Yes, ma'am, I do feel better."

"Good." Sister nodded and then turned back toward the stove, glad to have gotten the pleasantries out of the way. "Let's get some good, hot food in you. You are lookin' a little poor lately. You're down to skin and bones."

Shelby grinned as Sister placed a plate piled high with bacon, fried eggs, grits, and biscuits.

"Joshua left early this morning for the fields, but he gave me strict orders to go to your house and get all of your clothes. I reckon you'll stay here until your mama gets back. He also told me to get Homer and Sarah."

"That's great," Shelby replied enthusiastically as she stopped eating and looked up in surprise.

"Yeah, I guess it's kind of hard on your papa, trying to run the store and look after you young 'uns at the same time. It's awful good of 'im to try and take on all that responsibility in the first place."

"Yes, ma'am," she managed to mumble as she put down her fork. She wasn't hungry anymore.

"Joshua told me to make sure and go alone to your house. He said I should leave you here." Sister had been bustling around the kitchen, cleaning up the dishes. She stopped and looked directly at Shelby and continued. "Why do you think he said that?"

Shelby felt her heart drop. "I—I don't know," she muttered as she dropped her head and stared down at her plate.

Sister stood for a moment and watched intently as Shelby fidgeted with her food. The silence grew uncomfortable. Finally, Sister dropped her gaze and began clearing away the dishes from the table.

"Don't mind Joshua," she said, trying to sound cheerful. "Men are funny that way sometimes—getting silly notions in their heads. Why don't you go outside and sit on the front porch and make a list of all the things you want me to get from your house while I finish up in the kitchen?"

*　　*　　*　　*　　*

Shelby stumbled out of the kitchen and onto the front porch where she sank wearily into a chair. She clasped her shaking hands in her lap in an attempt to steady them. She took a deep breath and looked out over the yard, lush with green grass. Next, her gaze went to the nearby fields and then to the rolling mountains, blue-gray in the distance. There wasn't another house in sight. Normally, she enjoyed the seclusion of the farm, but today the absence of neighbors felt lonely.

Why had Sister asked such a strange question? Had Joshua not told Sister what happened? Why wouldn't he tell her? An unbidden thought penetrated into her consciousness, sending icy needles of fear prickling down her spine. *Maybe Joshua didn't believe her. Was that why he didn't tell Sister?* She shook her head incredulously. When Joshua had returned the night before, he had quietly told her Papa was fine, and everything would be all right. It had never occurred to her that Joshua might doubt her word. Of all people, she had been absolutely sure she could count on him. *If Joshua, my own uncle who knows me so well, doesn't believe me, then how can I expect anyone else to?* She stared unseeingly into the horizon and for the first time in her life, felt totally alone.

*　　*　　*　　*　　*

Shelby awoke to the distant sound of hoofs. She stifled a yawn and then sat sleepily up in the bed and stretched. Was Sister back already? How long had she slept? After Sister had left to fetch Homer and Sarah, Shelby walked aimlessly around the yard, trying to sort things out. Getting nowhere, she finally decided to take a nap. Sister told her she had errands to run before picking up the children. Shelby assumed they wouldn't return until after lunch and had resigned herself to an afternoon of boredom. She heard the front door open. Excitedly, she jumped out of bed and ran into the living room, ready to throw her arms around Homer and Sarah.

"Well, hello you two," she said as she came bounding into the room, a big smile on her face. In an instant, her smile froze, and her heart leaped in her throat as she took a step backwards. "Papa!" she managed to exclaim. "What are you doing here?"

"Girl, get yourself in the wagon."

Shelby's feet froze to the floor. She looked up in terror at the purple bruise across Papa's forehead.

"Did you hear me?" he snarled. "From now on, you're gonna do what I say."

Shelby shrank back against the wall as tears trickled down her cheeks. She shook her head defiantly, knowing full well what horrors would await her at home. Her voice sounded small in her ears. "No, I'm stayin' here 'til Mama gets back."

Frank's jaw squared as his face grew black.

She turned to run, but he grabbed her around the waist and dragged her into the kitchen and shoved her into a chair. She tried to get up, but he slapped her hard across the jaw. She put her head down on the table and sobbed, her breath coming in broken gasps. Papa strode across the kitchen to Sister's desk and pulled out a sheet of paper and a pencil. He walked over to Shelby and grabbed her by her hair and pulled her up to a sitting position.

"Stop that whinin'," he barked, "or I'll give you what you really deserve! Now you listen to me. I've had just about enough of you and all the trouble you caused. I ought to tie you to a tree and give you a good horse whippin'."

Terror clawed at Shelby as she looked at his savage expression. She hardly recognized this beast who used to be her papa.

"I tried to do this the easy way, but you won't let me. I'll fix you. I'll send you so far away, you'll never get home." Frank's eyes hardened into flint steel as he continued. "You will pick up that pencil and write what I tell you. Do you understand?" he hissed.

Too stunned to speak, Shelby picked up the pencil with a shaky hand and began to write. When she finished, he led her outside.

The fight gone out of her, she numbly followed his orders, as if in a daze. He pushed her into the back of the wagon and ordered her to stay under the cover. "If I see so much as one hair of your head, so help me I'll..." He left the sentence unfinished as Shelby quickly scampered into the wagon and pulled the cover over her head.

Chapter Three

Gretta Sharp leaned against the open window and peered out as the afternoon sun cast its fading rays over the freshly mowed lawn. It was this time of the day she enjoyed most. The sweet scent of grass mingled with the fragrant azalea bushes planted underneath the window caught her attention as she looked at the bordering bushes and noted with satisfaction how they looked neat and orderly, planted exactly two feet apart just as she had instructed. Absently, she ran her fingers across the heavy drapes hanging to the side. The gray drapes, dull and drab in their appearance much like the rest of the office furnishings, had been hung only out of necessity to keep out the relentless, noonday sun.

She looked around the room. Her eyes fell on the battered desk and chair, and she felt a sudden kinship with the objects. Like her, they were once shiny and new. But that was long ago, and now only a fragmented shell of what they once were is all that remained. The old desk and squeaky chair seemed out of place here in this modern facility. Gretta supposed that when funds were available, they would be replaced with their more updated counterparts. She moved away from the window and sat down at her desk, running her fingers respectfully over its grainy surface. Yes indeed, this is one of the few old relics left behind as a reminder of a past soon to be forgotten.

"Miss Sharp?"

Lost in her thoughts, the knock at the door startled Gretta, and she was annoyed as she looked up to see Shirley. Peering over her spectacles in a gesture she used to indicate disapproval, she motioned for Shirley to enter.

Shirley scuffled into the room, red-faced. "I'm sorry to disturb you, but I wanted to let you know that I informed all of the staff about the meeting tomorrow morning."

"Good. Did you tell them that it will begin promptly at eight A.M.?"

"Yes, ma'am. Here is your paper," Shirley said.

Gretta seemed to have forgotten about Shirley's presence as she thumbed through the paper. Shirley stood for a moment and then turned to leave.

"Today is June 2nd."

Shirley stopped, not sure where the conversation was heading but knew better than to question her superior. She waited for Gretta to continue.

"Today is my father's birthday."

"That's nice," Shirley offered.

"Not that I care," Gretta countered, changing the subject. "Have you read this article on the front page?"

"No, ma'am."

"It says here that 'Birmingham is a thriving, prosperous city nestled comfortably between a mountain of coal on one side and a mountain of iron on the other.'" A humorless laugh, sounding more like a snarl, escaped her lips. "Yes, it is prosperous for some. Have you seen those luxury houses on the side of the mountain?"

Shirley nodded.

"I've always found it amusing that those houses weren't built quite high enough to escape the smoke billowing up from the smokestacks below. But I suppose when the rich tire of breathing in the filthy fumes, they can leave their patios and go inside and close the doors. I've never been that lucky."

Shirley looked down at the floor.

Gretta turned and stared out the window. "There was a time when Birmingham was little more than a small, crossroads town of Jones Valley. I came here with my parents thirty years ago. We were like all the other wide-eyed immigrants who came in search of prosperity. My father got a job in the mines, and my mother took in laundry to help make ends meet. After a while, my father grew tired of the endless work and measly wages and took solace in the bottle, spending what free time he had in bars with loose women. One night, he didn't come home."

Shirley's face flamed. She'd never heard Miss Sharp speak this openly about herself.

"My mother got a job in a factory. It wasn't much of an income, but we survived. I was fifteen when my mother contracted tuberculosis. She died a few months later."

"I'm so sorry."

Gretta was jolted to the present. "I'm boring you."

"No, I don't mind," answered Shirley.

Gretta waved her hand in dismissal. "Enough of that. I am sure you have plenty of work to do before you leave," she added, putting Shirley back in her place.

"Yes, ma'am."

Gretta felt a twinge of guilt for her harshness toward Shirley. She wasn't displeased with her secretary but neither was she overly impressed. This was one instance in which the creator made a person's outside appearance match the inside.

In capability and appearance, Shirley was average. She was five-feet-five with mousey, brown hair that fell loosely on her shoulders. Perfectly straight bangs were cut high on her forehead, emphasizing her square face. Her squinty eyes were spaced too far apart from her pug nose. She couldn't really pinpoint what it was about Shirley that bothered her and why she felt the need to unnerve her. Maybe it's because she's so easily intimidated, she decided.

"I'm going to get the new girl settled before I leave for the day," Shirley said. "Unless, that is, you need me to do anything else."

"No, I don't have anything else for you today," Gretta replied curtly. "You may leave after you take care of the new student."

As Shirley turned to leave, Gretta called out to her, "Do you have her file?"

"I put it in your basket for you to go over."

Gretta leaned over her desk and picked up the file. She leafed through it and then placed it back on her desk. "What do you think of her?"

Shirley looked surprised. She wasn't accustomed to being asked to give her opinion. She shifted her feet back and forth. "She seems different than the other girls."

Gretta studied Shirley. "How so?"

"Well, from what I can tell so far, she is very quiet and sort of distant. But she does have a certain bearing about her." Shirley scrunched her nose and wrinkled her eyebrows as she sought for the right words. "She just seems like she'd be more at home sipping lemonade at a Sunday social than here learning record-keeping and farming."

Gretta pursed her lips together. "That's interesting. Thank you, Shirley. I'll see you tomorrow."

Realizing she was being dismissed, Shirley turned and hurried out the door.

Gretta picked up the file and gazed at its contents. What sort of girl was this Shelby Collins and what turn of events precipitated her arrival? As interesting as she found the girl to be, it was the girl's father who captured her attention. At five-feet-eleven, Gretta was as tall as most men and accustomed to towering over other women. She had always felt her height gave her a physical as well as an intellectual advantage and found it ironic and slightly unnerving that her encounter with a complete stranger, who incidentally was a little shorter than herself, could've left her feeling ruffled and out-of-sorts.

She had just come back from lunch and intentionally left her afternoon free to catch up on some paperwork. Just when she was starting to make progress, Shirley poked her head in the door and told her she had a visitor.

"Who is it?"

"His name is Frank Collins. He has a young girl with him. I think he wants to enroll her."

"Did you give him an application to fill out?"

"Well, I—"

Gretta's disdainful expression left no doubt that she was growing impatient with the conversation. "You know I don't see potential students without a prior appointment. Have him fill out the necessary paperwork, and I'll review it and submit it to the board for approval."

"Miss Sharp, I think you ought to see—"

Gretta cut her off. "You know my policy. No exceptions!"

"He says he came all the way from Cartersville, Georgia," Shirley injected timidly.

Gretta pursed her lips as she decided what she would do.

Her indecision gave Shirley the encouragement she needed to continue. "And will only be in town for one day."

"Oh, all right. Very well. Send him in."

Shirley halfway smiled but stopped short when she saw Gretta's stern expression.

"Let's get one thing clear," Gretta huffed, "I don't like having my orders disobeyed."

"Yes, ma'am," Shirley croaked.

From the moment he entered the room, Gretta could see why Shirley had a difficult time turning this gentleman away. He strode in with purpose, his head held upright. Clearly, he was a man who was used to getting his way.

"Good day," replied Gretta, briskly. "Please have a seat."

"Thank you."

His gray suit had a faint pinstripe and looked as if it had been custom tailored to fit perfectly. It enhanced his olive skin and dark hair. A few gray streaks were starting to show around his temple. *Why do men with gray hair look distinguished but women look old?* Gretta wondered. Suddenly, she felt uncomfortable in her plain button-down blouse with its dingy collar. She sat up in her seat a little higher and cleared her throat.

"What can I do for you Mr...?"

"Collins. Frank Collins."

Gretta nodded and continued. "Mr. Collins, my assistant told me—"

He smiled slowly. "Please call me Frank."

"Yes, of course," she replied, her cheeks slightly reddening. "My assistant told me you are in town for today only."

He nodded.

"How may I help you, Frank?"

He rested his arm on the back of his chair, and she couldn't help but notice his slender hand and neatly trimmed fingernails—not the rough hands of a laborer. Instead of answering her right away, he glanced first at her—his eyes lingering on hers long enough to cause her to blush—and then around the room. His casual, debonair manner seemed to suggest he had all the time in the world. Finally, he spoke. "I am a very rich man."

She stared at him in surprise as he continued. "I realize that may sound boastful, especially since we've just met, but you strike me as a no-nonsense woman who likes to get straight to the point."

"That is correct," she said, pleased that he had perceived her correctly. "Continue."

"I want my daughter to attend your school. After looking at other places and considering other possibilities, I feel this is the best place for her."

"Mr. Coll...Frank, I am flattered that you are impressed with our facility, but I believe there has been some sort of misunderstanding. Are you familiar with the Mercy Place?"

"No."

"The Mercy Place, a children's home, is an affiliate of this school. It is run by twelve members of the Women's Christian Temperance Union. The home assists women and children. My school, the Mercy Place Industrial School, is two years old and is run by those same women. It offers industrial education for white girls between the ages of thirteen and eighteen. You see, this school is not designed for the wealthy. It's a place for..."

He cut her off mid-sentence, his eyebrow raised. "It was my understanding that your school is supported by donations."

"Yes...but..."

He held up his hand as a signal for her to stop talking. "I realize that it must seem odd for a man such as me, a man of considerable...," he paused, "...for a gentleman of my standing to consider sending my daughter here. But I detect an authenticity here that I've been unable to find in some of the more prestigious schools. You teach young girls how to become useful to society—how to learn a valuable trade. My daughter has had enough pampering and fluff to last her a lifetime; she needs to learn the value of honest, hard work."

Gretta nodded her head thoughtfully, clearly impressed. "I see. I'll have my assistant get you an application to fill out."

She leaned over her desk and grabbed her calendar. "The admissions board will meet again in two weeks to review all new applications. If she is approved, she can begin the first of next month. How does that sound?"

He stood up and walked over to the window and gazed out it with his hands clasped behind his back. Finally, he turned and looked intently at Gretta. "I haven't always been wealthy. Like you, I know what it takes to rise from the dust and make something of myself."

Color rose in her cheeks. What was it about her that so apparently suggested she had come from poverty? Before she could articulate a response, he continued.

"I like you. You strike me as being a very practical and capable woman—one who can teach my Shelby to be useful, one who understands the urgency of my situation. I have a business to run. I have come here for the express purpose of enrolling my daughter in your school...today."

"While I do appreciate your situation, I hope you can understand that we have procedures and rules here that must be followed."

He cocked his head and raised his eyebrow in a condescending manner. "As head of this school, do you not hold the privilege of making some decisions of your own accord?"

She became ruffled. "Yes, of course I can," she huffed, "if I so choose."

He ran his fingers over the tattered filing cabinet, and she felt embarrassment over the worn appearance of her office furniture. "Perhaps we could make some sort of arrangement that would more than compensate for any inconvenience this situation could cause you."

She became intrigued and a little wary at the same time. "What sort of arrangement do you have in mind?"

Noting her suspicious expression, he laughed pleasantly. "One that is upright and noble, I can assure you."

She grinned sheepishly and wondered again how he could read her so clearly.

"I would like to make a substantial financial donation to your school in the hope that it can benefit my own daughter as well as help further this noble cause you have begun here."

He winked. "Let's make it worth your while, too."

Gretta pursed her lips together. "That's very generous of you. I will accept your offer," she then paused a moment, "but only for the good of the school."

He smiled. "Yes, of course."

They spent the rest of their meeting discussing the details of admission. When he turned to leave, she had extended her hand as a farewell gesture. He took her hand and held it for a second and then pressed it to his lips. "It has been a pleasure. I will be in touch."

Gretta raised her hand and looked at the back of it, remembering the delicate touch of his warm lips. She didn't know what had come over her. All her life she had followed every rule. And the first time a handsome man comes into her office, she turns to mush and throws caution to the wind. The donation he gave was substantial, she rationalized, and the school could use the funds. Still, it wasn't going to be easy to explain why she had admitted a student without prior board approval. *Even Shirley, daft as she is, can see the girl is different from the others. The board will be very impressed with the donation. I am the head mistress here; I should be able to make some decisions by myself. Oh well, what's done is done, I suppose.*

Even as she tried to figure her way out of the pickle she was in, she kept thinking about his commanding presence—his finely chiseled jaw—his money. She couldn't help but wonder when he would return and why he never mentioned a Mrs. Collins.

*   *   *   *   *

Shelby hung her head and dutifully followed the woman who was escorting her through the corridor and down a long, dark hall. Everything she had ever known seemed to fade into the distance as a bleak, sterile reality forced itself into the forefront of her consciousness. It was as though she was in the middle of a bad dream and was unable to awaken. She could hear the distant sounds of girls laughing. The sharp tone of her escort's voice jolted her back to reality.

"My name is Shirley Smith; I am the assistant to the head mistress, Miss Sharp. This is your room which you will share with thirteen other girls. Over yonder is your bed."

Shelby looked around the room. The plaster walls were stark white and completely bare except for a small needlepoint on the back wall. It was too far away for her to read. Except for a few books atop some beds and shoes placed neatly beneath, the room appeared devoid of any humanization. She could tell from the faint lemon scent that the floor had recently been cleaned.

"The girls are at supper right now. You may join them if you wish, or you may stay in here and get settled in."

Shelby was beginning to get hungry, but the idea of having to meet the other girls in the cafeteria seemed too overwhelming.

"I would like to stay in here tonight," she answered quickly.

"Bedtime is at nine P.M., and we awake at six A.M.," the woman barked. "These hours are strictly enforced. No exceptions! Do you have any questions?"

"No."

"While you are here, you will follow orders immediately and will always use 'ma'am' when answering your superiors. Is that clear?"

"Yes, ma'am."

Even as she spoke, she strained to keep her voice even to hide the overwhelming feeling of panic threatening to engulf her.

"Very well. Then I will leave you alone now."

Shirley could tell the young girl was on the verge of a breakdown, and she smiled smugly as she turned to leave. "Try to get some rest," she quipped. "You will need it for tomorrow."

Shelby sat down on the bed. Ignoring her pounding head, she tried to regain control of her emotions. Never in her darkest dreams could she have ever imagined herself here. The past few days seemed a blur. At Sister's house, she had almost managed to convince herself that everything had been a terrible misunderstanding. The familiar smells and comforting practicality of her aunt's home had been a temporary haven from her ugly reality.

She looked around at her foreign surroundings. The identical white beds, with their iron posts, looked sterile and impersonal. By instinct, her hands went to her neck to rub her necklace. She searched frantically before realizing that it was gone. She'd lost it—the only thing she had left of her mama and home, and it was gone. Loneliness encircled her like a shroud. She lay down and closed her eyes. *If I close my eyes tightly enough, maybe I'll wake up tomorrow and discover that this is all just a bad dream.* She tried to imagine her own room and the chirping birds outside her window but other images kept flashing through her mind—Uncle Joshua and Sister. They would probably be eating supper right about now. She tried to imagine them laughing and talking about the events of the day. *What must they think of me?*

It was at that moment that a sudden awareness struck her with enough force to take her breath away. Her life would never again be the same.

She would have to face the repercussions of her actions. Shame covered her as she remembered the evil glint in Papa's eyes and his slurred speech, and then she was overcome with bitterness. *I had no choice. Never could I have let that happen.* Images of Homer and Sarah flooded her mind, and she ached for them. *What will he do to Sarah?* She shivered. *Think of them,* she ordered herself. *I must be strong for them. When Mama returns, she will be shocked beyond belief.* Tears welled. *How will Mama ever find me?*

Chapter Four

Ellen slept uncomfortably in the chair next to her mother's bed. A movement at the bedroom door startled her, and she awoke suddenly and looked with concern at her mother, who was still sleeping soundly. She raised her hand to her head and massaged her forehead. *I must have fallen asleep.* She heard a knock at the bedroom door and turned to see Martha Baker peaking in.

"May I come in?"

"Of course," Ellen answered with a smile.

Martha walked over to Sue's bedside. "How is she? Any changes?"

Ellen shook her head. "None that I can see. Her coughing subsided a little last night, and she was able to get some sleep. Maybe that will help build her strength."

"Yes," Martha nodded in agreement. "I hope so." She sat down in the chair across from Ellen and scrutinized her from head to toe, her keen eyes taking note of Ellen's pale complexion and gaunt appearance.

"Have you been sleepin' in that chair all night?"

Ellen nodded. "I didn't want to leave her alone. I was afraid she might need something."

Martha raised one eyebrow, causing a ripple of wrinkles to spread across her forehead, and her voice suddenly grew stern. Ellen's mind turned back sixteen years, and she felt like a child who had just gotten her hand caught in the cookie jar as Martha continued.

"I've already told you that Paul and I can take turns sittin' with her at night. If you keep goin' at the pace you've been goin' for the past couple of weeks, you'll need lookin' after yourself. When your mama gets well, she'll want to see a healthy, rosy-cheeked daughter, not a rack of bones with bags under her eyes."

Ellen looked startled for a moment, and then she leaned her head back and laughed, something she had not done since her arrival in Alabama. She had been too preoccupied with her mother and worried about leaving her children. "Goodness sakes, Martha, you have quite a way of putting things. Do I really look that bad?"

Martha smiled back, her eyes twinkling as she patted Ellen's hand. "You look just as lovely now as you did when you were sixteen. Paul's always fussin' at me for the way I carry on. He always says that a person can catch more flies with honey than vinegar. Maybe he's right," she winked. "But I'd never tell him as much. When you get to be my age, you forget about tact and say things the way they really are."

"I wouldn't have you any other way. You've been such a good friend to Mother over the years. It has been a tremendous comfort for me to know that you and Paul were always right next door. If anything should happen to her..."

"Shhh. Don't you let me hear you talkin' that way."

Ellen looked down and clasped her hands tightly in her lap as she tried to hold back the tears that were threatening to spill over.

"Sue's a strong woman," Martha continued, her voice husky with emotion. "She'll pull through this. We have to be strong and have faith." She paused and wiped away a tear. "If Sue weren't sleepin', she'd tell us as much herself."

"Yes, you're right," agreed Ellen as she wiped away her tears.

Martha took a deep breath and smiled. "We've cried enough tears for one mornin'. Don't you think? Why don't you let me take over for a while? Sue's sleeping now, and when she wakes up, I'll see that she gets everything she needs."

"Are you sure?"

Seeing the uncertainty in Ellen's eyes, Martha added, "Just the other day Sue mentioned that she'd been havin' a hankerin' for some blackberry cobbler. This Indian summer we've had has caused the blackberries to bloom early this year. The Millers have oodles over at their place, and Margie told me to pick some for a pie."

Ellen stood and smoothed her wrinkled dress. "I think I'll do just that. And I need to mail a letter to my family. They're probably wondering why they haven't heard from me yet. Thank you, Martha— for everything."

Ellen was grateful for a break, but she felt guilty for leaving her mother, even in the capable hands of Martha Baker. She breathed deeply and savored the sweet smell of honeysuckles as she walked down the red, dusty road. Just over the hill, she could see burley trees framing the pasture and cows grazing lazily in the distance. It was still early enough in the day that the air felt warm against her face but not sticky. A gentle breeze brushed her hair against her cheek. She had forgotten how much she missed this place.

A clutch of anxiety tugged at her as she thought about Frank and the children. She wondered how they were getting along without her. She'd been in such a hurry to leave Cartersville, had been so afraid that her mother would die before she could see her again. She wished again for the thousandth time that her children were here with her. She'd suggested it, but Frank had flatly refused, telling her they would only be in the way.

"Shelby is capable of running this house," he had said. "It'll be good for her."

Frank's argument had seemed reasonable enough at the time. But now, thinking back, she wondered if he had an ulterior motive. Was he afraid she wouldn't return if she took the children with her? Oh, she'd thought about leaving him often enough, especially when he drank. It was one of those notions that would seem so plausible, but then she would lose her nerve. Frank had provided a secure life with all of the comforts money could buy. Sometimes though, she wondered if the security was in reality a shackle that kept her bound to a man she did not love.

She shook her head in an attempt to purge the negative thoughts from her mind. Such thoughts were dangerous. She'd chosen her path long ago. There was no deviating from it. It didn't matter how she felt. She had to think about her children and what was best for them, and that meant staying with Frank. She would put one foot in front of the other, taking each mindless step the same way she had done for the past nineteen years. Yes, that was the answer.

As she made her way across the pasture, she detoured to a nearby stream. When she got closer, she could hear the musical sound of water flowing over the rocks. She looked down at the ground; the grass was just as lush and thick as it had been when she was a little girl. She looked up at the old, sturdy oak tree leaning across the stream. It seemed unchanged by the passage of time, as if waiting for her to come and play on its knobby, bent branches. She closed her eyes and could almost hear the laughter of summers long ago forgotten. Gazing around at the peaceful scene, it seemed ironic that she had once been eager to leave this place. How could it have remained the same when she had changed so much?

Chapter Five

Sister sighed deeply and fought the urge to cover her ears as Sarah's shrill voice echoed around the room for what seemed like the hundredth time.

"Sister! Sister!" she wailed.

"What is it now?"

"I want a drink of water, and Homer said I couldn't have one!"

"She's had so much water already this morning she's drunk the water jug dry," Homer answered indignantly. "It's completely empty!"

Sister looked at the little pudgy face, now red with fury, and nodded her head in agreement. "I think Homer is right. You've had enough water, honey."

Every thirty minutes or so Sarah would drink as much water as she could possibly hold and would then start wailing that she had to go. She and Sister would then have to take another trip to the outhouse.

"But I'm thirsty!"

"Why don't you go outside and play?"

Sarah began crying and jumping up and down. "I don't want to go outside! I want a drink of water!"

Homer turned his head in disgust. "Sarah, stop crying! You're being a big baby!"

Sarah shoved him in the stomach. "I am not being a baby!"

Before Homer could retaliate, Sister intervened. "Homer, would you please take Sarah out to the well and get another bucket of fresh water?"

"But, Sister—"

"We'll need some more water for supper." Sister's tone became authoritative, and Homer knew that he'd lost.

"Oh, all right," he huffed. "Come on Sarah," he barked.

Glad to have gotten her way, Sarah skipped happily behind him.

Sister watched them go out the door and prayed it would take them a while to fetch the water. There had been a time when she had yearned with all her heart to have children of her own. Finally, she'd accepted things the way they were and stopped hoping. Now, after two long weeks of taking care of Homer and Sarah, she had decided that maybe the good Lord knew what He was doing when he made her childless. She didn't know how much more her nerves could take. Her home, usually neat and orderly, was becoming disheveled, and a film of dust now covered her furniture. Every time she would start to get some things done, she would get interrupted. She didn't know how a little, three-year-old girl could have so much energy.

She had to admit that Homer had been a big help with Sarah. His only vice was his incessant talking. He talked from dawn to dusk and was always questioning everything. Most of the time, Sister just nodded her head and added in an occasional *really* or *uh-huh* to pacify him. That worked most of the time but not always. The most difficult question she'd had to answer for him was why Shelby had left. That was a hard question—one for which she had no answer. Homer had been so upset over Shelby's leaving that Sister hadn't wanted to hurt him further by reading him the note she had left. But after a few hours of constant badgering from Homer, she finally broke down and read it to him. She had hoped that would make things better, but it only made things worse. He insisted that there had been some sort of mistake.

"I know my sister wouldn't have left like that. She told me that she would always be here with us."

Sister had gently tried to explain to him that Shelby had written the letter. "Her decision to leave was of her own accord, dear. That doesn't mean she loves you any less. People often make mistakes. She just made a mistake by leaving. That's all."

In response, Homer had jutted out his chin and repeated the words he'd often heard his mother say, "I don't mean any disrespect, but I don't believe you."

She had talked to him until she was blue in the face, but nothing she said had in any way changed his mind. He kept stubbornly insisting Shelby wouldn't have left like that. Finally, Sister had given up. "I swear that boy could pester the hind legs off a mule."

Despite it all, Sister had to admit Homer had a point. In the past, Shelby had always proven to be sensible. Leaving suddenly seemed totally out of character for her. *It was a very dimwitted thing for her to do. She could have at least waited until she told me and Joshua where she was going instead of leaving us a note.* When Joshua had read the note, his face became dark, and he had stalked out the door, muttering about how he had failed Shelby.

Later that night, she had questioned him about his remark, but he had remained evasive. When she pressed him for an answer, he had finally told her that *some things are better left alone.* The knowledge that Joshua was keeping a secret from her was painful. *He knows something about Shelby's hasty departure, and it's tearing him up inside,* Sister thought. One of the things she'd always loved about Joshua was his strong character. He could be very affectionate and open with his feelings when he wanted to be, but there was another side of him—a self-possessed, hidden side he kept bottled up. He was like two separate people sometimes. She loved him deeply and accepted him as he was, but it didn't keep her from becoming frustrated on occasion.

From the time that Shelby was a young 'un, she and Joshua had developed a close relationship. At first, it had bothered Sister that the two of them shared something of which she was not a part. She had felt excluded and a little jealous when she realized Shelby confided in Joshua—not her. However, over time she had come to accept their closeness and even began to realize that their relationship had helped compensate for Joshua's inability to have a child of his own.

What does Joshua know that he's not tellin'?

I'd better make good use of my time while the young 'uns are gone. She decided to dust her furniture. *What was Shelby doing out at night all by herself when Joshua found her in the garden? And was she alone?* Judging by her appearance, Sister feared she might've been attacked or taken advantage of. Sister had never paid much attention to outward beauty, but even she had noticed that Shelby was strikingly beautiful, with her lustrous hair and dark eyes. She'd probably attracted the attention of just about every hot-blooded male this side of the Mason-Dixon Line. Shelby had always acted and dressed too maturely for her age. And that could only lead to trouble.

She shook her head woefully. *Why can't young girls learn not to lead fellas on?* Just the other day, Sister had heard a sad tale of a young girl over in Rome who had gotten in the habit of taking nightly walks by herself with a young man she had been courting. She had let him get too familiar with her and had then declined his advances. He became angry and forced his attentions on her. Afterwards, he had walked her home as if nothing had happened. The poor girl had been too scared and embarrassed to say anything right away. She kept her terrible secret to herself for a few weeks until she began to have stomach trouble every morning. Finally, she had to tell her family the truth. They sent her up North to stay with relatives for the duration of her confinement.

Sister's heart began to pound. *Had Shelby gotten into a similar situation? Was that why she left so suddenly?* Sister knew that only time would tell.

The dusting now done, she decided to turn her attention to mopping and cleaning her baseboards. *When would Ellen return?* She had spoken to Frank the other day at the store, and he told her he had finally received a letter from her. She had written that her mother was worse than they had at first thought, and she wasn't sure how much longer she would need to stay. For all their sakes, Sister hoped that she would be returning soon. Frank had looked unusually tired and haggard. His appearance and brusque manner had alarmed her. She had invited him to supper the past three nights in a row, but he had declined, saying he had too much work to catch up on at the store. Homer and Sarah kept asking why their papa hadn't been by to see them, and she kept making excuses for him.

She figured the real reason for his unwillingness to come to supper was the tension between him and Joshua. She dipped the mop into the pail. *How much longer could she keep things together? I really should do a better job of cleaning my baseboards,* she chided herself. *They're caked in dust.* She grabbed a rag and got down on her hands and knees to scrub. At the same moment, Homer and Sarah ran back into the house.

"What are you doing?" asked Homer.

"I'm tryin' to get this filthy house clean. I just mopped, so be careful. The floors are slippery."

Homer bent down. "Hey, it's Shelby's necklace."

"Where did you find that?"

"Right here. Behind the cupboard."

"She must've taken it off and dropped it."

"No, ma'am. She never takes it off," Homer answered matter-of-factly. "It was a gift from Mama." He handed the necklace to Sister. "Look, it's broken."

Sister's eyebrows wrinkled. Her pulse quickened as she held the necklace up to the light and examined the broken chain.

* * * * *

"Mr. Collins, Joshua came by the store while you were gone. When I told him you weren't here, he said he'd be back in about an hour."

"What time did he come in?" asked Frank a little too hastily.

Peggy eyed her boss suspiciously. She had worked as his assistant long enough to be able to detect his edginess. "About two o'clock. Is everything okay?"

"Yes, of course." The tone of his voice clearly indicated that whatever was troubling him was not up for discussion. Peggy shrugged her shoulders nonchalantly and finished sweeping the floor.

A few minutes later, he grabbed his hat off the rack and adjusted his tie. "Peggy, I've got to run out for a few minutes."

She stopped working, a confused expression on her face. "I thought you had to get Mr. Whitaker's order filled by three."

"Take care of it."

"But last time I got it wrong and you said from now on that you would do it. I don't think I—"

"Peggy," Frank barked, "what do I pay you for?"

Her face turned white, and she stood dumbly looking at him. Finally she managed to squeak out a "yes, sir" as he headed out the door.

Frank pulled his hat further down on his head and looked guardedly over his shoulder. Seeing that the coast was clear, he quickly made his way down the back of the stairs and across the dusty road. He was glad Peggy told him Joshua was stopping by. He knew he would have to face him sooner or later, but at least it wouldn't be today.

He shook his head in disgust and scowled. A store owner and one of the leading citizens of Cartersville, he resented being reduced to sneaking around behind his own store like a common thief. This was going to have to stop. If only he hadn't been so stupid...or so drunk. For a while, it looked as though things were going to turn out all right. It had been easy enough to charm that pompous schoolmaster, Miss Sharp, into taking Shelby. He had figured that with Shelby out of the picture, he wouldn't have any more snags. That was before Joshua kept coming around asking questions he didn't know how to answer. The fact of the matter was he couldn't really remember what happened that night.

He kept mulling things over in his head and kept coming up with the same answer: All of the blame lay with Ellen. It was her fault he was all alone. She was the reason he went out drinking in the first place. If she had been home like she should have been, none of this would've happened. Why did Shelby have to run and blab to Joshua? And why couldn't Joshua just leave things be? Joshua had been a thorn in his side for some time now, and he was getting a little tired of it. The only thing that had kept Frank from putting him in his place was Sister. Sister or no Sister, things between him and Joshua couldn't continue like they were. He had finally gotten a letter from Ellen saying her mama wasn't getting any better. She wasn't sure how much longer she would need to stay but would write again next week and let him know. Ellen and her precious mama. *Why can't she be here for me when I need her?*

An image of Ellen, with her long, graceful neck and upright posture, flashed through his mind. He closed his eyes and pictured her dark hair and olive skin. He could almost smell her perfume, and he longed for her. In his mind, she was smiling, her smile not quite reaching her eyes. Then her expression turned to disdain. His eyebrows creased, and he longed to wipe the smirk off her face. *She's always been a little too proud. Maybe she thinks she's better than me.* He knew one thing for sure: There wouldn't be any more long trips to Alabama for Ellen. He was gonna make her pay for all the trouble she'd caused. Things were gonna change. He was the man of his house, and when she came back, he would put her in her place like he should've done a long time ago. He felt a thrill of power shoot through him. In his resolve, his back became a little straighter and his step more sure. He forgot his troubles for a moment and started to whistle as he walked. Things were definitely gonna change.

Chapter Six

Shelby sat stiffly in her seat, her head erect, and tried to ignore the commotion going on in back of her. The windows were open, but the room was still hot and sticky. She could see a few of the teachers vigorously waving paper fans back and forth. Every morning, just after breakfast, all of the students gathered to have prayer and devotional. Shelby didn't mind beginning each day with a prayer; she had grown up doing the same. Having to listen to Reverend James drone on for a half hour, however, was an entirely different story. She heard a couple of the other girls saying that he only came two days a week, and she could already tell that two days was more than enough for her. She squirmed in her seat and then stifled a yawn. Relaxing her shoulders a bit, she leaned back in her seat. *I might as well get comfortable,* she thought.

"In the Bible, the Lord tells us to love one another. The book of Matthew tells us: 'Ye have heard that it hath been said, Thou shalt love thy neighbor, and hate thine enemy. But I say unto you, Love your enemies, bless them that curse you, do good to them that hate you, pray for them which despitefully use you and persecute you.' Now I would ask you, Who is your neighbor? Look to each side of you. Here are your neighbors!" While saying his last phrase the reverend raised his voice to a crescendo and slammed his fist down on the podium. He was a tall, portly man with thick, dark hair and fleshy cheeks who looked as though he might have tasted one too many cherry tarts offered by solicitous ladies at Sunday picnics.

He turned to Miss Sharp and smiled broadly, revealing large, gapped teeth. "It is a great privilege to be able to come here and speak. I want to give a special tribute to Miss Sharp; a lady whom I feel truly exemplifies the commandment to 'love thy neighbor.'" Miss Gretta Sharp acknowledged the reverend's compliment by slightly nodding her head.

"Don't let the good ol' rev fool ya, gals. The only thing ol' hawk-eye loves is herself," came a hushed whisper from behind.

Shelby's eyes widened in disbelief, and she turned her head slightly to see who had spoken. A skinny, blonde girl sat in the middle of several other sniggering girls, and Shelby guessed the comment had come from her. The girl looked pleased with her little joke, and when she caught Shelby's eye, she winked. Shelby quickly turned around.

When the sermon was finally over, the girls were dismissed. They all filed out the door as quickly as possible, and Shelby guessed they were all breathing silent gasps of relief. Once outside, she found herself standing face to face with the girl who had told the joke.

The girl was at least three inches taller than Shelby. Her hair was long and stringy, and she had a few freckles sprinkled across her angular nose. She would probably be pretty, Shelby decided, if she gained a few pounds. Sister would love to get a hold of her so she could fatten her up.

"Did you just get here last night?"

Shelby nodded.

"You looked surprised by what I said about Miss Sharp."

"It just caught me off-guard."

"It's true. The only thing that battleaxe cares about is herself."

"Do you talk about all of the teachers this way?"

"No, just the majority of them. A few weeks here, and you'll see."

"Is it really that bad?"

The girl paused for a moment and surveyed Shelby from head to toe. "How did a proper girl like you end up in a place like this?"

"I'd rather not talk about it." The girl's probing gaze made Shelby uncomfortable, and she looked down at the ground.

The girl shrugged her shoulders. "Suit yourself. What chore have you been assigned to this week?"

"Garden."

"Me too. Come on. I'll show you where to go. By the way, my name's Frankie. What's yours?"

"Shelby"

"That's a weird name."

"Not as weird as Frankie." Shelby answered, somewhat offended.

Frankie laughed. "Okay, okay, you've got a point. Come on. Let's go."

"How did you get the name 'Frankie' anyway?"

"I was named after my mother's second husband. He ran out on her right after I was born, so she named me Frankie so she could always remember him. She says she done right because I give her nearly as much trouble as he done."

Shelby chuckled. There was something refreshing about this carefree girl who was not afraid to speak her mind.

"Miss Sharp must really have it in for you to stick you with garden duty your first week here."

"Really?"

"Yeah, everybody hates it. It gets hotter than blue blazes out here. That's why they switched the schedule around. In the spring and fall, they hold the classes in the morning and do chores in the afternoon."

"I would rather get the chores done first."

Frankie looked at Shelby in amusement and raised one eyebrow. "Gardening is hard work. Have you ever worked in a garden before?"

It was Shelby's turn to be amused. "I can hold my own."

"All right. Let's go. I'll race you!"

Frankie shot off like a bullet. Shelby shook her head and took off in pursuit.

* * * * *

Ignoring the persistent stinging caused by fresh blisters on her hands, Shelby repeatedly attacked the hard ground, loosening it with each swift motion of her hoe.

"Hey, Shelby!" Frankie yelled. "You'd better slow down; you'll wear yourself out fast at that pace."

"Thanks for the advice, but I've worked in the garden ever since I was old enough to walk. It will take a while for my hands to toughen up though. At home, I always wear thick gloves so my hands won't get calluses. I guess that luxury is over."

"Yeah, you can be sure that old hawk-eye ain't gonna spend no extra money for gloves. She hordes every penny that comes into this place. We're lucky to have socks and shoes."

"What does she spend the money on?"

"Beats me."

Shelby gazed over the garden and saw a handful of other girls working. Frankie had introduced her to a couple of them. They were all dressed in identical drab, brown dresses that would have faded into the dirt except for the brightly colored handkerchiefs some of the girls had wrapped around their heads. She looked down with disdain at her own shapeless dress. Yesterday, Miss Shirley had given her three dresses exactly alike and told her that she would be required to wash them in the scrub tub every Saturday. "I don't know what your personal cleanliness habits have been in the past," she had said, "but at this school, we expect you to keep yourself and your clothing clean."

Shelby had merely nodded, all the while fighting the urge to laugh hysterically. Time and time again, her mama had affectionately told her. "Shelby, I appreciate all of your help around the house, but you don't have to keep everything looking perfect all the time."

"Cleanliness is next to godliness, Mama," she would quip.

"Water break! Water break!"

Shelby turned to see a young girl walking down the row carrying a big bucket of water and a dipper. "Good. I'm soaking wet with perspiration," she said, brushing her matted hair out of her eyes as she hastily put down her hoe and walked over to get a drink.

Frankie jeered, "My goodness, you are proper. Don't you mean wet with sweat?"

* * * * *

Shelby and Frankie worked side by side in the garden as time slowly passed. Neither the hot sun nor the exhausting work could quiet Frankie; she talked incessantly. Shelby learned that Frankie had been at the industrial school for two months. She was the third child in a total of six, most of whom had different papas. Her mother had been married three times and had lived with several boyfriends in between. Her latest beau and Frankie didn't get along and were always fighting. He beat Frankie's mama and had even hit Frankie a few times. Frankie's mama blamed her for the conflict. Finally, Frankie had enough and left home. Shelby had been amazed at this story. "Your mama just let you leave home just like that?"

"Ma said that times were hard and my leaving would mean she had one less mouth to feed."

Frankie had spent two months living on the streets, finding shelter wherever she could until she was arrested for vagrancy and a few other things she didn't care to mention. Finally, she was brought to the school.

Shelby shook her head in disbelief. She couldn't help but compare her own beloved mama to Frankie's. Mama had a special way of making each of her children feel cherished and special. In fact, she realized forcefully, she had spent her entire life seeing herself through her mama's eyes. This perspective had strengthened her and had given her an added sense of worth. Her mama had always taught her that no obstacle was too great to overcome.

"All it takes is faith and perseverance," Mama would constantly say.

Shelby had heard those words so often she would sometimes mimic them while her mama spoke. Those words were beginning to take on a new meaning. *Mama said no obstacle was too strong to overcome, but she hasn't seen my predicament. This may be too great—even for Mama.* She wiped away a hot tear, and silently, with all her being, uttered a prayer. *Please, Lord, help me to have the strength I so desperately need to get through this, and please help Mama find me.*

Chapter Seven

Joshua tipped his hat and curtly smiled to Mrs. Meriweather and her daughter Rachel as he passed them on the street. "Howdy do, ladies."

"Good afternoon, Joshua," they chimed in unison.

"How is Sister doing?" Inquired Mrs. Meriweather. "I haven't seen her in a long time. It has been a while since she has been to town."

"Sister is doing fine."

"Please tell her I said hello."

He smiled politely. "Will do. You ladies have a nice day."

"Thank you," they said as they passed on by.

Normally, Joshua would've taken the time to inquire about Hank, Mrs. Meriweather's husband. Someone had told him the other day that Hank had been a little under the weather for the past few weeks. Hank Meriweather briefly skirted the edge of his mind. Today, Joshua had more important issues that captured his attention. He really didn't have time to keep leaving the farm and coming into town, but he needed answers, and he wasn't about to wait any longer to get them.

Frank was obviously avoiding him. He had already been by the store twice, and Frank hadn't been there. The last time he had even told Peggy he would be back by in a little while. When he returned, Frank was gone, and Peggy gave some lame excuse about his having to run an errand. He took long, purposeful strides up the road to get to his destination. This time, there would be no excuses; he wouldn't go inside until he saw Frank there. When he got about 100 yards from the store, he stopped and peered inside. The afternoon sun was casting a glare off the window, making it impossible to see. He raised his hand and shielded the sun from his eyes, hoping that would help. He still couldn't make out anything, so he moved a little closer. The door opened, and a customer came out. The fraction of time the door remained opened was enough for him to catch a quick glimpse of Frank leaning against the counter. Joshua felt his chest tighten and his pulse quicken. He wished at that moment he could turn his back and walk away, never seeing Frank again. If he had been any less of a man, he would have. But Joshua was a man of strong principle, and there was Shelby to consider. She had always been like a daughter to him. He had to find out if she had tried to contact Frank. *Where did she go, and how could a young girl survive on her own? Did she take any money with her?* He doubted it.

He shook his head sorrowfully. *Oh Shelby, why couldn't you have trusted me? We would've worked through this whole mess.* Now, all he had to go on was Shelby's fragmented accusation, which she related the night of her attack. He knew Shelby well enough to know she was a straight-shooter. She wouldn't intentionally lie, that much he knew. *But was everything she told him absolutely correct, or could she have imagined things worse than they actually were?* He remembered her bare feet and the bloody scratches on her legs. *One thing was for sure, her distress had been real. She said she hit him with a skillet...and Frank did have a bruise across his forehead.* At least that part of her story rang true. Apprehension gnawed at the pit of his stomach. It was evident that Frank wasn't going to admit one dad-blasted thing. *It will be my word against his,* he reasoned. Maybe *I should go ahead and tell Sister.* He dismissed the idea. He couldn't burden Sister with this, at least not until he had all of the facts. He would wait until Ellen returned, and he would talk to her. *Ellen would know what to do.* Resolutely, he took a deep breath and squared his shoulders as he walked across the street and opened the door to the general store.

It took a minute for Joshua's eyes to adjust to the dim light inside the store. He gave himself a moment and then walked briskly toward the counter where Frank was standing.

"Well, I'll be. This is a pleasant surprise. What brings you to town this time of the day? I figured you be too busy plantin' to come in."

The familiar voice came from behind, and he turned to see Earl Davis and Luther Walker, two of Cartersville's most prominent and notable citizens. Earl ran the local bank next door to the general store, and Luther owned the only blacksmith shop in town. Joshua smiled cordially and shook hands with the two men. I picked a fine time to come here and butt heads with Frank, he thought. For a few minutes, he small-talked amicably with the two men as they discussed every insignificant topic, ranging from the weather to the fertilization of crops. All the while, the tension kept building inside him. From the corner of his eye, he could see Frank shifting uncomfortably and knew that he felt the tension as well. Mercifully, the conversation finally ended, and the two gentlemen went to get whatever it was they came into the store to buy. His jaw set firm, in a taut line; Joshua made his way over to the counter and stood facing Frank. He gave him a curt nod and a hard look.

Peggy was standing beside Frank. "Hello, Josh. What can we get for you today?" she asked.

Keenly aware that Earl and Luther were still in the store, Joshua decided to buy some time so he could speak to Frank privately. "Give me twenty pounds of sugar."

"Coming right up," she said cheerfully. "Would you like to put that on your account?"

While Peggy talked, Frank was bent over doing some figuring in a ledger. He stood up and looked steadily at Joshua and spoke loudly enough for everyone in the store to hear. "I can no longer finance your purchases. Your bill is past due. I'm afraid you're gonna have to pay with cash."

Peggy, who had gone to get the sugar, stopped dead in her tracks; Earl and Luther stopped what they were doing and looked at Frank and Joshua, astonished expressions on their faces. The words caught Joshua completely by surprise as if an invisible fist had sliced through the air and bushwhacked him. He gasped audibly and felt the heat of humiliation reddening his cheeks. "What're you talking about?" he growled. "We've had the same system for ten years. I always pay my bills in full come harvest time."

Frank blatantly ignored Joshua's explanation. Joshua would've liked to have pulled the spineless worm out into the street by the hair of his head and given him the bull-whippin' he deserved. With Earl and Luther in the store, his hands were tied, and he could only glower.

Frank sensed his advantage and went for the jugular vein. "Just because you're my sister's husband, doesn't mean that you don't have to pay your bills on time like everybody else." He let out a derisive chuckle. "What have you been spending your money on anyhow?" He looked over at Earl who was standing nearby and winked. "Maybe I should have a little talk with Sister."

Earl's eyes widened as he looked back and forth between Frank and Joshua and noted the black fury on the face of the latter. The situation made him uncomfortable, and he started fidgeting with a button on his shirt. Quickly, he turned and pretended to take interest in the reading spectacles in the display case.

Joshua's eyes narrowed into angry slits. "This ain't about money and you know it. Why don't you stand up for once and be a real man instead of slinking behind a bushel of lies?"

The brother-in-laws' conversation had everyone in the store's attention now, and Frank played up to his audience. He raised his hands in the air and smiled benignly, his eyes glittering like a snake poised to strike.

"I have no hard feelings for you, Joshua. Business is business. From now on, just pay for everything with cash—no credit." The words dripped silkily from his mouth.

For a moment, Joshua was too stunned to reply. He just stood there gaping at Frank. After he collected himself, he shook his head in revulsion as he felt bile rise in his throat. "You disgust me," he said hoarsely. Joshua wearily turned and made his way to the door, ignoring the stunned glances from those around him, feeling as though he carried the weight of the world on his chest.

*   *   *   *   *

Bedtime at the industrial school was strictly enforced—a fact Shelby did not mind. In the heat of the summer, humidity always made sleep uncomfortable. Back home, the shade trees covering her roof had kept the house cooler during the day, helping make the summer nights more bearable. There, occasional breezes flowing in through open windows had made some nights even pleasant. Here, there were no shade trees sheltering the building and few, if any, breezes. The added heat of all of the bodies made the room extremely hot and sticky. Her first few nights at the school were absolutely miserable. Mercifully, her body was beginning to adjust.

In the summertime, the students began their daily chores right after the morning devotional. Classes were held after lunch. This schedule was adopted so the garden work could be done before the heat of the afternoon set in. Shelby had been assigned garden duty every day since her arrival at the school. She was usually so exhausted after each daily routine that she often went to sleep right after her head touched her pillow. Tonight was no exception.

*   *   *   *   *

She was lost and couldn't find her way. It was dark. She groped in the darkness and felt something. *What was it? A door? But...where was the knob?* Frantically, she pounded on the closed door but to no avail. Sobbing, she screamed for help. The only sound she heard was her own voice echoing through the empty corridor. In the distance, she heard a faint sound. It was coming closer. *Footsteps!* She began to run wildly through the blackness, tripping and falling as she went. He was getting closer; she could hear him breathing. Suddenly, he grabbed her. In her terror, she was paralyzed. She tried to move, to scream, but couldn't. He was shaking her.

"Shelby!"

"No! Please, leave me alone," she sobbed.

"Shelby! Wake up! Keep your voice down. Do you want to wake up the entire room?" Frankie hissed.

Still half asleep, Shelby turned to see Frankie kneeling beside her bed.

"Who? What?"

In an instant, she was bolted into the present. "Oh," she whispered, somewhat embarrassed, "I must have been dreaming."

Frankie grunted. "It must've been some dream. Why were you crying?"

Shelby ignored the question. "What are you doing up this time of the night?"

"Shhh! Keep your voice down!"

"Okay."

"I need you to go for a walk with me."

"Right now?" Shelby asked incredulously.

"Yeah, I'll explain on the way."

"Where are we going? We'll get in so much trouble. Let's go for a walk tomorrow."

"Come on. Get dressed. We ain't got much time."

Still dazed, Shelby put on her dress and shoes and followed behind Frankie. Before going out the door, she turned and glanced around the motionless room. She could hear regular breathing and a few snores. A sudden movement from across the room startled her. She looked over and saw a girl toss and then turn over in the other direction. She bolted out the door and caught up with Frankie. Carefully, they made their way down the hall and into the night. Breathing a sigh of relief, Shelby glanced at Frankie.

"Where to?" she asked.

"We're going to the shed beside the garden."

Shelby was puzzled. "Why?"

"I've got a friend who's gonna meet us there."

"In the middle of the night? Why don't you meet with her during the day?"

"It's not a her; but a him and his friend that we're meetin'."

"Are you crazy?"

Frankie smiled and shook her head. "No, just looking for a little company. That's all."

Realization dawned, and Shelby suddenly understood. Her apprehension grew as she absorbed the full scope of the situation. Frankie said that her friend was bringing someone with him. Surely Frankie didn't think... She had never given her that impression...had she?

The muggy air pressed on Shelby as she glanced up to see a luminous, full moon. She normally would have taken the time to marvel at its perfectly round shape or its brilliant beams, lighting up the path before them. Now, she wished for darkness. Her anxiety increased with every step. Why had she let Frankie talk her into this? Even as she pondered the question, she already knew the answer. It was the nightmare. Tonight was the second one this week. Forcing herself not to think about it, she looked down at the ground and followed behind Frankie.

Frankie suddenly stopped, causing Shelby to stumble and almost collide into the back of her. "Shhh!"

"What? I don't hear anything." *Not that I could hear anything other than the sound of my chest pounding in my ears*, Shelby thought. She looked at Frankie and marveled at how calm she was.

"Listen!" Frankie barked.

Shelby strained her ears and heard a faint whistling in the distance. As the sound grew closer, she realized what she was hearing. It was a song. Someone was whistling a song!

"Get down!" Frankie grabbed her arm and pulled her behind a tree. They both listened as the melodic tune of *Dixie* floated gently in the wind.

Shelby shot Frankie a questioning glance, and Frankie shrugged. "I don't know who else could possibly be out this late," she whispered.

Shelby rolled her eyes in disgust. "Anyone else would have more sense."

They waited. The whistling grew louder and was soon accompanied by footsteps. Shelby peered into the distance. Her eyes widened in surprise and she instinctively shrank deeper into the cover of the tree. Coming toward them was the largest colored man she had ever seen. He was wearing blue overalls and heavy work boots. Even though his face was partially hidden in the shadows from the moon, his disposition seemed pleasant, and she could imagine he had a broad grin under his prominent nose. As he lumbered past them, she realized he had a slight limp.

"It's just Grover."

"Who?"

"Grover. He lives behind the school." She pointed. "Just there. He takes care of the yards and helps on the farm." They waited until the whistling had completely faded, and then Frankie took Shelby's hand and pulled her out from behind the tree. Together, they made their way down the path to the garden. Shelby's fear began to subside a bit, and her heart beat normally. She could then more accurately assess her present situation. She wiped her sweaty hands on her dress and took a deep breath as she pushed a strand of hair from her forehead. She glanced sideways in Frankie's direction, and her heart lurched as the familiar fear returned. Swallowing hard, she rubbed her tongue across her parched lips.

Frankie didn't seem concerned about their situation. On the contrary, her feverish excitement was intensifying with each passing moment. Her flaxen hair, normally stringy and unkempt, was neatly brushed and shining in the moonlight. Even though it was dark,

Shelby could see a mischievous sparkle in her hazel eyes. Frankie looked almost pretty in the moonlight.

What have I gotten myself into? Shelby wondered.

"I think they're already here. Let's hurry!"

Frankie quickly grew impatient with Shelby's pace and bounded on ahead. For a split second, Shelby started to catch up but then thought better of it. She'd get there soon enough.

The moon rose full overhead, casting eerie shadows as she walked. Crickets and katydids broke the stillness of the night with their incessant chirping, and Shelby had the fleeting impression they were screaming at her. She could see the shed looming in the distance, its tin roof casting a soft glow in the darkness. She rounded the corner and gaped when she saw Frankie and her friend entangled. He held her tightly around the waist in a dipped position, her long hair flowing behind. His lips were tightly pressed to hers. Suddenly, he jerked her forward and twirled her around.

"Frankie, my girl, I thought you would never get here," he said joyfully. The two clasped hands and started twirling each other around and around until they fell to the ground laughing. Like Frankie, he was tall and lanky and nimble on his feet. His sun-streaked hair was slightly longer on top, causing it to flutter around like the end of a mop with each movement as he danced around. The pair seemed perfectly matched. She stared at the two in fascination, feeling as though she were watching two pixies frolicking in the moonlight.

There was a movement off to her side Shelby felt more than heard. Startled, she whirled around. She had been so mesmerized she had forgotten someone else was here. He was leaning against the shed with one foot propped against the wall. She strained to see his face, but it was covered in shadows. Her face burned and her heart pounded as she realized that while she had been intently watching Frankie and her friend, he had been watching her. She glanced over at Frankie and the boy; they sat on the ground facing each other. Suddenly, as if by some unspoken agreement, the two jumped up and ran off together, leaving Shelby all alone with the stranger.

Shelby debated a few moments about what to do. Should she leave or stay? She was furious with Frankie for dragging her out in the middle of the night and then leaving her alone. Resolutely, she squared her shoulders and lifted her head in the air as she walked over to a nearby log and sat down. She decided that rather than approach the boy, she would let him come to her. She figured he would come and introduce himself, but he stayed against the shed. They both sat in silence. Shelby shifted around uncomfortably. With a concentrated effort she peered into the darkness. She still couldn't see him because he was covered in shadows, but she guessed he could see her. Why was he just standing there? Was he staring at her? Icy prickles of fear crept up her spine. Just as she was about to leave, he stood up and came over to where she was.

"Hey, howya doin? My name's Harlan."

"Hi."

The first thing Shelby noticed was the contrast between his light eyes and suntanned skin. He had a strong jaw and rugged features. He was thin, but not frail; tall, but not massive. She glanced at him and guessed that he couldn't be much older than she. His erect posture and graceful movements radiated confidence. His features were too angular to be what she considered classically handsome, but there was something striking about him—a confidence, an air of authority—suggesting he would be completely in control of any situation. *Yes, he is attractive and very sure of himself.* She disliked him immediately.

He sat down close beside her, and she quickly scooted away, putting distance between them. He didn't seem to notice.

"It's a nice evening."

"Yes, it is," she agreed.

"You didn't tell me your name."

"My what? Oh—Shelby."

"Pleased to meet you...Shelby."

"Thank you."

Shelby didn't look in his direction as she spoke but kept staring into the darkness, hoping Frankie would return soon.

"Where are you from?"

"Georgia."

"You're a long way from home."

"Yeah." She fidgeted with her hands as she spoke. "Where do you think they went?"

"Who?"

"Frankie and the guy she's with."

Instead of answering her question, he laughed and gave Shelby an appraising look that made her blush. She held his intense gaze for a moment and then looked away.

He reached out and touched a strand of her hair. "You have beautiful hair."

She pushed his hand away and jumped up.

"What's the matter? You act like I just struck you with a hot poker. I was only giving you a compliment."

Somewhat embarrassed, but nervous nonetheless, she stammered, "T-this was a mistake. I shouldn't be out here."

"Oh, I see."

"See what?" Her voice rose.

"Just a little cold feet."

"What do you mean by that?" she demanded angrily.

He stood up and faced her. "Why did you come out here?"

She looked up at his face and realized what he was getting at. "Not for the reason you think."

The crickets' incessant chirping had stopped, making the night seem even more solitary. Once again Shelby was keenly aware that she was out here in the dark—alone with a stranger.

"When a girl sneaks out late at night to meet someone out behind a shed, I can think of only one reason for her motive. Correct me if I'm wrong."

Shelby's face flamed, and sparks flew from her eyes as she replied with all the righteous indignation she could muster. "You most certainly are wrong. I am not that kind of girl. I didn't come out here for..." Her voice faltered, and she was unable to finish.

His eyes twinkled in amusement, and he chuckled, "You're even prettier when you're angry."

"I've had enough of your lewd remarks. I'm leaving now!"

"Just one thing before you go." He grabbed her around the waist and pulled her to him and pressed his lips to hers.

She felt the familiar fear return and stood frozen in place as he kissed her. Finally, he let her go. "That's more like it," he drawled.

Her fury rose, and she slapped him hard across the jaw. She then turned to run up the path back toward the school but tripped on a root protruding slightly above the ground. He tried to help her up, but she pushed him away and got up and fled, sobbing as she went.

Chapter Eight

Lucy Pearl paced angrily back and forth across the sidewalk of the schoolhouse. Her arms were tightly crossed, hugging herself, and she had a grim expression on her face. Normally, she wore her raven hair tightly pinned on top of her head. Tonight, it flowed loosely around her shoulders making her look much younger than her age of twenty-three. She was a teacher but could almost have been mistaken for a student herself. Her mammy had always told her that she had a hot temper. She shook her head. She had shown it today. If any of her students could've read Lucy's mind they might have been surprised to learn that their pleasant, level-headed teacher would describe herself as hot-tempered.

Among the students, she was definitely the most well-liked teacher at the school. Part of her success could be attributed to her quick wit and ability not to take herself too seriously. She emanated a zest for life that drew others to her, and she had the unconscious knack of putting people around her at ease. These qualities no doubt aided her in teaching, but the real key to her success was the deep compassion she felt for her students. She genuinely loved teaching. Her motto had always been, "Education is the only true road to success." She herself was highly educated and could've easily gotten a job teaching at a more prestigious school with better pay. But money had never been a great enticement to her. She was single and didn't need much to live. She had wanted to go where she could make a real difference in the lives of those she taught.

Two years ago, when it had opened, she had come to the industrial school with high hopes. She had asked herself: *What better place could there be to help those who could truly benefit from education?*

Lately, she had begun to question her decision. How was she supposed to teach her students without adequate books and supplies? The material was old and outdated. There weren't enough books to go around, so some of the girls had to share. This meant she couldn't give them any homework assignments that required the use of their books.

Earlier today, an event had occurred that was the straw that broke the camel's back. She had stepped out of the room for a moment. When she returned, two of her students, Tessie and Rachel, were rolling around on the floor. They had gotten into an argument that had come to blows. After pulling them apart, she discovered the reason for their disagreement. Rachel had stolen Tessie's book because she was tired of sharing with one of the other girls. Lucy knew that part of the problem could be attributed to the girls' upbringing. Still, in an institution whose sole purpose was to educate, it seemed ridiculous that there weren't enough textbooks to go around. All afternoon, she had stewed over the situation and had finally grown so frustrated she had confronted Gretta Sharp about it. That had been a big mistake. When Lucy went to Gretta's office, her secretary Shirley had snippily told her she would have to make an appointment.

"You know the rules. Miss Sharp doesn't see anyone without a prior appointment."

Lucy had felt her blood boil. Somehow, she had managed to keep her voice even when she spoke. "Shirley, I have something to say to Gretta, and I will not leave without seeing her. Kindly tell her I am here, or I will barge into her office this instant!"

Shirley became flustered. "You don't have to be rude about it. Have a seat, and I'll tell her you're here."

Once inside Gretta's office, Lucy had cooled her temper enough to plead her case rationally. While she spoke, Gretta had looked several times at her watch. She informed Lucy in no uncertain terms that the funds were stretched as far as they would go. "Miss Pearl, you are just going to have to do a better job managing the resources you have been allotted so that in the future you won't have to come in my office begging for more money. You have such grand ideas; unfortunately, these lofty ideas are unnecessary and expensive."

Lucy's voice rose, and she spat out her words. "How can you possibly think that wanting each of my students to have her own books is a frivolous request? As a learning institution, if we do nothing else, we should at least provide books."

"I believe you are forgetting your place, Miss Pearl. I have given you my answer. Like the rest of us, you are just going to have to make do."

Lucy gave Miss Sharp a withering look, and without another word, left her office, slamming the door behind her. Once outside the door, Shirley had furtively glanced at her then ducked her head. Lucy figured that she'd been right outside the door, hanging on every word. She guessed the yellow-bellied coward would spread every word of the conversation to the entire staff before the evening was out. *I hope she does*, Lucy thought. *It's about time someone stood up to the old biddy.* In all her years, Lucy had never met anyone as cold as Gretta Sharp.

For the first couple of hours after the encounter, Lucy felt giddy. However, as the afternoon wore into evening, she became uneasy. She asked herself why she stormed out of Gretta's office like that. *What if Gretta fires me? It wouldn't be the end of the world if she does. I could get another job.* Deep down, she knew the reason for her fears. Despite the difficult circumstances she faced, she really did love her job. She had seen more than a few girls take hold of their newfound knowledge and use it to make a better life for themselves. She was making a difference.

She looked up at the glittering stars. The air felt cool and moist, and she guessed it was after midnight. She knew she shouldn't be out this late alone, but she had been unable to sleep, and she enjoyed the quiet time to herself with no one else around. Out here beneath the velvety blanket of stars, she could think clearly.

What Miss Sharp told me makes no sense whatsoever. The industrial school is partially state funded. I know the state doesn't provide much, but the school also gets donations from the community and has held several fundraisers throughout the year. She reached up and massaged her stiff neck. *Where is all the money going?*

She looked at the red-brick schoolhouse with its large windows and sparkling white trim. It was stately. *Too bad Miss Sharp isn't as concerned about the inner quality of the school as she is about its outward appearance.* She paced back and forth a few more times. Suddenly, she felt very tired. She turned to go back to her room and then saw movement out of the corner of her eye. She turned and saw a girl running full speed in her direction. The girl was sobbing and looking at the ground. She didn't see Lucy in her path until they almost collided.

"Whoa. What's the trouble?"

As the girl gasped in surprise, Lucy instantly recognized her. "Shelby, what on earth are you doing out here this late?"

"Oh, Miss Pearl, I'm so confused—I don't know what to do." They sat down on the schoolhouse steps. Lucy put her arm around Shelby's shaky shoulders and tried to make sense of what she was saying. Shelby's words came haltingly at first as she described the events which had just taken place. Miss Pearl's sympathetic expression was balm to Shelby's wounded soul. Then, a dam broke loose inside, and her words came tumbling faster and faster until she had told Miss Pearl everything about the fateful night that led to her confinement at the school.

Miss Pearl listened intently as her eyes narrowed and her jaw became set in a firm, grim line. When Shelby finished speaking, they both sat in a comfortable silence as Miss Pearl collected her thoughts. Finally, she spoke. "From the first moment I laid eyes on you, I knew you didn't come here under the usual circumstances. You are well educated. You've obviously had a good upbringing, and in the short length of time you've been here, you've already mastered all of the skills we teach. Have you told anyone else about this?"

"No, ma'am."

"Does Miss Sharp know what happened to you?"

Shelby shrugged her shoulders. "My papa brought me to the school. He spoke to Miss Sharp. I don't know what he told her. I can only guess."

"Yes, you're probably right. We have to assume that whatever he told her was most assuredly not in your favor. Has she spoken to you about it?"

"Not really. She doesn't like me very much, so I try to stay away from her."

Lucy nodded in agreement. "That's wise. Have you tried to contact any of your family members?"

Fresh tears welled in Shelby's almond-shaped eyes. "No."

"Why not?"

"He—he told me I had better not try and contact anyone. He told me if I did…" Shelby was unable to continue. She buried her head in her lap.

"What did he tell you?"

Shelby lifted her head from her lap, the hurt emanating from her eyes. "That he would harm Homer and Sarah. Besides, it wouldn't do any good to try to contact anyone because they wouldn't believe me anyway because of the letter."

"The letter he made you write?"

"Yes."

Lucy chose her words carefully when she spoke. "Have you ever considered that maybe your papa only said those things to scare you?"

"I have considered that, but what if he's not bluffing?" Shelby paused, considering the possibilities. She shuddered. "I'm not sure I'm willing to risk it. And, even if I were, it wouldn't do any good. Miss Sharp screens all of the mail. She wouldn't let me get a letter through unless I addressed it to Papa."

"Do you know your aunt and uncle's address?"

"Yes."

"When was your mama going to return home?"

"She didn't know how long she would be gone when she left, but she should be back by now."

"Okay, here's what we'll do. Don't tell anyone else about this. Let's just keep it to ourselves. Write a letter to your aunt and uncle explaining everything. I'll mail it myself. How does that sound?"

"Okay, I guess." Lucy detected the doubt in Shelby's reply. "Is there another reason you don't want to write them?"

"The night Papa attacked me, I told my uncle Joshua what happened. I don't think he believed me. I know that my aunt Sister won't believe me. He has turned them all against me."

Lucy's heart wrenched as she listened to the deep anguish in Shelby's voice. She felt a growing animosity toward this man she had never met. She wondered what type of man—no, monster—did this to his own flesh and blood? She looked at the vibrant, young girl sitting beside her and asked herself the same worn-out question she often asked when considering the injustices of the world: Why should a young, innocent child have to carry such deep, cutting wounds at such a tender age? Would the scars ever heal? She had to help the girl. But how? She took a deep breath as she tried to find the right words to say.

"Shelby, I can't speak for your aunt and uncle. Maybe they believe you; maybe they don't. I can, however, speak for myself. I consider myself to be an excellent judge of character and am hardly ever wrong. You are a sweet and pure girl, the best this world can hope for, and who has been terribly wronged. I believe every word you have spoken and will do my best to help you any way I can."

"Thank you."

The gratitude in Shelby's voice was evident, but she stared unseeingly in the distance. Lucy decided to switch gears.

"What do you think of the school?"

Shelby turned and looked at her, surprise written all over her face. "What?"

"The school, what do you think of the industrial school?"

"I think it's the most horrible place on earth."

Lucy's eyes widened in surprise, and a smile played around the corners of her lips. She felt a surge of relief. There was still spunk left in this girl. She was stronger than she realized.

"Okay, you gave me a fair answer to a fair question. Now, let me tell you what I think—better yet what I *see* at this school. I see a wealth of opportunity and knowledge free for the taking. I see unfortunate girls who have grown up under the worst circumstances who have been given a second chance at life. I see education as a lifeline to a better life, and I see some of them grasping onto this newfound knowledge and pulling themselves to freedom—freedom from poverty and indigent circumstances."

It was Shelby's turn to be surprised. "I've never thought about it that way. I have been judging everything by my own circumstances."

Lucy nodded. "We all do that sometimes. Be it bad or good, perception is reality. You see, there are two types of people in this world: those who live in hope, and those who live in fear. Do you suppose that those who live in hope always have ideal circumstances?"

"I...I don't know. I've never considered it."

"Bad things happen to good people all of the time. Some people think because they've had it hard, the world owes them something. I shouldn't be saying this to you, but I will. Look at Miss Sharp; she had a hard life and has become bitter about it. She spends all of her time studying about what she can get out of life instead of what she can give to others. In saving her life, she actually loses it." Lucy stopped speaking and looked directly at Shelby for a moment. Gently, she continued. "You can't change the fact that you're here; that's beyond your control. But you can control the experience you have while you're here—or at the very least, your outlook on the situation. Who knows? Maybe something good will come out of this whole ordeal."

Shelby considered Miss Pearl's words. Somehow, they made her feel better, but she was still skeptical. "How can one hope when the situation seems hopeless?"

"Look around you. There's always hope. Sometimes, you just have to look a little harder to find it. Hope is evident in little things; things we often take for granted. No matter how dark the night seems, there's always a sunrise waiting a few, short hours away. Every winter the earth looks desolate and dead, but look what happens every spring. There's hope in every breath we take, in every smile." Lucy looked over and saw Shelby wipe away a tear. She smiled tenderly. "Yes, there's even hope in every tear. Starting right now, resolve to live your life in hope. Stop dwelling on the past; concentrate on the future, and things will get better."

Shelby digested the words she had just heard. She wanted to believe them, but could she? "It's something to think about," she replied as much to herself as to Lucy.

"You just keep that chin of yours up, and I'll see what I can do. In the meantime, I think you should consider writing a letter to your aunt and uncle. Everyone deserves a second chance. Don't you agree?"

"I'll think about it."

"Good. Now, about tonight..." Lucy raised one eyebrow as she spoke, reminding Shelby that even though she was her friend, she was her teacher as well.

"I'm sorry, Miss Pearl. I made a mistake."

"We all do. Just don't let it happen again."

"Don't worry," she said, sounding relieved.

"If you sneak back in very quietly, no one will even realize you were gone."

Shelby smiled, and Miss Pearl winked. "Hurry up now; you'll want to beat the sunrise."

As Shelby got up to leave, she turned on impulse and hugged Miss Pearl. "Thank you."

"You're quite welcome. And remember, the world is what we make it."

"I'll remember," whispered Shelby as she quickly made her way back to her room.

Chapter Nine

John Larsen gently pulled the reins signaling his horses to halt—not that they would've needed much prodding today. *They look as weary as I feel.* He got down from the carriage and walked up the path to the door. The sign on the front read "Dr. Larsen, Medical Doctor." But if the truth be known, the building didn't look like a doctor's office. The wood siding had never been painted and was now gray and weathered. Patches of rust covered the old tin roof, and the front door always squeaked whenever anyone opened it. Battered and dilapidated as it was, the condition of his building hadn't been a great concern to Dr. John Larsen. He bought the building, feeling his resources would be better spent on medicine and equipment rather than on a fancy office. Perhaps his purchase of the rundown little building was more deeply rooted. When he came back to Alder Springs he had wanted to distance himself from the past and everything he had been before. He really wasn't sure what he had hoped to find here.

"Dr. Larsen, it's good to have you back."

John Larsen turned and greeted his visitor with a hearty handshake and pat on the back. "Thanks, Jim. It's good to be home. These visits always wear me out. I don't know how much longer I can continue traveling all the way to Jackson County to treat patients. I'm not as young as I used to be."

Jim nodded sympathetically. "We're sure glad you're back, Doc. There's been lots of sickness going around."

John acknowledged the comment by shaking his head. He was used to getting these types of comments after being gone for a while. The townsfolk of Alder Springs were grateful to have a doctor in their community and did not like having to share him with patients in another county. "Who has taken ill?" asked John.

"Cynthia Whitaker has had stomach trouble."

John nodded as Jim named a half a dozen people with various illnesses. When he got to one particular name, John's brow furrowed in concern and he interrupted Jim mid-sentence. "Mrs. Duvall has been ill?"

"Yes. Mrs. Sue Duvall."

"How long?"

"I'm not sure, but it must be serious because her daughter came all the way from Georgia to look after her."

"Is there anything else?"

"Well, no...that's about it."

"I've got to go now. If you'll excuse me."

All trace of weariness was now gone from the doctor's voice. Without waiting for his visitor to respond, he quickly opened the door to his office and went inside, closing the door behind him.

Jim scratched his head and stared at the closed door for a moment. He wasn't sure how the conversation had ended so abruptly. He shoved his hands in his pockets and walked leisurely back down the front path.

*   *   *   *   *

Black clouds churned and rolled in the sky, matching John's emotional state. He drove his horses as hard as he could. Shortly after his conversation with Jim, he'd gotten a message from Martha Baker asking him to come to Mrs. Sue's house right away.

John was very fond of Mrs. Sue, and the news of her illness disturbed him. But what surprised him the most was the intensity of emotion he felt when he learned Ellen had arrived in town to take care of her mother. How long had she been here? He was a doctor; his first concern should be for his patient, but Ellen was all he could think about. He had dreamed of the day that he would see her again. What would he say to her? What would she look like after twenty years? Images of Ellen as he had last seen her floated into his mind. So full of life, with her huge, brown, sparkling eyes and mischievous smile. It's strange the little things he remembered, like the wisps of brown, curly hair escaping from her bun, and the way she moved her hands when she talked. But most of all he remembered the hurt in her eyes when he told her he had to leave immediately to go back to Atlanta to take care of some business.

John's and Ellen's courtship had begun spontaneously. He had just arrived in Alder Springs to start his medical practice. As he was hammering his shingle on the front porch of his newly painted office, the most fascinating creature he had ever seen turned the corner of the drugstore sidewalk. During all of his time in Atlanta, he had never seen anyone more poised or beautiful. He watched her as she walked across the street with her head held high. Her tiny form seemed to float toward him. Then she turned, and their eyes met. She had the most expressive eyes he had ever seen. Her quick smile revealed sparkling white teeth. Oh, but those dimples were what stole his heart.

"Hello, sir," she said, slightly tilting her head. "My mother sent me to get something from the new doctor for a headache. Would you so kindly tell me where I may find him?"

John smiled broadly. "That would be me."

Ellen introduced herself and explained that she wasn't expecting someone so young to be the new doctor. From that time on, they became inseparable. At the time, he had not thought it necessary to tell Ellen about his past, especially about Mary.

It had been a beautiful, crisp fall day. In fact, he had been contemplating that very day to ask Ellen to marry him when the telegram from Atlanta came. It was from Mary's parents. As fate would have it, instead of asking Ellen to marry him, he had to tell her he would be leaving for Atlanta to attend to some business.

"What kind of business, John?" she asked.

Afraid to tell her the truth, he became evasive. He could tell from the hurt expression on her face and the doubt in her eyes that she didn't believe his flimsy explanation. "I just have to tie up a few loose ends. That's all, nothing really important. I won't be gone long. I promise."

He had then kissed her lightly on the forehead as he got in his wagon. As he rode away, she stood watching him through the tears in her eyes. He promised himself he would set things right as soon as he returned. Those were the last words they had spoken. When he returned, Ellen was gone—gone from Alder Springs and gone from his life.

He should've told her why he was leaving. What a fool he'd been. He should've told her about Mary. Funny, he had not even thought of Mary after he had met Ellen. Mary was a part of his past. Why had the telegram come on the very day he had planned to ask Ellen to marry him?

He had met Mary while he was in medical school in Atlanta. It was cold the day they met; the sleet and snow made it almost impossible for him to see. Mary was standing on the side of the street, waiting for a carriage to take her across town. She had been visiting the library at the University he attended. He instantly felt compassion for Mary. She was so small and frail. He asked her if she would like to share a carriage with him, and she accepted his offer. Her enormous blue eyes seemed too large for her pale face. Even though Mary had a pretty smile, it never seemed to reach her eyes. John felt sorry for her and asked her out to dinner. After that day, the two attended several concerts, plays, and parties together. John sensed how deeply Mary cared for him and was careful not to lead her on. Purposefully, he talked about the day he would graduate from school and leave Atlanta. Mary never commented. She just smiled and nodded at him.

He later learned that Mary and her parents undoubtedly had different ideas. Mary's parents were prominent and having a doctor join the family would have been fine with them. After all these years, he still winced as he remembered the terrible scene that took place the night he went to dinner at Mary's home to tell her he would be leaving shortly. Until that day, no one had spoken to him about Mary's health. She often looked fatigued but would make up some excuse about having a cold or having stayed up too late the night before. John arrived at the Phillips' home at 6:00 P.M. The butler asked him to wait in the sitting room. John found this odd; he had always been greeted by one of Mary's parents in the past. After a while, Mary's father came into the parlor.

"John, we're so glad you're here. Mary has had a little setback."

John was puzzled. "What do you mean? A setback from what? Is Mary ill?"

Mr. Phillips turned as pale as Mary. "Why, John, did Mary not tell you that she is in remission from tuberculosis?" His voice broke.

"No, she did no such thing; this is the first I've heard of it," he said, his voice rising a fraction.

"Surely, during all of the time you and Mary spent together, you must have noticed that she is ill. You are, after all, a doctor."

John's voice was barely above a whisper as he answered. "Yes, I knew that Mary was a fragile girl, but I had no idea she had a serious illness. She kept it hidden from me," he added in an attempt to defend himself.

"John, this is all irrelevant. You're here now. That's all that matters"

"Sir..." John's voice trembled, "Mary and I are just friends."

Mr. Phillips was becoming flustered. "I thought you and Mary were.... Exactly what are your intentions?"

"I came here tonight to tell her that I have found a post in Alabama and will be leaving shortly to take up residence there."

Mr. Phillips gasped. "That's impossible. You can't leave now. She needs you—we need you. You must reconsider."

John couldn't believe his ears. He had tried to befriend Mary, but that's all. How could Mr. Phillips expect so much of him? "I can't," he finally said. "I have to leave. I've already accepted a position."

"She'll die without you."

The comment struck John like a glass of cold water in the face. "There are wonderful doctors here. She doesn't need me. I'm not even a doctor yet. Please say goodbye to Mary for me."

Mr. Phillips sputtered as John turned to leave. John knew that he didn't understand, that he would never understand.

He left Atlanta shortly thereafter, putting everything in the past, until the day Mr. Phillips' telegram arrived in Alder Springs telling him that Mary was seriously ill and calling for him. He knew what he must do. He went to Atlanta and stayed with Mary's parents, by her side, for four months until she quietly passed away.

*   *   *   *   *

The clouds had broken, and rain was pelting down like bullets. John could hardly see Mrs. Sue's house. He unbridled the horses and unhitched them from the buggy. They would be safe from the storm in the barn. By the time he arrived at the front door, he was sopping wet. He suddenly felt old and tired. *What has gotten into me? I'm behaving like a lovesick schoolboy. Twenty years ago, Ellen and I had something together. That was a lifetime ago. I've got to get a grip on myself. Ellen is now a grown woman with a husband and three children of her own.*

Just as he was about to knock on the door, it swung open. His breath caught as he stood face to face with Ellen. He felt a little better about his own nervousness when he saw her face pale. For an instant, their eyes met, and he felt like he had gone twenty years back in time. She stood, staring at him as if he were a ghost. Finally, after an uncomfortable silence, she shifted her stare.

"Um—hello, Ellen."

No response.

"May I come in?"

Ellen recovered her composure. "Yes, please come in," she replied. "You are soaking wet. Let me get you something dry to put on."

Without saying another word, Ellen quickly hurried up the stairs toward the guest bedroom. It only took the top of the stairs for her to realize that she definitely wasn't thinking clearly. What was she thinking? Her father had been dead for several years; there would be no reason for her mother to keep his old clothes. Ellen's head swam. *I must have been missing more sleep than I realized,* she thought. She slumped down on the bed. Earlier in the day, Martha had told her the doctor was back in town and she would ask him to stop by. Ellen had no idea it would be John! The last she heard was that he had taken over a practice somewhere in South Alabama.

The sound of the rain on the tin roof had become louder. John stood looking out the picture window. Water was pouring in buckets off the side of the house. He had known that Ellen would still be attractive, but was unprepared for the beautiful woman that had taken the place of the girl he had loved so many years ago. Ellen's sudden departure both perplexed and amused him. Whose clothes was she expecting to find in her mother's house? It was no surprise when she came back empty-handed. "I'm sorry I wasn't able to find you anything to wear. Here, dry off with this towel so you won't catch cold."

By this time, Ellen had completely regained her composure and was acting the part of a polite hostess. He decided that he'd better get a hold of himself. He dismissed all preliminaries and went straight to the reason for his visit. "Is Mrs. Sue in her bedroom?" he asked, assuming his professional voice.

"Yes," Ellen answered quickly. "She's expecting you."

"How has she been?"

Ellen related all the events which had taken place and how she had come right away when she received a letter from Martha. "When I arrived, Mother was confined to her bed and could hardly breathe. That was a couple of weeks ago. Not much has changed since then. Some days she seems to be getting better. Other times...other times I'm not so sure." Ellen dropped her hands by her side in a gesture of defeat.

"Is she coherent?"

"Part of the time. Most of the time, she just sleeps."

Ellen seemed more reserved and sedate than he remembered. Her eyes, however, were still just as expressive, and he could see the concern looming from them. He wished he could somehow erase the hurt. "I'll go in and have a look at her."

*　　*　　*　　*　　*

Shelby swiftly removed the pins from the bodice she had basted. The powder-blue fabric was sprinkled with dainty, yellow daisies. Next, she would gather the skirt and attach it. She carefully picked it up and admired her handiwork with satisfaction. Mama had taught her to sew at a young age, and her skill had always been adequate. But thanks to the mandatory dress-making class she was required to take, she had become quite good—a benefit from being at the school. Ever since her conversation with Miss Pearl, she had tried to improve her outlook on her situation; and for the most part, it seemed to be working. Every day, she tried to find at least one thing to be positive about. At first, this had been ridiculous; however, with great effort and additional pestering from Miss Pearl, she was starting to make progress.

"Well, look at you and that pretty dress. Yours looks great. I'll trade ya." Frankie was holding up what was supposed to be her bodice; it was all twisted, and the checks on the fabric were mismatched.

Shelby giggled. "Maybe you should just start over."

Frankie playfully shoved her and then placed her hands on her hips and mimicked Shelby. "'Maybe you should just start over.' Just because you can sew doesn't make you 'Miss High and Mighty.'"

Both girls laughed.

"Let me help you fix that. You know how strict Miss James is. She's going to pitch a fit when she sees this. And we're going to have to model our dresses for the teachers after we're done."

Frankie lifted her sharp chin and stuck her arm in the air, with her bodice held close, as she twirled around. "You don't think this looks good?" When Shelby didn't answer, she sighed and then groaned, "Okay, you've made your point. You'd better get busy helping me if you know what's good for you."

Frankie talked big, but all the while she spoke, her eyes twinkled and a smile curved slightly on her thin lips. Shelby looked at her friend appraisingly. Frankie seemed to take each day as it came with hardly any thought for the morrow. After their midnight escapade, Shelby had resolved to stay away from Frankie. However, the next day, Frankie profusely apologized and begged for forgiveness. Finally, Shelby forgave her on the condition that Frankie never again include her in any mischief. Shelby decided that she needed a good friend as much as Frankie did, so the two put their differences aside and agreed to disagree.

Shelby suspected that Frankie was still sneaking out at night to meet the boy with the mop hair and asked her about it once. Frankie told her the boy's name was Jed. She wanted to ask Frankie about Harlan, the boy she had met, but never could figure out a way to phrase the question without appearing interested in him. Shelby worried about her friend's nighttime adventures but finally decided that she had enough problems of her own without worrying about Frankie.

Time was slowly passing. Sometimes, it seemed hard to believe she had been at the school for a month. Other times, it seemed as though she had been there forever. The raw hurt she felt when she first arrived had subsided a bit. As long as she immersed herself in her daily routine, she was okay. The nights were still hard; many mornings she would awaken to find her pillow wet with tears. She had finally gotten up the nerve up to write a letter to Joshua and Sister, telling them where she was. Miss Pearl had mailed it for her.

That was two weeks ago, and she had not heard anything back. She wasn't sure how long it took for the mail to get from Birmingham to Cartersville. How much longer was she going to have to wait?

*   *   *   *   *

John quietly shut the door behind him as he left Mrs. Sue's room. He was deeply concerned about his patient. She had been completely unaware of his presence, and her breathing was shallow and raspy. The recovery rate for pneumonia was normally good, providing that the illness was diagnosed and treated at an early stage, and that the patient was healthy before the onset of the sickness. Unfortunately, Mrs. Sue didn't have either of these benefits. If only he had been in town when she first got sick. A wave of guilt rushed over him, and he pushed it away. Those poor folks in Jackson County had needed him badly during the epidemic, he rationalized.

Despite all of his years practicing medicine, he still found it hard to watch someone he cared about suffer. Mrs. Sue was in a precarious state. At this point, only time would tell the outcome. He would provide the best assistance he possibly could, and he would hope—for Ellen's sake—for the best.

He walked through the house until he found Ellen in the kitchen. She had a pot of tea on the stove. As soon as he came into the room, she took one look at John's face and braced herself for the bad news that was sure to come. She poured him a cup of tea and invited him to sit down. He took a seat directly across from her. His light eyes were troubled, and his mouth was drawn in a frown, emphasizing the deep lines etched around his thin lips. He had changed so much over the years. When she first met him, his face had been boyish. At first glance, she hadn't found him exceptionally good-looking. His features were too plain and sturdy for that. It was afterwards, when she took a second look, that her perception of him changed. He had a way about him that commanded her attention and eventually endeared her to him. His practical outlook on life and wry sense of humor had made her laugh.

He once jokingly remarked, "Girls want one of three things in a man—they either want him to be rich, handsome, or funny.

Considering that I am a complete failure in the first two aspects, I might as well try for the third."

"What?" she asked in mock seriousness. "You don't consider yourself handsome?"

He made a face. "Even my own mother once told me so."

She had looked at him dubiously. "Really?"

"Yes, ma'am. That's right. She told me that I have a good, honest face." He grimaced. "Not handsome or interesting, but a good, honest face."

Ellen laughed. John raised his hands over his head in an animated fashion. "See, you have just proven my point!"

She enjoyed being with him because of the way he made her feel. Life had been brilliant and rich through John's eyes.

Ellen looked across the table and over at John. Where were these thoughts coming from? Time had been good to him—his face was now leaner and his features more chiseled. His sandy hair, still thick, was now sprinkled with gray, especially around the temples. His green eyes sparkled with a maturity and wisdom only life's experiences can bring. The young boy was gone, and in his place was the capable, distinguished doctor.

She didn't want to hear any more bad news about her mother but knew she had to ask. Her pulse quickened as she cleared her throat. "What do you think about Mother?"

John struggled to find the right words. He always found it difficult to discuss disturbing news with the family members of his patients, and his connection to Ellen further compounded the situation.

"The pneumonia has weakened her system. The fluid in her lungs is making it difficult for her to breathe. I believe that she is strong enough to survive this. But at this point..." His voice trailed off. "At this point all we can do is wait."

Ellen looked down at her cup. Stinging tears began to rise. "I understand," she mumbled.

John reached over and placed his hand over hers and took a deep breath. "I am so sorry about..."

Ellen interrupted him mid-sentence. "Thank you," she said, her eyes still glistening. "I appreciate your concern for Mother."

John shook his head. "I am sorry about Mrs. Sue. More so than you may realize. She has been a dear friend to me since I came back to Alder Springs."

Ellen nodded.

He looked directly into her eyes. "But what I was going to say was that I am so sorry about what happened between us."

His apology caught her off guard. She quickly withdrew her hand from underneath his grasp.

"Ellen, you must realize. We have to talk about what happened. We have to try and resolve things."

Instead of answering him right away, she propped her elbows on the table and buried her head in her hands. Finally, she lifted her head. "Not tonight, John. I can't talk about it now. I just can't handle anything else. Not tonight."

Chapter Ten

Longingly, Harlan looked up toward the sky in the hope that he would see a thundercloud. All he could see were billowy clouds drifting in front of a pristine, blue sky. He shook his head ruefully and cast aside any further hopes of an impending thunderstorm and began mentally preparing himself for the grueling physical task ahead. He wiped the perspiration from his brow and smoothed back his sandy hair as he carefully placed the hot leather football helmet on his head. Coach Hill always insisted that all of his players wear helmets for protection—even during practice. Harlan decided that he would prefer to leave off the stifling thing and take his chances.

On days like today, he often second-guessed his decision to join the football team. He joined the team the previous year, just before the start of fall season, because he felt it would be an easy way to meet new friends. His plan had worked better than he had hoped and he became fast friends with Jed Williams, the quarterback of the team and one of the most popular guys at school. When the other guys saw that Jed had taken him under his wing, they quickly followed his lead, accepting him as one of them. Harlan liked being on the team, and he was good. Coach Hill started him playing linebacker but moved him to half-back on the offensive side when he discovered how quick he was. Harlan liked the notoriety he received from the coaches and other players but was glad this would be his last summer of practice. He would graduate next year.

Harlan still found it hard to believe he had lived in Woodlawn, a suburb of Birmingham, with Aunt June for an entire year. He moved to Woodlawn two days before school started last year. All things considered, he had fared quite well. *I've become a city boy*, he chuckled to himself. At first, living in the city had been intimidating. Tucker, where he was born, was a small town located in south Alabama. His previous years of school had been spent with a handful of other students in a crowded, one-room schoolhouse where they sweated out the heat of early fall and huddled around a coal stove in the winter. His new school was much larger and more sophisticated than his old one—so were his friends.

He really liked Jed and the other guys, even though they made him anxious on occasion. When he was with them, he always felt as like he was swimming in water a tad too deep for comfort. He thought back a couple of weeks to when he'd gone with Jed to meet the girls at the school. Jed had met Frankie, and Harlan had met Shelby. Harlan hadn't really wanted to go; the idea of sneaking out late at night to meet some unknown person made him uncomfortable, although he never would've admitted that to Jed. He had met Frankie before and could tell she was the kind of girl who had trouble written all over her. More than once, he had wondered what Jed saw in her. Curiosity finally got the better of him, and he had asked, "Why are you wasting your time with her?"

Jed had pushed back a strand of long, blonde hair and flashed a boyish grin that was known to send hopeful flutters through the hearts of three-fourths of the female student population at Woodlawn. He smiled at Harlan for a moment without saying a word. Finally, he shrugged. "Me and Frankie have fun together." Harlan let it go at that. He knew exactly what type of fun Jed was referring to, and it could only lead to trouble. His thoughts returned to the night he met Shelby. She had been something he hadn't counted on. He had expected to meet someone the equivalent of Frankie; boy was he wrong. As he remembered her dark eyes and wistful expression, his heart skipped a beat. Several times throughout the past couple of weeks, he had caught himself thinking about her. Why did he keep thinking about someone he met only once? Maybe it was guilt for the way he treated her. He hadn't meant to scare her the way he did. Her haughty attitude toward him had made him angry, and yet he felt excited and drawn to her at the same time. His kiss had been spontaneous, surprising himself as much as her. Even when she ran off, he hadn't felt bad. The guilt had come later after he found out from Frankie she really hadn't met him there on purpose. Frankie had been thoroughly amused when he told her and Jed what had happened. Harlan had wanted to strangle her and wipe that sly grin right off her skinny face.

"Hey, Harlan, you'd better stop daydreaming and line up for sprints."

Harlan turned to see Jed, a jovial smile on his face. Harlan smiled back. "I guess I'm just trying to talk myself into it. It sure is hot."

Jed slapped him on the back. "That just goes with the territory. Let's go." Jed started jogging slowly over to the middle of the field where the rest of the team was lining up. Harlan bent over and gave his shoelaces a quick tug to make sure they were securely tied and then caught up with Jed.

"Hey, where were you last night? I missed you at the diner."

"I was with Frankie."

Harlan nodded. "You and Frankie are becoming inseparable. What does your family think of her?"

Jed was the only son of the honorable Charles Williams, a man of strong stock with a long pedigree of ancestors whose accomplishments nearly matched his own. Charles Williams expected his only son to follow closely in his footsteps.

Jed's eyes widened and then he let out a gasp of disbelief that turned into howling laughter. "You're a funny man! Do you think I would ever be crazy enough to introduce Frankie to my old man?" He laughed so hard that it brought tears to his eyes. After the laughter died down, he assumed an air of mock seriousness. "Frankie and I have fun together. It's no more or less than that. She knows that. Come on, we've gotta get lined up. Coach Hill will make us run laps if we're not there by the time he blows the whistle."

Harlan followed behind Jed. *I hope you're right my friend,* he thought. *I surely do.*

*　　*　　*　　*　　*

Joshua raised his sleeve to his forehead and wiped away the beads of perspiration. His cheeks were deeply flushed, and he was breathing heavily. He had worked in the heat all his life, and he couldn't remember it ever affecting him this much. He looked steadily at his young field-hand to see how he was faring. James had a sweaty brow too, but his eager expression suggested he could go strong for a couple more hours.

"I can stay longer and finish things up if you want me to," he called.

Joshua shook his head admiringly and nodded. "Go ahead and finish up. We need to get these last rows hoed and chopped today." In long strides, he walked to the edge of the field and put down his hoe, then flashed a brief smile tinged with sadness. "I wish I could stay with you, but I guess I'm just not as young as I used to be."

James gave Joshua a hasty nod and then turned his attention back to the task at hand.

Wearily, Joshua trudged up the field toward home. His chest felt tight, and he massaged his throbbing arm tenderly. I must have hurt myself hauling feed yesterday. He really was tired. He walked over to the edge of the field and sat down by one of the terrace rows. Like most farmers, Joshua used a method called "terracing" to prevent erosion. A terraced or raised row was planted around the edge of each field. His gaze swept over the majestic, red fields. Even in his weary state, he couldn't help but admire the neat rows of cotton, level across the top, with the corn rising high in the background. The dark green foliage of the cotton plants was studded with a profusion of tiny, white blossoms. He scooped up a handful of dirt; it smelled clean. He let the dirt trickle through his fingers and fall back to the ground as he rose and dusted off the seat of his pants. These tired spells seemed to be coming closer together. Sister noticed and had urged him to see Doc Godbee.

"You take things like this too lightly. You aren't as young as you used to be."

This irritated Joshua—mostly because he knew she was right. He had always been healthy as a horse and had never had much use for doctors. As he neared his house, he saw the mailman walking down the dusty road.

"Hello, Joshua," Clyde said, heartily. "I'm glad I caught you. I was just coming to the house to bring you a letter."

"You didn't have to go to the trouble to come all the way out here to deliver something. You should've just put it in my box."

He smiled. "The last time I did that it sat there for a month. Besides, it was no trouble."

Joshua chuckled. He knew Clyde was right. Because his and sister's mailbox was located a mile up the road, they only checked it when they made visits into town.

Clyde quickly handed Joshua his mail and then turned and began walking back toward town. "I would love to stay and sit a spell with you, but I have a few more deliveries to make."

"Thank you," Joshua yelled after him. He turned over the letter he had received. There was a return address but no name over it. *Who do we know in Birmingham?* He walked to the edge of the yard and sat down under a shade tree. His breath caught as he opened the letter and pulled out its pages. It was from Shelby. He frowned. *What in the world is she doing in Birmingham?*

As he read the letter, he shook his head in disbelief. Then his astonishment turned to anger, and his cheeks burned. A deep rage pulsed through his veins, and he knew what he must do. He rose up and then fell back to the ground as a heavy weight pressed on his chest. He gulped for air and attempted to rise again and then staggered backwards as he collapsed on the ground, clutching the crumpled letter in his hand.

* * * * *

Sister went into the house to fix Joshua a glass of lemonade. She had seen him coming up the field earlier and was alarmed by his haggard appearance. Things had been really stressful in their household with the children. Frank told her yesterday that he had received a letter from Ellen saying that her mother was still critical and that she had to stay longer. Sister almost wept in desperation at the news. She didn't know how much longer she could tolerate watching Homer and Sarah. It wasn't that they were bad children. In fact, they were well-behaved. It was the combination of things, she reasoned, that was getting to her. Sister looked forward to the day when her life would return to normal. She squeezed an extra lemon to make the lemonade extra tart, just the way he liked it. As she walked out the front door, she gaped at what she saw. The glass slipped from her hand and shattered as Sister ran across the yard and threw herself down beside Joshua. It only took a moment for her to realize he was gone. In that instant, her life changed, and she wept bitter tears for her beloved and for all of the time they would not be together.

Chapter Eleven

B etty Lou, what is one-fourth plus one-fourth?"

Betty Lou turned sharply in her seat and looked guiltily at Miss Pearl. She hadn't been paying attention and had been too busy talking to Abigail to hear the question. She nervously cleared her throat. "Um—could you repeat the question?"

Instead of repeating the question, Miss Pearl stood in front of her errant student with her hands on her hips and a frown on her face. Betty Lou had a ruddy complexion to begin with, but as the silence continued, color kept rising into her pudgy cheeks, making her look like a cherry tomato. Miss Pearl softened as she looked at the silly sight, but her face remained stern. The two girls had been snickering and talking amongst themselves the entire class, and she wanted them to realize that she would not tolerate it. Abigail knew she was in hot water too. She sat rigidly behind Betty Lou, hoping Miss Pearl wouldn't single her out.

"Girls, I expect you to pay attention during class. Betty Lou, I will repeat the question this time. Next time, however..." She paused. "Let's just make sure there is no next time. Is that clear?"

"Yes, ma'am," came the reply in unison.

Miss Pearl's shoulders felt tight. The class ran smoothly after she'd sat Betty Lou and Abigail straight, especially considering that Gretta Sharp had been present the whole time. Ever since Lucy confronted her about the lack of books, Miss Sharp had been dropping in on her classes nearly every day. Her ominous presence could be felt by Lucy and her students, making everyone ill at ease. Miss Sharp wouldn't ever say anything to Lucy or the students. She would sit silently in the back, observing the class while taking notes. Lucy knew Miss Sharp was trying to intimidate her, and admittedly she had been intimidated at first. It didn't take long, however, for Lucy's heckles to rise. She refused to be bullied. Now, she was even more determined to make her classes better than ever. *Maybe some good will come out of this. The old bag would have to be blind if she couldn't see how desperately we need new books and supplies.* Lucy Pearl didn't relish the idea of going head to head with Miss Sharp again but knew she must for Shelby's sake. Ever since the night she learned about Shelby's predicament, she had vowed to help her somehow. Lucy had felt certain that Shelby's uncle and aunt would come to her aid if they knew her situation. She mailed the letter Shelby wrote. That was some time ago—plenty enough time to have received a response by now. Lucy shook her head. *It's a shame that her own kin have forsaken her.* Another idea crossed Lucy's mind, and she had been mulling it over in her mind for a few days. *It just might work.* Miss Ramsey, the matron of the Mercy Place, was in desperate need of an assistant. As soon as Lucy Pearl learned about the open position, she had known Shelby would be perfect for it. Shelby would enjoy working in the children's home, and Miss Ramsey would benefit from her help. The trick was how to get Miss Sharp to release Shelby from the school. Technically, a student enrolled by a parent couldn't be released without parental consent. However, if the story Shelby told about her hasty enrollment was indeed correct, then Miss Sharp had no right to allow Shelby in the school to begin with. Shelby didn't fit the profile of the typical applicant. Something didn't seem right. Lucy Pearl didn't know how long the assistant job at the home would remain open. If she were going to make things happen, she would have to act soon. She stacked the books on her desk and straightened up her desk. *Well, there's no time like the present,* she decided. *I might as well go ahead and talk to Miss Sharp today.* Her heart pounded in her chest as she headed out the door.

*   *   *   *   *

Miss Pearl straightened her dress and smoothed her raven hair. "The driver is here with the wagon and right on time. I would expect nothing less from Miss Ramsey. She always does exactly what she says she will do," she said admiringly. Shelby climbed into the wagon with her bag of belongings clutched tightly in her hand. As the wagon began to move down the bumpy road, Shelby turned and looked back at the school. *I'm glad I'm leaving this terrible place.* She caught a glimpse of Miss Sharp staring down at her from her office window and turned around quickly to face forward. *Look forward*, she told herself, *not back.*

Shelby glanced at Miss Pearl who was chatting amiably with the driver. For the first time, Shelby looked at the driver. Much to her surprise, it was same colored man she had seen on the way to the garden the night she and Frankie sneaked out. All Shelby could remember about him was his massive size. He was a large man, his expression was friendly, and he had a wide, toothy grin. He and Miss Pearl were obviously well acquainted. Shelby was a little surprised to see Miss Pearl chatting so openly with a colored man. She had never considered herself prejudiced against coloreds but had followed the unspoken rule and behaved respectfully while keeping her distance. If Miss Pearl were aware of the generally accepted custom, she chose to ignore it.

"Grover, I would like for you to meet Shelby, my star pupil. She is going to be one of Miss Ramsey's assistants."

"Pleased to meet you," Grover replied. "Any friend of Miss Pearl is a friend of mine."

"It's nice to meet you too."

Shelby still wasn't sure how she should act around Grover, but she liked him instantly. His gentle manner toward the horses pulling the wagon reminded her of Joshua. The sun shone brightly overhead. As the wagon rumbled down the dusty road, a twinge of excitement crept over Shelby. She settled back and listened to the jovial banter of her companions.

*   *   *   *   *

The home was located on the corner of 12ᵗʰ Avenue North and 25ᵗʰ Street. It was only about seven miles from the industrial school, but it might have been a different world. Because the industrial school had been built in the middle of six acres of land, it seemed isolated and disconnected from the rest of the city. Since the day of her arrival at the school, Shelby hadn't left the grounds.

As they rumbled down the busy street, she was amazed at all of the new sights and smells surrounding her. The pungent smell of tar, mingled with leather, invaded her senses as they passed a busy blacksmith shop. Never in her life had she seen so many automobiles in one place—and such fine clothes. The wagon stopped abruptly as a lady pushing a baby carriage passed in front, and Shelby looked in wonderment at her fancy dress and matching feather hat. On both sides of the road, people were walking briskly in and out of stores. They rode farther past the stores to a residential section, where the houses were built close together. The yards were neatly kept. Some had picket fences in front. A window-box filled with purple and yellow petunias caught her eye. As they drove further along, Shelby saw a group of small girls taking turns using a jump rope, their hair bouncing in the wind.

The wagon pulled to a stop. "Okay, ladies. This is where I let you out."

"Thank you, Grover. It was great to see you again." Miss Pearl hastily got out of the wagon. Shelby quickly followed.

"What do you think?" Miss Pearl asked eagerly.

Shelby stood looking at the grand facade directly in front of her and felt her confidence wane. "It's very big." Shelby looked at Miss Pearl's anxious expression and knew she had expected a more positive response. "It is a beautiful building," she added.

"Yes, indeed." Miss Pearl smiled broadly. "I just know you're going to love it here."

Shelby knew Miss Pearl had gone to a great deal of trouble to get her an assistant position at the Mercy Place. When Miss Pearl told her about the opportunity, Shelby had been surprised. "How did you manage to convince Miss Sharp to allow me to leave the school?" she asked.

"Let's just say that she came to the conclusion your leaving would be very beneficial to her position."

Shelby had been confused by that answer. "What do you mean? How could I affect her position?"

Miss Pearl smiled wisely. "You should never have been admitted to the school in the first place without board approval, and the board would've never approved you. Your education exceeds our curriculum, and you aren't poverty stricken like the rest of our students. Miss Sharp broke a rule, and I just reminded her that she didn't need a constant reminder of her folly walking around the school for everyone to see. It was as simple as that."

Miss Pearl always made everything sound reasonable, but Shelby felt sure that things had not gone as smoothly as Miss Pearl described. She shuddered as a mental picture of Miss Sharp filled her mind. "I hope this isn't going to cause you any trouble."

"Not any more than I already have from her," Miss Pearl reassuringly answered.

A sharp tug on her arm brought Shelby back to the present. "Are you all right?" Miss Pearl asked.

Shelby smiled. "I'm fine. It's just that everything is happening so fast."

Miss Pearl gave her a sympathetic nod and grasped her hand, giving it a comforting squeeze. "Remember, love, the world is what we make it."

"Yes, ma'am. I'll try."

"Good. I'm going to go on in and let Miss Ramsey know you're here."

Miss Pearl walked briskly up the front steps. Shelby lagged behind and took in the full scope of the Mercy Place. It was truly magnificent, with its deep, red brick and green shutters. The home was only two stories high, but it appeared taller. Maybe that was because it had a partially underground floor below and an attic above covered with two steeply arched gables. At least a dozen windows covered the front of the home, and there were countless more on the sides. She could see another building directly behind the house but couldn't tell whether or not it was connected. Four big chimneys jutted prominently from the roof. The house swallowed Shelby as she looked up at it and felt very small in comparison. She didn't know whether to laugh or cry. Admittedly, it was good to be away from the industrial school, but what would she find here? Miss Pearl had told her that the Mercy Place housed an average of eighty inmates at any given time. Shelby found her choice of the word "inmate" peculiar. Now the term conjured up waves of foreboding feelings. She had spoken honestly when she told Miss Pearl the home was beautiful. Indeed it was. The industrial school had felt cold and impersonal, with its perfectly laid brick, but not this place. It looked ancient and full of character with its steep roof and twin gables. A wide, covered porch extended across the front with six evenly-spaced posts. Wide steps led up to the entrance. Shelby had the impression that if its sturdy walls could talk, they would tell a thousand tales of the residents who had lived here before. She wondered what her story would be.

*   *   *   *   *

Shelby slowly made her way up the stairs. The front door was made of mahogany with intricate panes of thick glass across its top half. She grasped the doorknob, not sure what to do. Should she wait outside for Miss Pearl or go on in? Suddenly, the door pushed open, knocking her to the side. She gasped in surprise as a small boy ran down the stairs. He was so busy hooting and hollering that he wasn't paying any attention to where he was going. Before he reached the bottom, he fell and skinned his knee. He dropped to the ground and started wailing. On impulse, Shelby rushed down the stairs to his aid.

"Are you okay?"

"My knee hurts!"

"Let me have a look at it." She tenderly pulled his leg out and examined his knee. It was bleeding, but Shelby could tell it was only a superficial scratch. The boy was still crying but had stopped wailing. He seemed to sense that he was in good hands. "I think you're gonna be okay. Let's get you inside, so we can wash it."

Miss Ramsey and Miss Pearl heard all of the commotion, and they both came outside just in time to see Shelby comforting the boy.

"Miss Pearl, I believe she's going to fit in just fine here."

Shelby looked up the steps to see who had spoken.

"Miss Ramsey, I would like for you to meet Shelby."

Shelby reached up to shake Miss Ramsey's hand and was surprised at the firm grasp that the frail-looking older woman had. Her silver hair was curly. It parted in the middle and was pinned up in the back. Loose ringlets framed her square face. Little, round spectacles accentuated her kind, sparkling eyes which were etched in wrinkles. As Miss Ramsey looked intently at Shelby, her eyes seemed to penetrate into Shelby's very soul.

"Welcome to the Mercy Place. I hope you will soon consider this your home."

Shelby was touched by the sincerity of the older woman, and she looked down quickly as she felt tears rising. "Thank you, Miss Ramsey," she muttered.

"Please, call me Mother Ramsey."

"Mother Ramsey, I hurt my knee!" The plea from the young injured caused all to focus their attention on him.

"Charles, what were you doing running out of the house like that? You need to be more careful."

"Yes, Mother Ramsey. I know."

"Go inside and tell Miss Janice to wash your knee." Charles gave Mother Ramsey a hug, which she returned affectionately. As he ran into the house, she gave him a slap on his bottom.

"Charles doesn't like to be cooped up. Every time the door opens, he runs out of it like a wild Indian." She smiled at Shelby. "You'll get used to the commotion."

Shelby smiled back. "I like it already."

"Good. Let's get you settled in. Lucy, do you have time to visit for a while?"

Miss Pearl nodded. "I sure do."

Shelby gathered her suitcase and followed the two women in the door. Maybe things would turn out all right after all.

Chapter Twelve

Ellen opened the screen door and started down the steps leading to the back yard. She stepped onto the first step and lost her footing. She stumbled and then caught herself from falling. Her first instinct was to be grateful that she hadn't been hurt; her second instinct was to berate herself for her carelessness. A sprained ankle was the last thing she needed. She carefully made her way down the remainder of the steps and then sat down at the bottom. The flower gardens her mother had planted on each side of the steps were overgrown with weeds. She remembered how much her mother loved her yard and her beautiful flowers. In her mind's eye, she could see her mother bent over, painstakingly pulling weeds. A wave of sadness flooded Ellen. *How things change*, she mused. *I'll clean up the flower gardens tomorrow*, she vowed. Just promising that to herself made her feel a little better.

Ellen had always taken great satisfaction in her ability to remain composed in any given situation. But she had to admit that seeing John the night before had thrown her off balance. Feelings that she had long ago dismissed were surfacing, and she wasn't sure how to deal with them. No one told her that he had returned and taken up residence here.

She got up from the step and slowly walked across the yard. Without thinking, she made her way through the pasture to the stream where she had spent many long, lazy summer afternoons as a girl. The moss around the stream was starting to turn brown. She sat down near the stream and breathed in the sweet scent of honeysuckles. Spontaneously, she kicked off her shoes and took off her stockings and began to wade in the cool stream. She laughed to herself. How silly she must look—a grown woman holding up her dress and wading in the stream. Her attention was quickly diverted when she heard someone coming. She had almost made it back to her shoes when she looked up and saw John.

"Hello there."

Ellen's heart felt as though it would jump out of her body. She reached her shoes in two steps and sat down on the grassy slope and John sat down beside her. Instantly, she became aware of his closeness. She started to move away from him and then chided herself for being silly and stayed where she was.

"How did you know that I was here?" she began.

"Martha told me that you were taking a short walk, and I remembered that this used to be our favorite place to hide." He smiled broadly. "So, I took a chance, and here you are."

His friendly banter made her forget her uneasiness, and she smiled back. "I'm glad you're here. I wanted to apologize to you for last night. Things have been so difficult lately with mother's illness. I'm afraid I just haven't been myself."

John chuckled, and Ellen's face flushed as she realized what she had just said. John hadn't seen her in years. How was he supposed to know how she normally acted? She became flustered. "What I'm trying to say is—"

He interrupted her before she could explain. "You don't owe me an apology. I owe you one. I had no idea that you didn't know I was your mother's doctor. You had every right to be upset. I can only imagine what a shock it was to see me so unexpectedly."

She looked him squarely in the face. "Why did you come back?"

John reached to his side and picked up a rock. He slung it into the stream and watched it skip across to the other side. "In every person's life there comes a time for self-evaluation. One day I looked around and asked myself what in the world I was doing. I was a prominent doctor in an affluent town with a long list of prestigious patients. I had a big house and every comfort a person could ever want. And yet, I had nothing." He took a deep breath. "So, I decided to come back here, to offer my services to people who really need help." He shrugged his shoulders and smiled grimly. "And that's about all there is to it."

Ellen nodded and looked at the ground. The two sat in silence and watched the water ripple over the rocks. Finally, John spoke. "We need to talk."

She raised one eyebrow. "What do we have to talk about?" She kept the tone of her voice light; only the look in her eyes betrayed the tumultuous emotions churning inside. How well John remembered those expressive eyes. She was trying hard to put up a good front. It reminded him of a frozen lake during wintertime where a thin sheet of ice was all that covered the raging waters below. He cleared his throat and decided to plunge right in.

"You know darn well what we have to talk about."

"It all happened so long ago. Why can't you just let it be?"

John shook his head and gently grasped Ellen's arm. "I told you that I had business to take care of in Atlanta; and when I returned, you had left and married that Mr. Collins or whatever his name is."

Ellen jerked her arm from John's grasp. Her cheeks began to burn. "Don't you think this conversation is a little late? Why didn't you tell me you were involved with someone in Atlanta? Why didn't you tell me that the 'business' you were going to take care of was another woman?"

John was taken aback by Ellen's response. He brushed his hands through his hair and continued in a calm tone. "Ellen, I was not involved with another woman. She misunderstood my intentions. She was only a friend."

"What did you expect me to believe? Your mother told me about the telegram, and then you didn't return."

"But all those letters I wrote you. You sent them back all unopened."

"John, I was so young...and foolish."

John walked over and sat down beside a tree. His face was dark and his voice full of remorse. "Ellen, what have we done to our lives? Are you happy?"

"I have three children I love who depend on me. I have a husband and a home in Cartersville."

"Are you happy?" he asked again.

Ellen looked at him pleadingly. And then her hesitancy gave way to resolution. She squared her jaw and summed up all of the courage she could. "I have to be happy; I don't have any choice."

It didn't take long for Shelby to feel completely at home in her new surroundings. From the moment she arrived at the Mercy Place, Mother Ramsey put her straight to work. She spent most of her time performing domestic tasks. There always seemed to be one more child to dress, another bed to make, or one other hug to give. Just as Miss Pearl had told her, there were approximately eighty residents at the home, not including the staff. This number would increase in the fall due to the fact that a number of the children were allowed to take short vacations in the summer. Shelby had been surprised at this. Mother Ramsey had told her that additional funds and donations were always set aside specifically for this purpose.

"It promotes well-balanced and happy children. These precious children have had so much sadness in their lives, they deserve a little sunshine."

Shelby soon learned that the home even owned a retreat on Shady Mountain, located a few miles outside the city, for the children and staff.

The other members of the staff seemed friendly and glad to have an extra hand on board. All of the staff members were females except for Grover, and he didn't live at the home. He worked at both the industrial school and the home and consequently, spent much of his time running back and forth between the two. All of the women were much older than Shelby except for Janice, who was seventeen. On the first day of Shelby's arrival, Mother Ramsey had instructed Janice to show her around. It seemed to Shelby that the two had been paired together ever since. Janice could be bossy at times—interpreting Mother Ramsey's counsel of "showing Shelby around" to include instructing her about the proper way to do things around the home. This bothered Shelby a little, but overall, she liked her. Janice had brown hair and green eyes, and a fair complexion. Her nose had brown freckles splashed across it and tilted upward slightly on the end. She was taller than Shelby and of medium build.

The Mercy Place was the only home Janice could remember. "Mother Ramsey found me in a basket on the doorstep wrapped in a pink blanket. The only thing that gave any indication of my identity was a note which read: 'Please take care of my little Janice. It torments my soul to give her up. My sweet, little princess is the joy of my life.'"

Tears glistened in Janice's eyes as she spoke, and Shelby felt compassion for her. "Janice that is a beautiful story."

Janice nodded and wiped away a tear. "Yes, it is beautiful. Mother Ramsey has been like a mother to me, and yet I can't help but wonder sometimes where my real mother is and what she is like."

Shelby thought of her mama so far away and felt a stab of pain. "It must be hard to not know about her."

"Yes," Janice agreed. "I see her sometimes in my dreams." She looked wistful for a moment and then her voice became practical. "All of that happened a long time ago. I've had a good life here. That's what matters." Shelby nodded in agreement, but she couldn't help but wonder what life must have been like for Janice at the home. She knew that Mother Ramsey and the other staff members tried hard to make all of the children feel loved, but could they adequately compensate for a real home? She thought about her own home and wondered if Mama had returned. Miss Pearl told her that she would let her know if a letter arrived for her at the school from Uncle Joshua. Shelby still continued to hope, but deep down she was not expecting a letter to come. It had been too long. All she could do at this point was pray for a miracle.

Even though Shelby liked the staff at the home, it was the children who kept her going. Most of them only stayed at the home for a few months. Some even had parents and relatives who came to visit on a weekly basis. This really surprised Shelby. She just assumed that all of the children were orphans. This wasn't the case at all. In fact, most of the children's parents were alive and living right here in Birmingham. Each child came attached with his or her own story. Some of the parents were too poverty-stricken to care for their children, others too sick, while others were simply neglectful or unfit. There were several groups of siblings at the home. One such case involved a group of four, two girls and two boys, whose parents had been sent to a tuberculosis camp.

Shelby usually stayed too busy to dwell on her own situation. Today was different; she had been melancholy all day. She decided it would do her some good to get out of the stuffy house, so she went into the back yard. The infirmary was located directly behind the school in a separate building. Shelby had only been in there once. Thankfully, it was vacant. There had been the occasional cold over the summer, but none of the children had been seriously ill. As Shelby took off her shoes and stepped onto the cool grass, her spirits lifted a little. She loved the back yard; it was her favorite part of the home. There was a vegetable garden in the far back corner and a play area for the children on the other side. She walked over to the big oak tree in the middle of the yard and sat in the swing attached to one of its lofty branches. She began to swing very slowly at first, and then faster. A burst of exhilaration ran through her veins as she sliced through the air. She was enjoying herself so much that she didn't hear the movement behind her. A voice from behind caused her to quickly put her feet on the ground in an attempt to slow herself down. She looked around in surprise as Mother Ramsey walked around the tree and stood facing her.

"Mother Ramsey, I didn't know you were there. I was just—"

The elderly woman smiled. "I've been in the garden. You were enjoying yourself so much that I didn't want to disturb you."

Shelby's eyes widened in surprise, and her cheeks colored. She hadn't realized anyone else was outside.

"I would've joined you myself a few years ago. There's nothing like sailing through the air with only the wind at your feet."

Shelby had a hard time picturing Mother Ramsey sailing through the air, and it must have shown on her face.

Mother Ramsey chuckled. "Don't look so surprised. I haven't always been this old and wrinkled."

"I'm sorry. I didn't mean to imply. I mean..."

"Yes, age takes its toll on the best of us. Sometimes I look in the mirror and wonder who that old woman is staring back at me. I've been piddling around in the garden. Would you like to see it?"

"Yes, I would love to."

Shelby quickly put on her shoes and walked with Mother Ramsey over to the garden.

The older woman reached over and picked a cherry tomato off of the vine. She then wiped it on her apron and popped it in her mouth. "I love cherry tomatoes right off the vine."

"Me too," Shelby agreed.

"Here, have one."

Shelby picked a tomato and bit down on it, the tangy flavor bursting in her mouth.

"How do you like my garden?"

"It's lovely."

"Yes, it is lovely, and it helps feed the children."

Shelby looked at Mother Ramsey admiringly. "The work that takes place in this home is really impressive. Where would some of these children be if it weren't for the Mercy Place?"

The two walked through the rows of the garden as they talked.

"Some of them would still be with their parents despite their desperate circumstances, and others would be on the street. It is a great work to feed and clothe these children, but that only provides a temporary solution to the problem. If we provide these children with good training in their impressionable years, then they will never forget it. Our children are our future citizens, and every little one we help—and every small victory we have—will do much to help create a better society." Mother Ramsey stopped walking and stood still. She looked at Shelby intently. "Miss Pearl has told me a little about your situation. I want you to know that God doesn't make mistakes. Providence brought you here."

Shelby stared down at the ground to hide the tears in her eyes.

"Come over here. I want to show you something." They walked over to the edge of the garden as Shelby looked where Mother Ramsey pointed. "What do you see?"

Shelby looked over to see a jumbled group of weeds. "It looks like weeds," she said carefully.

Mother Ramsey's eyes smiled. "Yes, it does look like weeds. Look closer and then tell me what you see."

Shelby looked more closely and noticed a small cluster of purple violets growing under the weeds.

"Do you see them now?" Mother Ramsey bent down and lovingly touched one of the blossoms. "When this tiny bloom opens up, it will be a violet—a brilliant violet growing amongst the weeds. The weeds have done their best to choke out this little clump of violets, but they have failed." She looked at Shelby intently. "There are many violets in my midst. They have all dealt with their share of weeds but have survived. They continue to hope when everything around them teaches them to despair. You are like the violets. One day, you'll realize your own strength, and then you, too, will blossom."

*   *   *   *   *

"When are you leaving to go to the show?"

"In about forty minutes."

Janice raised her eyebrows and looked doubtfully at Shelby. "And you're sure you know how to get there?"

Shelby sighed deeply. "Yes, Janice," answered Shelby, with more patience in her voice than she felt. "I know how to get there. Miss Sanders gave me directions."

"All right," Janice huffed. "If you get lost, don't blame it on me." She stood to leave. "I have to go and supervise supper."

As Shelby watched her leave, she shook her head. "She's going to drive me crazy," she muttered under her breath.

She and Janice got along just fine as long as Janice felt like she had the upper hand. She enjoyed reminding Shelby that she had been in the home her entire life and knew the correct way of doing things. Shelby knew that Janice was feeling put out because she wanted to be the one to take the children to the show. Shelby had noticed the stricken look on Janice's face when Mother Ramsey asked her to go instead of Janice. She understood and even sympathized with Janice's reaction, but she was getting a little tired of having to walk on tiptoes just so Janice wouldn't get her feelings hurt.

Shelby was very excited about going to the Alcazar to see a show. Cartersville didn't have a picture show. She could remember going to one in Atlanta when she was very little. She had been enchanted by all of the lights and by the delicious smell of fresh popcorn. *I'm not going to worry about Janice,* Shelby told herself. *She's just going to have to grow up a little bit, that's all.*

Shelby pulled her dark hair up in a ribbon and scrutinized her reflection in the mirror and decided she looked dowdy. She was wearing the powder-blue dress she had sewn while at the industrial school. Miss James, her sewing instructor, had chosen the fabric. She rarely wore pastels because they made her look washed-out. She preferred rich, vivid colors. But the blue dress was all she had other than the beige sacks that had been given to her at the industrial school. Anything was better than those. Mother Ramsey had suggested that Shelby take part of her earnings and buy fabric to make herself a few more dresses. Her assistant position didn't pay very much, but it did give Shelby some money of her own. She swished her skirt back and forth and turned slightly to look at her back reflection. *I think I will go and buy some fabric—something red,* she decided. She gave herself one last look and pinched her cheeks before quickly hurrying out the door.

*   *   *   *   *

Shelby and her small group made it to the show without any difficulty. Mother Ramsey had asked her to take five of the older children. The youngest was nine and the oldest twelve. The picture show was even better than Shelby remembered. There were two boys in the group and three girls. As could be expected, the boys got a little noisy right before the show started, and she had reprimanded them. On the whole they had been very good and easy to manage. The girls giggled amongst themselves most of the trip.

When the show was over, Shelby gathered her small group and headed back toward the home. They walked for a while, chatting about the movie and the sights of the city. After they had walked about twenty minutes, Shelby realized with a sinking feeling that they were lost.

"Are we lost?" asked Matthew, the older of the two boys. "None of this looks familiar."

Shelby looked at her group and noted the growing anxiety on the faces of the girls. "Yes," she admitted. "We must have taken a wrong turn."

She looked up at the sky. It was beginning to get dark. She was growing nervous, but tried not to show it because she didn't want to alarm the children. "Everything is okay. We'll just backtrack."

The cheerful chattering ceased, and their faces grew somber as they turned around and headed back in the direction they had come. The walked until they came to an intersection. Shelby couldn't remember if they had turned right or left. She tried to keep her voice calm. "Does anyone remember which way we turned?"

The group looked at one another with nervous expressions and shook their heads.

"Very well," answered Shelby, trying to sound confident, "I think we came from this direction."

The evening slowly grew darker, and the group walked close together as the landscape changed from neat, well-kept houses to shabby, broken-down dwellings. Up ahead they could see a saloon. A few people were already lumbering in. They passed a woman standing on the curb with a bottle of liquor in her hand. Her lipstick was so bright it glowed.

"Aren't you young-uns' too little to be out without ya mamas?" she leered. She eyed the two boys and then let out a loud howl of laughter. "Ah, what the heck, ya ain't ever too young. Come on over here. Aunt Sally'll take real good care of ya."

Shelby shooed the group on down the road. All of their faces looked panic-stricken, and she felt the same way. They had been walking for at least an hour and were more lost now than ever. She felt the tears well up and then pushed them back. *It won't do any of us any good if I break down*, she told herself.

"Matthew," she said, "I want you and Peter to pay close attention to each street we come to." It was dark now. The lights from the saloon had been comforting, but Shelby wanted to keep them away from the drunks.

The group kept walking farther away from the saloon. Shelby didn't know for sure when she first heard footsteps behind them. Maybe she had only felt them. A couple of blocks earlier she saw a shadow out of the corner of her eye. When she turned to look, no one was there. She had even thought she imagined it until one of the boys quietly mentioned it to her. As she tuned her ears, she could hear soft, steady footsteps behind them. She turned to look, but no one was there. Her heart raced, and the group started moving faster. As they got faster, so did the footsteps. Finally, the group began to run. They turned a corner, and Shelby gasped as she ran head-on into their attacker. The boys shrieked, and the girls began to cry as Shelby kicked the attacker hard in the shins. He bent over in pain as Shelby struggled to break free from his grasp.

"Run!" She yelled to the children. "Run!"

"Wait a minute. Hold it! I'm not gonna hurt you. I just want to help!"

The voice sounded strangely familiar. Where had she heard it before? Just as her mind was trying to register what was happening, she looked up to see Harlan standing in front of her.

Shelby stood dumbfounded as relief flooded through her. Finally, she managed to speak. "It's you."

"Did you recognize me right away? Is that why you kicked me in the shin?"

She started to fire back a sarcastic remark until she looked up and saw that he was smiling.

"What are you doing here?"

"I was just going to ask you the same question."

Before she could explain, the children realized Shelby knew her so-called attacker. They had all stopped running and were gathered around Harlan and Shelby.

"Do you two know each other?" Peter asked.

"Yes," answered Shelby dryly, "we've met."

"It looks that way," Matthew added, and the girls began to giggle.

Shelby was confused for a minute, and then she realized that Harlan was still holding her arm. "Umm, excuse me. Would you mind?"

"Not a 'tall." Harlan answered. He held her arm a second longer than necessary before letting it go. "It looks like you're in need of a little assistance."

"We're lost," said Matthew.

Harlan smiled broadly. "And I thought you were just out for a nightly stroll."

"We went to the picture show," said Julia, the oldest of the three girls.

"Me too," said Harlan.

Shelby raised her eyebrow. "You were there?"

"I was," Harlan answered and then changed the subject. "This isn't exactly the best part of town to be in." He looked directly at Shelby and grinned wickedly. "You seem to have a talent for ending up in unusual places at night."

Shelby just glared at him, her dark eyes blazing.

Harlan ignored her and turned his attention to the children. "Why don't I help ya'll get home safely?"

"Yes, please!" they chimed.

On the way home, Harlan talked and joked with the children as Shelby walked silently a few steps behind the group. She had been on the verge of hysteria when she thought she was being attacked. And, when she discovered it was Harlan, she had been so relieved that her knees had gone weak. As she watched him walk with the children, she couldn't help but notice the way his sandy hair curled slightly around his suntanned neck. She reminded herself how he forcibly kissed her in the garden. *He's a brute.* The girls were all speaking to Harlan in an animated fashion, as if he were the first boy they had ever seen. She even saw Julia bat her eyelashes at him. He seemed to take it all in stride, as if it were an everyday occurrence. *He expects every girl he meets to fall down at his feet. Well, I won't give him the satisfaction.* She lifted her chin in the air at the thought.

Despite her resolution, she glanced at him several more times as they walked. *He is very good with the children,* she had to admit. She had heard somewhere that children are a good judge of character. She looked at the children all huddled around him as they walked, each one trying to get his attention. They absolutely loved him.

When they turned onto 25th Street, the boys decided to run on ahead, and the girls quickly followed. Harlan fell back with Shelby. The two walked in silence for a few minutes until Shelby finally spoke. "I'm not sure how we managed to run into you tonight, but I'm glad we did."

Harlan looked over at Shelby. "Do you mean you were glad to see me?"

"No, I mean... What I meant was that I don't know what we would've done if you hadn't come along and helped us get back to the home. What I'm trying to say is thank you."

"You're welcome."

"How did you happen to be in that part of town the same time we were?"

Harlan shrugged. "I recognized you at the show, so I decided to follow you."

Shelby looked perplexed. "Why?"

"To apologize."

His answer caught Shelby off guard, and she didn't know what to say. It had been much easier thinking of him as a brute.

"Look, Shelby. I'm not very proud of the way I acted the night we met. I misjudged you. I'm sorry."

Shelby looked at Harlan, a slight upward curve on her lips as she studied his hazel eyes, flecked with gold. His expression appeared sincere. "I accept your apology." She shrugged her shoulders. "I guess I at least owe you that for tonight."

"So, can we start all over? Fresh?"

They were now standing in front of the home. Shelby stopped and studied him carefully without saying a word.

"Well?" demanded Harlan.

"I don't even know you."

"So, get to know me. Ask me anything."

Shelby swung open the front gate and walked in. Harlan followed closely behind her. "Okay," she said, "I'll ask you a question. What would've happened if I had been a little more cooperative that night in the garden?"

Harlan stopped dead in his tracks, a stunned expression on his face. "What do you mean?"

"What I mean is this: How often do you meet girls alone at night? Is it a nightly ritual?"

"I could ask you the same question," Harlan shot back.

"I was there because of a misunderstanding. What's your excuse?" Harlan didn't know what to say. He just stood there looking at Shelby, so she continued. "I just don't know that I want to be friends with someone who has so little respect for others as well as himself." She gave him an angelic smile and opened the door and walked inside. "Good night, Harlan," she said sweetly, "and goodbye."

She would've closed the door behind her, but he had already followed her in. He watched her walk quickly up the stairs, and he shook his head and smiled. *If this were baseball, I would be out for sure. Strike one–a slap across the jaw; strike two–a kick in the shin, and strike three–a tongue-lashing.* He opened the door to leave but stopped as he heard the voice behind him.

"Young man, I believe we owe you our gratitude for what you did tonight for the children." Harlan turned and saw an older lady with her hand outstretched. He reached out and shook it.

"Thank you, ma'am. I'm just glad I could be of help."

"We don't have much to offer you for your kindness except for our hospitality. The older children missed supper tonight, so they are making themselves something in the kitchen. Won't you please join us?"

He was going to gracefully decline until he saw Shelby standing at the top of the steps with a horrified expression on her face. "I'd be most grateful, ma'am."

"Mother Ramsey. Please, call me Mother Ramsey."

Mother Ramsey saw Shelby standing at the top of the stairs and motioned for her to come down. "Shelby, come and eat supper with us. I want to hear all about your adventure."

Shelby came haltingly down the steps, her face flushed.

A loud cry came from upstairs. "Mother Ramsey! Samuel took my blanket!"

Mother Ramsey smiled and shook her head. "There's always a heap of trouble at bedtime. I'd better go settle the children down. Shelby, would you please take our guest into the kitchen?"

Harlan bowed slightly. "I'd be much obliged."

Shelby stared straight ahead as she began walking toward the kitchen with Harlan following behind, smiling like the cat who had eaten the canary.

Chapter Thirteen

I'm so glad you're feeling better, Mother," said Ellen as she leaned over and tucked in the last corner of the bed with one deft movement. She ran her hand over the top of the cool spread, smoothing out the last wrinkles, humming as she went.

Mrs. Sue sat quietly nearby, gazing out the window, her expression a reflection of tranquility like a still summer morning. Ellen's tune caught her attention, and she turned and smiled at her daughter. "I used to hum that tune to you when you were little. Do you remember?"

Ellen searched her memory for a moment. "I do remember. It's strange how being here has brought back so many memories." She sat down on the bed facing her mother. "I'm so glad you're feeling better."

"Every day that I live is a blessed gift from the good Lord," said Mrs. Sue. She was about to say more but instead looked out the window again, a wistful expression on her face. After a moment, she drew her eyes away from the window and looked at Ellen earnestly. "I want you to know that even though I am grateful that my stay here is lengthened, when that time comes, I will be ready." She smiled tenderly at her daughter's stricken face. "I don't mean that I am not enjoying life. I love you and the children so much. It's like the tune you were just humming. Every time I see you carrying on a family tradition I taught you, I realize that I will never die. A part of me will go on." She paused as she searched for the right words. "I just miss Luther." Her eyes grew misty. "We had a good life together. I know he's up there waiting for me." She chuckled. "And rather impatiently, I'm sure. You know how impatient your father always was."

"You really loved him, didn't you?"

"Yes, dear," answered Mrs. Sue, "even death cannot change that."

Ellen nodded and then looked at the ground. She was touched by her mother's display of affection for her father, but it only made her more keenly aware of the void in her own life.

Mrs. Sue reached out and touched her on the shoulder. "Ellen, are you all right?"

Ellen pulled herself together quickly. "Yes, Mother. I just think it's so wonderful that you and Daddy had such a special relationship. I just wish..." Her voice faltered.

"You just wish you could find the same thing in your life," her mother finished for her.

"Yes, I guess I do," said Ellen.

"You'll find it," said Mrs. Sue with such certainty that Ellen somehow believed her.

"How?" she asked more to herself than to her mother.

Mrs. Sue smiled wisely. "You will have to find your own way."

Ellen nodded. "You think I need to go home, don't you?"

Her mother grasped her hand and smiled lovingly. "Yes, dear. I think it's time you went home."

*   *   *   *   *

Shelby cocked her head and looked incredulously at Janice. She couldn't believe what she had just heard. "What did you say?"

Janice straightened herself up and tilted her nose in the air. "I said that you're just jealous because Harlan talked mostly to me at supper last night."

Shelby shook her head. "I say I don't like Harlan, and now you're telling me that you think I'm jealous? Well, that makes a lot of sense," she snapped, her voice tinged with sarcasm.

Janice bristled. "You don't have to get so upset. I was just making a simple observation."

"You're wrong," Shelby responded huffily.

Janice looked at Shelby quizzically. "Why are you being so sensitive? Don't you think he's cute?"

Shelby shrugged. "He's okay."

Janice squealed in delight. "He's much more than okay. I can't wait to see him again."

"Again? What do you mean? When are you going to see him again?"

"He's going to be helping with the renovation for the new kindergarten room."

Shelby's mouth dropped in astonishment. "Are you sure? When did you hear that?"

Janice was beginning to grow impatient with Shelby. "Yes I'm sure. I heard Miss Patterson talking about it with Mother Ramsey. Miss Patterson is the head of the kindergarten guild," Janice went on to explain. "She—"

"I know who she is," Shelby snapped.

"Mother Ramsey suggested that Miss Patterson hire Harlan to help with the plastering and flooring," said Janice, her eyes sparkling with excitement.

Shelby let out a groan and sat down in a chair. *Why does he keep showing up everywhere?* She sat quietly for a moment and then exploded in laughter.

Janice eyed her suspiciously. "What's so funny?" she demanded.

Shelby was laughing so hard that tears began streaming down her face. Finally, she managed to get control of herself enough to speak. "I was just laughing about my crazy, mixed-up life. That's all."

"Oh," Janice answered, unconvinced and feeling as though she'd been the butt of some joke which eluded her. "Anyway, Harlan talked to Mother Ramsey about working here during supper last night. You would've heard it yourself if you hadn't gone to bed so early."

Shelby knew Janice was right. She had excused herself and gone upstairs shortly after she had led Harlan into the kitchen at Mother Ramsey's request. The shock of getting the children lost had given her a headache, and she had grown tired of watching Harlan flirt openly with Janice. That little scene in the kitchen confirmed all her suspicions about him.

"When will he start working?" she asked casually.

"This afternoon."

Shelby's eyes widened. "Well, he certainly doesn't waste any time, does he?"

"Undoubtedly not," Janice answered as she floated out the door, humming as she went.

Poor Janice, Shelby thought. *He'll just add her to his long list of conquests.*

* * * * *

Shelby stayed away as long as she could and then curiosity got the better of her, and she made her way up the staircase toward the kindergarten room. When she got to the top of the stairs, she could see Harlan inside the room bent over a pail of plaster. She got up to the door and realized she had made a mistake and quickly turned to leave, but it was too late. Harlan looked up and saw her, so she entered the room. He looked Shelby over from head to toe and then turned his attention back to his work. For a split second she feared he was going to ignore her, and she wasn't sure what to do. But then he spoke.

"How's your headache?"

"Fine," Shelby stammered. "I guess I just needed a little rest."

Her flimsy excuse amused him, and he flashed a quick smile and raised one eyebrow. "Oh? I just thought you were trying to get away from me."

Shelby knew he was teasing her and didn't rise to the bait. "I was surprised to hear that you're working here," she said, keeping her voice even.

Harlan shrugged. "Mother Ramsey offered me a job, and I need the work."

The tone of his voice suggested that the subject was not up for discussion, but she was not satisfied with his answer. "I guess it was very fortunate for you that you saw me at the show yesterday," she continued.

Her comment caught his full attention, and he stopped working and stood facing her.

"Yes, Shelby. It was very fortunate. For me and you."

He took a step closer to her, causing a charge to pulse through her veins. She took a step backwards as she broke her eyes away from his penetrating gaze. Just as she was trying to figure out what he meant by that comment and how she should respond, Janice came into the room. She walked over to the two of them, instinctively aware that she had interrupted some sort of exchange between them.

"Well, hello, Harlan. Miss Patterson asked me to come up here and see if you need anything." Her eyes rested on Shelby. "But it looks as though Shelby beat me to it." Her words were innocent enough, but their meaning was clear.

An amused interest twinkled in Harlan's eyes, and he looked at Shelby for her reaction.

Shelby took another step back from Harlan. "I'm sure you two have much to discuss, and I have work to do," she said in a cheerful voice that mimicked Janice's earlier tone. Without another word, she lifted her chin in the air and walked out of the room.

Chapter Fourteen

There was a time when Dora Helton's chestnut hair had been beautiful. Rich, shiny tresses had danced lively around her lovely, heart-shaped face. But that was a long time ago. Now her hair was dull and lifeless. The tattered shawl she had draped loosely around her shoulders seemed to engulf her skeletal frame. Dora wasn't thinking about her weary appearance or about the beauty she had lost. Her only concern was the welfare of her precious children. Carefully, she spooned the last morsel of food in the house into her youngest child's plate and then turned and stared vacantly out the window.

"Mama? Mama, are you okay?"

The persistent tugging of her oldest child brought her back to the present. She looked down at her hands and realized that she had been wringing them again. "I'm fine, Tobias. Mama is fine." Gently, she directed him toward the table. "Go finish your supper."

"I only ate part of mine tonight," he said proudly. "I gave the rest to Lily. She was crying for more."

Dora hugged Tobias fiercely and fought the urge to cry out. She knelt down and looked deep into his sad, dark eyes. There was a time when his little cheeks had been robust and rosy, but they had grown pale and gaunt. His eyes were dark, hollow caves surrounded by sunken circles.

"You gave up part of your dinner for your sister?"

Tobias nodded.

"Your father would've been so proud of you," said Dora as a tear trickled down her cheek. A pang gnawed at the pit of her stomach. It was not a hunger pain, however, that drew her attention. She had long since learned to suppress those. It was a deep, burning hurt that penetrated her to the very core. Her children were suffering, and she was powerless to help them. The sickness was ravaging her body. She shivered as perspiration rolled in rivulets from her aching frame. *I have to get through this. What will become of my children if I don't?* It was growing harder and harder for her to concentrate, but she forced herself to think clearly. The children had finished their meager supper. The younger ones were now crying for more.

"My belly hurts," whined Martha.

She leaned over and stroked Martha's hair. "I know your belly hurts. It will be all right." She turned toward Tobias. "Go and look on top of my bureau in the bedroom. There are a few pieces of candy left. The children can suck on those. It will help ease their hunger pains."

Tobias nodded. He was only nine but was intelligent beyond his years. Poverty makes a child grow up too fast. Dora was so grateful for his help but yet couldn't help but feel sorrowful for his loss of innocence. She looked at the children and smiled. "I've got a surprise for you." She had been saving the candy as a last resort. She probably shouldn't give it to them tonight. But she was so tired, and they were so hungry. If only they could all get some rest tonight. Things would seem better in the morning. She would get better, and then she would find some work. Even in her resolve, she could feel her head spin. Tobias had given the children the candy, and they seemed pacified.

"I'll get everyone to bed, Mama," said Tobias. "You rest."

Dora nodded and then sat down in her chair. She was seeing sparkles and knew that a fainting spell was coming on. *I'll be better in the morning,* she reassured herself. Even as she repeated the words in her mind, deep down, she feared the worst. But she had to continue to hope. As blackness settled in, she continued to reach for that small glimmer of hope, shimmering right there in the distance, just beyond her grasp.

* * * * *

Shelby sat up in her bed and rubbed her eyes. "What time is it?" She moaned. Still groggy, she glanced around the room to see what had awakened her. She figured it was either Janice or one of the other girls. They were all still sound asleep. She had been dreaming of home. Not surprisingly, many of her dreams were of home. But this one was different. It had seemed so real. She could still smell the fresh scent of biscuits baking in the oven. She was going to a barn-raising and was excited about the dance afterwards. She had chosen one of her favorite dresses. It was crimson-red and had a snow-white, lace collar around the top. She had begun to get ready but no matter how fast or how hard she worked, she couldn't seem to get dressed to make it there on time.

She chuckled and then lay back against her pillow. Maybe now she could stop worrying about getting ready for the dance and get some sleep. Deliberately, she closed her eyes tightly shut. She tossed and turned several times, trying to get comfortable. Sleep just wouldn't come. Finally, she quietly got out of bed and tiptoed out of the room and down the stairs in search of some warm milk. When she got down to the first floor, she was startled to see the front door standing wide open. In two steps she covered the distance from the landing to the door.

A group of people was standing near the road. She caught a glimpse of Mother Ramsey's silver hair as she made her way down the front steps toward the commotion. As she neared the group, she saw that Mother Ramsey, Miss Patterson, and a few of the other ladies were gathered around an automobile. *No,* she corrected herself, *they were gathered around an ambulance.* Whatever it was they were discussing amongst themselves was so intense they didn't even notice when Shelby walked up and stood beside them.

She stood on her tiptoes and looked around the shoulder of one of the ladies. Her breath caught when she saw the object of their interest. A tear-streaked, young boy was stubbornly clinging to the ambulance door, refusing to budge. A cluster of smaller children stood huddled together off to the side. Some of them were quietly whimpering. Mother Ramsey was kneeling beside the boy. It looked like she was trying to coax him away from the door so the driver could leave. Shelby strained her eyes and could barely make out the silhouette of a woman lying inside the ambulance. She nudged her way through the circle until she was standing directly in front of the pitiful scene.

Mother Ramsey placed one hand gently on the boy's shoulder.

"Dear, you must let go and come inside," she urged. "Your mother must get to the hospital. She is very sick."

The boy shook his head fiercely, causing his dark hair to wave back and forth.

"I can't leave Mama. She needs me," he said stubbornly.

"Please try to understand," Mother Ramsey began again—this time more urgently. "Your mother needs you to be strong, and your brothers and sisters need you."

Shelby's heart wrenched as she followed the boy's dark eyes as his gaze went first to his mama and then to his siblings. He was frail and helpless, yet there was something noble about his unwillingness to leave his beloved mother. Shelby felt tears rise in her own eyes as she watched those haunted eyes shift back and forth between the two objects of his affection. He wasn't sure what to do.

The ambulance driver was growing impatient. Mother Ramsey motioned for him to let her try once more. Reluctantly, he agreed. On impulse, Shelby stepped forward and tugged on Mother Ramsey's sleeve.

"Would you mind if I try?" she asked timidly.

Mother Ramsey looked for a moment as if she would refuse but then stood up and nodded her head in approval.

Shelby bent down so she could talk to the boy face to face. "What is your name?"

"Tobias," he replied, haltingly.

"I'm Shelby."

Silence.

Shelby looked into the boy's eyes. "I know what it's like to be separated from someone you love."

Her comment caught his attention, and he looked searchingly into her eyes. He seemed to be sizing her up to see if he could trust her.

"You do?" he finally asked with such pain in his voice that Shelby had to resist the urge to throw her arms around him.

"Yes, I do," she answered truthfully. "If you'll let go of the door and come inside with me and your brothers and sisters, I promise you that I'll go with you to the hospital to visit your mother." Shelby glanced over at the driver and realized that he wasn't going to wait much longer, even if he had to pry the child away from the door himself.

Tobias looked back at his mother once more and then at Shelby. "Can we go tomorrow?" he asked suspiciously.

Shelby looked at Mother Ramsey for approval. She nodded. This time Shelby grabbed the boy's arms. "Yes," she whispered fervently. "We'll go tomorrow."

Tobias stood quietly. Ever so slowly, he released the door handle. Before he could change his mind, the driver hastily got into the ambulance and pulled away. Shelby put her arm around the boy. Together, they watched the ambulance drive away until they could see it no more. Tobias stood stone-faced as tears flowed down his cheeks. Mother Ramsey was attending to the other children huddled nearby.

"Let's get you children..." she was about to say "in bed" and then a thought struck her. She looked at their gaunt faces. "Have you children eaten anything today?"

Miserably, they shook their heads no as if they were to blame.

"Let's go to the kitchen and get some milk and biscuits." Their longing expressions brought another wave of sympathy from the other ladies.

Shelby kept her arm around Tobias as she led him into the house. Once they were in the kitchen, she sat nearby and watched as the children eagerly devoured the biscuits and sorghum syrup placed before them. She paid special attention to Tobias. His dark eyes were a stark contrast to his pale skin. She watched in admiration as he interacted with his siblings. They depended on him for everything. She had only caught that vague glimpse of their mother and even then could tell she was very ill. She had been unconscious and oblivious to the drama unfolding around her. How long has this young boy had to be strong? His courage in the face of his hopeless situation touched her. He was definitely a fighter.

After the children were put to bed, Mother Ramsey pulled Shelby aside. "What you did tonight..."

"I know I acted out of turn. I'm sorry."

"I was going to thank you."

Shelby gaped in surprise at this spunky woman whose views often seemed incongruent with her age. "I just thought..."

Mother Ramsey smiled. "You acted on impulse. Is that so terrible?"

Shelby was puzzled. "I'm not sure."

"These children are going to need lots of love and attention. Their mother is very ill. She and the children were found in a destitute condition. From what I gather, she had been ill for quite some time. The older child, Tobias, has been looking after her and the children. When his mother passed out and he couldn't revive her, he went to the neighbors to ask for help."

Shelby nodded and then formed the words she was almost afraid to ask. "Will she get better?"

Mother Ramsey shook her head. "I don't know. We can only hope and pray. In the meantime, we have to make sure we take special care of these little children. You will take the boy to the hospital tomorrow. I'll get Grover to drive you there in the wagon. They may not even let him in to see her, but at least we can keep our promise to him."

Shelby swallowed hard. "I guess I shouldn't have made such a promise."

Mother Ramsey reassuringly placed her hand on Shelby's shoulder. "You did what you thought was right. He trusts you. He sees the goodness in you, just as I do. Now go and get some rest, my dear."

Shelby turned to leave. She got no further than the stairs before Mother Ramsey stopped her. "Shelby?"

She turned back. "Yes, ma'am?"

"How did you know what was going on outside?"

Shelby shrugged her shoulders. "I couldn't sleep, so I came downstairs to get some warm milk."

Mother Ramsey looked at her questioningly.

"It was just luck," Shelby continued.

Mother Ramsey looked thoughtful. "Yes, I suppose that was all it was. Good night, Shelby."

*   *   *   *   *

Ellen stepped down from the train. She couldn't help but notice the sun setting in the West behind the trees, its brilliant, orange rays setting the sky ablaze with a myriad of vivid colors. She felt a twinge of sadness as she hesitated and watched the last bit of color fade. It was as if a door was closing in her life, and her last hope for happiness was vanishing. How different her arrival home was from her hasty departure to her mother's house. She didn't even feel like the same person anymore. For so long she had lived a surface life, simply existing. Seeing John had opened up a part of herself that she had long ago forgotten about. Having opened herself up to her feelings, she was having difficulty suppressing them now. An image of John smiling tenderly flashed into her mind, and she was almost overcome with emotion. Angrily, she pushed the thought away. The sooner that she forgot about everything that had happened in Alder Springs the better off she would be. Now, she was back—back to reality, and back to Frank.

She looked expectantly beyond the other passengers greeting their families. When would her beautiful children arrive to greet her? She had doubted that Frank would come but had hoped that he would change his mind and bring the children. She imagined Homer with those twinkling eyes running to her, Sarah hugging her legs, and Shelby kissing her cheek.

Ellen soon found herself alone as the last passengers made their way out of the train depot. *Surely Frank received my telegram.* Lugging her heavy bags, she made her way to the blacksmith's shop. Perhaps Frank had left her a buggy there. Even if he didn't, she would be able to rent a carriage there. With every step, Ellen fought the awful dread in the back of her mind. *Something is terribly wrong. Something has happened.*

It was completely dark by the time she reached home. She figured that Frank was getting back at her for going by not showing up at the station with the children. As she drew up the rented carriage in front of the house, the terrible feeling intensified. The house was dark and looked bleak and cold. As she walked up the sidewalk, she noticed that weeds had overtaken her flower beds. Shelby would never let that happen. Panic was beginning to overwhelm her. There was no sign of life anywhere.

His voice pierced Ellen's thoughts and startled her as she mounted the steps. "Well, the Queen did return," Frank sneered. "I hope that Her Majesty had a wonderful vacation."

His comment hit Ellen like a runaway mule. It wasn't like Frank to be so blatantly rude. "Frank, what in the world is going on? What are you talking about? Why didn't anyone answer my letters? Where are the children?" Ellen asked as she tried to keep her voice even.

"You mean why didn't your precious Shelby answer your letters, don't you?" Frank hissed.

Ellen's heart began to pound in her chest. As she passed Frank in the doorway, she could smell alcohol on his breath. His hair was disheveled, and his clothes were dirty. In all the years she had known him, he looked worse tonight than she had ever seen him.

"Frank, where are the children?"

Ellen could see Frank's face for the first time as he lit the lamp in the kitchen. She gasped. Thick, dark stubble covered his normally smooth jaw-line, and his expression was strained. He looked as if he hadn't slept for weeks. The circles under his eyes added years to his appearance. He had obviously been under a lot of stress. Surely all of this stress hadn't been caused by her absence. She couldn't possibly have guessed that he had anguished over her return ever since receiving her telegram. She ran up the stairs, calling each child's name.

Ellen walked back into the kitchen. Frank saw a mixture of loathing and fear in her dark eyes. "Frank, for the last time, where are my children?" she begged.

When he didn't answer her, Ellen started back toward the door. Frank grabbed her arm. "Where do you think you're going?"

"You're drunk!" She wrenched her arm away from him and ran out the door and down the steps. She could hear his hollow laughter echoing behind her. She had to go to Sister's house and get some answers.

*   *   *   *   *

As she rounded the bend, the first thing Ellen noticed were the bright lights surrounding the house. Carriages and wagons lined the driveway. She could hardly breathe; her panic had mounted to the point of frenzy. Why were there so many people at Joshua and Sister's? What in the world had happened? Where were the children?

She jumped down from the carriage and hurried up the steps. She stopped dead in her tracks when she saw the funeral wreath hanging on the door. *Who had died?* Her hands flew to her mouth.

Something had happened to one of the children! That's why Frank was drunk! Her world swirled around her. The blinding-white snow lilies in the wreath were the last thing she saw as she crumpled to the ground.

When Ellen came to, she was bewildered to find herself surrounded by a room full of people. She heard the voices of Homer and Sarah, and felt the warm sensation of relief flood through her body as they rushed to her side.

"Mama has come home," they chimed.

Ellen gathered them in her arms as hot tears flowed down her cheeks. "I have missed you so much," she said.

"Did you bring Shelby with you, Mama?" Sarah asked. A sharp stab of fear returned, causing Ellen's heart to jump in her throat. Somehow she managed to get the words out. "What do you mean? Isn't Shelby here?" Her head started spinning again like a top, and she couldn't speak or think clearly.

She heard someone say: "It's a good thing that Ellen was able to make it home in time for the funeral."

Ellen remembered the funeral wreath on the door. *Who had died? Where was Shelby?*

*　*　*　*　*

Ellen had never seen so many people at one funeral. There had been standing room only inside the church. She stood stoically beside Frank, her expression masked, as she watched the pallbearers slowly lower Joshua's casket into the ground.

Ellen had loved and respected Joshua, but she hadn't realized the tremendous impact he had made on their community. She glanced up at the trees; the leaves were beginning to fall from the willowy branches. She watched as a gust of wind plucked several leaves from the branches. They twisted and twirled sporadically before falling softly to the ground. Soon the branches would be completely bare.

The last few days were a blur. The night of her fateful arrival home, she had tried in vain to question the children and Frank about Shelby's whereabouts. The children didn't know, and Frank kept stubbornly insisting that Shelby had run away.

JENNIFER LEIGH YOUNGBLOOD & SANDRA POOLE 123

I should've taken the children to Mother's with me, she told herself. *I've been a fool to stay gone so long. I should've come home sooner. I've been so selfish. If only I'd been more concerned about her children instead of myself.* There were times when she felt her guilt would consume her. She knew that such thoughts were unproductive.

She looked across the open grave to the crumpled, grieving widow who was being supported on each side because she couldn't even stand up by herself. Ellen was desperate to find some answers. Maybe Sister knew where Shelby was, but Ellen knew she was going to have to wait a few days before questioning Sister.

The two days following Joshua's funeral seemed eternally long to Ellen as she waited to talk to Sister. On the third day, she decided she couldn't wait any longer. She watched Frank leave for the store and then packed a basket full of freshly baked bread and jam and headed to Sister's house.

"Mama, can we go inside?"

Ellen shook her head. "No, Sarah. It's best if you stay outside with Homer."

Sarah's countenance fell, and her bottom lip jutted out in protest. She was about to start wailing until Ellen knelt down and looked into her eyes. She smiled and then gave her little daughter a big hug. Sarah had been extremely clingy since Ellen's return. She didn't want to let her mama out of her sight.

"Be a big girl for Mama. Okay?"

Sarah furrowed her eyebrows in a frown. "Oh, all right," she huffed.

Ellen looked up at Homer and smiled. "I won't be long."

She turned and knocked on the door. She waited expectantly a few moments before knocking again. When Sister didn't come, she turned the handle and let herself in. Once inside, she was alarmed to see that the room was dark. It was past noon, and Sister hadn't drawn the shades to let the sunlight in. As her eyes grew accustomed to the darkness, she became aware of the other presence in the room. She put down her basket and walked across the room to where Sister sat rocking slowly back and forth in her rocking chair.

Sister's hair fell flat around her face and draped down below her shoulders. From a distance she could almost pass for a young girl, with her loose, flowing hair were it not for her aged face. The contrast was stark, making her look disjointed. Her cheeks were tear stained and her eyes puffy. The appearance was unsettling to Ellen. At first, she wasn't sure whether or not Sister was even aware that anyone else was in the room. Ellen's heart dropped as she questioned for the first time how Joshua's death had affected Sister's mental capacity. Finally, Sister slowly shifted her gaze to Ellen.

Ellen cleared her throat. "Sister, I'm not sure what to say. I want to tell you...I want you to know how sorry I am." The words sounded empty to Ellen. "I've brought you some bread."

Sister didn't reply.

"I can't even imagine what you must be going through. Joshua was a fine man, a fine husband." Her voice faltered, and she dropped her eyes to the floor. The silence was becoming oppressive. Her heart hammered in her chest, and her palms grew moist. She felt terrible about questioning Sister, but she had to know. With every passing day, her chances of finding Shelby decreased.

She drew a deep breath, and looked squarely at Sister. "I'm not sure how to ask you this, and I know it's not the right time. Please forgive me, but I have to ask you about Shelby."

If Ellen's question caught Sister off-guard, her eyes registered no surprise. Instead of answering the question, she slowly got up from her chair and walked out of the room. Ellen didn't know what to think. Sister's behavior wasn't making any sense. Just when she decided that she had better leave, Sister came back into the room. Without saying a word, she walked over to Ellen and pressed a crumpled letter into her hand.

Chapter Fifteen

The builder of the Mercy Place never dreamed that the large
ballroom on the east side of the house would one day be
used as an eating area for homeless children. Nevertheless, as is often
the case in such matters, after a few minor alterations, the ballroom
was surprisingly well suited for the needs of the children. Constant
chatter and a few intermittent giggles echoed around the room as
the children ate. Shelby studied Tobias and marveled at how rosy his
cheeks were becoming. It seemed hard to believe that this sturdy,
precocious boy reaching for his third helping of supper could be the
same waif who had come to the home only two short weeks ago.
Normally, she ate her meals with the other assistants, but tonight, at
Tobias' request, she decided to eat with the children.

She looked at her young friend admiringly; he definitely had a
knack for making friends quickly. It took most children a while to
get adjusted to their new environment, and yet Tobias was telling
jokes—acting as though he'd been here forever. From an outsider's
perspective, it might seem that he would be perfectly content to stay
at the home indefinitely, but Shelby knew better. Behind his friendly
smile and jovial banter was a serious little boy who was deeply
concerned about his mother. Almost as if he were reading her
thoughts, he looked up. "When are we going back to the hospital?"

"The nurse said we could go back next Tuesday."

"Next Tuesday?" he asked incredulously.

"Yes, next Tuesday," she answered, trying to sound authoritative.

"I don't understand why they won't let me see her," he huffed.

Even though he was being insolent, she understood his
frustration. They'd made the trek to the hospital, clear on the other

side of town, twice already only to be turned away at the lobby. Secretly, she feared that his mother's critical condition was the reason behind them keeping him at bay. She tried to come up with an answer to appease him. "The nurses don't want us to bring in any germs."

"I think the whole thing is stupid," he barked angrily as he pushed his plate away from him.

She was about to reprimand him but thought better of it. He had been through a tough time, so she decided to try a more gentle approach. "The doctors and nurses just want what's best for your mother, and so do you."

Tobias looked down at his plate. He knew she was right.

"Just be patient," she continued. "She's getting stronger every day. I'll bet they'll let you in next week."

He brightened a little. "Do you really think so?"

There was such hope in his voice that she hoped with all her heart that she was telling him the truth when she answered. "Yep, I do."

Both Shelby and Tobias' attention was instantly diverted from their conversation as they watched Harlan come in the door.

Shelby's breath caught and she straightened in her seat.

"Hey, Harlan!" one of the boys yelled. "Come over and sit with us."

"Sorry, Danny," he said, smiling as he shook his head, "but I already promised Tobias I would sit by him tonight."

Tobias beamed as Harlan made his way over to the table and sat down directly in front of Shelby. He reached over and ruffled Tobias' hair. "Hey, Toby." He looked at Shelby. "Hello."

"Hi," she mumbled back. She turned to the boy and asked sternly, "Tobias, why did you invite me to have supper with you when you had already invited Harlan?"

Tobias smiled shyly and shrugged. Before he could defend himself, Harlan came to his aid. "He asked me this afternoon if I would stay after work and have supper with him. I told him I would—on one condition." His hazel eyes sparkled mischievously, emphasizing the specks of gold in them. A smile was playing around the corners of his mouth. "I told him that I would have supper with him only if he brought along the prettiest girl at the home."

Color flooded her cheeks, and her eyes widened. She wasn't sure how to respond. Tobias was smiling broadly, first at her and then back at Harlan. She looked back at Harlan. He was smiling too, but his smile seemed, surprisingly enough, sincere.

"Thank you," she whispered. Their eyes locked, and she felt warmth rush over her. As quickly as the moment had come, it left as the three of them laughed and talked together. Then, Shelby did something unusual. She relaxed and allowed herself to be pulled in by Harlan's charm and the lively conversation of the boys around her. Several times throughout the remainder of the meal, Shelby glanced furtively at Harlan in an attempt to study him. One moment his jaw would be firmly set and then another moment he would break into a smile, lighting his whole countenance. His sandy hair had been lightened by the sun and emphasized his tanned skin. The boys were reveling in the attention he was giving them. He flashed a quick smile at her, and she smiled back.

"Harlan is teaching me and Jim how to play football," Tobias said.

"Is that right?" She wrinkled her nose. "Can Harlan play football?" she asked in mock surprise.

The boys looked at her with such disbelief that she couldn't contain herself any longer. She laughed, and Harlan began to laugh with her.

When Miss Patterson came into the room and gave the signal that supper was over, Shelby felt slightly disappointed. The boys got up to leave. Tobias reached over and gave her a hug. "I'll see you tomorrow." He looked over at Harlan. "Good night."

"Good night, Toby. You make sure you practice that pass I taught you."

"Yes, sir," he answered as he waved.

All the children left, and an awkward silence passed as the two found themselves alone. Harlan was the first to speak. "Thanks for having supper with us."

"It was fun."

"Let's do it again."

Her mouth dropped slightly. "What?"

"Come to the show with me this Saturday."

She swallowed hard. "This Saturday?"

He began to talk faster. "Yes, I would ask you out Friday, but I have a game that day."

He was nervous; it was the first time she had seen him ill at ease, and she felt herself soften. "Okay, I'll go."

"You will?" he asked incredulously and then caught himself. "Okay, what time can I pick you up?"

"I'll have to ask Mother Ramsey's permission. If she says okay, why don't you pick me up at 6:00?"

*   *   *   *   *

Shelby got up from her chair and pushed aside the lace curtain and looked down at the empty street below. She then smoothed the imaginary wrinkles out of her starched dress for the hundredth time and wrung her hands together as she paced back and forth in front of the bed. Finally, she walked over to the door and peeked out. Miss Bissell from the nursery guild was walking by.

"Excuse me," Shelby called to her. "Can you tell me what time it is?"

Miss Bissell stopped and pulled a pocket-watch from her dress pocket. "It's a quarter of six."

"Thank you," Shelby said as she stepped back into her room and shut the door. How was she going to get out of this? She didn't know what had made her agree to it in the first place. She only knew that she had to think up something—and fast. At first, her main concern had been Janice's reaction when she found out. Her anxiety quickly turned to relief on that account when she realized that the children and most of the assistants were going to an ice cream social. She had almost written him a note to be delivered when he came to the door, but she didn't want to appear cowardly. No, she would tell him face to face.

She sat on the edge of her bed and berated herself for accepting the date to begin with and then got up and walked over to the window and pulled up the curtain once more. This time, she caught a flicker of sandy hair. *I may as well get this over with.*

She had just made it to the stairs when she met Miss Bissell going the other direction. "You have a visitor downstairs."

Shelby nodded. "Thank you," she replied, ignoring the flicker of curiosity in the older woman's eyes.

Harlan was waiting in the parlor with his back turned away from her. Her pulse quickened as she waited for him to turn and face her. She had her excuse on the tip of her tongue.

"Hello, Harlan."

A quick turn and they stood face to face. Their reactions to each other were simultaneous. He lifted an eyebrow as he did a slight double take, and her mouth dropped. All notions of breaking their date vanished when she saw what he was holding in his hand.

He spoke first. "You look beautiful."

"Thank you," she murmured as her hand went up to brush back a loose strand of hair.

"These are for you."

"Yellow roses." She took the bouquet and held it up to her nose, letting their sweet scent fill her nostrils. "They are lovely. Thank you. I haven't seen any yellow roses since..." She paused. She was about to say *since she left home*. "Well, it has been a long time. Where did you get them?"

He smiled, softening his angular jaw. He had wondered how she would react to his gesture, and he was pleased that she was so appreciative. "My Aunt June grows them in her garden. She has lots of different colors."

"And you like yellow best?"

Caught off guard by her question, he shifted uncomfortably. He looked directly into her dark eyes when he spoke, hoping she would believe the sincerity of his words. "Aunt June told me that yellow roses are a symbol of friendship."

His knowledge of flowers caught her attention, and she looked up at him in surprise. "What else has your Aunt June told you about roses?"

A playful grin turned up the corners of his mouth as he shrugged his shoulders. "She sends white roses to the church whenever anyone dies."

She giggled. "Uh huh, but that's not the only time you give a white rose."

"Tell me, ma'am, what else do they mean?" He was teasing her now, and she grinned.

"They are sometimes sent during times of great sadness. Tell me, sir. If you know so much about roses, what does red mean?"

He took a step closer to her. "They represent love," he replied, his voice only slightly louder than a whisper.

She took a step back to recover herself. "Remind me to ask you for advice the next time I send flowers," she replied, keeping her voice light. "If you'll excuse me for a moment, I'll go and put these in water."

He chuckled as he watched her walk gracefully out of the room, her shiny curls bouncing on her shoulders. "Maybe I'll give you a red rose someday," he uttered under his breath.

When Shelby came back into the room, Harlan was making himself at home in the parlor. Miss Bissell was seated directly across from him. He must have been telling her a joke because shrills of laughter were erupting from her, causing her plump belly to jiggle. Both parties stopped talking, then turned and looked at Shelby.

Miss Bissell removed her spectacles and wiped the tears from her eyes. "I'd better let you two get to the show, and I have work to do before the children return." A hint of laughter was still in her voice as she spoke.

Harlan stood. "Are you ready?"

As he opened the door, Shelby was unprepared for the cold blast of air that assaulted her. It was early fall, and the days were still warm, so she had assumed the evening would be warm as well. Seeing her shiver slightly, he glanced up and down at the thin cotton dress she was wearing. "Are you going to be warm enough?"

"I'll be fine."

The two walked toward the Alcazar in silence. Shelby glanced at him out of the corner of her eye several times. Even though the silence was making her uncomfortable, she wasn't sure what to say. He'd mentioned his aunt earlier. "Where does your aunt live?"

"Six blocks south of here on West Elm."

She nodded in acknowledgment, although she had no idea which direction that was.

"It's that way," he said, pointing his finger and grinning.

She smiled sheepishly. "Is your home nearby?"

He had a blank look on his face.

"Do you live near your aunt?"

Realization dawned, and he became hesitant. She watched his jaw clench slightly. "You might say that," he replied vaguely.

"Where do you live?"

"Six blocks south on West Elm," he replied mischievously. He pointed his finger again. "South is that way."

"Oh," she answered, slightly embarrassed. "You live with your aunt."

"Exactly."

Her curiosity was piqued. "Does your family live here also?"

"Nope. Just me." She could tell from his short answer that he had no desire to discuss his family, but she was becoming more and more fascinated with this Harlan Rhodes she knew so little about.

"Where is your family?" she probed.

"The sky is clear tonight. Just look at all those stars."

He was right. There wasn't the slightest haze covering the glittering night. It was a splendid sight, but she wasn't interested in the stars, and she knew he wasn't either. Clearly, he was trying to divert their conversation to another topic. Somewhere in the back of her mind, a red flag went up. *Why doesn't he want to talk about his family?*

As if in answer to her question, he continued speaking. "Back home the sky is always clear, but here the bright lights always drown out the stars."

"Yes, I know what you mean. I used to sit on my porch swing and look at the stars, but here—" She caught herself and stopped abruptly. The last thing she wanted to do was to talk about her own family and where she was from. She glanced sideways at him and caught a flash of curiosity in his golden eyes and looked away.

"How long have you been at the home?"

"Long enough," she answered curtly, hoping to curtail any further questions. She began walking faster, forcing him to lengthen his stride to catch up with her.

"How did you end up at the school anyway?"

"I don't want to talk about it," she snapped. "Let's just enjoy our date and not ask each other any more questions, okay?"

Grabbing her by the arm, he turned her around to face him. He was so close to her that she could feel his warm breath on her cheek. His mouth was drawn in concern. "What are you hiding? What happened to you?"

Terror filled her eyes for a second, and she shrank away from him. Her voice became cold as she jerked her arm out of his grasp. "I do not wish to discuss my past or my family."

Harlan looked puzzled and a little hurt. She saw the hurt in his eyes and relented. "Let's just go and have fun together, okay?" She said softly.

His lips tightened into a smile. "Whatever you say. Let's go and have some fun together."

They walked the rest of the way in silence. Shelby's mind was screaming at her. *How could I have been so careless, and why did I panic at the mere mention of my family? I've done it this time. Now he thinks I'm a raving lunatic.*

Several times during the show, she caught Harlan staring at her out of the corner of her eye. She became acutely aware of his nearness as his arm brushed against hers. At one point, he eased his hand over hers, and she didn't pull away. When the show ended, he continued to hold her hand. She wasn't sure how to act, so the two just sat their in silence for a moment as the other patrons left. The energy was building, and it scared her. She tried to pull her hand away from his, but he grasped it tighter and then turned in his seat so that he was facing her. His warm breath against her cheek sent a shiver—half excitement, half fear—running up her spine. Her heart began to pound, and he gave her that crooked grin of his that was becoming very familiar.

"Shelby, I..." he whispered and then changed his mind about speaking. He moved so close that his lips were grazing hers. Just as their lips touched, she panicked and withdrew her hand from his grasp and stood up.

"I guess we should leave. Everyone else has gone."

"Yes," he agreed hesitantly, glancing around the room as if he had just noticed. "I guess you're right. Let's go."

*   *   *   *   *

Harlan was quiet on the walk home. The night had turned downright cold, and Shelby shivered as the wind cut through her cotton dress. "I should've insisted that you bring a sweater earlier," he said, shaking his head.

"It's my own dumb fault."

"Here, let's walk close together, and I'll shield you from the wind." A look of concern touched her expression, and he held up his hands. "No funny business. I promise."

His humor was reassuring, and she huddled next to him as he put his arm around her. Side by side, the two of them walked with their bodies ducked to avert the cold wind. She felt warm and protected and scooted closer into his muscular shoulder.

Harlan stopped abruptly, causing her to fall into him. "Did you feel that?"

"What?"

"Raindrops!"

No sooner had he spurted out the word, when Shelby felt one drop and then another. A gust of wind picked up around them, and then the bottom dropped out of the sky as sheets of rain poured down.

"Let's go! We only have a few blocks left." He grabbed her by the hand and began to run, pulling her behind him. She was no match for his long strides, so she let go of his hand. She stepped off a curb to cross the street, and her foot gave way underneath. She landed square on her hind end in the middle of a puddle of water. He was halfway across the road before he realized she wasn't there. He turned and saw her in the puddle. His eyes grew wide as he rushed to her side. "Are you okay?" He reached to help her up but lost his balance when his foot slipped like butter across the wet pavement, causing him to fall directly on top of her. Normally, she would've been appalled at their predicament until she looked up and saw the horror in his face just before he landed. The situation struck her as funny, and she began to laugh. His eyes narrowed for a second, and then he began to chuckle, too.

"You didn't tell me we were going swimming after the show."

"It was a surprise. Are you surprised?" he asked, his eyes twinkling with amusement.

"Very," she added.

He got up and then helped her up. "As much as I would like to continue our little swim, I think we'd better get inside before we catch our death."

She snickered. "Whatever you say."

They began to run through the rain holding hands. Despite the cold, Shelby found the experience exhilarating. When they got to the door, she reached for the handle to turn it. He grasped her arm and turned her around to face him. Before she could retreat, he slipped his arm around her waist and lowered his face to hers and kissed her gently on the lips. A warm sensation flooded her body, and her knees gave way, forcing her to lean into him to keep from falling. When she recovered, she was about to say something smart until she realized that he had been affected by their kiss as much as she was.

"Thank you for going to the show with me," he said.

"I had fun," she answered sincerely.

He was still holding her, and he leaned his head down close to hers. A pulse of energy raced through her veins when she realized that he was going to kiss her again. She leaned backwards, causing his lips to miss their mark and graze her on the cheek. Calmly, but firmly, she extricated herself from his grasp. He chuckled.

"I'd better go inside, and you'd better be getting home." She looked up at his sandy hair. It was matted to his forehead, and water was dripping into his face. "Are you going to be all right? Would you like to come inside and get dried off first?"

He leaned over the porch and held his hand out past the roof. "No, thanks. It's eased off a bit, and I don't have far to go."

"I know," she said, pointing as her lips curved upward. "It's six blocks that way."

"Six blocks south," he corrected her with a wink. He backed down the steps, then turned and ran toward home. She watched him for a moment and then went inside.

Breathing a sigh of relief, Shelby slipped inside her room and closed the door behind her. She looked around. Thank goodness it was empty. Janice and the other girls must be downstairs. The last thing in the world she needed was to have to answer questions by well-meaning assistants and children as to why she had been out in the rain. She went over to her bed and started removing her wet clothes as fast as she could.

She jumped as the door opened, and Janice walked into the room. Janice looked her over from head to toe, her eyes resting briefly on Shelby's flushed cheeks. She then plopped herself down on her bed. "What happened to you?" She asked, wiping all trace of interest from her voice.

"Oh, I just got caught out in the rain," Shelby replied, keeping her voice even. "How was the ice cream party?"

"It was all right, that is if you like trying to make small talk with the members of the Ladies Aid Society while trying to keep the children from smearing their ice cream all over the floor," she responded sarcastically and then glanced at Shelby speculatively. "So, what were you doin' out in the rain?"

"I was out with a friend."

"A friend? What friend was that?" Janice asked innocently.

"No one important. Just someone I went to the show with, and we got caught out in the rain."

Fury smoldered in Janice's eyes, and she averted them so Shelby wouldn't see her expression. "I hope you had fun."

"Yes," answered Shelby, her face glowing, "I had a nice time."

*   *   *   *   *

"Isn't it a beautiful day? Just look outside. I've never seen the leaves turn such brilliant colors before. Don't you want to come to the window and see?"

"Not really," answered Janice, dryly.

Shelby pulled her by the hand, and dragged her over to the window. "Just look!" she exclaimed.

Janice rolled her eyes in disgust. Shelby was unaffected by the young woman's sour mood. She cracked the window and put her hand underneath it as she felt the crisp, morning air rush in. The rain the night before had cleared out the humidity, making everything seem fresh and new. It had been a long time since Shelby had felt so good, and she knew that her date with Harlan was responsible for her rejuvenated spirit. She smiled inwardly and felt warm all over as she remembered how he had kissed her good night. How could she have been so wrong about him? She walked over to the table beside her bed and picked up her bouquet of roses and inhaled their fragrant scent. She allowed herself a few more moments to linger around the room before reluctantly getting dressed. Today was Sunday, and helping get eighty-eight children ready for church was no small task.

Out of the corner of her eye, she looked over at Janice who was making her bed. She was going to have to somehow break the news to her about Harlan. Janice would be upset of course. It was common knowledge that she had a crush on him. But she would understand, wouldn't she? Anyway, she wasn't going to address that concern today. Today, she wanted to relish in her newfound happiness. She would keep her secret to herself a little while longer.

Chapter Sixteen

Dear, would you please take this basket of rolls and honey to the kindergarten room? The men are working awfully hard up there; I'm sure they would appreciate something to eat."

Shelby smiled warmly at Mother Ramsey as she reached for the basket. "I'd be happy to."

The older woman's eyes glittered. "I trust that you had a nice time at the show the other night?"

"Yes, ma'am," she answered, grinning shyly as color crept into her cheeks.

"I'm glad you're enjoying your time here," said Mother Ramsey as she placed her hand over Shelby's and squeezed it. She then let go and patted her on the shoulder. "Now go ahead. We don't want to keep hungry workers waiting."

Shelby nodded as she turned and walked up the stairs. She hadn't really given it much thought lately, but she was enjoying being at the home. Nothing of course could ever compare to back home with her family. Still, the children were all so easy to love, and they seemed to blossom if given the slightest bit of attention. She was glad Mother Ramsey had asked her to take the basket because it gave her an excuse to see Harlan again. Her pulse quickened. Since their date Saturday night, she hadn't seen him. She had assumed he would drop by the home Sunday afternoon, but he had not. She had planned to stay near the front door so she could see him when he came to work but had gotten involved in helping Miss Patterson cut out gingham material to make dresses for six of the older girls.

She couldn't believe how wrong about him she had been. She bounded up the last few steps—taking two at a time. They had had such a fun time together. She couldn't believe how many times over the past couple of days her thoughts had been drawn to him. When she got near the door, she halted a moment to smooth her hair and pinch her cheeks. She opened the door, ready to greet him, and her smile froze as the color drained from her face. Time seemed to stop, and her feet felt glued to the floor. She blinked, hoping her eyes were playing tricks on her. But no, this wasn't the case for Harlan and Janice were indeed standing near the window kissing each other. She didn't know if it was the sound of the door opening or her own gasp that caused them to turn and see her.

As she dropped the basket and fled the room, she didn't see Harlan back away from Janice as if he'd been burned by a hot poker. Somehow, Shelby made her way up the stairs and into her secret room. She sat down in the corner and pulled her knees to her chest and buried her head as she tried to block out the image of Harlan and Janice together.

*　*　*　*　*

After Shelby had exhausted all of her emotions, going from disbelief to rage to tears and finally disappointment, she promised herself that she would hold her head high and never let him see how much he had hurt her. She came to the conclusion after careful introspection that the person she was most disappointed with was herself. She had known since the first night she met him that he was a scoundrel. She had even felt sorry for Janice for falling for him, and yet she had allowed herself to follow the same path. He was smooth, no doubt about it. On their date, he'd appeared so kind and sincere.

At first, she had been angry with Janice, but her anger soon turned to pity. After she had run out of the room, Janice had confronted her about it later on in the day. "Shelby, are you okay?" she had asked, concern dripping from her voice. "You didn't have to run out of the room like that. All we were doing was kissing."

Shelby had felt her fury rise and had fought for control. "I don't wish to discuss it," she answered, trying to keep the resentment out of her voice.

Janice's voice took on a tone of superiority. "I don't know what it's like where you come from, but from where I come from, it's perfectly acceptable and proper for a couple who are courtin' to kiss one another."

Shelby's eyes widened in exasperation. Was Janice really that naive or just plain stupid? Could she not see what was happening? He was playing them both for fools. She turned and looked Janice squarely in the eyes. "And you think you're the only one?"

"What do you mean by that?" she stammered as her cheeks grew flushed.

She was on the verge of telling Janice that Harlan had been out with her the other night but then clamped her mouth shut as an image of a small abandoned baby left on the cold, hard steps flashed through her mind. Janice had been through so much. She deserved better than this. No, she wouldn't say anything hurtful to her. Her quarrel was with Harlan—not Janice. "I just don't trust him," she finally said. "You deserve better."

The relief was evident in Janice's expression as a smile spread across her freckled face. "I'm a big girl. I think I can take care of myself."

"Just promise me you'll be careful."

"I will."

Shelby turned and left the room feeling a little better. She would've been shocked had she turned around to see the object of her pity sitting on the bed with a satisfied smirk on her plain face.

* * * * *

The back yard of the Mercy Place with its giant oak trees and tall hedges was the closest semblance Shelby could find to home. Whenever she began to feel stifled with the close quarters, she would come outside to be alone. Today, she knew no one else would be outside because it was cold and overcast. After her conversation with Janice, not even the dark clouds, hovering like a blanket in the sky, deterred her from going out. She dragged her feet through the leaves on the ground as she walked aimlessly around the yard. Finally, she went to the shed and grabbed a rake.

"Why are you out here raking leaves? You should let me help you."

His voice startled her, and she turned around to face the person who had been the center of her thoughts. She glared at Harlan for a moment, her dark eyes smoldering, and then turned her back on him. "I have nothing to say to you," she barked.

He walked around to face her. "What do you mean you don't have anything to say to me? We had plenty to talk about the other night."

Fury flew all over her. "I can't believe you have the gall to come out here and say such a thing to me after what I saw," she said, her voice rising.

"Oh yeah, tell me...what is it that you think you saw?" he shot back.

Instead of answering him, she shook her head, her dark hair flying wildly, as she threw down the rake and walked away from him. He caught up with her at the back of the yard. "Tell me what you saw," he demanded.

She spun around to face him. "Don't play games with me," she huffed, her voice hard with anger. "I won't give you the satisfaction of putting it into words when we both know what I saw. Tell me, Mr. Rhodes, do you always take such pride in manipulating women?"

Harlan flinched at the bitterness in her voice. "What would you say if I told you that I didn't kiss Janice? She kissed me."

"What?" she spat. "Do you think I'm stupid? Do you actually think you can tell me a pack of lies and that I'll believe you?" Her voice was rising, but she didn't care.

"It's true."

She shook her head. "You disgust me."

"What have I done that is so terrible? Why are you always so quick to believe the worst in me?"

For a split second, her eyes filled with uncertainty. Could it be true? Was Janice kissing him? She couldn't remember.

He sensed her thoughts and began to relax. "Shelby, you know how I feel about you," he said gently.

She looked up at his handsome, rugged face and felt herself soften. She did want to believe.

"This is all just a terrible misunderstanding," he continued, placing his hand on her arm. She felt the familiar warmth rush through her veins at his slightest touch and lowered her eyes so he wouldn't see how he was affecting her. Before she knew what was happening, he circled his arm around her waist and pulled her next to him. She felt his breath on her hair, and he bent down to kiss her as she closed her eyes expectantly. Janice's long, frail arm clasped around his neck flashed through her mind, and she stiffened. What was she doing? She was furious with herself for being taken in by him again. She was beginning to think she was just as helpless as all of his other conquests against his devilish charm. In a huff of anger, she extricated herself from his grasp.

"What did I do?" Harlan asked, dumfounded.

"This stops here and now," she said hotly. "You won't add me to your list of conquests." She lifted her chin defiantly in the air. "I won't have it!"

"What?" He couldn't believe his ears. "Is that what you think? You think you have it all figured out," he said sarcastically.

She met his angry glare. "Don't I?"

His face was white with emotion, but he managed to keep his voice even. "I've told you how I feel about you. I'm tired of playing your silly games—one minute you're hot and the next you're cold. When you grow up a little bit and start to see the big picture, you let me know." He turned and walked away.

Still reeling from the sting of his accusation, Shelby walked over to the swing and sat down. She wasn't sure if it was relief or disappointment she was feeling as the realization dawned that she would no longer have to worry about Harlan bothering her.

*　　*　　*　　*　　*

Upon close inspection, it was visible from the outside. In fact, the small, nondescript window was directly centered above the second-story windows. She had gone outside and checked, just to see. Because the house was so large, it was often hard to tell from the outside which window went with which room. Most residents of the home seemed unaware of its existence. Maybe it was because three-fourths of the year, the window was partially covered by leafy branches. She had discovered the attic a month ago when Mother Ramsey sent her upstairs to look for extra blankets. At first, she would come up and rummage through the old trunks, but lately, she used the attic as a place of solitude.

When the leaves were on the branches, it would be almost impossible to see past them. But now that the branches were almost bare, she had a bird's-eye view of the front. Today, the street below was vacant. Red, yellow, and brown leaves littered the ground. She sat staring out the window with her elbows propped up on the open window, her chin resting in her hands. An old refrain she had once heard kept running through her mind. *Time ebbs slowly by, especially for those who have no future.*

With the exception of her first week at the industrial school, this had been her hardest week so far. It had all started with her argument with Harlan and had gone downhill from there. At first, she had wondered how she was going to avoid him but soon realized that he evidently didn't want to be around her any more than she wanted to see him. He had skillfully avoided her the entire week— not that she minded. She was glad to be rid of him. Still, it was hard to watch Janice bask in her triumph. Somehow, she had managed to keep her face expressionless as she listened to story after story about the wonderful times she and Harlan were having together. "He even told me I was the prettiest girl he'd ever kissed," Janice had blushingly admitted.

Shelby gently massaged her throbbing head. A slight shiver ran down her spine as she felt the wind pick up, sending a gusty draft through the window. Reaching up, she pulled down the window and clasped it shut. She knew she shouldn't be up here wallowing in self-pity, but she couldn't seem to break out of the despondent mood. Resolutely, she got up and moved away from the window and plopped herself down on the dusty, feather bed as the old springs groaned under her weight.

No one had ever come up here to find her. Didn't anyone ever wonder where she was? *Maybe they just don't care.* She closed her eyes and let herself drift off to sleep.

"It's not a permanent job but at least it's work." Bill Summers put down his tools and then went over to the window and sat down. He pulled out a cigar, lit it up, and took a draw. A slight breeze was blowing in through the open window.

It felt good.

Over the past few months, Bill had worked so many odd jobs in various places that he was beginning to lose count of them all. That was okay, though, because as long as he could find work, that would mean Bessie and the children would be taken care of.

He enjoyed working at the Mercy Place. The constant noise and sounds of laughter reminded him of his own house, and Mother Ramsey was one of the kindest, most loving people he'd ever met. He laid his cigar down on the nearby windowsill and looked up as Joe, one of the other workers, stuck his head in the door.

"How are we doin' on plaster?"

"I just used the last of it," Bill answered.

"Come on," Joe urged, "let's run and get some more."

Bill stood, and the two men left the room. Neither of them saw the wind catch the curtain, fluttering it lightly before depositing it directly on top of the lit cigar. Nor did they see the curtain a moment later when it burst into flames.

* * * * *

Startled, Shelby bolted up in the bed and looked around in a daze. At first, she thought she was having a nightmare. Then she began to cough hoarsely, trying in vain to take a deep breath. As she was jarred fully awake, she realized that the air was filled with smoke. She got off the bed and looked toward the window; it was dark outside. Panic began to rise as she made her way to the door. The smoke was so thick that she was finding it hard to breathe. She pulled up the hem of her dress and held it to her mouth as a filter, but it did little good. Fire! The house is on fire! Her mind screamed as she made her way to the door.

She willed herself to remain calm—tried to remember what she knew about fires. *It will be okay*, she told herself. *Once I get out the door, I can make my way down the stairs.* She felt for the door and almost sobbed with relief when she realized it was cold. That meant the fire wasn't right next to her. She grasped the handle and pulled. The door didn't budge. It was stuck! She yanked it again with all of her might, but it still wouldn't open. The smoke was stinging her eyes. She gulped the air and then doubled over as her body racked in a spasm of coughing. How could this be happening? She'd been up here at least a half-dozen times, and the door had never jammed before. *Why now?* In desperation, she began beating on the heavy wood.

"Can anyone hear me? Please! Help!" She knew it was useless. The door was so thick that her beating barely made a sound on the heavy oak. She fell to her knees and began crawling back toward the window.

The hopelessness of her situation hit her full force. No one knew where she was. If she could make it to the window, she could scream for help and maybe even go out on the roof. She couldn't see a thing because of the smoke and could feel herself losing consciousness. *It can't end this way*, she thought. *There are so many things I want to do. If only I could see my family one more time.*

Just when she was about to abandon all hope, she heard a loud crash. Someone was coming. Strong arms lifted her up, and she held onto her rescuer with every ounce of strength she had left. She must have then passed out because the next thing she knew she was outside on the grass in Harlan's arms. He was hugging her, and they both were crying.

"I thought I'd lost you," he said fiercely.

"You saved my life. You risked your own life for me. But how did you know?" Tears of gratitude were streaming down her face.

"Where you were?" he asked as he cupped her face with his hand and gently wiped away the tears as they fell.

"Uh huh," she murmured, looking in his eyes.

"You've been going up there every afternoon for a week."

She didn't know what to say. She just shook her head. "Why would you care where I was going?" She stopped. "Unless..."

"I love you. I have from the first moment I saw you. Please say you love me too. I don't think I could stand it if you didn't."

His eyes pleaded with hers, and she felt as if her heart would burst with emotion. "I love you, too," she blurted out and then was shocked at the wonderment of it all. She did love him and was realizing it for the first time.

All of her hostility toward him melted away, and she began to see things clearly as his lips found hers, and he kissed her tenderly. She pulled back and looked into his eyes. "Thank you," she said.

"For saving you? You're welcome."

She smiled playfully. "For loving me."

The children, captivated by the billowing smoke rising up from the roof, had all gathered as close to the burning house as the firemen would allow while frantic assistants scurried around them, trying to maintain order. Shelby and Harlan, oblivious to the other people around them, hugged and kissed again. And as he held her in his arms, she knew her life would never again be the same.

Chapter Seventeen

The fire had completely destroyed the new kindergarten room and a portion of the attic. Luckily, the firemen had arrived in time to keep the fire from spreading to other areas of the house. All of the children and staff had gotten out safely. At first there was concern over whether or not the children would be allowed to stay in the home while it was being repaired. But Mother Ramsey had insisted that the children would be perfectly safe as long as the damaged areas were blocked off. This was a relief to the children and assistants because it meant that life would go on as usual.

Shelby gave her hair one last swift brush before putting down her hairbrush and picking up the necklace. She held it up to her neck and admired it in the mirror. How could she explain to Harlan how she was feeling? Just when she thought everything was great and that she could truly be happy, nagging thoughts would surface.

Ever since the fire, she and Harlan had been inseparable. They took long walks in a nearby park and had even gone to the fair together last week. When she was with him, everything seemed right. It was afterwards—when she was alone—that the doubts began to surface. One thing she knew for certain about Harlan was that he was a man with purpose—never letting anything stand in the way of something he wanted. In every kiss and in every embrace, she could feel his yearning for something more. She began to fear that he might ask for a part of her—a commitment she couldn't give, at least not yet.

If she could just see her mama, Homer, and Sarah again, then maybe she could sort out her feelings for Harlan. Their relationship had deepened to the point that marriage was the next logical step.

Even though he had not yet proposed, she knew it was imminent. And what would she say? His love for her was true—that much she knew. Still, she knew nothing about him or his family, and he knew nothing about hers. Could two people really make a go of things under such circumstances? She didn't want to lose him, but she wasn't sure if she was ready for marriage. Maybe he wouldn't want her if he knew why she'd been sent to the industrial school. She wondered what Harlan would think if he knew that Papa had tried to rape her. What would he think if he knew that she'd almost killed Papa? She shuddered.

And then there was his family. Every time she had tried to question him about his family, he had grown evasive. What was he hiding? She shook her head. Maybe they were just two misfits trying to make a whole. She wrinkled her nose. That couldn't be a good thing, could it?

A knock sounded. Shelby turned to see Miss Bissell standing in the doorway.

"Harlan's here."

"Thank you, Miss Bissell. Please tell him I'll be right down."

* * * * *

"You look beautiful tonight."

"Thank you," Shelby replied, lowering her eyes slightly, causing her thick eyelashes to flutter against her cheeks. She had taken special care in getting ready for her date with Harlan, choosing her favorite dress—a simple, red dress that tapered in around the middle, emphasizing her slim waist. Its v-neck accented the delicate pearls against her milky-white skin. Harlan touched her necklace, lightly brushing her slender neck.

"The pearls look nice. I knew they would. They look as good on you as they did on my mother."

"You shouldn't have given them to me."

"Don't you like them?"

"Of course I do," she answered quickly, touching them protectively. "They're the most beautiful things I've ever seen. I just feel awkward wearing your mother's pearls—she should be wearing them."

A flicker of pain flashed across his face, and he grabbed her hand as they walked in silence through the park. It was dusk, and the last glimmer of daylight was fading against the trees. A gentle wind was rustling through the fallen leaves as they passed another couple walking in the other direction. He led her to a bench where they both sat down. She looked sideways at him but couldn't make out his expression. All she could see was his taut jaw. Tension began to build inside of her. What did she say that upset him?

He took a deep breath and exhaled slowly. "My mother is dead."

Her breath caught. "I'm sorry," she began. "I had no idea."

"It's okay. You had no way of knowing," he said as he turned to face her. "Those pearls were a gift to her from my father. They were her most prized possession." He smiled ruefully. "Except for her children, I mean."

She reached up and touched the pearls as she pondered the significance they played in his life. Her forehead creased. Funny, she had never considered that he might have siblings. "You have brothers and sisters?"

He nodded. "Four—one brother and three sisters. I'm the oldest."

A thousand questions tumbled into her mind. She waited expectantly for him to go on, but he didn't. He seemed to be staring at some unknown object, his mind far away in another place.

"Would you like to talk about it?" she finally asked.

He cleared his throat. "My mother's name was Hazel Jean. She and my pappy ran a general store in Tucker."

Her eyes widened. They had so much in common and hadn't even realized it.

"Mama had never been sick a day in her life. So when she started having stomach trouble, we assumed she had a touch of the flu. Pappy made her go to the doctor. She came back and told us everything was all right. But it wasn't." His voice broke. "She died of stomach cancer two months later."

Shelby placed her hand on his back and rubbed it gently. "Does your family still live in Tucker?"

"Yes. After she died, Pappy withdrew into himself. He kept late hours at the store. Mary Beth, my oldest sister, looked after the little ones." He shook his head. "I should've helped her more. I was just so torn up inside, too. I started hanging out with the wrong crowd—

staying out late at night." He paused. "Anyway, you get the idea."

Her eyes widened, and she shook her head, not sure what to think.

"Four months went by, and then Pappy brought Violet Kimball home to meet us. Only six short months after my mother went to her grave, he married again," he finished bitterly.

Shelby started to inject her opinion but then realized that he was speaking to himself as much as he was to her. She clamped her mouth shut and waited for him to continue.

"Violet is ten years younger than Pappy and has two boys of her own. They all came to live with us. She's hot-tempered and sharp-tongued—as different from my mother as anyone could possibly be. From the moment she set foot in the house, she tried to control me. I wasn't gonna have it. She had no right." His voice took on a pleading quality. "One morning, we had words. I lost my temper and pushed her up against the wall. Pappy came into the room and pulled me away from her. That's when he sent me here to live with Aunt June."

She pulled her hand away from his back and clasped it in her lap. Nothing could've prepared her for this. She shook her head.

"I'm not proud of what I did." He leaned his head down and rubbed his fingers through his hair and then looked back up at her. "Haven't you ever made a mistake?" he asked remorsefully.

Her mouth went dry as she tried to formulate her fears into a single question. Her voice sounded hoarse in her ears. "Do you think you would've hurt her if your pappy hadn't come in?"

Harlan shook his head. "I don't know," he answered, his voice heavy with anguish. "I've asked myself that over and over again. I was so angry—at her and Pappy."

She hesitated. "I'm not sure what to make of this. What would you do to me if you ever got angry?" she asked, feeling very small.

"I would never hurt you," he answered vehemently. "You know that."

She searched his eyes for reassurance and found fulfillment there. Yes, she did know. She leaned against him, and he placed his arm around her as he linked his hand in hers. They sat in silence and listened to the crickets. After a while he spoke. "I wasn't gonna tell you any of that."

She turned and looked up at him. "Why did you?"

"Because I never want to have any secrets between us."

She nodded and swallowed hard. He had trusted her with his secret. Why was she having such a difficult time telling hers? He may have been waiting for her to tell him about her past, but when she remained silent, he didn't press her.

"I had intended to talk to you about something far more important than my sordid past," he began.

Her eyes widened.

"Do you know what I want to talk to you about?"

She stiffened. "I'm not sure," she answered nervously.

He placed his finger on her lips and traced a pattern around the edges. His lips came down on hers, and he kissed her hard, taking her breath away. "You know what I want to ask you."

She nodded.

"What is your answer?"

Instead of answering, she placed her fingers on his lips to silence him before kissing him back lightly. "I just need more time," she whispered.

He smiled, but she could see the disappointment in his eyes. "Just don't make me wait too long," he whispered back as his lips sought hers once more.

*   *   *   *   *

"When do you reckon we'll be ready to leave?" Sister asked.

"Will everything be finalized this Friday?"

Sister nodded.

Ellen did some quick calculating in her head. "I don't have much more to do." She smiled apologetically. "I can't contribute much financially to our venture. I wish I could do more."

"Just letting me go with you is enough," said Sister.

The two women smiled briefly and then directed their focus to the task at hand. They'd lived a couple of miles apart from each other almost their entire married lives, and yet they'd grown closer together over the past month than they had in the last twenty years. Sister was selling the farm to Virgil Weatherby and would use the earnings to pay off her debts. They would use the meager remainder to finance their trip first to Birmingham to pick up Shelby and then on to Alder Springs. Shelby's letter gave the address where she was. Ellen had almost contacted the school to let them know she would be coming but then changed her mind. She wasn't sure how much contact Frank had with them and didn't want to arouse suspicion.

They couldn't go until Frank left in two weeks for Atlanta to purchase supplies for the store. From the moment Ellen read the crumpled letter, she knew she was going to retrieve Shelby come hell or high water. She had wept with relief when she realized Shelby was okay. In the place of her sorrow, a deep burning rage had taken root. Sister told her about the night Joshua found Shelby in the garden, and Ellen had gasped in horror as they pieced together the events that had taken place.

"I figured Shelby had gotten in trouble with some boy," said Sister. "I misjudged her. I had no idea." Remorse hung heavy in the air as she spoke. "Joshua knew what had happened all along. How could I have been so blind?" she asked angrily. "I could've helped him. Why didn't he tell me? I'll never be able to forgive myself." She paused. "And I'll never forgive Frank as long as I live." She spoke with such forcefulness that Ellen, had she not witnessed it firsthand, would've found it hard to believe the words had come from Sister. She understood her though—only too well.

"How do you think I feel?" Ellen asked.

Sister looked surprised. "What?"

"Don't you think I blame myself every second for being gone? Here I was off gallivantin' around while that snake in the grass took my daughter off to rot in some school."

Sister quickly came to Ellen's defense. "You were taking care of your mother. I hardly see how any of this could be your fault."

"I should've come home sooner," said Ellen resolutely.

"And I shouldn't have been such a blind fool. I would give anything to just hold Joshua one more time." Tears erupted, and Sister burst into sobs.

Ellen put her arm around her and let her cry. Finally, Sister lifted her swollen eyes.

"Sister, I want you to listen to me. Neither of us can do anything to change the past. Joshua loved you, and you loved him. Nothing, not even death, can change that. He would want you to be happy—to start a new life. And I need you."

"We need each other," Sister clarified, "and Shelby needs us."

"It's settled then. We leave in two weeks."

*   *   *   *   *

Ellen soon discovered that the hardest part of getting ready for the trip was hiding her preparations from Homer. Keeping him on a steady routine helped some to occupy his busy mind. Even so, he had already asked her why she spent so much time with Sister and why Sister had begun to pack her things. She had answered him as honestly as she could, telling him that Sister couldn't run the farm on her own and that she was going to sell it. Her answer seemed to appease him.

While she detested keeping secrets from her children, she knew that one inadvertent slip of the tongue to Frank could lead to disaster. So far, everything was taking place right on schedule. If Frank sensed that anything was amiss, he hadn't let on. On the contrary, he seemed pleased that she had stopped questioning him about Shelby's disappearance. He even remarked that he was glad to see her settling back into her routine. She tried not to think about what would happen if he somehow found out. Her nerves were bothering her so badly the night before last that she had awakened sick at her stomach and had slipped out of the house, behind the outhouse, where she vomited until there was nothing left. On and on she went, going through the motions each day, outwardly composed while her insides churned with apprehension and fear.

*   *   *   *   *

It had come to her on the way back from the hospital to visit Tobias' mother. The news had been good. Dora Helton was in the recovery stage of her illness, and, with a little luck, if everything went as smoothly as the doctors' predicted, she would be released to come home next week. Tobias, bouncing up and down in the wagon beside her, had hardly been able to contain his excitement over the news.

As Shelby had watched the frail woman reach up from the bed to embrace her son, tears of gratitude had surfaced, threatening to spill out. She was truly glad that something good was happening for them, but the feeling was bittersweet. If only she and Harlan could be reunited with their families. Life is too short to be separated from the ones we love. She couldn't do anything to change her situation, but Harlan certainly could. Goosebumps rose on her arms as the answer hit her full force. If she could convince Harlan to go home and mend things with his father maybe that would help her feel better about her own situation. That's what she must do—convince him to go back and set things right. And, she admitted, it would give her some time to examine her own feelings about marriage.

She reached over and gave Tobias a hug. He grinned broadly. "I can't wait to tell my brothers and sisters the news," he said.

"Yes," she nodded. "It has been a good day. I'm so excited for you." She grinned. *And for me and Harlan too.*

*   *   *   *   *

Ellen had almost finished the supper dishes when Frank came into the kitchen. She had to fight with herself to keep her hands steady. Everything was happening so fast—tomorrow Frank was leaving for Atlanta. Her heart skipped a beat as he put his arms around her waist. His lips grazed her ear, and she had to fight the urge to recoil from his touch.

"Sugar, you're working too hard," he said in a syrupy tone. "Why don't you come over and sit down at the table and talk to me for a few minutes?"

She felt fear rise in the pit of her stomach. He hadn't called her sugar in years. What in the world was he up to? Hesitantly, she wiped her hands on her apron and sat across from him.

He scrutinized her. "Are you all right?" he asked. "You look a little pale."

"I'm fine. Just a little tired."

"I've been thinking about this trip to Atlanta, and I've decided it just wouldn't be right to go off and leave you here—especially with Shelby gone and all. I think I'll wait another week."

She looked down to hide the bitter disappointment she felt. It was as if a vice were clutching her heart. *Remain calm,* she willed herself. *He couldn't possibly know.* She raised her head and looked him steadily in the eye. To her astonishment, he was staring back at her with a benign smile on his face, and she knew that she was married to a monster. He knew what he had done to Shelby, and now he was toying with her. Her anger gave her courage. A thin smile etched its way over her mouth.

"No dear," she said, keeping her voice neutral. "Don't worry about me. I plan to spend a lot of time with Homer and Sarah. They missed me when I was away—more than I realized at first."

She could tell from his expression that he was weighing every word she spoke as he made his decision. "Well, I really do need supplies. If you think you'll be okay..." His voice trailed off, and then he smiled, portraying the perfect image of a concerned husband.

Relief flooded Ellen's body, and she managed to smile back.

* * * * *

Harlan shook his head in exasperation. Why was Shelby being so stubborn?

"Give me one good reason why you won't come with me."

"I've already told you," Shelby replied, letting him down as easily as she could. "You need to do this on your own. This is between you and your papa. I would only be in the way." She paused. "They wouldn't want me there," she finished gently.

"Who cares what he wants? It's what I want," he huffed, but deep down he knew she was right. He just couldn't bear the thought of being away from her. And there was something else—a feeling of dread.

She scooted up next to him on the park bench and picked up his arm and placed it around her neck. He felt his anger melt away as he reached up and stroked her hair. He looked sideways at her profile, memorizing the outline of her soft cheek. "I guess you'll have to come here and listen to the crickets all by yourself while I'm gone," he sulked.

"No," she replied, shaking her head. "I won't come here without you. This is our place." She nestled into his shoulder.

He grinned slightly. "Good."

"How long will you be gone?"

"About a week and a half," he answered before raising an eyebrow. "You wouldn't be trying to get rid of me now, would you?" He kept his voice light so she would know he was teasing. But, for some reason he needed reassurance.

She punched him in the arm, and her dark eyes began to spark. "How could you say such a thing?" she asked incredulously. "You know how I feel about you. I wish you didn't have to go away at all..." Her voice trailed off.

"But?" he finished for her.

"But you need to do this—for you—and for us."

"I know," he whispered, pulling her as close to him as he could. She sighed. "I'll miss you."

There was so much he wanted to say. He wanted to tell her that from the moment she suggested he go home, a deep, unexplainable dread had come over him. The intensity he felt for her scared him. Maybe he was experiencing the jitters because he had finally found the woman he wanted to spend the rest of his life with and feared deep down that he might lose her somehow. He chided himself for being so superstitious. It was only a week and a half. "I'll miss you too" was all he said as he hugged her once more, savoring the sweet scent of vanilla on her skin. "Just do me one favor."

She looked at him quizzically.

"Promise me you'll be here when I get back."

Her eyebrows furrowed, and she wrinkled her nose. From the tone of his voice, she had figured he wanted to ask her something serious. This was easy enough. She smiled. "I promise."

* * * * *

Homer and Sarah were in the back yard playing when Frank's wagon finally lumbered down the road. Ellen's anticipation was building to the point of frenzy. She calmly waved him off. There was so much to do and so little time.

As Ellen packed the last bag, she heard Sister coming up the stairs. Perfect timing. With any luck, they would be gone before anyone missed them. "Sister, come on in. I'm almost finished," she yelled.

"Well, well, what have we here?" Frank hissed. "Going on another vacation, I see."

Her face turned crimson as she whirled around to face him. His face was black with rage. "Frank," she began, "what are you doing here?"

"Sorry to interrupt," he sneered.

Before she could respond, he slapped her on the jaw, sending her sprawling across the room. Her head whirled as white light flashed before her eyes. She was so stunned she couldn't move. He stepped forward to pick her up; he wasn't finished with her yet. He clinched his fist to strike her again.

The click of the chamber sounded like a bolt of lightning. Frank jerked around and saw Sister standing above him with a double-barreled shotgun aimed directly at his head.

"Leave Ellen alone," she said in a voice so hoarse and low it was almost inaudible.

"Give me the gun," he ordered. "You know you couldn't hurt a fly—much less me."

"I said back off!" she yelled.

He flinched and then his eyes rested on her trembling hands. When he spoke, his voice was steady and condescending, as though he was speaking to a child. "Sister, this doesn't concern you. Put down the gun and go home." He took a step toward her, and she raised the gun and tightened her grasp.

"No," she barked. "You have destroyed too many lives already." She narrowed her eyes. "And if you have any doubts about my intentions, you just remember that Joshua is lying in a pine box because of you."

He could tell from the look in her eyes that she couldn't be reckoned with. His best bet was to back off. "Go ahead and leave—both of you! I don't need you anyway. It won't be long before you'll be crawling back, beggin' for my help," he sneered as he turned and bolted down the stairs.

Sister helped Ellen up from the floor. "Are you okay?"

Ellen's left cheek and eye were already swelling from the hard blow across her face. "I'm going to be okay as soon as we get out of here," she whispered. "Is he still around?" Her voice quivered as she steadied herself on her feet.

"No, I heard him take off on one of the horses," replied Sister, trying to sound confident, although her own knees felt so weak that she could hardly stand.

"Get the children," Ellen said in a strong voice that surprised even her. "We're getting out of this place before he changes his mind and comes back."

Chapter Eighteen

"M iss Shelby! Miss Shelby! Come quick! Something happened to Iris."

"Where is she?"

"She's sittin' in the corner crying."

Shelby sighed and looked sternly at her little messenger. "Agnes, have you two been fighting again?"

Agnes nodded sheepishly and then looked down at the ground, causing her long braid to bounce.

"What have I told you two about quarreling? You're gonna have to learn to get along with each other."

That's all it took for big tears to well up in Agnes' eyes. "I know. I'm sorry."

Shelby softened. "It's okay."

Agnes shifted back and forth. "Miss Shelby?"

"Yes Agnes?"

"Do you think I'm gonna go to the devil for fightin' with Iris?"

Shelby stifled a grin. She kept her face masked as she looked into the eyes of the little, mischievous urchin standing before her. "You are a good girl, Agnes. I don't think there's any danger of that."

Relief spread across the little rosy cheeks. Shelby smiled and placed her arm around the little girl. "Now come on. Let's go see about your sister."

Shelby was still chuckling to herself about Agnes' comment as she made her way up the stairs. It took all of a minute and a half to solve the quarrel between the two sisters. When she left them, they were holding hands as they skipped happily off to play. *If only it were that easy for grown-ups to put aside their differences. How was Harlan's visit with his father going? Did he make peace with him and his stepmother?*

After Harlan left, Shelby decided she would be better off to keep herself busy. The mornings were easy enough. There was always so much that needed to be done at the home she hardly had enough time to breathe, much less to dwell on his absence. Afternoons and evenings were harder. She was missing him more than she realized she would. The days seemed mundane and colorless without him.

Janice's change of attitude had been the biggest surprise of all. At first, she had reacted with anger and resentment over the news of Harlan and Shelby but now seemed to accept their relationship. She, more than anyone else, had been extremely solicitous, going out of her way to make sure Shelby was okay during Harlan's absence. Her compassion touched Shelby, especially considering the situation.

"I've been looking all over for you. You have a visitor downstairs in the parlor," Janice panted.

Shelby took a quick assessment of her friend. Her cheeks were flushed, and she was out of breath. What visitor could she possibly have that was important enough to make Janice run up the stairs to find her? "Who is it?"

Janice smiled slyly. "Why don't you come down and see?"

Shelby's heart skipped a beat and a clutch of anxiety tugged at her. Was it Harlan? He wasn't supposed to return until next week. Had something happened? "Is Harlan back?"

"You'll just have to see," said Janice, grabbing Shelby by the hand as she practically pulled her down the stairs.

By the time the two made it down the stairs, Shelby had convinced herself that Harlan was waiting for her at the bottom and that something had gone wrong. She came down the landing and stopped dead in her tracks. It couldn't be! The image she had most longed for was standing directly in front of her. Her eyes registered shock, and she felt as though the wind was knocked out of her. It only took a second for her eyes to brim with tears. A sob erupted from her throat as she ran and embraced her mother. She was so overcome with emotion at first that she couldn't speak. Finally, she caught her breath. "I can't believe you're really here. I've dreamed of this moment for so long."

"Me too, Shelby," said Ellen, wiping away a tear.

Shelby searched her mother's beautiful face as she reached and touched her swollen cheek. "You hurt yourself. What happened?"

Ellen placed her hand over Shelby's. "It's not important. I'm fine now."

She looked in her mother's eyes. What was she seeing—fear—sadness?

"I thought I'd never see you again," said Shelby, her voice cracking with emotion. She asked her next question and then held her breath as she listened for the answer. "Is Papa with you?"

"No," Ellen reassured her. The relief that washed over Shelby sent a wave of guilt rushing over Ellen. No child should have to go through what her own daughter had endured. "You don't have to worry about that anymore," Ellen added with conviction.

"How did you find me?"

Ellen smiled wearily. "That took some doing." She motioned toward Sister. "I wouldn't have found you if it hadn't been for Sister."

Shelby shook her head dubiously. "Sister?" She'd been so overwhelmed at seeing her mother that she hadn't even noticed her standing there. She looked past Sister and squealed with joy as she ran and embraced Homer and Sarah. She was crying again. "Look at you two. My how you've grown. I've missed you both so much."

Homer's face was beaming. She then turned and hugged Sister. She had so many questions and didn't know where to begin.

All of the commotion had attracted the attention of the other residents of the home as a circle began to form around them. Mother Ramsey was the first to step forward. "Now I see where Shelby got her stunning beauty," she said, her eyes twinkling. "You two look just alike."

Shelby smiled radiantly, and Ellen blushed. "Thank you," they both chimed.

Mother Ramsey motioned toward all of the children who were curiously watching the scene. "As you can see, all of us love to see a happy reunion."

A wave of compassion flooded Ellen, Shelby, and Sister as they glanced at the children and nodded, all of them acutely aware that they were some of the privileged few among the group who had been blessed to be together again.

Always the perfect hostess, Mother Ramsey began to attend to the needs of her guests. "Shelby, take your family into the parlor and make them comfortable. I know you have much catching up to do.

I'll ask Miss Patterson to bring you some iced tea in a few minutes."

"Thank you," murmured Ellen graciously. The long trip and emotional reunion had both taken their toll, and she suddenly felt very tired.

After Miss Patterson brought in the tea, everyone began to chitchat in the parlor—mostly because all of them were a bit unsure how to begin the discussion of the topic that lay directly beneath the surface. Shelby tried to clear her thoughts, but she was burning with a feverish excitement, and her head was spinning wildly. She finally couldn't contain herself any longer. "How did you find me?" she began.

A flicker of concern crossed Ellen's features as she looked over at Sister. Ellen cleared her throat and then began, "Mother was ill for quite some time. I ended up staying there longer than I had anticipated."

Shelby nodded. "How is she?"

"Much better."

"Good."

Ellen went directly back to her narrative. "When I returned home, Sister showed me your letter."

Shelby sat up quickly and leaned forward. "You got my letter?" she asked eagerly and then grew thoughtful. "But you never responded. I thought..." She stopped short, her face coloring. She didn't want to hurt Sister's feelings.

Sister nodded her head in understanding, and her mouth became a firm line, emphasizing the lines around her mouth. "It's okay dear," she finished for Shelby. "I can only imagine what you must've thought about me and Joshua. I only wish we could've helped you sooner" Her voice was strained.

Shelby scrutinized her aunt. She looked older and very vulnerable. A wave of tenderness rushed over Shelby as she placed her hand over Sister's. "It's okay. I was just so afraid," her voice cracked, and she fought for control as she took a deep breath and began again. "I was so afraid that you didn't believe me," she finished as a tear trickled out from the corner of her eye.

Sister was fighting her own emotions as well. "Joshua never doubted you for a moment. He knew the truth from the very beginning. He didn't know where you went or why you disappeared."

She bit her lip and pressed her hand to her lips as a muffled sob escaped. "I'm so sorry. I didn't know. He didn't tell me, and I never dreamed that Frank would be capable of doin' such a thing."

Shelby's eyes were glistening. She understood. "It's okay," she said, feeling as though a weight were being lifted. All she had wanted was for them to believe her. She sniffed and then raised her head. "Where is Uncle Joshua?"

Concern shadowed Ellen's features, and Sister only shook her head. A chilling fear clutched Shelby as she looked back and forth between the two, waiting for an answer. "He's okay, isn't he?"

Ellen shook her head, and Sister began to cry. The truth hit Shelby full force, and she began to shake her head as tears started to flow. "He's gone?" she managed to squeak, affirming the truth to herself. Ellen nodded as Shelby buried her head in her hands and wept.

*　　*　　*　　*　　*

The joy Shelby felt seeing her family again was partially swallowed up by the pain she felt from the loss of Joshua and the sadness of being separated from Harlan. She walked over to the window and pulled back the lace curtain and looked down at the street below, committing the scene to memory as her eyes took note of the tall hedges framing the rock wall that led to the street below. She then looked at the trusty, towering oak tree just outside her window. How many nights she'd lain in her bed and studied its intricate network of branches silhouetted against the moonlight. It had been a comfort to her somehow. Almost all of the leaves had fallen from the tree, making its sturdy branches look naked against the hazy sky. She raised the window, welcoming the air that splashed her on the face. Even though the days were still relatively mild for late autumn, a certain chill in the air gave the indication that winter was lurking just around the corner. She stayed there for a moment until a shiver ran up her spine and then she turned away.

Mama and Sister were waiting for her in the parlor. It had been decided that they should leave as soon as she was able to gather her things. She had waited for this day for so long. And now? Now she wasn't sure. She was sure of one thing, however. Now that Mama had found her, she wasn't going to let anything ever come between them again. The room darkened as a cloud passed over the sun. The gloom that had immediately descended on her when she first thought about being apart from Harlan deepened. Her heart ached as she pictured how he would react to the news that she was gone. If only she hadn't made the promise to him. She was being silly. No one could've foretold the events which had taken place during the past few hours. Harlan would understand. She clenched her fists. Her family had come for her. They were her life, and she'd simply die if she didn't go with them. He must understand.

There wasn't much time. She sat down on her bed and wiped her sweaty palms on her dress. Her head was still whirling as she began to write.

My Darling Harlan,

So much has happened. I hardly know where to start. I hope with all of my heart that you will understand the reason for my hasty departure, and that you will find it in your heart to forgive me. When we were together, I could never bring myself to tell you about the events which brought me to the home—and now the reasons no longer seem important. I will always treasure the time I spent here because it brought me to you. My mother and my family came to the home today to get me. I thought they were lost to me forever, and I am overjoyed to be reunited with them again. I hope you will understand that I have to go with them. Even so, my heart aches at the mere thought that we will be apart for a time. I live for the day when we can be together again. Please come for me as soon as you can. I love you with all my heart and will always be yours truly.

Shelby

She skimmed quickly over the letter before adding in the address of the place where she would be. There were so many things she wanted to tell him, but she couldn't get the words to come out right on paper. She folded the letter and placed it carefully in an envelope and then sealed it. It was done. Hastily, she began stuffing her clothes in her frayed suitcase. She swallowed the lump which rose in her throat as she carefully wrapped her milky, pearl necklace in one of her dresses and placed it on top before closing the lid. She then latched it shut, picked it up, and walked to the door. Her hand on the knob, she hesitated and skimmed the room to make sure she hadn't left anything. Her bed, neat and tidy, and the small table tucked beside it looked sparse and cold without her things—almost as though she'd never been there at all. She shook her head as she mentally shrugged off the despondent thoughts and forced herself to think about the future. Mama was here. She had come for her, and Harlan would come too. She just knew he would! A glimmer of hope rekindled within as she resolutely closed the door and walked down the hall.

*   *   *   *   *

Mother Ramsey had no doubt said many goodbyes during her years at the Mercy Place, but for Shelby the experience was a heartrending, yet tender event she would never forget. Shelby fought back the tears as she looked at the kind eyes shining back from behind the round spectacles. She hugged the bony frame and then drew back and tried to memorize the wise, wrinkled face framed in gray ringlets.

"I will never forget you," Shelby whispered.

Mother Ramsey smiled. "Nor I you, dear. Just remember that life hands us many experiences—some good and some bad. But none are ever in vain. There's always a lesson to be learned if we'll only take the time to pay attention."

"I'll remember," she promised fervently. Shelby suddenly remembered something. "I didn't get a chance to say goodbye to Miss Pearl. Would you tell her I said goodbye, and thank her for her kindness?"

The older woman nodded. "Of course."

Shelby searched the faces behind Mother Ramsey. "Where is Janice? I didn't get to tell her goodbye."

"I'm not sure where she is."

"Will you tell her I said goodbye?"

"Yes."

"It makes me so sad when I think about her, wrapped in a pink blanket, left all alone."

Mother Ramsey looked confused. "What do you mean?"

"She told me the story about how you found her on the steps when she was a baby."

"You must be mistaken dear. Janice didn't come here as a baby. Her mother brought her to us when she was a young girl. She comes to visit her every once in a while," she said shaking her head. "At first I had hoped that her mother would get her life in order and come and get her, but I don't see any hope of that now."

Shock registered on Shelby's face.

"Are you okay?"

Shelby smiled weakly. "Yes. I guess I must be thinking of someone else." She hugged Mother Ramsey once more, and this time the tears began to flow. Reluctantly, she let go of her friend and allowed herself one more look at the majestic house before turning to go.

"Shelby! Wait!"

She turned to see Tobias running down the sidewalk toward her. He ran and embraced her, almost knocking her over in the process. He buried his head in her arms for a moment and then broke away. "I'll miss you," he said, his voice cracking with emotion.

She looked into his dark eyes. "I'll miss you too. I was afraid I wasn't going to get to say goodbye. You've been at the park."

"Grover just brought us all back, and Miss Patterson told me you were leaving, so I ran out here as fast as I could," he explained, still trying to catch his breath. He quickly grew serious. "Will I ever see you again?"

She looked into those dark eyes burning with intensity and knew she had to answer him honestly. "I don't know," she finally said.

He nodded and looked down at the ground to cover up his hurt. Gently, she lifted his chin so that his eyes met hers. "No matter where we go, we'll always have a part of each other." She put her hand over her chest. "Right here." She paused and then continued. "I have to go now." She smiled through her tears. "And you have a family to take care of."

His chin set with renewed determination. "I know," he answered. She hugged him once more, then turned and walked to the wagon where Mama and Sister were waiting.

Shelby wiped her tears and climbed in next to Homer. "Are we going to pick up Papa next?" he asked.

"No, Homer," Ellen said.

Homer looked puzzled and then concerned. "Why not?" he demanded.

"Papa is staying in Georgia," Ellen answered in a tone that was so resolute Homer was taken aback for a second. He started to argue until he saw the look of warning on Shelby's face. He crossed his arms over his chest and pressed his lips together in a thin line as he withdrew into himself. Shelby looked over at Ellen and saw that she was watching him. Did Shelby imagine it? Or did a flicker of sorrow flash over her mama's expression?

Ellen and Shelby looked at one another, and a look of understanding passed between them. Ellen patted Shelby on the knee reassuringly and smiled at her. "Let's go home to Alder Springs."

* * * * *

Janice thought back to the day of the fire. It had been easy to lock the door to the attic. Because no one ever ventured up to the top floor, she had felt confident in knowing that she could easily slip up and down the stairs without anyone seeing her. She'd had to act fast. Earlier in the afternoon, she had seen Shelby going up the stairs. Shelby had probably thought no one knew about her little, secret place. Janice smirked to herself. She had known, but then again, there wasn't much that escaped her attention.

It wasn't until later, when Janice heard the children and ladies hollering about a fire, that a brilliant plan began to take shape. While the ladies were hustling the children down the hall, she'd slipped by them and up to the attic and locked the door. Her plan would've worked too if Harlan hadn't saved her. This time, there would be no mistakes. She had figured Shelby would try to write Harlan a letter, and she had been right. She had stood outside the bedroom upstairs and had watched her seal it and had then secretly followed her downstairs to make sure she put it in the mail bag. Timing was essential. If anyone looked in the bag before she could retrieve it.... She wouldn't think about that, she vowed. She just had to get there in time.

She looked furtively over her shoulder before slipping stealthily down the hall to the front office where the mail bag was kept. Her heart was pounding wildly as she made her way into the room. She edged next to the window and pushed aside the lace curtain just enough to peer out and still remain unseen from the outside. She let out her breath in relief. They were all still outside watching Shelby's wagon pull away. Quickly, she made her way to the desk to retrieve the letter from the bag.

At first, when she saw Shelby writing the letter, she had been afraid that she would do something intelligent for once like give it to Mother Ramsey to deliver. Her plan would've been foiled then. But Shelby had never been that smart—pretty maybe, but no brains. *It's a shame*, Janice thought, *that beauty should be wasted on the stupid.* She shook her head sorrowfully. What she could've done with such looks.

Oh, Shelby was a good enough person all right—too good. In fact, she was so full of goodness, kindness, mercy, and benevolence that it made Janice sick. *Was it benevolence?* Janice frowned. She couldn't remember for sure if that was the exact word that she'd overheard Mother Ramsey use when she heard her talking about Shelby to Miss Patterson. But there was no way she could miss the point. Shelby had cast a spell over Mother Ramsey the same way she did over Harlan.

Images of Harlan with his slow, easy grin and golden hair flooded through her mind, causing a warm sensation all over. She could easily imagine him kissing her and caressing her tenderly with those piercing eyes. Her revelry turned to rage when an image of his hand touching Shelby's dark curls invaded her daydream. *He should've been mine*, her mind screamed fiercely. *No*, she corrected herself, *he will be mine.*

She grabbed the bag and pulled a handful of letters out. It only took a second for her to recognize the clear, careful handwriting.

"Janice, what are you doing in here?"

She flinched and almost dropped the letter as a hot, prickly fear covered her. She swallowed hard and quickly tucked the letter into the pocket of her dress. With a smile plastered on her face, she turned around. "Oh, Miss Bissell, you startled me," she said, trying to keep her voice light. "I just couldn't handle anymore long goodbyes, so I decided to come inside."

Miss Bissell looked unconvinced. "What are you doing in the office?"

Janice laughed nervously. "I was just checkin' to see if I got any mail," she replied, wondering if her voice sounded unnaturally high-pitched.

"Well, you're lookin' in the wrong place. If you have any mail, it will be in there," she said, pointing to a large basket sitting on the other side of the desk.

Janice relaxed. She could've kissed the little, chubby woman for her daftness. She rolled her eyes and shrugged her shoulders. "I never can keep these bags straight—one day it's on the desk and another time it's on the floor," she said flippantly. She walked over and leafed through the incoming mail while Miss Bissell watched her curiously. She finally turned around and smiled apologetically. "Nothin' today. I guess all that work was for nothin'."

"I suppose so," echoed Miss Bissell. "Just remember that from now on you're not supposed to be in this office without permission."

"Yes, ma'am. I can assure you it won't happen again." Janice nodded politely at Miss Bissell and then quickly scurried out the door. It wasn't until she made her way up to her room that the full exultation of what she had accomplished swept over her. She pulled out the letter and lay across the bed. Eagerly, she tore it open and began reading.

Her eyes sparkled with a grim satisfaction as she tore the letter to pieces.

Chapter Nineteen

In a remote section of the woods, tucked at the base of the mountain and obscured from sight by kudzu in the spring and snow in the winter, sat a tavern known by the locals as the Bloody Bucket. Someone passing by would never notice the old tavern except for the glimmer of light emitted from the solitary lantern hanging from the low ceiling. The bottom section of the clapboard was dry-rotted, causing as much as a four-inch gap in some places, but no one seemed to care. A threadbare, dingy-white curtain, barely hanging, was the only feminine touch to the place, lending the impression that some effort had been extended to make the place homey at one time but had long ago been dismissed. Spit cans for chewing tobacco rested on the dusty, wooden floor, and a scent of stale whiskey and cigar smoke hung heavy in the stagnant air.

Despite its decrepit appearance, the Bloody Bucket was a place of great importance to the scoundrels who frequented it. Many lives had been altered within those four walls with the flick of the wrist as the fateful cards cast their fortune or destruction across the grainy tables.

The young man could feel the beads of perspiration forming on his upper lip in spite of the cold. He knew that the moonshine flowing in his veins was not the only thing causing his heart to pound wildly and his face to flush. His hands were quivering slightly, and he willed himself to steady them. *Please, let me stay calm.* He was so close now to getting what he wanted, he could almost taste it. He had stacked the deck perfectly. *Let the old man play out this last hand,* he prayed, *and I will have what I came here for.* He managed to keep his face passive as he looked around at the other players. They were also getting tired of waiting for the old man to make his move.

"Come on, old man," one of them bellowed. "Play your cards."

"What's wrong with you anyway?" another one grumbled. "We've been waitin' fer ya all night, and I wanna go home. By golly, if you ain't got nothin', just fold."

The old man's hands were trembling as he looked around the room at the gamblers' expressions and then back at his cards. What had he gotten himself into? Maybe he was in over his head. He'd lost almost everything. He had to win this hand. It was getting harder and harder for him to stay focused. The long hours of gambling and moonshine were not only taking their toll on him physically—but also mentally. How would he explain this to Jane?

The old man had just about decided to fold and go home. He was about to get up from the table when the door opened, blowing in snow from the outside. A young boy with a shock of red hair stepped in quickly and closed the door behind him. He looked worried and tired. His ragged coat was a size too small, and his bare hands were red and chapped from the cold. He walked directly over to the old man. "Paw, we've been lookin' all over fer ya all night long. Maw is worried sick."

The old man looked at his son. The alcohol and fatigue had clouded his thinking, and rage rose up like bile in his throat. How dare she send his boy up here to follow him and embarrass him in front of his friends?

"Ted, what the devil are you doin' here?" he slurred. "What did I tell you about follerin' me?" He rose from his chair and almost fell as he raised his hand to hit the boy. It didn't take much effort for the boy to move out of the old man's way.

The whites of the boy's eyes popped out of the dim light as he looked wildly between his paw and the men sitting around him. "Paw, Maw told you these people ain't honest," he cried. "They'll cheat you, Paw. They will!" he wailed pitifully.

"Go on. Git out of here. Go home and tell your Maw that I'll be there when I git darn good and ready." Then, trying to salvage what little dignity he could from the situation, he turned and smiled at the group. The boy ran out of the Bucket and slammed the door as the old man slouched back in the chair. "Now where were we?" he began with renewed energy, forgetting that he, himself, had thought about leaving a few moments earlier.

"It's your play," the young man said steadily, trying hard to keep the eagerness out of his voice.

A toothless grin spread across the thin, wrinkled face as the old man spread his cards. "I call—two pairs—aces and jacks," he said proudly.

"Not so fast, old-timer," the young man said in a low tone as he spread his cards across the table. "I have a full house."

There was a collective gasp around the table, and then all of the players except the old man began to whoop and holler.

All of the color drained from the old man's thin, withered face. A gurgled sound started deep in his throat and then rose to a fevered pitch. "You cheated! You cheated!" he screamed over and over.

The young man smiled and shook his head sadly at the pathetic wretch. The old man continued to scream obscenities at the young man as the other men laughed, while shoving him out the door into the cold. They bolted it shut behind him. He continued to holler and bang on the door for a few more minutes. He could still hear the laughter inside as he slumped to the ground in despair. Everything was gone—even the farm—Jane's farm. Somehow he finally managed to get to his feet. The pain in his heart was almost more than he could bear. He didn't feel the bitter wind or snow on his face. His only thought as he staggered and stumbled through the snow was how to tell Jane.

*   *   *   *   *

"Well, what do you think?" Ellen asked as they drove the wagon into Alder Springs.

Shelby looked first at her mama's hopeful expression and then at the town. She'd been here before to visit her gramma, but she had been too young to remember very much about it.

"It looks a lot smaller than Cartersville," Sister grumbled. The trip had been long and tiring for her, and she had grown irritable.

"Yes," Ellen agreed reluctantly, "it is smaller, but there's a bigger town, Albertville, only about seven miles up the road from here."

"Look over there." Ellen pointed. "There's the cotton gin. Do you know what kind of bushes those are growing around it?" Ellen asked the question, not really expecting anyone to answer. "Those are alder bushes," she continued. "And just over that hill is a spring."

"Alder Springs, that's why it's called Alder Springs—because of the bushes and the spring," Shelby exclaimed, putting it all together.

Ellen smiled proudly. "That's right. There's the general store. Hershel and Mindy Miller run it. I remember going there with my mother when I was a little girl."

Homer looked surprised. "Really? Is it that old?"

Ellen laughed. "I suppose. Now, over there is the train station and the bank."

They passed another building and waited for Ellen to point it out. When she didn't, Shelby asked. "What's that?"

Ellen's face colored. "That's a doctor's office."

Sister looked impressed. "Really? A doctor in a town this small? That's nice."

"Is the post office inside the general store?" Shelby asked.

"Yes," Ellen answered. "Guess where we are now?"

"At Gramma's house!" Homer yelled excitedly.

Shelby climbed out of the wagon and stretched her stiff legs. She was glad their trip was finally over. How would Harlan react when he realized she had left? She would go to the general store tomorrow and find out the length of time it would take for a letter to get from Birmingham to Alder Springs.

Chapter Twenty

"Ouch! You're hurting me."

"Well, hold your head still," replied Shelby, slightly releasing her grip on Sarah's hair. "You said you wanted to look nice for church tomorrow."

"How long is this gonna take?" grumbled Sarah.

"I got the sides done; all I have left is to tie up the back."

Sarah folded her arms and scowled.

"It hurts to be beautiful," Shelby quipped.

"I didn't think it would hurt this much," countered Sarah.

Shelby grinned and suppressed a giggle. She looked across the kitchen and caught her mama's eye. Ellen was also amused at Sarah's comment. When she was a baby, Sarah's hair had curled on its own. The older she got, the straighter her hair became. She had asked Shelby to tie it up in rags so it would be curly for church the following day.

Ellen looked appraisingly at her two daughters. They were both so different from each other. Shelby was so dignified, always choosing her words carefully before she spoke. Sarah, on the other hand, was free-spirited with a sharp tongue.

The past two years since they'd come to Alder Springs had been eventful. At first, Ellen had feared that Frank would never consent to a divorce. She had geared herself up for a big battle—which never came. One month after her arrival in Alder Springs, Ellen had received signed divorce papers from Frank, along with a newspaper clipping announcing his upcoming marriage. The news of his wedding came as a shock to the children and to Sister, but Ellen had been relieved. She counted her blessings, signed the papers, and married John three months later.

She'd come very close to not marrying John. Shelby had been supportive of the marriage and Sarah too young to care. But the transition was traumatic to Homer. John had stubbornly insisted that Homer's reaction was normal and that he would eventually accept the marriage, but Ellen hadn't been so sure and had vowed that she would never again sacrifice her children's well-being for her own happiness. Her loving mother advised her to go ahead and marry John. "Homer is confused right now," she had said. "He's a good boy. He'll work this out in time."

Ellen's eyes misted. If only her mother knew how many times she'd leaned on those words.

A few days before her mother's death, she had told Ellen, "I can finally rest now that you have somebody to take care of you."

"Okay, I'm done," Shelby sighed.

"Finally," Sarah huffed, hopping out of the chair.

Ellen looked at the clock hanging on the wall. "It's two o'clock already. Shelby, you'd better go and get cleaned up. Is your basket ready?"

Shelby nodded. "Are you sure you don't want to come?"

"I'm sure. John won't be finished seeing patients until this afternoon, and I don't want to go without him." Ellen smiled. "Don't worry about me. I want to stay here and relax. You go and have fun. He'll be expecting you."

Shelby smiled back. "Thanks Mama."

*   *   *   *   *

For most of the residents of Alder Springs, Decoration weekend was a time of great excitement. Saturday was when relatives and friends alike came from all over to pay respects to their deceased by visiting the cemetery to place fresh flowers on the graves. Sunday was the day when everyone took extra care in donning their Sunday best as they crowded into the little white church on the hill, fanning themselves like mad to stay cool, while they listened to the honorable Reverend Clayton Tucker deliver what everyone hoped would be one of his best fire-and-brimstone sermons of the year. The crowning event of the entire weekend was the annual supper-box auction held Saturday evening on the grassy lawn beside the church.

Reverend Tucker shifted slightly in his seat as a stream of perspiration trickled down his back between his shoulder blades. It was late enough in the day that the sun was just starting its trek back down behind the mountains, but the air was still thick, making him want to breathe in deeply just so he could catch a good breath. His clothes were sticking to him. He leaned forward and tugged at his pants and then pulled out his handkerchief and blotted his high forehead as he looked out over the growing crowd. His wife caught his eye and gave him a meaningful smile, telling him that he'd better wipe the bored expression off his face. He quickly sat up and began nodding courteously to the people around him as he waited for the festivities to begin.

The Reverend was sitting beside Hugh Walker, the auctioneer. Hugh had been doing the supper-box auction for as long as the Reverend could remember—his loud booming voice made him a shoe-in for the job. With the exception of when he delivered his fiery sermons, the Reverend rarely raised his voice. In fact, his tone was so subdued that those listening to him speak had to often strain to catch all of his words.

He pulled out his watch. It was five o'clock on the dot—definitely time to start. His eyes gazed out over the crowd. Wagons, some pulled by horses, others by mules and a few automobiles were still arriving. He didn't have much use for crowds and would've felt more at home sitting down by the stream organizing his thoughts for a sermon, but he knew that events such as these were beneficial for his flock. The ladies were in all of their finery. He could count at least a dozen frilly hats dotting the field of moving bodies like splashes of wild flowers. His thoughts then left the crowd as his gaze fell upon his pride and joy—the little white church standing prominently against the sky. He looked at the delicate panes of glass on the windows and sturdy wooden door on the front before gazing upward. There was only one thing missing—a steeple. The proceeds from the auction were always donated to the church, and he hoped they would be enough to pay for the steeple.

His stomach growled as he looked at the beautifully wrapped

boxes on the tables. The aroma of fried chicken and fresh apple pie filled the air. From the eager expressions on the faces in the crowd, he guessed that he wasn't the only one who was affected by the food.

Hugh stood up and cleared his throat. Everyone got silent. It was time to begin.

* * * * *

"Isn't that your box next in line?"

"I don't know," Shelby replied to the middle-aged woman seated next to her as she craned her neck in a polite attempt to look toward the table, even though she already knew it was hers. She'd been watching it nervously for the past fifteen minutes. "Yes, I believe it is my box," she said, managing to keep her voice light despite the fact that she was seething inside.

"What types of flowers are on top? It's hard to tell from here."

"Buttercups," replied Shelby, smiling thinly.

Louise smiled back knowingly. "How clever. You must've put those in there so that dashing fiancé of yours would recognize your box."

Shelby's face flushed.

"Is he here? I haven't seen him."

"Perhaps something came up."

"Yes, that must be it," replied the woman, doubtfully.

Shelby shifted in her seat and turned to stare straight ahead so that she wouldn't have to see the look of pity in Louise Sutherland's eyes.

Hugh held Shelby's box up and inspected its contents. She had spent all that time meticulously preparing Rayford's favorite foods, and he wasn't even here to bid on it. What was so important that he couldn't make it? He knew how much this meant to her. They'd even laughed together as he'd spouted off the large amounts of money he would bid for her supper. She glared at the box. It suddenly looked ugly and deficient. The buttercups, still tucked into the ribbon, were a perfect reminder of her wasted effort. She had noticed them growing in bunches beside the church and had added them to her box right before the auction had started. She had felt so light-hearted and witty at the time; now her last minute gesture seemed childish and ridiculous.

Hugh's booming voice cut into her thoughts. "Ladies and gentlemen, we have some good vittles here—fried chicken, corn on the cob, apple butter, and sweet potato pie. Um, um, good. What'll I get for this one? Let's start it out at a nickel. Who'll give me a nickel?"

"One nickel," said a voice from the back."

"One nickel," Hugh rattled off. "Who'll make it a dime?"

The price for the box kept steadily rising until it finally leveled off at seventy-five cents. Shelby's heart sank, and a burning shame covered her. All of the other boxes had fetched at least one dollar.

"I have seventy-five. Who'll make it a dollar? A dollar. Anybody? All right. Seventy-five goin' once. Seventy-five goin' twice..."

"Three dollars!"

A gasp rippled through the crowd as Shelby turned to see who had placed the enormous bid.

Even Hugh was taken aback. He cleared his throat in an attempt to recover. "Three dollars," he belted. He didn't even bother asking for anymore. "Three dollars goin' once...twice." He slammed his fist down on the table. "Sold to the gentleman in the back for three dollars."

"Who was that?" asked Louise, wide-eyed.

Shelby shook her head. "I'm not sure," she stammered as her heart hammered away in her chest. The momentary surprise of the event was quickly forgotten by the crowd as the attention was turned to the next box up for bid. But Shelby's mind was reeling with the possibilities that were beginning to take shape. It couldn't be, her reason argued, but her heart already knew. *It was.*

* * * * *

It was all Shelby could do to sit still for the remainder of the auction. Fortunately, there were only three more boxes following hers. When the last box was sold, she got up and inched her way through the crowd toward the table full of boxes.

"Your box fetched quite a high price," said a loud shrilly voice.

She turned to face the Reverend and his wife, Mildred. Sheepishly, she ducked her head slightly as her face colored.

"I believe that was a town record," echoed the Reverend in his more subtle tone.

"Who is that young fella who bid on your box? I haven't seen him around these parts before," Mildred finished with a look of open curiosity on her rouged, round face.

"I'm not sure. I wasn't able to get a good look at him from where I was sitting," Shelby finished lamely.

Mildred Tucker considered herself an expert at keen observation—there wasn't a person or event of significance within ten square miles of Alder Springs that escaped her attention. Her green eyes raked Shelby up and down, making special note of the young girl's nervous behavior and flushed cheeks. She'd bet her right eye there was an interesting story here. "Where is Rayford?" she asked sweetly. "Is he here with you?" The Reverend gave her a sharp look of reproof, which she blatantly ignored. "I haven't seen him this evening."

"Neither have I," Shelby answered as her head shot up. Her cheeks were blazing. "If you see him, tell him he missed a wonderful auction."

Mildred looked surprised, and the Reverend chuckled.

"If you'll excuse me."

"Of course," said Mildred.

Shelby shook her head and wondered what had prompted her to say such a thing to the Reverend's wife. She looked straight ahead to avoid any more curious stares as she made her way to the table. It was almost cleared off. She got as close to it as she dared and then turned and surveyed the crowd. A few more minutes went by, and her box was the only one left on the table. She inched up to it and peered inside to see if any of the contents had been taken.

"Is it all there?"

His voice was slightly louder than a whisper. He was so close that his breath on her ear caused a tingling sensation to pulse down her spine as she jerked her head sideways and saw that he was leaning over her shoulder, also looking in the box. She quickly turned to face him. There he was—the same fair hair—those same forceful eyes. Her gaze rested briefly on his taut jaw and crooked smile. She must have seen them a hundred times in her dreams. She studied his face, not quite sure what she expected to find. His expression remained unreadable, his eyes shadowed like a gray mist hovering over a golden pond.

Her face paled, and she took a step backwards and almost knocked over the table. He reached over and took her arm in an attempt to steady her.

"Do I get to eat this supper I paid top dollar for, or are we gonna stand around all night long looking at it?" he asked.

She gaped at him in surprise, and he smiled briefly, lighting his features. She straightened herself up and smiled back weakly. "Of course. I know a place we can go."

He lifted the box off the table and tucked it under one arm and offered the other arm to her. She slipped her arm through his as he led her to his wagon. He seemed to be oblivious to the attention the two of them were attracting. Once on the wagon, he was silent, and she only spoke to give him directions. Butterflies were turning summersaults in her stomach, causing her to feel almost as giddy as she had felt when she had gotten thrown off the Bakers' horse last spring.

Why was he here? She had waited so long for some type of word, anything. She looked sideways at him. He felt her gaze and looked over at her and flashed an easy smile which caused her breath to catch. She couldn't deny that he still had an effect on her. She looked quickly away and down at her hands. What did she feel for him? Wasn't it only yesterday that she was chiding herself for believing she had loved him? What about Rayford? Her two worlds were colliding. A fear seized her, causing her to feel as though she was about to break out in a cold sweat. *I am engaged,* she reminded herself. Fury began to rise as she glanced over again at Harlan. He seemed so calm and sure of himself. Did he really believe he could just waltz right back into her life as though the last two years didn't even take place?

"Pull over here," she said coolly. "We can eat under the weeping willow tree."

He swiftly pulled the reins and maneuvered the horses to the side of the road. They walked over to the tree, and Harlan pulled an old tarp from the back of the wagon and spread it over the ground.

"It's not very pretty, but it's clean," he offered in the way of an apology.

She shrugged. "It's fine."

They sat down, and she began taking the food out of the box. Just as she was putting the last item on the tarp, he placed his hand over hers. She looked at him questioningly. He moved his hand and reached up and brushed a curl away from her face.

"You haven't changed a bit. You're just as beautiful as I remember." Her eyes blazed, and her chin jutted out as she tried to remove her face from his touch. He chuckled as he lowered his hand. "And just as stubborn, I see," he finished, shaking his head.

She looked at him squarely in the eyes. "Are we going to eat this supper you paid top dollar for, or are we going to just sit around and look at it?"

His eyes widened in surprise, and then he laughed. Some of the tension began to ease as they ate in silence. Shelby watched Harlan polish off his third piece of sweet potato pie. When he finished, he scooted over next to the trunk of the willow tree and leaned against it. He then propped his arms behind his head. "So who was the lucky fella you fixed all that food for?"

She had just taken a bite of pie and almost choked on it. "What are you talking about?" she managed to get out.

"This food," he said, motioning with his hand. "I'm glad I got to enjoy it, but I just can't help but think it was meant for someone else."

She fidgeted with her pie, not saying a word, so he continued. "I saw you pick the buttercups."

"That's how you knew which box was mine," she blurted out.

He nodded. "You still didn't answer my question."

"Question?"

"Who is the lucky man?"

Her heart began to pound. Why did she felt so guilty? "What are you doing here?" she demanded.

"Can't I look up an old friend?" he asked innocently enough, but his words were tinged with sarcasm.

"Why do you care who I made this supper for?" She began.

He shrugged his shoulders and reached up and tugged at one of the strands of the willow tree. "I don't."

His remark cut, making her want to lash out at him. "I made this supper for my fiancé," she said smugly.

Her words hung in the still air, and she watched as a look of hurt washed over his features. She wished she could take the words back, but it was too late. "Why did you wait so long to come?" she asked.

"You promised me you'd be there when I got back, and you weren't," he said simply.

She shook her head in confusion as the words tumbled out. "I explained to you why I had to leave. I thought you'd understand. I..."

He cut her off. "Yeah, you explained it all really well. I came back from a trip, which you asked me to take, by the way, only to find you gone, and that you'd left no word."

She cringed at the bitterness in his voice. "I wrote you a letter," she cried, trying to defend herself. "I asked you to come for me."

He stood and shook his head. "A letter? What do you mean you wrote me a letter?"

"I did!" she said in exasperation. "I wrote you a letter explaining how my mother showed up at the home to get me." Tears filled her eyes. "I know I promised you that I wouldn't leave, but I had no idea that she would come for me. If you only knew how many nights I have lain awake at night wondering where you were and why you didn't come for me." She used the back of her hand to wipe away a tear.

"I didn't get any letter," Harlan said obstinately, but his anger was relenting.

"I wrote it right before I left. I went down to the office and placed it with the other mail."

Harlan sat down next to her on the tarp. "You really wrote me a letter?"

She nodded and then looked at him, her eyes pleading with his to understand. "I didn't want to leave you without any word. I had to go with my mother, and I didn't know what else to do." Her voice trailed off, as they both considered the possibilities.

"Who—what—what could've happened?" he asked as much to himself as to Shelby. "Did it get lost?"

She shook her head. "I don't know. It must have."

Harlan shook his head and ran his hands through his hair. "Mother Ramsey told me where you'd gone, but I was too upset to go searching for you."

"What? You knew where I was all this time?"

Harlan nodded. "When I came back and discovered that you had gone, I talked to Mother Ramsey. I asked her where you went, and she told me that your mother had come for you. As I was leaving, Janice stopped me. She told me that you had said that you were starting a new life and that meant putting everything, including me, behind you."

"But that's not true," Shelby exclaimed. "Why would Janice tell you that? She knew how I felt about you. I never said those things to her. When you didn't come, I just figured that our relationship never really meant that much to you."

Harlan clenched his fists. "How could've I have been so stupid? I should've known better than to believe Janice. She probably destroyed the letter."

"I wouldn't put it past her," Shelby added dryly.

"Well, we'll never know, and I guess it doesn't matter now anyway."

The silence stretched between them until Shelby spoke. "Why did you come now?"

"What?"

"What made you change your mind? Why did you come now?"

"I'm engaged, too."

She was stunned. She swallowed hard as her heart sank. "I see." She stared off in the distance, trying to collect her thoughts. "Maybe it's all for the best."

"What?" he asked sharply.

"What is she like?"

"Who?"

"Your fiancée. What is she like?"

"Oh, she's nice. Very pretty, smart."

Shelby resented herself for feeling jealous. "Where did you meet her?"

"At my pappy's store."

"Did you get things worked out with him?"

He nodded. "I guess I have you to thank for that. After I went back to Birmingham and you weren't there, I went back home and started working at the store."

She touched him on the arm. "I'm glad you got things worked out."

He looked at her for a moment and then stared down at the ground. Finally, he lifted his head. "I guess things have a way of working themselves out."

"I suppose so," answered Shelby as a knot formed in the pit of her stomach.

Harlan looked at the sky. "It looks like rain. I'd better get you home."

*　　*　　*　　*　　*

Shelby lay on her bed, listening to the sound of the pouring rain pelt down on the tin roof as she repeated the encounter with Harlan over and over in her head. The numbness that had settled in right after she had watched him drive away was ebbing. They had parted like strangers. How could things have gone so wrong? Seeing him again so unexpectedly had been such a shock. There were so many other things she had wanted to say. She shook her head and tried to think of Rayford.

After all, Rayford had been good to her. He was a good catch. She'd seen the jealous glances that other women cast in their direction whenever they were together and knew that any one of them would gladly take her place if given the chance. She'd been content with her engagement to him. Still, he'd never evoked the tumultuous feelings which Harlan's very touch had the power to do. She brushed aside the thought. Her decision had to be based on logic, not attraction. Her relationship with Harlan took place a long time ago. So much had happened since then. She was a different person now.

There were other things to consider. Why had Rayford not gone to the supper-box auction? Could some of the rumors she'd heard about him be true? Was he out drinking or gambling? She considered the possibility and then pictured Rayford's polite smile. No, it was absurd; Rayford wasn't doing those things. There had to be another explanation for his absence today.

Finally, she drifted off to a restless sleep. She dreamed that she was picking apples. Sarah and Homer were helping. She pulled a tall ladder over and showed Homer how to climb up it while balancing his bucket in the other hand. No sooner than she had gotten him settled, she looked around and realized that Sarah was gone. Where did she go? She listened intently and heard a peculiar noise. She followed the noise to the edge of the orchard. Sarah was throwing apples against a large, tin washtub leaning against one of the trees. "Sarah! What are you doing?" Each time an apple hit the tub it made a sharp pinging sound against the glass. Glass? Shelby was confused. She had thought it was a tub. The pinging sound was becoming louder and getting very annoying.

She turned over in her bed and opened her eyes. She sat up and looked out her window. At least the rain had stopped. She was about to lie back down and go to sleep when she heard the pinging sound again. This time she knew she hadn't dreamed it. It took her a second to realize it was coming from her window. She got up and looked out. She rubbed her eyes groggily and looked again. The moon was partially concealed behind the heavy clouds. Below her window was a shadowy figure barely visible. She pressed her face to the glass and strained to see. The fair hair was unmistakable even in the dark. A surge of excitement and wonder rushed through her veins as she lifted the window.

"What are you doing?" she asked, keeping her voice barely above a whisper.

"Come down here."

"Why?"

"We need to talk."

She stood staring down from the window long enough to make him wonder if she would actually come out. Finally, she spoke. "Okay. I'll be right there."

*   *   *   *   *

The house seemed unusually still to Shelby as she quietly made her way down the stairs and out the front door. When she got outside, she found Harlan waiting on the front porch swing. She walked over and sat down beside him.

"What are you doing here, and how did you know which room was mine?" she asked, a little out of breath.

He smiled. "Lucky guess." His expression then turned grave as he took a deep breath and exhaled slowly. "I couldn't leave you like that." He turned to face her. "Not without telling you how I really feel."

She was too stunned to speak.

Tenderly, he gathered her hands in his. "It doesn't matter what happened with the letter or whose fault it was. What matters is that I love you." He searched her eyes. "And I believe you love me too. Shelby, I've tried to put you out of my mind time and time again. I came back here because I had to settle things. I had to know how I felt. And more importantly, how you felt."

She blinked in an attempt to fight back the tears which were threatening to spill over.

He scooted closer to her. "Please say something," he begged.

She shook her head and pulled her hands from his clasp, shaking her head sadly. "It's no good."

"What do you mean 'it's no good?'" he demanded. "I'm here and you're here. What else could we ask for?"

She tried to make him understand. "After you drove away this afternoon, I thought about us. Harlan, a lot has happened in the past two years." She sought for the right words. "I am engaged to be married." She paused as she watched his face darken. She finished quietly. "I gave my word. I made a commitment."

"Well, break it!"

"I can't," she whispered hoarsely.

"Do you love him?"

Her eyes widened, and she leaned backwards in an attempt to protect herself from her emotions as he pressed harder.

"Do you love him?" he repeated.

"I thought I did, until today."

"And now?"

"Now I'm confused. Before today, I had my whole future planned out. I felt secure. Now, I don't know what to think."

He shook his head. "You're a coward."

Her temper flared. "What?" she fumed. "How dare you show up here on my doorstep after two years and have the nerve to call me a coward? I didn't know why you didn't come for me. I had to start over. I moved on."

He grabbed her by the arms and shook her. "Shelby, don't you see? We were meant for each other. I knew that the first moment I laid eyes on you. It doesn't matter what happened before. We can start fresh right now. Pappy has promised me the store."

Her eyes filled with uncertainty. It was all happening too soon. "I can't."

"I'll do anything," he said fiercely. "Just tell me that you love me too."

Before she could answer, he gave way to his pent up emotions and kissed her long and hard. It wasn't a kind and gentle kiss, but a harsh, demanding one. When he finally let her go, she was trembling. His kiss had unleashed a powerful longing she didn't completely understand, and it frightened her. "I-I think it is time for you to go," she said resolutely.

"Shelby," he began again, "I shouldn't have kissed you like that. I don't know what came over me. I just want you to understand how I feel." His voice quivered with emotion. "I don't think I can live without you."

She was touched by his intense display of emotion. "You told me earlier that time has a way of working things out. I hope you can understand. I have made a commitment, and I will stand by it. I will always remember fondly the time we spent together, and I wish you much happiness," she said woodenly. "Don't go anywhere. I'll be right back." She ran into the house. When she came back she was holding the strand of pearls he had given her. She pushed them into his hands. "I can't keep these. They belong to your fiancée."

As he took the pearls, his face went white, and he stood up and backed away from her. She might've been a poisonous snake that had just struck. He stood facing her for a moment. It was the image of her, tear-streaked with loose tendrils of hair escaping from her braid, that would remain etched in his memory forever. The wind blew gently, causing her white nightgown to cling to her soft form.

At that moment, he loved her so much it hurt—loved her and hated her at the same time. He loved her because she filled every part of him and was everything he could ever want. He hated her because she was taking it all away. He had opened his heart and laid bare his soul to her, and she was rejecting him. He felt as though someone had taken his insides and twisted them all in a knot. How was it possible for him to love her so much and she not love him back?

His anguish gave way to rage, and he allowed it to permeate his soul. It was better to hate than to feel such bitter pain. At least now the hurt would be deadened. He got to the edge of the drive and then turned and watched her walk into the house. She didn't even bother to look back. He got in his wagon and tugged on the reins. This time there would be no coming back.

* * * * *

It had taken every ounce of self-control for Shelby to keep from showing her emotions when she'd handed Harlan his pearls. She closed the front door behind her and crumpled in a broken heap against the door where she wept bitter tears. She didn't know how long she stayed that way, but she finally wiped her face and got up to go to bed. She only got two steps before stopping dead in her tracks when she looked up and saw Mama sitting on the sofa watching her intently.

"How long have you been there?"

"Long enough. Come over here and sit down," said Ellen as she patted a spot beside her.

Shelby's head was beginning to throb, and her eyes were puffy. She had thought that she had cried so much that there couldn't possibly be any tears left, but as she looked at the concerned expression on her mama's face, fresh tears began to fall. "My life is such a mess."

"Why don't you tell me about it?"

So Shelby started at the beginning and ended with the events which had just taken place.

Ellen listened carefully. She stared into the distance and then looked at Shelby. "Why didn't you tell me about Harlan?"

Shelby sniffed. "You were going through so much at the time that I didn't want to burden you with my problems. When he didn't write, I just figured it was all in the past, that it didn't matter anyway."

Her mother nodded. "Shelby, do you love Rayford?"

Shelby's eye's widened in disbelief. "Of course I do," she sputtered.

Ellen looked thoughtful. "Are you sure?"

Shelby only shook her head. The truth was she wasn't so sure. She wasn't sure about anything anymore.

"I can't tell you what you feel in your heart," Ellen began tenderly, "but I can tell you that I watched you and that young man out there on the porch." Shelby's almond eyes became wide circles, and her face began to burn as Ellen continued. "I only watched you for a couple of minutes, and I could see the difference." Ellen grasped her daughter's hand. "You've sat here and told me all of the reasons why you should marry Rayford. In all of your talk, I keep waiting for you to say the one thing you haven't."

"What?"

"That you love him. Shelby, you always let your head guide you in all of your decisions. What does your heart tell you to do?"

"I'm not sure."

"I think you are. My mother once told me something very important. She told me that I would have to find my life my own way."

"Is that why you left Cartersville and came here to marry John?"

Ellen nodded. "I think you already know what your heart is telling you."

"Are you saying that I'm supposed to break my engagement with Rayford and marry someone I haven't seen in two years? Is that what you're telling me to do?"

Ellen smiled.

"I love him, Mama."

"I know you do. I think it's time you told him."

Shelby's hand flew up to her mouth. "But it's too late. He's gone."

"It's never too late. He's staying at the Main Street Inn in Albertville.

"But—what—how did you know?" Shelby squeaked in utter amazement.

Ellen chuckled. "How fast do you figure the word got around town after Mildred Tucker saw you two get into his wagon after the auction?"

"But you didn't say anything to me about it."

"I figured you would tell me when the time was right. Now go upstairs and get some rest. John left a couple of hours ago to make an emergency house call. Jenny Lynn is having her baby. Hopefully, he'll be back before too long. I'll get him to take you into Albertville first thing in the morning."

Shelby hugged her mother. "Thank you," she whispered.

"You're welcome. Now go on and get some sleep so you can get an early start. Let's not keep this young man waiting any longer than we have to."

*   *   *   *   *

Ellen searched Shelby's pale, nervous face. "Are you all set?"

Shelby nodded, and then hugged her mama tightly. "Thank you," she murmured.

"You're welcome," Ellen answered, returning the hug. She turned toward John. It had taken a lot longer at the Smith's home than he had anticipated. He looked so haggard and worn out. She hated to ask him to go into Albertville as tired as he was. "John, make sure you go with her inside the inn. She needs your support."

He nodded. "I'll take good care of her," he assured Ellen as he leaned over and kissed her tenderly on the forehead. "You go back to bed and get some rest. You haven't slept all night, either."

Ellen agreed, saying she would go back to bed, but John knew that she probably wouldn't take his advice. She would stay up just get a head start on accomplishing some task she felt needed to be done. He smiled lovingly at her, and she returned his look of affection as she shooed him out the door.

*   *   *   *   *

When they finally arrived at the Main Street Inn, it was barely dawn. The inn was two stories tall with a restaurant in the bottom section. The aroma of fresh biscuits and sausage invaded John's senses when they opened the front door. His stomach growled, and he remembered that he hadn't eaten since noon the day before. Shelby, on the other hand, seemed oblivious to the smell. She walked quickly past the tables and over to a desk pushed against the back wall. John followed her. They stood in front of it for a few minutes, hoping someone would come and help them.

"It doesn't look like anyone is working right now," said John as he turned and surveyed the room. "Excuse me," he called across the room to a red-haired lady who was placing silverware on one of the tables.

If she heard him, she chose to act as though she didn't. He furrowed his brow. "Excuse me, ma'am," he said much louder. This time, the woman couldn't ignore him. She placed her hands on her hips and turned around to glare at him. "Could you possibly get us some help over here?" he asked, his voice tinged with frustration.

"Bo!" the woman yelled at the top of her lungs. "Will ya get out here? You've got some customers waitin' at the desk." She then turned her back on John and Shelby and went back to setting tables.

John looked at Shelby and rolled his eyes. A couple of seconds went by before a stocky, balding little man came scurrying out from the kitchen. He reminded Shelby of a mouse as his eyes darted back and forth between them both. The little man cleared his throat and pushed his glasses back up on his nose. "Yes, how may I help you?" he asked briskly.

"We're looking for someone," John said and then motioned for Shelby to continue.

She stepped forward. "His name is Harlan Rhodes, and he is staying in your inn.

"No need," answered the man. "He's gone."

Shelby's face paled, and she swallowed hard. "But there must be some mistake. Are you sure you have the right person?"

"Can you check your ledger?" John asked.

This irritated the little man, and he started blinking rapidly. "I don't need to check my ledger to know that Harlan Rhodes woke me up at two o'clock in the morning, demanding to be checked out."

John took one look at Shelby and realized she was on the verge of shock. He turned back toward the man and smiled tightly. "This is a matter of great importance. Are you sure you have the right person?"

"I'm absolutely positive, but if it will make you feel any better, I'll ask Winifred." He motioned to the red-head. She sauntered over. "Could you describe the young man who was staying with us to these folks?"

She frowned hesitantly.

"The young man you were talking to at breakfast yesterday," he clarified.

Recognition dawned, and her red lips smiled broadly. "Oh him. He's not easy to forget." She winked at Shelby. "No wonder you're here lookin' fer 'im."

John's expression told the woman that she'd better stick to the facts.

"Yeah, I remember 'im. Young fella." She looked at Shelby. "'Bout yer age. Light hair, nice smile, friendly. Came in a huff, woke everybody up, and checked out." She shrugged. "Did I leave anything out?"

Stars exploded in Shelby's head as her knees buckled. She would've landed on the floor if John hadn't caught her. He helped her to a table.

"Honey, are ya okay?" asked Winifred.

"She'll be all right," said John. "She's just had a little shock. Could you please get her a glass of water?" He knelt down to get a good look at Shelby, and felt her skin. It was clammy. Her pulse was weak and rapid, and her eyes were dull. "Shelby," he began calmly, "everything is going to be all right. Just try to relax."

She reached up and squeezed his arm. "I'm okay. I don't need any water. Could you please just get me home?"

Chapter Twenty-One

"Where are you going?" Ellen looked her oldest daughter up and down, her eyes resting briefly on the floppy, brimmed hat on top of Shelby's head and her long gloves. If a thunderbolt had suddenly broken through the clear, blue sky, it would've surprised her less than seeing Shelby walking down the stairs. "I thought you were resting," Ellen added before Shelby could answer.

Shelby tugged on her gloves, trying to make certain every inch of her milky arm was covered. "I heard you telling Sister that the tomatoes need picking so we can get them put away. I know how busy you've been, and I just can't stand the thought of them sitting out in the garden going soft."

Ellen raised an eyebrow. "Are you sure you're up to it?"

Shelby's eyes narrowed and she lifted her chin slightly. "Mama, I heard John telling you that I should stay in bed for a couple of days, but I can assure you that I am perfectly fine." She could tell her mother needed further reassurance, so she smiled.

Ellen's brow creased in concern. Even the tight smile on Shelby's face couldn't disguise the dark circles under her eyes or her pale pallor. They walked into the kitchen, and Ellen watched as she grabbed an apron and tied it around her waist. It broke her heart to see Shelby acting as if nothing had happened. She had tried to discuss things with her yesterday when she came back from the hotel, but Shelby had refused. She started to press her, and then bit back the words she wanted to say as John's words from the night before came back to her. "Be patient," he had urged. "Give her some time."

She decided to try a more subtle tactic. "Why don't you sit down and drink a little something? It's hot outside, and I don't want you getting sick."

"Thanks, but I'm not thirsty."

"You need to eat something. You haven't eaten anything since yesterday," Ellen pleaded.

"I will eat when I get hungry," Shelby answered emphatically. She looked at her mama's worried expression and softened. "Please try and understand. I will have to get over this thing on my own terms. If I continue to stay cooped up in my room—well, I'll go crazy."

"Okay," Ellen conceded. "Just remember I'll be here whenever you need me."

Shelby nodded. "I'll be outside."

As Ellen watched Shelby turn to go, she had an idea. "We can pick the tomatoes this evening when it gets cooler. If you really want to be of help, maybe you could take the wagon over to Miller's and pick up a bolt of fabric for me. Mindy ordered it a few weeks ago. It should be in by now. You could get us some more cocoa too."

Shelby considered the request. It didn't really matter to her what she did as long as she did something. She shrugged. "Okay, but I don't need the wagon. A walk will do me some good."

* * * * *

Summer held on as long as it possibly could, and just when the townsfolk of Alder Springs felt they couldn't take another sweltering day, the weather slowly got cooler until one day the promise of autumn could finally be felt in the air. For Shelby, the change of season represented a new birth of sorts. For a while after Harlan left, she would catch the shadow of his smile lingering on smiling faces around her or it would be his laugh echoing through her ears whenever John would laugh. She had wondered if she would ever be capable of experiencing any amount of happiness again, but time has a merciful way of healing even the most wounded of hearts.

Rayford had been by almost every day during the summer to check on her, despite her best efforts to put him off. She had put off setting a wedding date on the vague excuse that she had gotten ill and was having a difficult time recovering. She had thought that would get rid of him, but he still continued to come. Pretty soon she found herself looking forward to their afternoons together. They would sit together on the swing and drink cold lemonade as they watched Sarah play in the front yard.

"I went out to the farm yesterday." Rayford looked out of the corner of his eye to get Shelby's reaction, but her face remained blank.

"How does it look?" she finally asked.

"Lonely. Like it's waiting for us to live there."

Shelby didn't answer, and they continued to swing back and forth. Rayford scooted closer, and she turned to look at him.

"Will you ride out there tomorrow and let me show you?"

The excitement in his voice caused her to smile, giving him the encouragement he needed to continue. "It's a beautiful piece of land, and it's all ours," he said, his dark eyes glittering with satisfaction. "The soil is rich and fertile. We'll plant cotton—acres of it," he said eagerly. "Think about what it means to be landowners. You won't ever have to want for anything. I'll see to that."

As Rayford continued to describe the farm confidently, she took note of his sculptured features and generous smile, framed by thick, dark hair. He was strikingly handsome; she had to give him that, and he seemed to be genuinely concerned about her. Not many men would've hung around as long as Rayford had, waiting for her to come around. Harlan certainly hadn't. She forced herself to concentrate on what Rayford was saying. Despite herself, she felt a tingle of anticipation and a fragment of her old self returning as she listened to him talk about his farm.

"Will you go out there with me tomorrow?" he asked again.

She smiled, lightening up her face. "Yes, I think I will," she said as much to herself as to him.

He visibly relaxed and leaned back in the swing. A second later he reached for her hand, linking his fingers with hers. She didn't pull away.

*　*　*　*　*

"Don't uncover your eyes."

"Are we there yet?" she responded, excitement creeping into her voice.

"Yes, we're here," remarked Rayford, as he pulled the horses to a halt. "You can look now."

"Oh, Rayford, it's beautiful," she breathed, seeing past the grounds and pastures overgrown with weeds. Instead, she imagined how the rolling hills would look covered with lush, green grass. The house was set on a hill surrounded with huge maple and oak trees.

"Let's go see the house," she said.

Shelby took only slight note of the flaking paint as her eyes went instead to the wide porch and large windows. As she walked through the house, only the things she loved made an impression on her mind: the huge bay windows, the beautiful hardwood floors, and the spacious rooms with the high ceilings. She could make a home here.

"I love this place!" she whispered as she examined each room.

"And what about me?" Rayford joked, trying to sound jovial.

"Of course, silly," she replied, ignoring the uneasy feeling in her stomach. The mood was broken. "Let's go home now," she added hastily.

Shelby could not help but feel irritated on the way home. Why would Rayford ask such a strange question? And why did she feel so guilty? He should know by now that she loved him. She turned her thoughts away from Rayford and focused on the farm. She would make it a showplace. No, she corrected herself, she and Rayford would make it a showplace. Then she felt better.

*   *   *   *   *

"Why aren't you happy for me?" Shelby demanded.

"I just feel like you're rushing things a bit. Why not give yourself a little time to..." Ellen's voice trailed off. She wasn't sure how to approach the subject of Harlan to her daughter without opening old wounds, but she had to talk some sense into her.

Shelby picked right up on her hesitation. She leaped off the couch with clenched fists. "Some time?" she exploded. "Time for what? Don't you think it's time I got on with my life instead of pining away over something that never will be?" Her voice rose to a fevered pitch. "Harlan is gone!"

"You know where he is," countered Ellen. "We could plan a trip."

Shelby's eyes grew wide. "No!" she exploded. She thought back to the morning that she'd gone to the inn to find Harlan. An image of the tawdry, red-headed waitress with her insinuating smile and snide remarks flashed through Shelby's mind. She again felt the hot needles of shame. "I've made a big enough fool of myself as it is. I've run after him once. I'll not make the same mistake twice."

Ellen was at a loss for words. She shook her head sadly as she watched her daughter stomp back and forth across the floor. After a few minutes Shelby's anger began to diminish, and she sat back down on the couch facing her mother. Her anger continued to fade, draining all the color from her face as well. It broke Ellen's heart to see how pale and fragile she had become.

"I'm sorry," Shelby finally said. "I had no right to act that way to you. You're only trying to help." Her voice sounded hollow and flat.

Ellen wanted to help, but she didn't know how. She had tried to reach Shelby, but it was no use. It was as if the essence of her vibrant self had left with Harlan on that fateful night, leaving only an empty shell behind. There was so much she wanted to say. Why was Shelby torturing herself? Why wouldn't she open up her heart and let Ellen help? If only she would realize that it was not a sign of weakness to hurt or trust. She had hoped that Shelby's outburst would yield some type of lasting emotion, but as she looked back at the rigid, tight smile on Shelby's pinched face, she knew that the demons her daughter was facing were beyond her reach. She felt as though Shelby were on a high cliff, perched precariously near the edge. *If only she would reach out her hands, I might be able to save her,* Ellen thought, *but no, she just keeps standing there, alone.*

Shelby's placed her hand over her mama's. "I know what I'm doing. I know it might not seem that way now, but I really do. Yesterday, when Rayford took me to see his farm, I felt a part of my old self returning. I looked out over the rolling hills and felt a sense of belonging." She paused. "And I haven't felt that for a really long time."

Ellen looked surprised. "Honey, you know you belong here with us. Have we ever made you feel like you don't belong here?"

"No, Mama. You haven't," Shelby answered quickly. "It's just that I think it's time. What I mean is that I feel like it's time that I started my own family."

"Oh, Shelby," said Ellen tenderly, "I know you want that, and I want that for you. I want you to find the happiness that John and I have found. I just want to make sure you're not rushing into anything. Why don't you wait until the spring to get married? That will give you time to make sure."

"I don't need any more time." The words were spoken kindly enough, but the edge in Shelby's voice was unmistakable.

"You can't get married to Rayford because you love his farm."

Shelby looked as though she'd just been slapped. She shook her head incredulously. "You're not suggesting..." she began, and then Ellen cut her off.

"You told me a few moments ago that you felt as though you belonged at the farm. What about to Rayford? I haven't heard you profess any love for him."

"Well, of course I care for him," Shelby blustered. "That goes without saying." She sought for the right words to try to make Mama understand how she felt. "Rayford is a good man. He loves me, and I know he will take good care of me. We'll be happy together."

Ellen looked unconvinced. Shelby took a deep breath and prepared herself for what she knew she must say. She had never told her mama a lie before. She straightened herself up, hoping her cheeks weren't flaming like a beacon. "I love him." *Or at least I hope and pray that I will someday*, she added to herself. Shelby looked up to see Ellen's reaction. The latter's face was masked, so Shelby continued. "This experience with Harlan has been good for me. It has helped me realize that I can't keep chasing rainbows. I have to focus on what's real. Rayford is here." Shelby's voice went flat. "He stood by me. Rayford is real."

"Shelby," Ellen said as her eyes grew misty, "you can't ever lose sight of your dreams. You have to hold onto them. Our dreams give our lives meaning and hope."

"I have to get on with my life," Shelby said stubbornly. "Rayford has thrown me a life-line, a chance for happiness, and I'm going to take it."

Before Ellen could say anything else, John walked into the room. He took one look at the two of them and then turned to make a quick exit. "I'm sorry. I didn't mean to interrupt."

Shelby jumped up. "It's okay. You don't have to leave," she said, glad that his entrance had gotten her off the hook. "I was just telling Mama the happy news."

John looked dubiously at his wife and her daughter. "Happy news?"

"Rayford and I have decided to get married next month."

A look of surprise washed over his face. He didn't know what to say for a moment. "So soon?"

"Yes," Shelby answered quickly, "we want to get settled in before the winter hits, and Rayford wants to start planting in the spring."

"Congratulations," John murmured as he looked over at Ellen and noticed that her smile was forced, and she was wiping away a tear.

Chapter Twenty-Two

"If you make your bed, then you have to lie in it." Shelby had heard that quote from her gramma, along with many others, all of her life. But not until this past year had she realized the full implication of what she had meant. Her relationship with Rayford had taken a turn for the worse the last few months. The newlywed stage had worn off. And with a baby coming, it was only natural for Rayford to worry more. At first, she assumed that perhaps his moody and sullen manner was her imagination; she had heard that being pregnant did all sorts of things like that to women. Then she noticed that he was staying away from home more and more and taking less interest in her, the baby, and the farm.

Maybe it was her fault. She had been really demanding lately. She was determined to make things better between them.

As usual, she left Rayford sleeping in the bed and got up early. She put on one of her gingham work dresses and expertly piled her brown curls high on her head and secured them with a silk ribbon. She set aside a royal blue freshly starched dress and a crisp, white apron. She would put her nice dress on after she did the morning chores. Except for her little round tummy, she could've passed for a child.

The first order of the day was to milk the cow and feed the chickens and other animals. She had heard some of the ladies at the church complaining about having to get up so early to milk the cows, but she didn't mind. This was her favorite time of day, and she loved the animals. A patch of fog was still nestling in the valley up against the mountains. Sunlight shone on the morning dew, spreading a sparkling blanket across the grass, and the air was cool and crisp.

What she did mind, though, was carrying in the heavy wood from the shed to start a fire for cooking breakfast. Until recently, Rayford had made sure that she had plenty of wood to cook with, but this was the third time this week that she had had to lift the heavy wood and bring it in from the shed. She made a mental note: When the time was right, she would discuss it with him.

Shelby's earlier optimism about her day waned a little by the time she finally got the fire started, changed into her blue dress, and cooked breakfast. She tried to sweep the negative thoughts out of her mind as she hummed her favorite tune and set the table, using her lace table cloth and floral china. Rayford's favorite breakfast was hot biscuits served with fresh butter, applesauce, sausage, and steaming coffee. She knew that he would be pleased. The aroma could be smelled a mile down the road.

The table was situated in front of the bay window where the first morning rays of sun spread across the room. Shelby loved this spot in her house most of all. The morning sun always gave her hope for a beautiful day, and she took particular delight in the rays on this morning as they spread across the table and fell onto the floor.

She was still admiring her tablesetting and the green plants in decorative pots that lined the window seal when Rayford came into the kitchen. "Good morning," she chimed cheerfully as she poured a cup of coffee before turning to face him. Her next sentence stopped in mid-air. "I have the clothes ready to—" she began and then stopped. "Why are you dressed in your nice clothes? I have the clothes ready to be separated for washing. You promised to set the pots up for me and build a fire this morning." She stammered in exasperation.

"Well, something has come up, and the clothes will just have to wait another day, darling," he drawled with that smile she was beginning to despise. "I have to go into town early this morning, so I won't be eating breakfast." He picked up the coffee cup and took a long sip while looking at her above the rim of the cup.

Her face started to blaze. She had spent at least an hour cooking breakfast for him! "You've made promise after promise to me all week and haven't hit a lick at a snake," she flung at him, her resolve to make everything work quickly fading. How dare he expect her to keep their house and clothes clean and run the farm without any help? She tried to calm down. "Look, I didn't mean to lose my temper.

Rayford, you know I am seven months pregnant, and I need your help."

He sneered. "Miss Perfect, everything has to be just right. You're always nagging me to do something. You don't have to wash today. Other women don't wash every week. You think you're better than everybody else. That your stuff has to be better—cleaner! You're just a spoiled little baby," he shouted as he slammed down the coffee cup and bolted out the back door.

She stood for a few seconds, her mouth hanging open in shock, as she stared at the back door. What in the world was that all about? It then occurred to her that he was gone again, and she didn't have a clue where he was going or what he was going to be doing. Hot tears filled her eyes and spilled down her face as she looked at her beautifully set table and the hot food that was now getting cold. She finally slumped down in the chair and let the tears flow freely. Unfortunately, they couldn't wash away the hurt. She felt that same sinking feeling in the pit of her stomach she had felt when her papa had abandoned her at the school.

She didn't know how long she cried, but the sudden movement in her belly reminded her that she couldn't sit around feeling sorry for herself all day. Even though she wasn't the least bit hungry, she picked up a biscuit, placed a piece of sausage inside, and shoved a big bite in her mouth. She chewed it up and swallowed it; it tasted like glue to her. But she would need all the strength she could get for the washing.

*   *   *   *   *

Drops of perspiration fell off Shelby's dark curls and onto her face and clothes as she wrestled with the big iron pot. She wiped her forehead with the back of her hand, leaving a smudge of black soot. Prickles of pain spread from her back and down through her legs, causing her to feel chilled even though it was warm and she was perspiring. Each movement was a great effort. A wave of nausea enveloped her, and she was suddenly aware of the swelling in her ankles. She'd felt so heavy the last few days. Tears ran down her face as she tried to level the huge pot. She could feel the baby's feet in her side as she continued to pull and tug at the pot. Finally exhausted, she was able to get the pot into place and fill it with water.

All in all, it had taken her almost an hour to balance two pots, fill them with water and start the fire just so that she could get started. The morning was almost gone, and she was not even halfway done yet.

She had carefully positioned the tubs so that the smoke would not blow toward the clothesline. As she carefully shaved a cake of lye soap into the water, she tried to make some sense of her life.

Her stomach began to contract; she needed to sit down for a moment and let it pass. She sat down on a bench that Rayford had built for her when they were first married. It was ironic how solid and sturdy it had remained—not like their marriage. She looked down at her dress and hands. She was covered with black smut from the pot. She didn't have time to worry about how she looked right now. She would feel better if she could relax and clear her head for a second. Her cheeks were flushed with anger. She knew that feeling angry with Rayford would not help the baby or her.

She looked across the yard and a little ways down the road and cringed at the thought that entered her mind. After the morning she'd had, she could just see Mama and John driving up and seeing her right now. She knew what their reaction would be, and she didn't want to deal with that. Then a more horrible thought came into her mind as she imagined the Reverend's wife riding by in her carriage and spreading the word like wildfire to the other ladies in the community that she saw Shelby, big as a barrel, working like a field hand. She almost laughed at the thought and felt a little better.

She got up and carefully separated the clothes into three piles: one for whites, one for coloreds, and one for work britches and rags. As she examined each piece of fabric, she noticed one of Rayford's shirts had a dark smear on the sleeve. She meticulously applied the paste of lye soap and baking power that she had made earlier in the week and rubbed it vigorously up and down the scrub-board. There, that stain was gone. She wished it were that easy to remove the stains Rayford had put on their marriage and on her heart.

Rayford strolled into the tavern and smiled his handsome, debonair smile, his white teeth glistening against his dark skin. It was impossible to tell that he had been riding for almost two hours. He looked totally refreshed.

He had not expected the blowup with Shelby, but the two-hour drive had been ample time for him to put her out of his mind. She had really been getting on his nerves lately. She wanted everything to be perfect, including him. She knew how he was when she married him, and by golly he wasn't about to change for her or anyone else. There was more to life than working that farm!

He glanced around the room. No one would ever recognize him this far from home.

"Well, hello darling," he drawled as he approached the bar.

"Hello. How are you, baby?" the girl replied.

"Is there any action going on around here?"

"No baby," she crooned, "but we can start some."

Rayford could not help but think of Shelby for a split second when he put his arm around the girl and brushed against her brown, curly hair.

Chapter Twenty-Three

You sit right here on the steps, and don't go anywhere," Shelby repeated the third time.

Aaron flashed a smile at her—the same one he'd seen his father give. "I won't, Mama. I promise."

Shelby smiled back warmly. It seemed like only yesterday that she was changing his diaper and now here he was, old enough to sit out on the steps. Even at the tender age of five, Aaron looked so much like Rayford with his dark, thick hair and dazzling smile. She gave him a quick kiss on the cheek, and he ducked away bashfully. "I'll be right back," she said as she walked up the stairs and into the bank.

*　　*　　*　　*　　*

"Mr. Fisher, there is something wrong with this balance," Shelby said. "I should have over fifty dollars in that account. Are you showing all of my deposits? Let's see," she said, checking her ledger. "I made a deposit of eight dollars in milk money last month, and the month before that..."

The man's mustache twitched as he carefully looked over the account. "Mrs. Carter," he replied in a condescending tone, "perhaps, you should talk to your husband. It looks like he has made a sizeable withdrawal from this account since your last deposits."

Shelby's blood turned cold, but her face blazed with embarrassment. How dare Rayford make a sizeable withdrawal and not discuss it with her? He knew how tight they were until the crops came in.

"Yes," she said in an almost inaudible voice, "I will check with him."

Shelby left the bank and went directly to John's office. She found him sitting at his desk, poring over a medical book. As soon as he saw her, he stood up and smiled broadly and then looked around for Aaron. "Well, to what do I owe this visit? Where is Aaron?"

"He's playing out front."

John noticed that Shelby's face was flushed. "Are you feeling okay, Shelby?"

"Yes, John, I feel fine," she continued, "but I do have a little problem that you may be able to help me with."

"Are you sure everything is all right?"

She was beginning to think that she had made a mistake by coming to John, but she didn't know where else to turn. "John, I need some help on the farm," she finally stammered.

"Is something wrong with Rayford?" he asked.

"No, he's all right" she replied, trying to sound as convincing as she could. "I think he just needs a little space right now."

John shook his head. He'd never been overly impressed with Rayford. "A little space for what?"

"Please, John, I need your help, and I don't want to worry Mama," she pleaded.

"What kind of help do you need?"

She sat down in a chair. "Do you remember when Rayford had the falling out with the Abrams?"

He nodded. "I thought he was going to get another family to take their place."

"Yes, he was, but he hasn't gotten around to it," she replied evasively. "I need someone to take their place and work in the fields." Shelby tried to hold back the tears.

John noticed for the first time how exhausted Shelby looked. Even though he'd never believed in resorting to violence, at that moment he would have loved to get a hold of Rayford and pound some sense into him. "Shelby, let me see what I can do. I heard of a family in Boaz that is looking for a place to move. They got into some type of disagreement with their landlord, and he's kicking them off the place."

"What did they do?" she asked.

"It's the same old story. They claim, they didn't do anything," he replied. "No one really knows because ol' man Brown won't comment on why he's kicking them out."

Shelby thought for a second. "When can you get in touch with them?"

* * * * *

From the moment she laid eyes on Otis Wilkerson, Shelby knew she had made a serious mistake. And just as she knew for a surety that she would probably regret the day he stepped foot on her property, she knew with equal clarity that she couldn't turn his family away. Standing just behind Otis, her face partially covered by the baby she was holding, was his petite wife. Tiny as she was, her dress still looked snug and worn, as if it had almost totally exhausted its wear. Upon first glance, Shelby guessed his wife was about her mama's age, but after a closer inspection, she realized with a jolt that the woman was actually closer to her own age. It was the deep wrinkles around her sad eyes and her stooped posture which made her seem older.

The family was standing close together in front of the broken down shack, waiting to see if they would pass inspection. Shelby felt embarrassed about the poor condition of the shack this desolate family would have to call home. How she wished she could've given the faded, dry wood the whitewashing it so desperately needed or at least planted a few petunias to make the place seem more inviting. There was simply not enough time—or energy.

She looked again at the pitiful family and felt embarrassment for them that they had been reduced to such a life, so dependent on her decision. What would happen to them if she turned them away? She looked at the oldest boy, trying hard to hold his bony shoulders straight under her gaze, despite the fact that his little sister was tugging on him to pick her up. He couldn't have been much older than Aaron, she decided. There were two other small children huddled behind the folds of their mother's dress. They looked dirty and unkempt.

It seemed like only yesterday she had come to this farm innocent and naive, ready to spend a life of bliss with a husband to look after her. It should be Rayford standing here trying to handle this situation—not her. She looked at Otis and squared her shoulders, and she felt as though the weight of the world rested on her. What was it about him that made her skin crawl? Something in his expression let her know that he would perceive any gesture of kindness on her part as a sign of weakness. She had to appear tougher than him.

He was only about an inch taller than Rayford, but his wiry frame made him appear even taller. His skin looked like leather, caused no doubt by working all his life in the blistering sun, picking cotton. The overalls he was wearing had holes in the knees and were so faded they hardly had any trace of color left in them. Patches of red whiskers dotted his sharp chin, and he was missing his two front teeth, causing him to speak with a slight lisp.

It was the bitter expression in his cold, blue eyes that caused a shiver to run down her spine. Was it her imagination or did they also hold a hint of mockery in them? He seemed to be condemning her, as if she were responsible for his situation. John must've sensed the hostility too. He pulled her aside. "Are you sure you want to hire this family?" he whispered.

Her eyes filled with doubt. The truth was, she wasn't so sure. "What are the chances of finding another family this close to picking time?"

John shrugged, his expression thoughtful. "I'd say your chances are pretty good. Times are hard. I'm sure we could do some more checking around. There are always families willing to work the land. Do you want to keep looking?"

She hesitated and looked over at the children. The smaller two had come out from behind their mother and were now playing in the dirt. The oldest boy had finally picked up his little sister and was balancing her on his hip. His pants weren't quite long enough to reach his dusty feet. She looked out across the distant field as an image of Mother Ramsey filled her mind. Mother Ramsey wouldn't turn them away. "No, I don't want to keep looking," she said finally. "I think we should give them a chance."

John weighed Shelby's words while trying to make up his own mind. "Well, at least this will get you through the season," he mused.

"All right. Let's see what we can work out."

Otis had gone over and sat down on the porch of the shack where he was chewing on a piece of grass. His body language suggested a lack of concern, but underneath his straw hat, his keen eyes were surveying the exchange between John and Shelby with interest. He stood up and spit out the grass when they approached. Clearly, it was time to get down to business.

"Do you have a plow or a mule? Anything you could bring into the contract?" Shelby asked, even though she could tell from looking at them that they barely even had clothes on their backs, much less anything else.

Otis shook his head.

"Well, in that case," she continued, "I'll furnish you with a credit of ten dollars at Miller's Mercantile. You probably noticed it on your way into town. You can buy enough food and other necessities to tide you over until pickin' time next month."

He nodded but remained silent.

"Since you are starting right before the season, I will pay you three cents a pound for the cotton you and your family pick, minus the credit I'm furnishing you right now. If things work out, we can renegotiate things for next year. Is that agreeable?"

Otis still didn't speak. This ruffled John's feathers. "I believe the lady asked you a question," he said brusquely.

Otis spit on the ground. "Three cents, huh?"

Shelby nodded.

Otis knew it was a fair price. "We'll pick by the pound fer now, but I'm gonna want to keep two thirds of the profit next year."

His open challenge caught her off-guard, and her heart began to pound. John started to speak, but she spoke first. This is where she had to take control. "Mr. Wilkerson, we haven't even decided how much acreage you will be allotted at this point and time. When and if that time comes, the only way that I would even consider paying you two-thirds would be on the condition that you provide your own mule, plow, tools, fertilizer, and seed. Are you prepared to bring those things into the contract?" she finished firmly, her steady voice surprising even herself. She looked him straight in the eye until he finally looked away.

"I cain't offer them thangs and you know it," he replied angrily.

"Those are my conditions. Take it or leave it."

He was beaten, and he knew it. "Yes, ma'am. I reckon that'll do," he replied slowly with a grin, but his eyes remained cold.

"Good, then it's all settled," Shelby replied as she looked over at Mrs. Wilkerson who immediately ducked her head to avoid any eye contact. She turned and climbed into the wagon.

"Welcome to Alder Springs," she said to no one in particular.

*　　*　　*　　*　　*

To say that Shelby was sad wouldn't have been the whole truth but neither was she fully happy. She found herself wandering day by day in that interim between sleep and wakefulness. Most of the time, she stayed so busy looking after Aaron and the farm she hardly even noticed the empty space that was growing somewhere deep inside of her. But sometimes, in the quiet moments, she felt the tide of loneliness mound up and knew she would have to patiently wait for it to ebb away.

Rayford was gone most of the time, and even when he was home, his mind was somewhere else. This way of life between them had become so customary that Shelby had to search her memory to see if it had ever been any different. Yes, things had been different. He'd been interested in her once, but any hope of them having a semblance of a relationship was dashed after the birth of Aaron. She had her suspicions, of course, but sometimes things were better left in the dark. Maybe she didn't have the courage to bring her fears out in the open. That would mean she would have to face them, and she just didn't want to do that right now.

*　　*　　*　　*　　*

"Well, hello, Ruthie. I believe you're getting prettier every time I see you."

Ruth's face flushed as she smiled and ducked her head slightly, acknowledging the compliment. Rayford flashed a brilliant smile back at her. He was glad it was Ruth at the counter today and not

Mr. Fisher. The last time he had been in to make a withdrawal, the man had gone so far as to ask him if Shelby knew he was making the withdrawal, as if he had to ask permission from his wife before taking money out of his own account. Rayford nearly scoffed out loud before turning his attention back to Ruth.

"How may I help you today?" she asked eagerly.

He studied her face carefully, taking note of the open admiration in her big, blue eyes. At this point, he could've asked her for the moon and she wouldn't have objected. A glint of satisfaction sparkled in his dark eyes, and he leaned a little closer into the counter. "I need to make a withdrawal," he said conspiratorially.

She smiled. "How much do you need?"

"I think ten dollars ought to do it."

"Give me just a moment."

He chuckled and gave her an intimate smile that caused a shiver of delight to run up her spine as she walked away from the counter to take care of his request.

When she returned, he noticed that she was empty-handed and frowning. "I'm sorry, Mr. Carter. I don't know quite how to tell you this—" she began.

His face darkened as his smile faded. "Tell me what?" he interrupted.

"There seems to be some sort of problem with your account."

He raised an eyebrow. "Problem?"

She nodded, and the words came tumbling out. "There appears to be a hold on your account. I asked Mr. Fisher about it, and he said that you must have Mrs. Carter's permission before making any withdrawals." She looked nervously at his darkened face. "I can ask Mr. Fisher to explain it to you."

It was all he could do to keep from exploding in anger. He let his breath out slowly. "I have never heard of anything so absurd. I have withdrawn money here on numerous occasions without my wife's permission. I demand to know the meaning of this," he said, his voice rising.

This sent the teller scurrying. "I'll go get Mr. Fisher right away."

Mr. Fisher looked every bit the part of a banker. He was tall and lanky with an eternal grim expression on his face. His dark hair was oiled and parted carefully down the middle and brushed straight down on each side. The only break in his sallow complexion was a pencil-thin mustache that curled slightly upward on each side. "What can I do for you today, Mr. Carter?"

Rayford's patience was wearing thin, and it was starting to show. "I wanna know where you get off tellin' me I can't withdraw money from my own account. What's the meaning of this?" he demanded.

Mr. Fisher's expression remained bland; the only sign of his discomfort was the small splotches suddenly apparent on his long neck. "Miss Shelby gave us explicit instructions that no amount of money was to be withdrawn on any condition without her approval."

Rayford's face was bright red now. "What?" he exploded. "I have every right to withdraw every cent of that money if I choose to do so."

There was now a look of disdain on the banker's face. "Your wife opened the account with us. She makes the deposits—and always has, I might add. She has given me specific instructions, and I will abide by them." There was a note of finality in the banker's voice.

Rayford's mouth twisted in a snarl, and he shot Mr. Fisher a look of pure hatred. "We'll just see about this," he said as he turned and left the bank.

*   *   *   *   *

After leaving the bank, Rayford's first impulse had been to go straight home and take his frustrations out on Shelby's hide, but as his temper cooled, his nerve faltered. He wasn't gonna let that hussie get the best of him. She thought she could keep him at home by cutting off his money. She wanted him to come begging to her to take the hold off of the account. We'll, he would never give *Miss Shelby* the satisfaction. He'd show her. He smiled grimly. There was more than one way to skin a fox.

Chapter Twenty-Four

No one really knew for sure where Bobby Ray Ledford had come from. Some folks said he came from northeastern Alabama, clear across the other side of Sand Mountain. Others jokingly remarked that they could've sworn he just dropped from the sky one day. He was private and elusive. Like the sneaky snake slithering on the ground, Bobby Ray appeared perfectly harmless, until you picked him up and put him in your pocket.

When the church had needed a piano a few years back, Bobby Ray made sure they had one. When Sherman Benson's house burned down last fall, Bobby Ray organized a house-raising. Any time the school needed books and supplies, it was Bobby Ray's money that bought them.

There were rumors, of course, of bootlegging, gambling, and extortion, but none of the rumors had ever been substantiated. Most people were either too busy with their own problems, too grateful for his generosity to the community, or perhaps too scared to investigate. It was said by some that there wasn't a tavern or saloon within twenty miles radius of Alder Springs that didn't pay a friendly gift to Bobby Ray just to keep Sheriff Myers and his cronies lookin' the other direction.

Yes, Bobby Ray was quite the model citizen. The last person who crossed him ended up on the bottom of the Tennessee River.

*   *   *   *   *

As Rayford stepped up the stairs leading to the Bloody Bucket, he could feel his pulse increase. When he grasped the wooden door, a jolt of adrenaline raced through him. Even though the Bucket was the closest tavern to Alder Springs, he didn't go to it very often on account of Shelby and the rumors he was sure would circulate through town. So, he'd always taken the trouble to travel to other places where people wouldn't recognize him. Fresh anger welled up again inside him when he thought about the incident at the bank earlier today. A dour smile stole across his face, looking more like a grimace as he opened the door and stepped inside. Thanks to his darling wife, he wouldn't have to worry about being so careful after all.

He forgot his anger for a moment and gawked at the scene unfolding before him as his eyes adjusted to the darkened room. "Wow," he uttered under his breath. He'd heard that Bobby Ray had cleaned up the Bucket, but he hadn't expected this. The wooden floor had been shined to perfection, and a piano now stood in one of the far corners. All of the tables were placed around the edge of the walls, leaving the center of the floor empty. Rayford assumed this was for dancing in the evenings. He looked toward the piano again, and caught the eye of the lady who was playing it. She was wearing a bright-colored dress with a tight-fitting bodice. Her cheeks were heavily rouged and tight, corkscrew curls were bouncing wildly as she pounded an upbeat tune. He smiled at her, and she winked back at him.

He casually strolled over to the bar and pulled up a stool, acting as though he didn't have a care in the world. He had to play this just right—dangle the bait at just the right moment, making sure the big fish would bite. He ordered a drink and then let his gaze travel around the room. There was a game going on over in one corner. He recognized two of the players as fellow farmers. Any other time, he would've been tempted to join them, but not today. He must remain focused. He slouched down in his seat, assuming a conversational tone with the bartender. "Any action goin' on around here?"

The bartender was a large, burly man with a ruddy complexion and dark whiskers. He raised one of his thick eyebrows and looked suspiciously out from underneath his heavy eyelid before shrugging. "I dunno," he replied carefully. "It depends on what you're lookin' for."

Rayford took a swig of his whiskey. "Sure is good whiskey." He shook his head. "Hasn't been anything this pure around these parts. Must be a mighty good still."

This really got the bartenders back up. "Just what're you gettin' at?"

Rayford figured the bartender outweighed him by at least seventy pounds. He felt the first prickle of fear creep up his spine as he noticed that the man's face was darkening, but he knew he had to see this thing through. He smiled benignly. "I was just makin' an observation. That's all."

The bartender's eyes narrowed as Rayford tried to figure out what to say next. He could feel the man's penetrating gaze as he scrutinized him. The bartender grew puzzled. "Hey, don't I know you?"

Rayford looked up in surprise. He didn't recognize the man but didn't know whether or not he should admit to the fact.

"I do know you. You're Rayford Carter," exclaimed the man as his face stretched in a broad grin. "You don't remember me, do you?"

"You look kind of familiar," Rayford admitted.

"I used to run around with Dave Williams and his bunch." When Rayford's face still looked blank, the man pointed to his chest. "Jerry Danielson. But my friends all call me J. D."

Rayford smiled. "J. D. Of course," he answered warmly, though he still had no idea who the man was. "It's good to see ya."

"Where've ya been? It's been years since I've seen you. I heard that you settled down and got yourself a little wife who leads you around by the nose." He winked.

Rayford smirked, the comment hitting a little too close to home. "That just goes to show you that you can't believe every rumor you hear," he said dryly.

J. D. shook his head and laughed heartily. "I guess so." He looked speculatively at Rayford. "What brings you in here?"

Rayford picked up his whiskey glass and swirled the liquid around. He placed it on the table and motioned toward the glass with his eyes. He paused just long enough to fully capture J. D.'s attention, and then he purposely lowered his voice so that J. D. had to lean in to hear him. "I'm lookin' for some work."

Understanding dawned. He looked at Rayford carefully and then shook his head. "I dunno," he said, looking furtively over his shoulder to make sure no one else was listening. "When a man comes lookin' for work, he has to be sure that he's up for the task, if you know what I mean. Once you start, there's no backin' out." His voice dropped to a whisper.

Rayford strummed his fingers on the table and then looked directly at J. D. "I am well aware of the risk, and I can assure you, I don't back down from nothin'."

J. D. looked steadily at Rayford, sizing him up. Rayford held his gaze until the other man blinked and looked away. "All right. Give me a few minutes. Let me see what I can do."

*　*　*　*　*

"What in the world?" Shelby muttered under her breath. "Aaron," she called out from the kitchen, "can you come here for a minute?"

In a couple of seconds, Aaron came running. "Yes, ma'am?"

"Honey, did you take one of the pies off the windowsill?

Aaron looked confused for a moment and then shook his head vigorously. "No, ma'am."

She looked at the sincerity shining from his dark eyes. "Are you sure? I put three apple pies up on the sill to cool, and now there are only two."

Aaron shrugged. "Maybe Uncle Homer took it."

Shelby chuckled and tousled his hair. She looked thoughtfully up at the partially open window and the lace curtain gently moving in the breeze. She stood on her tiptoes and looked outside. "Maybe you're right. I'll have to ask him about it."

Aaron nodded. "Can I go play now?"

Shelby smiled at her young son and nodded before turning her attention back to her baking. *Maybe Homer did take it,* she mused. A grin flittered at the corners of her mouth. She shook her head. The two ponds and stream on her property were more than enough temptation to keep her younger brother coming around on a regular basis. *That boy loves to fish more than anyone I know.* She smiled as she remembered a conversation she'd had with her mama about him. She'd asked her mama if Homer had ever shown any interest in dating. "He's fifteen years old," Shelby had exclaimed "I thought he'd have a girlfriend by now."

Ellen had chuckled. "I just don't think there are any girls around here who can measure up to the competition."

"What competition?" Shelby had asked dubiously.

"The fishing hole!" Ellen had exclaimed with a straight face, and then the two of them broke into peals of laughter.

The missing pie brought Shelby's thoughts back to the present. *Homer is a big practical joker. I wouldn't put it past him to steal a pie just to get a rise out of me. I'll be sure and ask him about it tomorrow at Sunday dinner.*

*   *   *   *   *

Despite all the uncertainty in Shelby's life, the one constant she could count on was Sunday dinner at Mama's and John's house. A great portion of Saturday was taken up in the preparation of the bounteous feast they would have the following day. There were always fried chicken, creamed potatoes, corn on the cob, green beans, fried okra, fresh tomato slices, biscuits, and an assortment of cakes and pies. After church, the whole family—John, Ellen, Homer, Sarah, Sister, Shelby, and Aaron—would gather at Ellen's house. Rayford had accompanied Shelby the first few months of their marriage, but that hadn't lasted very long. At first, John would inquire about his whereabouts and well-being. Soon, however, his absence grew normal, and no one seemed to miss him anymore.

Shelby frowned. She'd been expecting Rayford to get angry when she'd taken it upon herself to hire the sharecroppers. When she'd told him, he had acted strangely apathetic about the whole ordeal—oh he'd blustered around, fuming and fussing about it, but his heart wasn't in it. It was almost as though he were putting on a show—acting the way she'd expected him to react. And then there had been the bank episode. She'd been expecting a blow-up for several days now, but it hadn't come. If she knew anything about Rayford at all, she knew he would've attempted to make a withdrawal by now. He'd been his aloof self as usual, but there was a difference in him—a restlessness or excitement she couldn't quite put a finger on.

Just what was he up to?

Ellen placed the last dish of food on the table. Dinner was finally ready. Shelby stifled a grin as she caught a glimpse of Sarah across the table instructing Aaron to fold his arms before the prayer. She didn't feel as though she was getting older until she looked at her baby sister and realized how much she had grown. At eleven years old, Sarah was already a half-inch taller than Shelby. Her trim figure was beginning to show the first signs of budding womanhood. She still had that soft, blonde hair that had been such a strong feature of hers as a child, but it had turned a shade darker, making it look like golden honey. Her voluminous eyes had the same almond shape as Shelby's, but they were a dark, emerald green, except when she pitched one of those fits of anger she was famous for, and then they seemed to come alive with sparks.

Lately, Sarah had taken it upon herself to instruct Aaron on the rules of proper behavior. She was motioning sternly to him. He shot Shelby a look of hopelessness, and Shelby smiled back reassuringly. He rolled his eyes, but Shelby could tell the reassurance made him feel better. He then smiled as if to say, *I know she's overbearing, but I'll put up with her anyway.*

John got everyone's attention by clearing his throat. He bowed his head. "Let's offer thanks."

"Amen," they chimed in unison after the prayer was said. Bowls were then passed back and forth as everyone helped themselves to a hearty portion of food. Shelby listened contentedly for a moment to the lively chatter among her family before joining in.

"Homer," Shelby began, "did you go fishing yesterday at the farm?"

He picked up a drumstick and gnawed off a big piece. He then put it down and licked his fingers, bringing a sigh of disgust from Sarah. "No, I've been too busy helping Mama in the garden." Displeasure was heavy in his voice, causing Shelby and her mother to look at one another and smile.

"I was doing some baking yesterday," Shelby continued, "and I put three pies in the windowsill. The next time I looked, there were only two."

Homer shrugged. "It wasn't me, Sis," he said as a mischievous smile broke across his face, "but now that you've given me the idea..."

This brought a laugh from everyone at the table. Shelby just shook her head.

Ellen spoke up. "Shelby, how is the new sharecropping family working out?"

Shelby coughed as she nearly choked on her potatoes. She looked at John questioningly.

John's face turned red, and he shook his head. "I didn't tell her a thing," he offered in his defense.

Ellen chuckled. "I know more about the comings and goings of my family than you two may realize."

Shelby looked admiringly at her mama and grinned sheepishly. It was true. She was much too clever to not know what was going on. "It's too early to say for sure, but the family seems to be working out just fine. Of course the real test will come in a couple of weeks during harvest. I haven't seen them very often since I hired them. I took them some vegetables the other day. The wife is very quiet, but she seemed appreciative."

"How's the cotton looking?" John asked. "Any sign of boll weevil?"

Shelby shook her head. "No, thank goodness."

"I'm afraid you might need some additional pickers, even with the new family," John said between bites of chicken.

"I'm afraid you might be right," Shelby answered.

"Homer can help," Ellen interjected quickly.

"Oh, Maw!" Homer groaned. "I ain't pickin' no cotton."

Ellen saw the look on John's face and knew that he was about to scold Homer. She spoke before he could. The last thing she wanted was an argument at the dinner table. "You will help, and Sarah will too," she added.

"Girls don't pick cotton!" Sarah exclaimed as her eyes widened in shock. "My skin will burn."

"There will not be any more complaints at the table," said Ellen sternly as she looked back and forth between her two children. "You will both pick cotton, and you will do it without griping."

"Yes, ma'am," Homer replied glumly, staring down at his plate.

Sarah looked indignant, but she knew better than to talk back. She sighed heavily. "Yes, ma'am," she finally mumbled.

Shelby started to protest, but she also knew better than to question her mama's judgment, and she did need the help. She decided to change the subject. "Sister, how are things with the DAR?"

"We've been busy. Times are hard, and there are so many who are goin' without. Last week we bottled peach and strawberry jam. We aim to sell 'em at the harvest fair next month."

"That's great." Shelby looked at her aunt in respect. She knew Sister's happiness had weighed heavily on Ellen's mind ever since they'd moved to Alder Springs, especially when Ellen had married John. Ellen had been afraid that Sister would have a hard time adjusting to a new community. Thankfully, her worries had been unfounded. Sister had carved a life of her own, joining several charities and even serving as the president of the local chapter of the Daughters of the American Revolution. Every year these ladies sold bottled goods and home baked pies at the fall harvest fair. They used the proceeds to provide Christmas for needy families in the community. Sister always stayed busy, and she seemed content. But Shelby wondered how she dealt with the pain of living without Joshua. As she thought of her uncle, a wave of sadness rushed over her. If Shelby knew how Sister dealt with it, maybe she could learn how to better deal with the loneliness she felt. The thought fled as soon as it had come. She looked around the room and knew that, like Sister, she would never be alone—she would always have her family, no matter what.

John spoke next, rousing Shelby out of her thoughts. "Hershel Miller isn't getting any better," he announced sadly. "The cancer has moved to his lungs. I wish there was something else I could do, some other treatment, but I'm afraid there's nothing else. He doesn't have much time left." His voice trailed off, and he seemed to get lost in his own thoughts.

Ellen looked at her husband and nodded sympathetically. The worry etched around his eyes made him look older. He must've realized he was casting a somber mood over the group because he smiled. The transformation was instantaneous as the lines smoothed out and his countenance brightened, but Ellen could still see the concern in his eyes. His inability to save a life, especially that of a friend, caused him the most sadness. "He's in the Lord's hands now," she said softly.

"Yes," he murmured.

"I spoke to Mindy the other day," Ellen said. "She said she would be able to focus all of her concentration on Hershel now that she has sold the store."

This brought Shelby's head up sharply. "What?" she sputtered.

"She said she got a very generous price for it," Ellen continued.

Shelby was stunned. She'd always just assumed that the Millers would always run the store. How would this affect her credit? Hershel and Mindy had always been very willing to let her purchase goods on credit, and she'd always paid them back promptly at harvest time. They had even allowed her to extend credit to Otis Wilkerson. She stewed over the situation for a moment and then chided herself for being so selfish. She shook her head. Poor Mr. Miller was dying and all she could think about was her credit.

"Who bought the store?" Sister asked.

Ellen shrugged. "She didn't tell me the name, but I believe it's some out-of-towner."

Sister shook her head. "I sure do hate it for Mindy. I think I'll go and visit her this week."

Shelby looked up and realized that John was looking at her. He knew how hard she'd struggled the past few years and how much she depended on the store's credit to run her farm. "I'm sure the new owners will be as kind as the Millers," he said.

"Yes, I'm sure they will," Shelby repeated dully.

"It might be a good idea to go and talk to them as soon as possible," Ellen urged.

Shelby nodded. "Yes, I'll do that," she said. She'd go and try to arrange credit with someone she didn't even know. It was just one more thing she'd have to try to work out alone.

*   *   *   *   *

Her plan had worked perfectly. The windowsill was empty.

After Shelby found out that Homer wasn't the one who had stolen the pie, she knew then who the culprit was, or at least she suspected who it must be. She hadn't known for sure until she put another pie on the windowsill as a test. This time, she'd purposefully left the windows open while she was baking, in the hope that the tantalizing aroma would float outside and tempt the little bandit to try again.

She set out the pie and then went into the next room and stood by the window so she would have a clear view of the kitchen window. She had to wait about fifteen minutes before she saw him. He slipped stealthily up to the pie, his bare feet choosing each step carefully, as he looked furtively in each direction. In a flash, he snatched the pie and then took off running.

As Shelby watched him go, compassion welled in her breast. The dirty boy was skin and bones, making her wonder how much food the Wilkersons had. She'd given Otis the credit at the store but hadn't even to checked to see what he'd purchased. She had considered taking the family some produce from the garden but didn't want to make them feel uncomfortable. Then she thought of an alternative solution. If the boy takes pies from the windowsill, she mused, maybe he will take vegetables as well.

The next day, instead of a pie on the windowsill, the boy found a basket of green beans and tomatoes balanced precariously in the open window. Much to Shelby's delight, he took those, too. Every few days, she would set out another offering, smiling when, a little while later, the windowsill would come up empty.

*   *   *   *   *

A soft breeze rustled through the leaves and ruffled Rayford's hair as he walked along the windy trail. He looked up and could see intermittent patches of sky peeking above the thick grove of trees. A more astute observer might have noticed the lush, green moss growing beside the creek bed and the colorful contrast of yellow daisies grouped in clusters. But Rayford had other things on his mind. He was too busy trying to follow the trail that really wasn't much of one at all. The only markings were round spots on the trees about the size of baseballs where the bark had been carved away, revealing the smooth, white wood underneath. The trees were marked about every ten feet or so. A couple of times, he'd been forced to retrace his steps after realizing that he'd walked too far without seeing a marking. The soft pine needles covering the ground muffled any sound his steps were making, giving the eerie impression of being in a separate enclosure, cut off from the rest of the world.

He still couldn't believe how easy it had been to get set up in "the business" as J. D. had called it. It had been a stroke of luck that J. D. had recognized him. He had ushered him straight in to meet with Bobby Ray in a private room in the back of the Bucket. He really wasn't sure what he had expected Bobby Ray to be like, but the meeting with him had been unusual to say the least. Bobby Ray wasn't short, but his stocky frame seemed too big for his height, making him look awkward. His big, meaty hand dwarfed Rayford's hand when they had shaken hands, and it was moist. Several times during their short meeting, Bobby Ray had pulled out a handkerchief and blotted the beads of perspiration that kept continually forming on his forehead. His light hair was thinning on top and was damp like the rest of his body, and his soft jaw was sandwiched in the middle of two loose rolls of skin on each side of his face. He certainly didn't fit the profile of a man who exuded authority. But the biggest surprise came when Rayford heard him stutter.

Rayford changed his mind abruptly when he heard the tone of authority in Bobby Ray's voice, suggesting that first appearances can often be very deceiving.

The interview began with Bobby Ray asking Rayford a few surface questions about himself, and then he got right down to business. If the rumors were true, he'd probably already known all the questions about Rayford before he even asked them. Bobby Ray was too shrewd to come right out and say that he was hiring him to run whiskey. Instead he gave him vague directions to his Aunt Sadie Bean's house. "S-she l-lives out in the s-sticks," he said, "b-but if you'll watch the trees, you'll find your way j-just f-fine." He then sat down at the table and hastily scrawled something on a piece of paper and handed it to Rayford. "G-go to the d-door and ask for S-Sadie. Tell her I sent you and give her this," he said as he handed him the paper.

Rayford had about a thousand other questions, but he could tell that he was being dismissed.

"S-she'll be expecting you next T-Tuesday around dark," said Bobby Ray. He left one final word of caution. "Better head out t-there while it's still light s-so y-y-you won't get lost."

The two shook hands and that had been that. It wasn't until after Rayford left the Bucket that he realized there had been no talk of pay. He shrugged; he'd know soon enough.

It wasn't any trouble getting out early tonight. As usual, Shelby was busy doing chores and didn't even miss him. As he walked, he felt in his pocket to make sure the paper Bobby Ray had given him was still there. Just when he knew that he'd have to retrace his steps again, he saw the faint glimmer of tin in the distance. His blood pumped faster and he quickened his step.

This must be it.

He'd only taken one step out into the clearing, when something tackled him from behind. Before he realized what was happening, he was being pinned, face down, on the ground. A stab of pain wrenched through his arm as it was yanked viciously behind his back. He tried to free himself, but he couldn't even budge under the tremendous weight that was on top of him.

"Bird," he heard a voice hiss, "Git over here and look at what I got." He then heard the cracking of twigs as another person came running.

"Well, whadda ya got there?" asked a higher pitched voice.

Rayford began to struggle again and stopped abruptly when he felt the cold point of a blade of steel prick his neck.

"All right, buddy, you've got about two seconds to explain yourself before I carve you up."

"Bobby Ray sent me," Rayford uttered in gasps. His arm got yanked again, and he yelped in pain.

"Sorry," said the voice again, "you'll have to do better than that."

"He sent me to check on his Aunt Sadie Bean." The words sounded more like a plea than a statement.

The weight suddenly left Rayford's body, and he rolled over and clutched his arm. He reached in his pocket to pull out the paper. This caught the man's attention, and for a split second Rayford feared another attack. He quickly handed it to the man who looked at it briefly and then grunted in satisfaction. Rayford felt relief wash over him when he heard the knife flick back down in its case.

The man swore. "I sure do wish somebody would let us know when a visitor's comin'." He glanced at Rayford. "Before we almost kill 'im."

Rayford had collected his wits enough to roll to an upright sitting position where he could get a good look at his assailant. He was tall and big. His brown hair was clipped close to his square head. Despite his large size, he had pleasant features and wasn't nearly so frightening now as he'd been a few moments ago when he'd been wheedling the knife. The man laughed good-naturedly and extended his hand.

"Sorry about the little misunderstanding." His gaze went to Rayford's arm. "I'm Bo." He motioned toward the other man. "This is Ted, but we call 'im Bird."

Rayford took his eyes off the big man and looked at the one named Bird. He took one look and could guess how the man had gotten his nickname. He was tall and lanky with a shock of red hair that wasn't quite long enough to cover his large ears. His eyes were light blue and empty. Deep craters pitted the boy's fair skin. He guessed him to be around twenty-one or twenty-two years of age. He extended his hand first to Bo. "Rayford Carter."

The big man shook Rayford's hand and nodded in acknowledgment. Rayford then turned to shake hands with Bird. He grasped the boy's hand and had the fleeting impression that he'd met him before. "Howdy," he said.

The boy only nodded and quickly dropped his hand.

Bo reached down and grasped Rayford's hand again and heaved him to his feet and then slapped him on the back. "Come on. We've got work to do."

*   *   *   *   *

After his first introduction to Bobby Ray, it really came as no surprise to Rayford that the place where the whiskey was made was nothing more than a dilapidated shack with a rusty tin roof. If he'd not known better, he would've passed by the old place without as much as a second glance, and he figured that was the intent. Old crates, scraps of tin, and rags were littered all over the front. Some of the items had been there for so long that they were half buried, looking as if the earth were trying to absorb the foreign items under a protective cover of dirt and grass. There was only one small window on the front, and half of the panes of glass were either broken or cracked.

When Bo approached the house, an ancient-looking hound dog limped toward him. He reached down to pat the old dog, and the dog began to whimper with obvious pleasure. "Hey there, ol' girl." He turned to Rayford and grinned. "Allow me to introduce you to Sadie Bean."

Rayford looked down in surprise, and then his face reddened slightly when he realized the two men were laughing at him. He slowly smiled as he shook his head. "Forgive me, gentlemen, if I admit that I don't see much of a family resemblance between Bobby Ray and his aunt."

Bo sniggered at that. Rayford looked at Bird. The younger man scowled and stomped into the house. Rayford looked at Bo questioningly. Bo shrugged. "Don't mind Bird. He don't like very many people. He kinda keeps to himself."

The front porch groaned loudly as they walked, and Rayford found himself trying to walk lightly across the planks as they bent under his weight. The inside of the shack looked about like the outside. An old table and two chairs were in the center, and a cot was pushed over into one corner. Other than that, the place was empty. Bird lay down on the cot. Bo motioned for Rayford to follow him out back. "Come on out here, and I'll show ya where we do all the work."

Rayford followed Bo out the back door about fifty yards back into the woods and up a small hill. The hill dipped sharply on the other side, creating a valley that was concealed from view on three sides. There must've been at least ten fifty-gallon barrels—some of them full—sitting around in different areas. Rayford walked over to the closest one and peered into it.

"Go ahead. Get a whiff of it," Bo said.

Rayford leaned over and sniffed and then wrinkled his nose and shuddered involuntarily as the vile smell invaded his nostrils.

Bo got a big kick out of this. He leaned his head back and hooted. "Whadda ya think?"

"What is that?"

"Corn mash. It's been settin' in that barrel for about six days. In another couple of days, it'll be ready to distill." He pointed to another barrel. "This here's about ready. Smell of it."

Rayford really wasn't interested in smelling anything else, but he certainly didn't want to antagonize Bo. He leaned down and sniffed again. "This one smells like rotten peaches."

Bo smiled broadly. "Yep. This un's just about ready. I add the peaches in the mash to give it a better flavor. It's an old family secret. My mammy taught me," he said proudly.

"And this is where the magic begins," said Rayford as he walked over to the still and traced his finger along the copper coil.

Bo nodded. "The mash goes in the boiler, and then I start a fire under it. The liquid runs through the coil and comes out here," he said, pointing to the washtub. "Next, I run it through these," he said, pointing to some baskets.

Rayford already knew how whiskey was made, but he listened politely to Bo as he explained it in great detail.

"The first basket has cotton, the next has gravel, and the third has good oak charcoal."

"Charcoal?"

"Yep, this cleans the whiskey real good and removes the fusel oil." He pointed to several empty kegs. "Then, it goes in there."

"Where it gets distributed?"

"Not quite. There's one more step I take that makes my whiskey better than anybody else's."

"What's that?"

Bo shook his head. "Come on over here, and I'll give ya a taste of a batch I brewed earlier today." He handed Rayford a dipper full.

Rayford took a swig. "It's good."

"Good?" asked Bo, a little perturbed by Rayford's reaction.

"I told you I brewed that a few hours ago. Does that taste like new whiskey to you?" he asked, clearly exasperated.

Rayford wasn't sure what answer the man was looking for.

"It tastes at least four years old," Bo exclaimed impatiently. "Just after a day. That's the secret. I add a handful of white oak chips. After it sets for three days, it'll taste like ten-year-old whiskey."

"Impressive."

Bo scowled and waved his hand in frustration. "You hotshots are all the same, comin' up here to make some fast cash, and ya don't even know what it's all about."

Rayford wasn't sure how the conversation suddenly took a turn for the worse. "You're obviously very good at what you do," he offered, trying to appease the man. Bo didn't reply. "What am I supposed to do? Help make moonshine?"

"Naw, it takes more know-how than you got to do that. You're gonna transport it."

Rayford nodded, relieved. He found the prospect of hiding up in the hills hunched over a smelly barrel less than appealing, but he wasn't about to say as much.

"You and Bird are gonna transport these kegs."

Bird stepped down into the valley, almost as though he appeared on cue. Bo motioned at him. "Bird'll know what to do. You just do what he tells ya, and everything'll be fine."

Rayford wasn't too pleased to have to take orders from the boy, and it must've shown on his face. Bird sneered at Rayford and then turned his head and spit a wad of snuff on the ground. "We're gonna take this batch to Guntersville. We've gotta deliver five kegs to the Harbor House."

"How are we going to get them from here to the road?" Rayford asked in surprise.

"We'll carry 'em one by one about a quarter of a mile. I've got a car hidden by the road, and then we'll go by boat on the lake."

"A quarter of a mile?" Rayford asked, his eyes wide. "I walked at least six miles from the road to get here."

Bird was losing his patience. "Yeah, you idiot, you came the long way."

Rayford clenched his fist. He was about to grab up the skinny rat by the hair of his head and teach him a lesson. He took a step toward the boy, but Bo stepped in between them. "There'll be no more of that," he said fiercely. He turned toward Bird. "You're gonna be working with this man from now on. I would suggest that you learn how to get along with 'im."

"He'd just better learn who's givin' the orders," Bird sneered, but the statement lacked conviction and came more whiny than fierce. He knew better than to go up against Bo.

Rayford stepped back also. He glowered at Bird until the color of the boy's face matched his hair, and then Rayford turned away.

Chapter Twenty-Five

"Mama, why can't I go into town with you?" Aaron whined as he climbed into the wagon to sit next to his Shelby. "I wanna pick out a piece of candy from the store."

Shelby grasped the reins and gave them a swift yank. "I've already told you why," she answered a little impatiently as the wagon started rolling, "I have to go and speak to the new store owners, and I need to be able to concentrate."

"I wanna go with you," Aaron began again. "It's boring at Mamaw's house." He wrinkled his nose. "And Sarah always bosses me around."

"I don't want to hear another word," Shelby said sharply.

Aaron started to say something else and then took one look at his mother's face and decided he'd better not. His dark eyebrows knitted in frustration, and his mouth drooped in a frown. He looked so cute that Shelby felt herself soften. She knew how much he loved going into town, especially to the store, but she needed to do this without having to worry about him getting into things.

"I'll tell you what. You be a big boy and go to Mamaw's house without complaining, and I'll bring you back some peppermint sticks."

He raised one eyebrow as he considered the option. His frown changed to a smile. "Okay." He held up his little, pudgy hand. "Can I have five?"

Shelby smiled. "It depends on how good you are."

This seemed to appease him, and when they got to Ellen's house, he quickly leaped from the wagon and skipped up to the front gate. He was still trying to open it when Shelby reached him. She leaned over and flipped the latch, and he bolted like a racehorse to the front door. She chuckled. *For a little boy who thinks his mamaw's house is boring, he sure is eager to get there.* He had already flung the door wide open and run on inside by the time she got up the steps.

"Mama," she called as she stepped inside, her shoes clopping across the wood floors as she walked.

"I'm in the kitchen."

Shelby inhaled deeply as the tangy scent of strawberries invaded her senses. She stepped into the kitchen where Ellen was working away. "What are you making? Strawberry pie?"

Ellen turned around and smiled at her daughter. "Close," she answered, wiping her hands on her apron. "I'm bottling up some strawberry jam to give to the DAR. Sister said they could use some extra help." As she spoke, she quickly surveyed her eldest daughter from head to toe. Shelby was wearing a crimson dress that had a v-necked collar and a tailored waist. She was also wearing a red hat with tiny red, silk tulips nestled in the crease. Ellen reached out and hugged her. "You look beautiful."

"Thank you," Shelby murmured graciously. "I figured I'd feel better if I looked my very best to meet the new store owners."

"So you're going by yourself to meet them? Rayford's not going?"

Shelby kept her face expressionless and tried to ignore the butterflies churning in her stomach. "No. I'm going alone."

Ellen nodded, the look on her face conveying more than words ever could.

"I've been putting it off, but I need to get everything settled before picking time."

"When do you start picking?"

"Next week."

Ellen looked around. "Where's Aaron?"

"He must've gone upstairs to talk to Homer and Sarah."

"Has he eaten dinner yet?"

"No, we left in such a hurry that I didn't have a chance to feed him. I wanted to get to the store early."

Ellen smiled. "Try not to worry too much. Everything will work out."

Shelby nodded and returned a slight smile. "All we can do is hope."

"Take as much time as you need. Don't worry about Aaron. He'll be fine."

"Thank you, Mama."

* * * * *

By the time Shelby pulled up to the store, her hands were sweaty, and her heart was beating fast. What would the new owners be like? How would they react to having to deal with a woman? She had hoped that she might have a chance to talk to Rayford last night to see if he would accompany her, but he'd stayed gone all night long. She'd heard him stumble into his room about five A.M. They had long since stopped sharing the same room. It was as if they were two strangers living in the same house. She still took care of his clothes and fixed him meals, but that was about the only contact she had with him anymore. He seemed to be as uninterested in his son as he was in her. It broke her heart to see the hurt on Aaron's face when his father continually brushed him aside.

Shelby took a deep breath and wiped her hands on her dress. It wouldn't do for her to give the new owners a sweaty handshake. She had to appear composed and confident. How would she run the farm if they denied her credit? She pushed the fear aside. They would give her the credit. She straightened her shoulders and lifted her head. They just had to.

* * * * *

"Well, I'll be. This is indeed a surprise," said a high-pitched, syrupy voice that Shelby recognized instantly.

She plastered a smile on her face and waited for the lady to come out of the store. "Mrs. Tucker, how are you?" Shelby was glad she was going out of the store instead of in.

"I'm doin' just fine, honey. Where's that darlin' boy of yours?"

"Mama's watching him for me."

Mildred Tucker smiled brightly, emphasizing her large teeth. "Well, how nice. I'll bet you're gettin' ready for harvest."

Shelby nodded. "I'm just taking care of some last-minute errands before the onslaught begins."

"Yes," answered Mildred as her eyes raked Shelby up and down. "I just ordered some new fabric from the store." She looked down at herself. "I just get so tired of the same ol' dresses. That's a lovely dress you have on dear. It must be your favorite. You wear it quite often. Young girls can wear just any old thing and still look good in it."

Shelby raised one eyebrow. "Yes, I do like it, and I guess I'm not quite as fortunate as you to be able to have new ones made for every day of the week."

This flustered Mildred, and she was at a loss for words for a moment. Shelby suppressed a grin. "Well, it was good to see you. Please tell Reverend Tucker I said hello." She grasped the door and pulled it open. "If you'll excuse me, I need to be on my way," she said, leaving the woman standing outside the store with her mouth hanging open.

Shelby stepped inside and reached up and straightened her hat. Then she smoothed down her dress. She looked toward the counter, but no one was behind it, so she decided to look around. The shelves seemed to be stocked a little fuller than the Millers had kept them. She made her way over to the fabric nook and looked with satisfaction at the dozen or so new bolts. The Millers had only kept four or five different bolts of fabric on hand, so the selection was very limited. Anything else had to be ordered from the Sears and Roebuck catalog. Shelby ran her hand over the smooth blue and white calico fabric. It was certainly an improvement.

Next, she made her way over to look at the colorful display of hats. Two other women stepped to the display just as Shelby got there. One of them grabbed a hat and placed it on her head.

"Look at this green one, Ester. Wouldn't it look lovely with my flowerdy dress?"

"Yes," the other one murmured, "it's nice all right. How much is it?"

Henrietta pursed her lips and lifted the hat off her head and turned it over with a frown. "There doesn't seem to be a price tag. Oh well, it's probably too—"

"Much," Ester finished for her.

"Uh-huh," agreed Henrietta with a smug nod. "Just to be sure, we'll ask the new owner when he comes back out."

Both women turned and acknowledged Shelby as she approached.

"Well, hello there," they chimed in unison.

"Hello," Shelby replied, smiling at the two. They were sisters—even though the family resemblance was hardly apparent. Henrietta was tall and thin with sharp features and a long nose; Ester liked to refer to herself as pleasantly plump. Both of the sisters' husbands had passed away within two short years of each other, and since all of their children were grown, they had decided to move in together. The arrangement seemed to be working magnificently for them. They were rarely seen apart.

"We haven't seen you in a while," said Henrietta, speaking for them both. Ester was nodding beside her.

"I've been keeping very busy with Aaron and the farm.

The sisters nodded sympathetically. "I don't suppose it'll slow down anytime soon for you with harvest right around the corner and all."

"You're right about that. In fact, I decided I'd better come into the store before things get too hectic."

"Don't you just love all the new things?" asked Ester. "It's definitely an improvement over—" and then she caught herself. "Of course, it won't ever be the same as the Millers."

"Such a shame. Such a shame," said Henrietta, shaking her head.

Shelby nodded, the comment causing the butterflies to flutter again in her stomach. "Have you met the new owners?" she asked tentatively.

"Yes," they both nodded.

Ester spoke first. "He seems very..."

"Pleasant," Henrietta added.

Shelby was just about to ask about the wife when Henrietta started flailing her arms in the air. "There he is over there," she said loudly. "Yoo hoo," she sang out in her soprano voice, causing the whole store to turn and look at her. "Can we please have some help over here?"

Shelby looked at Ester to see how she was reacting to her sister's boisterous display. Ester was craning her short neck and standing on her toes behind Henrietta with an eager expression on her face.

"Is he comin'? Is he comin'?" she added.

Color crept into Shelby's cheeks as she saw movement out of the corner of her eye and knew that the owner was approaching. She turned her back on the sisters and pretended to study one of the hats. She didn't want the owner to group her with the two sisters.

"Yes, how can I help you?"

Shelby listened with interest as the man spoke to Ester and Henrietta. He didn't seem put-out by their rudeness and instead spoke to them as if they were his most important customers. His voice was rich and smooth. She listened in fascination as he confidently sold both women a hat, which was quite a feat considering that the sisters were known to be very tight-fisted with their money.

"Isn't he just a dear?" cooed Ester.

"Yes," agreed Henrietta "We'll have to have him over for some of my famous pumpkin pie."

"Your pumpkin pie?" huffed Ester as she put her hands on her round hips. "I'm the one who does all the bakin', and you know it," she blustered.

The two went back and forth for a second or two and then stopped abruptly when the man laughed. The warmth in his tone was infectious, and Shelby felt herself grin too. The calming voice somehow evoked such a sense of familiarity.

"I'd be honored," he continued, "to join you both for some pumpkin pie."

This seemed to please the sisters.

Shelby kept her back turned and her face averted until she felt a light touch on her arm.

"Excuse me, Miss," said the voice. "Can I help you?"

She took a deep breath and pasted a polite smile on her face.

Shelby turned and stood face to face with Harlan.

Shelby's eyes widened in shock, and her mouth flew open as the color drained from her face. She started to tremble all over. "It's you," she uttered incredulously. He reached out to steady her, and she took a step backwards and lost her balance as she tumbled backwards into the rack of hats. Shelby heard one sister shriek just before she landed in a heap on top of the rack. She was still trembling when she managed to get up on her feet.

"Goodness gracious, dear," said Ester. "You look as pale as a dishrag."

"Yes," agreed Henrietta, "quite so. The poor girl needs to sit down a spell. She looks like she fixin' to faint."

Harlan nodded, taking Shelby gently by the arm. "I'll take her in the back to my office and let her sit down while I get her a glass of water."

Shelby allowed him to lead her into the back of the store, all the while keeping her eyes firmly fixed on the ground. Numbly, she sat down in a chair and tried to pull herself together. Harlan returned with the water. He handed it to her and then sat down in the seat directly facing her.

"I'm sorry about the hats," she said, raising her eyes and looking at his face.

He waved the apology away. "No harm done. They can all be picked up."

She studied his face for a moment as he spoke. He looked more mature than she remembered. He was still lean but more muscular. His features were still rugged and chiseled, but his eyes and mouth had tiny creases around the edges. His hair was still just as fair, and it still curled slightly when it reached his neck. He must've realized she was studying him. He looked at her and for a moment their eyes locked. Was she just imagining things? Or was he really looking into the depths of her soul with those penetrating eyes of his, discerning the loneliness and innermost yearnings of her heart? She broke the gaze and looked quickly down at the ground.

"I'm sorry I gave you such a shock," he began.

She raised her head. "I came to the store today to speak to the new owners." She paused to study his expression. It was carefully blank. "Of course, I had no idea it would be you."

He nodded.

A sudden thought occurred to her, but she wasn't sure how to phrase the question, and the words came tumbling out. "Is your w-wife? I mean..."

"No," he answered quickly. "I'm not married."

She nodded, strangely relieved, although it really made no difference to her. She looked up and felt her cheeks grow warm when she realized he'd been scrutinizing her. "I guess I look older," she said, without thinking and then wished she could retract the words.

He smiled slowly. "You look just as lovely as you always did."

She looked at him carefully to see if the comment had been sincere or merely polite. She couldn't tell. "Thank you," she replied, feeling as though she'd just accidentally gone fishing for a compliment. "How did you end up owning the Millers' store?

He leaned back in his chair and casually crossed his legs. "I ran Pappy's store down in Tucker for a few years after he died, and then I decided that I needed a change of pace. Some new scenery. I've been looking to buy a new store for quite some time. I have an acquaintance who knows Herschel Miller and who knew about his poor health. It's not often that an opportunity to take over a well-established store comes along." He shrugged. "One thing led to another, and, to make a long story short, I couldn't pass it up."

Shelby's head swam. Did his coming back have anything to do with her? He seemed to read her thoughts.

"I almost didn't buy the store." He looked at her and watched her face begin to flame and continued. "I just want to assure you that I didn't come here to cause you any trouble." He looked carefully at her. "Whatever happened between us is in the past."

She nodded as the cold hard knowledge of his words encircled her heart and penetrated down to her toes. She sat up stiffly in her seat. "I'm glad we got that out of the way. And I hope you find whatever it is you're looking for," she finished quickly.

"Thank you."

"Like I told you earlier, I came here today to speak with the new owner. I had a very good working relationship with the Millers, and I would like to continue that with you."

He reached over and picked up a ledger from his desk and thumbed through it. "Yes, here it is. What would you like to work out?"

She felt a twinge of frustration. He clearly wasn't going to make things easy for her. Her mouth went dry. "I always purchased my fertilizer, seed, tools, and other goods on credit and paid the Millers promptly at harvest. I would like to establish the same system with you," she said, the words spilling out quickly.

He raised his hand and began absently stroking his chin with his finger as he studied the ledger. "It looks as though you had a difficult time paying off your debt in full a couple of years ago. What happened then?"

Shelby felt the first stab of fear. Thankfully, her temper then took over. "The boll weevil ate up most of my crop that year. I had a meager harvest, but I still paid the Millers what I could, and I have absorbed the balance into each year's payment. I will be able to pay the remainder in a few weeks after this coming harvest," she finished defensively. She then sat back in her chair and waited for him to speak as she tried to read his expressionless face. The silence stretched on for a couple of seconds.

"It does appear that you have made every effort to settle your balance while keeping current. And times have been hard for everybody. I believe we can continue the same arrangement you had with the Millers without any difficulty."

She felt relief wash over her, but she kept her expression bland. "Good," she said with an impersonal tone. Thinking their conversation over, she was about to stand.

"Who is Otis Wilkerson? It looks like he has purchased ten dollars worth of goods on your account."

"He is a sharecropper on my farm. I will pay that balance after harvest as well."

He nodded. This time she stood up.

"I just have one more question."

She looked down at him with one eyebrow arched, annoyance clearly written on her face. "Yes?"

"Why did you come here all by yourself today? Where is your husband?"

This comment cut deeply, and she had to fight to keep her voice even as her eyes began to blaze. "I run the farm, and I pay all of the bills. As you can see, I am clearly capable of both tasks. Any more questions?"

His gaze met hers, and she couldn't tell if she detected admiration or amusement in those golden eyes. A slow smile started at the corner of his mouth, and for a moment she felt sixteen again. "No, I don't have any more questions for you, Mrs. Carter. I will, however, be coming out to check the crops."

She wanted to scream insults at him to wipe away his smug expression. "The Millers never found it necessary to check my crops, but if it will ease your fears, you go right ahead." The words came out clipped and tense with only the slightest hint of sarcasm. "Good day, Mr. Rhodes," she added as she turned and left his office. She couldn't be sure but thought she heard him chuckle as she closed the door.

Chapter Twenty-Six

Every other time Rayford had made a moonshine run, it had been under the cover of darkness. So when he learned that the next one would be made in broad daylight, he was more than a little concerned. There were a few questions he wanted answered: Why the sudden change of plans? Why would they risk going during the day when the same run could be done at night? For a split second, he thought about asking Bird his questions but quickly changed his mind when he glanced over at him. As usual, the younger man had a scowl on his scrawny face. He felt Rayford's gaze and sneered contemptuously back at him. A surge of anger rose in Rayford, and he felt the hair on his neck stand on ends. He didn't know why the boy was so hostile toward him and why he was so bothered by it. He chuckled out loud and then turned his back on Bird. He wasn't about to give him the satisfaction of knowing he'd gotten under his skin.

A movement from behind caught Bird and Rayford's attention, and they turned to see Wendell Meyers, the sheriff, walking toward them. Unconsciously Rayford straightened himself up and stood a little taller as he waited for the man to approach. Wendell had only been the sheriff for a couple of months. He'd replaced Sheriff Andrews who'd been the sheriff for as long as Rayford could remember. The talk around town had been that Sheriff Andrews had resigned because he refused to take orders from Bobby Ray. But Rayford had overheard someone suggest this to the sheriff, and he'd scoffed at the idea. He said he was too old to be running a town and wanted to spend some time fishing. His explanation had seemed reasonable enough at the time, but seeing Wendell Meyers here made

Rayford wonder. This must be a pretty important run if the sheriff was getting involved.

The sheriff was of medium build and had short, thick hair that was more salt than pepper. His neatly trimmed mustache was as thick as the hair on his head and the same color. An intelligent light flickered in his gray eyes as he surveyed Rayford and Bird.

"Howdy," he uttered in a baritone voice that seemed to grumble from somewhere deep inside his barrel chest.

Rayford extended his hand. "Sheriff, this is indeed a surprise."

A brief smile, stopping short of his eyes, curved underneath the sheriff's mustache as he nodded curtly. If Rayford had expected a lengthy explanation as to why the sheriff was there, then he was sorely disappointed, because the sheriff quickly lost interest in him. He shook Rayford's hand, not bothering to make eye contact with him. Instead, his eyes scanned the transport truck. He walked over to it and pulled away the tarp and gave a low whistle.

"We shouldn't have any trouble runnin' the shipment with this," he said to no one in particular.

Rayford stepped up to the truck and peered over the bed. His breath caught as he realized what was lying in the bottom. "It's a coffin."

The sheriff laughed and then pounded the top once with his hand. "Yesiree, this here's a genuine solid pine coffin loaded full of one hundred fifty proof rye moonshine."

"Why are we runnin' this during the day?" Rayford asked. "And why in a coffin?"

"Word's out that the revenuers are on the prowl. A couple of men were picked up last night outside of Albertville. A couple of gallons of whiskey were confiscated."

This last comment caught Bird's attention. "A couple of gallons? That's small potatoes," he scoffed as he spit on the ground.

"Yeah," the sheriff continued, "unfortunately though, it's those small operators that make things hard for the rest of us."

"I thought Bobby Ray had an arrangement worked out with the revenuers so they wouldn't cause us any trouble," said Rayford uneasily.

"Some new big shot, probably tryin' to make a name for hisself, has been shootin' his mouth around town, saying that he's gonna find hisself a still," said the sheriff, looking at Bird as some sort of unspoken exchange passed between them. "I guess he don't understand how we do business in these parts," he added.

Bird chuckled. "He'll learn soon enough, I reckon."

Rayford was still uneasy about the whole situation. "Why don't we wait until things cool off to haul another load?"

"What's wrong, ol' man?" Bird goaded. "Are ya yella?"

Rayford shot Bird a hard look and focused his attention on the sheriff. "I just wanna make sure we're not runnin' into a trap."

"Trap or no trap, we've got a run to make," said the sheriff. "Our customers don't care about the revenuers. They want their whiskey, and they want it delivered on time."

"I dunno," said Rayford. He shook his head, his stomach knotting with apprehension. "I'm not too sure about this. Why not wait and run it tonight?"

The sheriff was growing impatient with Rayford. His jaw hardened. "Bobby Ray thinks it'll be safer during the day." He patted his pocket. "And I've got an order from the county health official forbiddin' the openin' of this here coffin." He looked at Rayford, his gray eyes narrowing dangerously, daring him to protest any further.

Rayford glanced over at Bird who was leaning against the truck using his knife to clean underneath his fingernails. A mixture of open curiosity and eagerness flickered in his cold eyes. Rayford realized with a start that he was alone with these two men. There wasn't another person or house around for miles. He felt like a piece of raw meat dangling between two coon dogs. "I don't have a problem with makin' the run," he said, trying to keep his voice neutral.

The sheriff eyed him for a moment, then his shoulders relaxed. Bird sensed the change too; he looked disappointed.

"I knew you'd see it my way," the sheriff said, slapping Rayford on the back. "Now come on. Let's get this show on the road."

*   *   *   *   *

Rayford grasped hold of the side of the truck to keep from being catapulted forward as the truck came to an abrupt halt, causing the heavy coffin to slide forward. He scurried over to the side and pressed himself into the truck to keep from being mashed by the heavy object. He rose up to see what was happening and felt his heart drop when he saw that the road was blocked by two cars up ahead. He counted four men. The sheriff got out the truck as one of the men came walking up to the driver's side to meet him.

"What's the trouble?" the sheriff grumbled.

The man ignored him and instead walked around to the back where Rayford was sitting.

"What ya got there?"

Rayford placed his hand above his eyes as a shield to block out the glaring sun as he tried to get a better look at the man. He looked to be in his early twenties and was short and small-boned. His pasty, white skin was a stark contrast to his dark hair. The man's most prominent feature was an inch-long jagged scar that traced the pattern of his angular cheek-bone. Rayford's blood chilled when he saw that the man was holding a rifle in his smooth, woman-like hands.

"I asked you what you're carryin'."

"What does it look like?" the sheriff snarled as another man with a rifle walked around the other side of the truck. Bird opened up the passenger door and got out.

"Open it up," demanded the small man, pointing at the coffin.

Rayford's face tensed.

"I don't think that would be wise," said the sheriff, pulling a paper from his pocket. "I have an order here from the county health official forbiddin' us to open this here coffin due to a highly contagious disease."

The man snatched the paper from the sheriff's grasp. He skimmed over it and then scoffed. "What disease does the body have?"

This caught the sheriff off-guard, and he looked at Bird for help. Bird just stood there speechless. Rayford found his voice quickly.

"Yellow jack," he blurted.

"That's right," the sheriff interjected quickly.

The revenuer eyed the three men warily. "Yellow jack, huh. What kind of a fool do ya'll take me for? Yellow jack hasn't been around these parts for at least twenty years. Now open it up!" he yelled, pointing the rifle at Rayford.

The sheriff was at a loss for words, and there was a glimmer of fear in his eyes. Rayford knew it was up to him to save them. "Are you sure about that?" he asked smoothly, despite the fact that his heart felt as though it would pound through his chest. The sliver of doubt he saw edge across the revenuer's face gave him courage to continue. He jumped out of the truck and stood in front of the revenuer.

"Maybe you're right." Rayford paused. "But what if you're wrong?" He shook his head. "I ain't willin' to take that chance." He looked at the sheriff. "That yellow jack is some nasty stuff. Remember Ed Polk? He was perfectly healthy, never seen a doctor a day in his life, and stone cold dead three days later. Started out havin' a headache and stomach trouble. Then he got a high fever." Rayford shook his head. "I still remember 'im sweatin' like a horse, shakin' and cryin' like a baby."

Rayford looked at the revenuer, who still looked unconvinced. He continued, "And that's when the pain started. Poor man hurt so bad in his loins. Well, you get the idea. And that's when he turned yellow."

The revenuer's eyes begin to fill with hesitation, and Rayford knew he was starting to believe him.

"Then he started bleedin'." Rayford noted with satisfaction that the man on the other side of the truck took a step backwards away from the truck.

"Bleeding?" the revenuer asked.

"Yeah, from his nose, ears, and every other place you can imagine. And in his final moments, he started vomitin'."

The revenuer's jaw slacked.

"Black vile with thick chunks. It like he was chokin' on his own insides." Rayford shuddered. "Like I said, I ain't takin' no chances, but if you want to..."

The revenuer was in a tight spot. He knew there was no way any of his men would dare open that coffin now, and he certainly didn't want to do it himself. He looked steadily at Rayford and then at the sheriff. "All right," he hissed, "get outta here. If I ever see you around here again, you'd better not be haulin' no coffin."

The three men nodded, and the revenuers walked back to their cars. The sheriff looked at Rayford with a new admiration, and as Rayford started to climb back into the truck, he grabbed his shirt.

"Bird," the sheriff hissed, "get in the back. Rayford's ridin' up front with me."

"You're going out? I thought you were going to stay home and have supper with us tonight. My family is going to be here. Don't you remember? We talked about it," Shelby said, trying hard to keep the pleading out of her voice.

Rayford looked up at Shelby, his eyes not meeting hers, and then looked back down at his shoes. He'd found that in these types of situations it was better to act preoccupied. Another time he might've relented and stayed home, but he had a run to make. "I'm sorry, darlin'. Something's come up," he answered while giving his boot a swift tug over his heel. Then he began tightening his laces.

Normally Shelby would've just given up, but her visit with Harlan had made her realize just how lacking her relationship was with Rayford. She had to try to do all she could to fix things. "It would mean a lot to Aaron if you'd stay." She paused. "And to me."

"Since when do you care what I do?"

She was always amazed at how quickly his anger could flare. He was like a stick of dynamite waiting for the littlest spark to ignite. She felt her anger surface and then pushed it away. Every time she tried to confront Rayford about anything he goaded her into becoming angry. She didn't want this conversation to end the same way. She had to get through to him somehow. She kept the tone of her voice even. "When we start the harvest next week, I won't get to see Mama or anyone for a couple of weeks or so. We thought it would be nice to get together here for a change instead of going over there. I just thought you might enjoy visiting with everyone, and I'm making sweet potato pie—just for you."

His dark eyes looked her up and down briefly and then back down at his boots. Even he had to admit that she was truly magnificent looking. "I should've known," he said nastily.

"Known what?"

"You never get dressed up for me." He stood up. "You never do anything for me. All that you care about is your precious family."

There was a time when his spiteful comments would've reduced her to tears but not anymore. "It's hard to care about someone who's never here," she said quietly. "Maybe if you could just stay home more, then we—"

His abrasive laugh interrupted her mid-sentence. "I probably would stay home." He made his way to the back door where he turned and looked back over his shoulder. "If I had anything worth staying home for." He then went out, slamming the door behind him.

Shelby stood for a moment, staring at the door until she heard a muffled sob from behind. She turned to see Aaron, his face red, trying to choke back the tears. She went to him and gathered him in her arms. "Your papa didn't mean those awful things, honey," she said as she stroked his hair. "He's just angry at me. Sometimes people say things they don't mean. You know that your papa loves you, don't you?"

He looked up at her and nodded, the hurt evident in his eyes.

"I am so sorry," she said, rocking him gently back and forth. This time the tears came, pooling in her eyes before flowing down her cheeks. But her tears weren't for Rayford; they were for her precious son whom she loved more than anything in the world. How could she explain things to him when she didn't even understand them herself?

*   *   *   *   *

"When are they gonna get here?"

Shelby wiped her hands on her apron and then looked down at Aaron and smiled. "They should be here any minute now."

Aaron began to jump up and down excitedly. "Good, 'cause I'm real hungry."

Shelby tousled his dark hair. "Me too," she agreed. "Why don't you go to the front window and look for them? Holler when you see them pulling up."

He let out a whoop and then ran out of the kitchen.

After the episode that had taken place earlier, she had wondered how Rayford's hateful words would affect Aaron. Thankfully, he was still at the age where he was very resilient. He was so excited about everyone coming to supper that he seemed to have forgotten all about it. Unfortunately for her, she couldn't forget. She had grown immune to the spiteful words and accusations he was constantly hurling at her, but seeing Aaron's anguish had nearly brought her to her wit's end. She brushed a loose curl from her damp forehead and leaned over to take her pie out of the oven. Rayford wouldn't have acted so hateful if he'd known Aaron was listening. He loved his son. That much she knew.

She took the steaming pot of potatoes off the stove and placed a plate over the top and held it just right as she tilted the pot over the sink to drain off the excess water. Then she removed the plate and began mashing the potatoes with her fork before adding a thick, chunk of fresh butter and some milk.

"They're here! They're here!"

Quickly, she transferred the potatoes to a bowl and then added a couple of dashes of salt and pepper. "I'm coming," she yelled as she wiped her hands and headed for the door.

*   *   *   *   *

Homer leaned back in his chair and patted his stomach appreciatively. "Sis, those were some mighty good vittles."

Shelby's face lit up as she smiled at the compliment. "Why thank you, Homer. I hope you saved room for some sweet potato pie."

"Yes, ma'am," he answered."

"I saved room too," Aaron answered."

"I hope you'll be cookin' meals next week when I'm here pickin'," said Homer.

Sarah rolled her eyes. She was still sore about having to help. "You can dream," she said nastily.

John chuckled and looked at Shelby. "Speaking of picking, did you find any help?"

"Yes," answered Shelby, nodding as she began clearing the dishes off the table. "I went over to Eastlake and rounded up some pickers."

"I hope you didn't go by yourself," Ellen interjected.

Shelby began slicing her pie and placing them on plates. She began handing them out. She did go by herself to Eastlake, but she didn't want to worry her mama. "Everything was fine," she answered reassuringly, looking at Ellen.

During harvest time, people would come by the dozens to a little place that was just outside of Guntersville known as Eastlake. It was named appropriately because it was nothing more than a little place on the east bank of Guntersville Lake. They would camp out for a month or so, picking cotton for the local farmers. Most came from Mississippi and Tennessee, but occasionally there'd be people who had come from as far as Louisiana. They would stay for the entire picking season, making as much money as they could, and would then pack up and head back to wherever it was they'd come from.

Concern flickered over John's lean face as he put the first piece of pie in his mouth. "You just make sure you keep a good eye out. Some of those transient workers can't be trusted. Are they going to stay here at the farm?"

Shelby nodded. "I told them they could make their camp down by the stream on the other side of the fields. That way they can have their own space, and we can still have our privacy."

"The whole thing makes me nervous," said Ellen.

"I don't especially like it either," said Shelby, "but we've been doing the same thing for several years now, and it has always worked out just fine. With the Wilkersons and the additional field hands, we should be in good shape."

"Don't forget about Homer and Sarah," added Ellen.

After everyone had eaten dessert, Shelby got up from the table and began washing the dishes.

Ellen nudged her youngest daughter. "Go and help Shelby dry those dishes."

Reluctantly, Sarah got up to go help.

"Shelby, how did your meeting with the new store owner go the other day?" John asked.

"Just fine," she answered as her face grew warm.

"I've only been in the store once, but he seems like a decent fellow. I figured it would work out. I'll bet that store owner took one look at you and could tell what a fine, upstanding young lady you are."

"Thank you," she uttered, barely looking over her shoulder at him. Her face was scarlet now, and she kept her back turned to John as he spoke and tried to concentrate on the dishes. She pulled out a dish too quickly, causing the suds to go all over Sarah.

"Hey, watch it," Sarah wailed.

"What is his name?" asked Ellen.

John scratched his head, trying to remember. "I believe it's Harry or Henry or something like that."

"It's Harlan," answered Shelby flatly.

"Yes," that's right," exclaimed John. "Harlan what?"

Shelby had dreaded this moment ever since she'd realized that Harlan was the new store owner. She'd almost convinced herself that Mama would never remember his name—after all it was so long ago. She took a deep breath and let it out slowly as she handed Sarah a dish to dry. "His name is Harlan Rhodes," she said as she plunged her hands into the soapy water to retrieve another dish.

Ellen's brow creased as she repeated the name to herself as she searched her memory. "Harlan Rhodes." She looked over at John. "That name sounds so familiar. Do we know him?"

John shrugged. "I don't think so. He's from somewhere down in south Alabama."

Homer decided to add his two cent's worth into the conversation. "Well, I'm not all that concerned about the new owner. Have you seen that pretty, little red-head that he brought with him? She's a real looker."

"Homer," Ellen exclaimed. She was about ready to sorely reprimand him, but the sound of breaking glass stopped her. Ellen looked up at Shelby in surprise just in time to catch the look of shock flicker across her daughter's ashen face. Ellen's eyes met Shelby's for a brief second, and then Shelby looked quickly down at the floor as she reached for a kitchen towel to pick up the pieces of the plate that she'd accidentally shattered into a thousand, tiny pieces all over the floor.

Chapter Twenty-Seven

He loved her. At least he acted as if he did.

Mary Kate sat perfectly straight with her back slightly arched as she let her long, silky, red hair curl around her brush. Mechanically, she finished her usual one hundred strokes as she studied her reflection in the mirror. She was pretty, she decided, as she batted her long eyelashes. Some might even consider her beautiful with her clear, green, even-set eyes and milky white complexion. In her youth, only her freckles had marred her perfect face; but now, quite to her satisfaction, only a hint of them remained, giving her face a unique, girlish quality which she rather liked. She looked down at her stubby fingernails and frowned. If only she could kick the habit of biting her nails. Her mind went back to the dilemma that had been plaguing her for some time.

She studied her reflection again and then formed her full lips into a pout as she thought about Harlan. It was hard to believe that she'd known him for over a year now; and yet, in some ways, she felt she hardly knew him at all. Just when she would think she was beginning to get through, he would get that faraway gaze in his eyes, and she would know that he was beyond her grasp.

It had been a rainy night in June when they had met. The rain had been coming down in sheets, and lightning lit up the sky as she drove her horses as hard as she could to try to find shelter from the storm. The wind was raging so fiercely she could hardly keep hold of the reins, and the hail was battering the top of her carriage. What in tarnation had made her think she wanted to move to Alabama? The tales her ma had told of Alabama over the years had been so romantic and exciting.

"A land of milk and honey," her ma had said. "Beautiful trees and flowers with lush moss on the banks of beautiful, rolling streams."

She scoffed at the memory. All that she had seen in Alabama since she had arrived from out west was red mud, lightning, and rain. If there were any flowers around, the hailstorm had surely taken care of that.

Mary Kate brushed the wet curls from her forehead as she jumped from the carriage and grabbed the reins. If she could just get under that covered bridge in the distance, she could wait out the storm there. With all her might, she tugged on the reins as the horses fought against her. She took a step backward and lost her footing and landed in the mud. Luckily, the reins were still wrapped around her wrist. She began shrieking and cursing at the horses at the top of her lungs, but her voice seemed to get swallowed up in the storm. Finally, she managed to get herself and the horses under the bridge where she stood shivering in the dark. The horses were still fussing over the lightning, and it took all of her effort to keep hold of the reins. Her hair was matted to her head, and her cloak clung to her voluptuous form.

"Hello there," said the soft, southern drawl of a male voice. Startled, Mary Kate turned to see the silhouette of a man so handsome she could hardly breathe.

"Well, hello to you," she countered without any inhibitions. Then she recognized the silhouette—he was the same man she had seen in the country store where she'd stopped to buy supplies earlier in the day. She had sauntered around him a few times so that he would see her, but he'd hardly seemed to notice she was alive.

Mary Kate's heart lurched as a bolt of lightning split a nearby tree. She jumped forward, just far enough to be standing nose to nose with the handsome stranger. "Fancy meeting you here," she said.

He smiled briefly, his tan, rugged face revealing straight, white teeth. Then, as quickly as it had come, his smile faded as he turned his attention to the horses. "You must've been driving these horses pretty hard."

It irked her that he seemed more interested in the horses than in her. "I was trying to get out of the storm," she said defensively. She was not used to being ignored in this manner. Where were those southern manners her ma had always talked about? Maybe her ma had dreamed up all that stuff she'd told all those years about polite, southern gentlemen.

Harlan stayed with her during the storm. Then he helped her get the horses to the blacksmith and even got her a room at the local inn. She waited around a few days to see if he would stop by and check on her. When he didn't, she went to the store.

The first comment out of his mouth when he first saw her was: "Well, how are those horses?" Then he casually mentioned that he could use some help at the general store if she needed a job.

That had been the beginning of their relationship. They were always together at the store, and when they started going places together, she'd assumed they would get engaged and eventually marry. But she never could seem to pin Harlan down. Whenever she broached the subject, he became evasive. And then out of the blue he told her that he was buying a new store in a dinky, little town she'd never even heard of.

"You can come along if you want," he had said. "I could always use your help."

So here she sat, pining away in some remote Alabama town, hoping for some teensy sign of affection or commitment from a man who was as elusive as the wind. He seemed to enjoy her company most of the time. Then she would see that faraway look in his eye that she was coming to dread. At first she'd dismissed it as a foolish fancy on her part. But now she wasn't so sure. It was as if she were battling with some ghost or phantom which she couldn't see, but which was very real nevertheless.

She walked over to the window and brushed aside the curtain. The leaves were just starting to turn. She watched the heavy branches sway back and forth in the wind and then let the curtain go. She was just being foolish. Maybe she was just antsy because for the first time in her life she'd fallen in love. Yes, she told herself fiercely, that must be it. Harlan wouldn't have asked her to come here if he didn't care about her. Maybe he thought this place would be perfect for them to start fresh. She'd never been much of a churchgoer but thought it might help speed things up a bit if she were more involved in the community. If everyone around them thought they were engaged, then it might push Harlan in that direction. She clenched her fists as her plan began to take shape. She was starting to feel better already.

Mary Kate left the window and sat down again in front of the mirror; and as she swept up her voluminous red hair into a chignon, she brushed all of her doubts aside.

Everything was right with the world again.

*　*　*　*　*

If Mary Kate had learned anything from the countless dull social gatherings her mother had forced her to attend during her growing-up years it was this: The best way to attract attention was to arrive at the function fashionably late. She'd learned from one of the customers at the store that church started at ten o'clock, so she intentionally arrived five minutes late. She wanted to let everyone else get seated before she made her dramatic entrance.

She tugged on the reins of the carriage for the horses to stop as she watched the last stragglers make their way into the church. She reached up and adjusted her hat so that it would sit properly on her head, and then she reached down and tugged at one of her stockings. She'd ordered the new dress she was wearing all the way from Atlanta. It had cost nearly half a month's salary, but she didn't care. From the first moment she'd seen it in the catalog, she'd known that the deep emerald color would set off her eyes perfectly, and besides, money had never been a big issue for her. She'd grown up wealthy enough. Harlan was always teasing her about being born with a silver spoon in her mouth. She'd never really been that concerned about wealth or social status. In fact, she'd really never been that concerned about anything—that is, until she met Harlan.

When she'd told Harlan she was going to church, he'd jokingly replied. "Those poor people won't know what hit 'em."

She had invited him to come with her, all the while knowing that he wouldn't.

Gingerly, she stepped down from her carriage. The dress was a little snug through the hips, and the last thing she wanted to do was to rip it getting out. When she got to the door, she took a quick breath before lifting her chin and sauntering down the aisle to the very front row.

"Let me be the first to welcome you to our little church," said Mildred Tucker as she walked over and extended her hand to Mary Kate.

"Thank you. It really is quite lovely," Mary Kate said as she glanced at the Reverend's wife and noticed the woman's bright, red hair. It was the color of carrots. A horrendous color job like that could've only come from a bottle. Mary Kate guessed she probably bought it from the peddler.

"I'm so glad to see you here," continued Mildred. "I heard some of the other ladies mentioning that it was such a shame that the new store owner and his...his..." She paused as she stumbled over her words, not really sure how to address Mary Kate.

"His fiancée," Mary Kate finished for her.

Mildred's eyes widened. "Oh, I didn't realize. Please forgive me, but then again," she looked down at Mary Kate's naked, ring finger, "I didn't see a ring."

In any other circumstance, Mary Kate would've put this meddling snob, who obviously had a much too high opinion of herself, in her place so quickly it would've made her head spin, but experience told her that if she wanted to get anywhere in this town it would be through this woman. So, she swallowed a scathing retort and smiled sweetly instead.

"Harlan has been so busy with the store that he hasn't had time to get me a ring." She sighed. "I suppose he could've gone to that sweet, little jewelry store over in Albertville, but because he knows that I have such peculiar taste, he wants to wait a few months until we take a buying trip to Atlanta," she finished as her eyes met Mildred's in an open challenge.

Mildred was clearly impressed. Her red lips formed into a big smile. "I agree one hundred percent. The right ring says so much." She leaned over and whispered. "You wouldn't be able to find anything worth having in that hole-in-the wall place." She stood back up straight. Her eyes flickered over Mary Kate's dress. "It's so refreshing to meet someone who has some fashion sense. Some of these poor people dress so dreadfully." She shuddered. Mildred cut her conversation short when she saw Henrietta Potts and Ester

Whitaker. She became annoyed when she realized they were making their way toward them.

"Now, Mildred, you need to stop hogging Miss Simpson all to yourself," said Ester.

"I was welcoming our guest," answered Mildred dryly.

Mary Kate extended her hand in greeting, and Ester reached and hugged her tightly instead. "It is so good to see you here today, dear."

"Where is Mr. Rhodes?" Henrietta asked.

"He couldn't come today. He is unloading some supplies that came in the other day." As soon as the words left her mouth, Mary Kate realized she'd made a serious mistake. Henrietta's smile turned to a tight frown and her dark eyebrows knitted together as she shook her head in disapproval.

"The Sabbath is a day of worship, not a day of work," she said stiffly.

"Now, Henrietta, don't be rude to our new guest," added Ester.

Mildred looked at Mary Kate and rolled her eyes as the two sisters began arguing back and forth.

"Our annual harvest party will be held in two weeks," said Mildred, interrupting the sisters. This diverted their attention, and they stopped arguing and looked at Mildred.

"I hope you'll come," said Ester.

"We could use some help serving refreshments," added Henrietta.

Mildred looked appalled. "I hardly think that it's appropriate to ask Miss Simpson to serve refreshments."

"Well, I always help serve, and if you ask me, I think it's a right Christian thing to do," replied Henrietta huffily.

Mary Kate winked conspiratorially at Mildred and then smiled brightly at the sisters. "I'd be honored to help."

The sisters moved on, leaving Mildred and Mary Kate alone again. Mildred linked her arm through Mary Kate's and patted her on the arm. "Come and meet my husband, and then I want you to meet the other ladies of the community. A group of us get together every Thursday afternoon for tea. I just know you're going to love it here," she cooed.

Chapter Twenty-Eight

Brown tobacco juice dribbled like mud down the corner of Otis' mouth. He wiped it off with his sleeve as he muttered to himself about Shelby. "Somebody needs to teach that gal a lesson. If she had a real man to keep her in place." His thoughts began to drift.

"Get goin'," he yelled at the horses as he jerked the reins. "We gotta get this cotton to the gin fore dark."

He'd thought it was going to be easy to outdo Miss Shelby that first day he'd come to the farm. How wrong he'd been. It seemed the harder things got on the farm, the tougher she got. He shook his head. She was always right there over his shoulder checking the weights and watching everything he did. It was her fault he had to resort to gambling and stealing. What else could a man do who had to work for a slave driver like her for practically nothing? He leaned over the wagon and spit. It didn't matter to him that she was paying him more than he'd ever been paid in his life.

Otis yelled at the horses again. He had taken too much time unloading the cotton in the shack outside town. Every time he took a load of cotton to the gin, he'd stop by the shack first and unload some of it. He frowned. Lately, he had begun to worry that she was on to him. It wasn't anything he could put his finger on, just instinct. His thoughts returned to his stash of cotton. Just a few more wagonloads were all it would take. Then he planned on taking his family and leaving in the middle of the night.

"Hello, Otis!" shouted Mr. Jenkins. "You're running late, aren't you?"

"Yep, I reckon so," retorted Otis, spitting tobacco juice as he spoke.

Mr. Jenkins' upper lip curled slightly in disdain. He disliked tobacco, and he disliked Otis even more. Why on earth did Miss Shelby put up with the likes of him?

"Pull the wagon up on the scales!" Mr. Jenkins hollered, not masking the disapproval in his voice.

Otis could see that Mr. Jenkins had a puzzled expression on his face as he studied the scale. "What's the matter?" he asked as innocently as he could muster.

"I'm not sure," answered Mr. Jenkins as he squinted. "Perhaps I'm misreading the scales. Wait a minute till I get my glasses." He finished the sentence in almost a whisper.

"I don't have all night," Otis huffed.

Mr. Jenkins carefully wrote down the weight, and then waved Otis off. "All right, that's it."

He waited until Otis left and then turned to his foreman. "Tom, something is wrong. This makes the fifth season I've ginned Miss Shelby's cotton, and her weights have never varied more than fifty pounds. This makes the fourth bale this season that has been almost two hundred pounds short. I think it's time she and I had a visit."

*   *   *   *   *

Shelby was up bright and early as usual. She wanted to get all the breakfast dishes cleared away before heading to the field to check on the workers and especially on Otis. He'd gotten home late from the gin, so she'd not had an opportunity to speak with him. Hopefully he was already in the field picking cotton.

A brisk knock on the back door gave her a start. She opened the door and was surprised to see Tom Brown, Mr. Jenkins' foreman standing on the steps.

"Mr. Brown, this is surprise. What brings you all the way out here this morning?"

Mr. Brown tilted his head toward Shelby and touched his hat. "Mr. Jenkins would like to speak with you, ma'am."

Shelby's eyes widened. "Today?" She knew it must be important because Mr. Jenkins, of all people, could appreciate how busy she was during cotton picking time. Her mind began to race. "Is something wrong?" she managed to ask.

"I'm not sure why he sent me," lied Tom. He wasn't about to tell her about Mr. Jenkins' suspicions.

"Tell Mr. Jenkins I'll be there as soon as possible," she replied. "I have some things I need to check on first."

"Yes, ma'am."

A feeling of foreboding enveloped Shelby as she watched Mr. Brown mount his horse, tip his hat to her, and ride off.

Shelby arrived at the gin shortly after lunch dressed in a tailored, navy dress and hat trimmed in white. Mr. Jenkins stood when she entered the room. He had seen many ladies in his time, but Miss Shelby was at the top of his list. She was truly the most beautiful woman, both inside and out, he'd ever met. His admiration of her had begun five years earlier when she had walked into his gin and negotiated a contract for her cotton. He had to admit that she was as smart as she was beautiful.

"Come in and sit down," he said almost breathlessly.

Shelby smiled. "Hello, Mr. Jenkins," she said as she held out a white, gloved hand. "I know this must be something of great importance for you to request an audience at this busy time of year."

Mr. Jenkins cleared his throat. "Miss Shelby, I think we have a real problem."

"I'm afraid I don't understand," she said, puzzled at his statement.

"It's your cotton," he stammered.

Shelby almost rose from her chair as she spoke. "My cotton is probably the highest quality I have ever seen in these parts."

"Oh no, it's not that" he interjected quickly. "The cotton is great. It's just that every bale Otis has brought in has been anywhere from 150 to 200 pounds short."

"But that's impossible," she cried. "Mr. Jenkins, we've been doing business for five years, and you know that I have never come up that short. I always check the scales myself before I send a wagonload to the gin."

"Yes, I know. That's why I wanted to talk to you." He paused and looked directly at her. "How well do you know this Otis fella?"

"Not very well. Or very long," she admitted.

He nodded. "That's what I thought. I'm afraid he's cheating you."

She shook her head. "But how?"

"Oh, I've seen this happen before. Some scoundrel like Otis steals a few pounds from each bale and stores it away until the end of the season. Then he takes the bale to a neighboring town where no one knows him and sells it as his own," he explained.

Realization swept over Shelby, bringing a wave of nausea with it. She stood up to leave. Mr. Jenkins' explanation would certainly explain Otis' behavior as of late. He insisted on going to the gin alone and always returned later than he should.

"Thank you, Mr. Jenkins," she said, smoothing the bodice of her dress. "Let me know how short I am, and I'll bring in the extra cotton."

*　　*　　*　　*　　*

Mary Kate's heart skipped a beat as she felt Harlan's arms encircle her waist. A thrilling sensation raced down her spine as his lips nuzzled her ear.

"What'cha say we close up a little early this afternoon?" His eyes surveyed the empty store. "We probably won't have many more customers today. Everyone's too busy pickin' cotton. And I'd like to take the prettiest girl in town to Albertville to get a bite to eat this evenin'."

Her eyes twinkled as she reveled in his compliment and in the excitement of going on a spontaneous outing. She turned around to face him. "This isn't like you," she teased, "closing the store early."

"So you don't want to go?"

She looked up in alarm for a split second, and then a broad smile broke out across her face when she saw the mischievous glitter in his eyes.

"Oh no," she said quickly before he could change his mind. "I want to go." She reached back to untie her apron. "I'll just go and get fixed up."

As soon as the words left her mouth, the front door opened and in walked a customer. She scowled and shot a nasty look at the woman.

This brought a chuckle and smile from Harlan. He had grown accustomed to Mary Kate's outbursts, and when he spoke his voice took on a soothing quality, as if he were speaking to a child. "Go and wait on her, and I'll go and put up the closed sign."

Her frown instantly disappeared and was replaced by a smile. "Mrs. Sutherland," she said brightly, "it's good to see you. What can I get for you today?"

Harlan stepped out the front door just in time to see Shelby pass by in her wagon going full speed. He stood and watched the wagon until it disappeared in a cloud of dust and then frowned. He couldn't put his finger on it, but something—maybe it was the way her jaw was set—just didn't seem right.

He walked back into the store and nodded curtly to Louise Sutherland and then turned to Mary Kate.

"Did Mrs. Drake's fabric ever come in?"

She nodded affirmatively.

"How about Mrs. Carter's?"

"Yes, it came in the same shipment with Mrs. Drake's fabric." She looked at him questioningly. "Don't you remember? You just unloaded it the other day. It's in the back. Why?"

"Something's come up. I've got to step out for a little while."

"What?" she exploded, forgetting all about the customer standing next to her. "What about our plans?" Her eyes narrowed angrily, and her full lips formed into a pout.

"It'll have to wait," answered Harlan as he walked briskly past her to the back of the store, ignoring the sour expression on her beet-red face.

* * * * *

Shelby lost no time in getting back to the farm. She got out of the wagon as quickly as she could, hurried up the steps, and went inside where she found Rayford sitting at the kitchen table finishing off a biscuit left over from breakfast.

"I'm so glad you're home," she said breathlessly.

He raised an eyebrow and didn't even bother looking up at her. "To what do I owe this greeting?"

She pulled up a chair and sat down across from him. "It's about the farm," she began.

He looked at her but didn't say anything, so she continued. "I just came from the gin. Mr. Jenkins thinks Otis is stealing from us."

His eyes turned back down to the table as he dipped his biscuit into a pool of sorghum syrup before shoving it in his mouth.

"Did you hear what I just said? Otis is stealing from us," she repeated slowly, her voice raising a fraction.

He shrugged and then polished off the last of his biscuit before getting up from the table and putting his plate in the sink.

She threw up her hands in frustration. "Don't you even care?" she cried angrily.

He turned around to face her and leaned his back against the sink. "What do you expect me to do about it?"

"I want you to go with me to confront him."

Rayford smirked. "Sorry, this is your problem. You hired him without my help so you can fire him without my help," he said as he undid his tie.

In another circumstance she might've wondered where he'd gone dressed in a shirt and tie, but today she was too upset to care.

"I should've known better than to think I could depend on you for anything!" she yelled as she stormed out of the kitchen. "I'll take care of this myself," she muttered under her breath as she went to her bedroom to change clothes. She sat down on the bed and angrily wiped away the hot tears which were spilling down her cheeks. "I have to get a hold of myself," she uttered, taking a deep breath.

She didn't know what had possessed her to ask for Rayford's help in the first place. She had known how he would react before she'd even asked him. Maybe she should get John to go with her. She quickly dismissed the thought. She hated to bother him. *He does so much already*, she told herself. Deep down she knew she wouldn't ask him because every time he came to her aid, it brought home the realization that he was forced to help because her own husband was too much of a coward to rise to the occasion.

She feared Otis' reaction, and an icy fear stabbed at her, which she tried to push away. Just take things one step at a time, she told herself as she stood up and walked over and opened the chifforobe to retrieve her work clothes.

Considering the day she'd had, it came as no surprise to Shelby when she couldn't find Otis or his family working in the fields where they should've been. She walked over to the section where Homer was working. He was bent over with his bag.

"Have you seen Otis or his family?" she yelled.

He wiped his brow and stood up. "Naw, Sis, haven't seen any of 'em all day."

She shook her head in disgust, her frustration reaching a boiling point.

"Do you want me to help find him?" Homer yelled, but his offer fell on deaf ears. Shelby had already turned her back on him and was heading back to her wagon.

*　　*　　*　　*　　*

Shelby headed to the house where Otis and his family lived. "Hello!" she yelled as she pounded on the door. A few seconds went by, and no one came to the door. She knocked again and waited. Nothing. Just as she turned to leave, Ola Mae opened the door.

"Ma'am, can I help you?" she asked timidly.

Even though Shelby wasn't very tall herself, she felt as if she towered over the shriveled woman.

"Is Otis here?"

Ola Mae's eyed darted back and forth nervously. "No, he ain't here right now."

"Do you know where he is?" Shelby asked impatiently.

"No, ma'am," Ola Mae answered, looking down at the ground.

"I looked for him in the fields, but he's not there."

Ola Mae stood silently staring at the ground.

"Why aren't you working today?"

Ola Mae looked pleadingly at Shelby. Shelby could tell that Ola Mae was trying to tell her something. The woman seemed to be growing more nervous by the second. What was she afraid of?

"I'm sorry," Ola Mae whispered.

This perplexed Shelby. "Sorry? Sorry for what?" Ola Mae shook her head. Shelby felt a twinge of alarm. "You know what Otis is doing, don't you?"

"He said he was goin' to get even with you," Ola Mae said quietly, looking from side to side, as if she feared that Otis was hiding out, listening to her.

"For what?" asked Shelby in astonishment.

"He don't have to have no reason, ma'am."

Panic gripped Shelby's heart. She knew Otis was mean, but to have his wife confirm her fears was almost more than she could take. She swallowed hard. "What is he going to do?"

Ola Mae shook her head.

Shelby grasped her shoulder. "You have to tell me," she begged.

"I cain't say no more." She retreated away from Shelby's touch as she closed the door in her face.

*   *   *   *   *

I'm going to be black and blue from carrying this wretched water bucket, Sarah thought as the heavy bucket hit against her leg each time she took a step. She reached up and pulled her collar away from her damp neck. Her skin was burning, and her head ached. She couldn't understand why anyone in his right mind would choose to live on a farm. She lifted her chin up sharply, causing her blonde hair to bounce lightly on her shoulders. She wouldn't spend her life wasting away on some farm. She was going to marry someone rich who had a nice house in town. Or maybe she'd become an actress. She smiled as she imagined all of the fancy dresses and hats she would buy, forgetting for a moment about the cumbersome bucket she was carrying.

When she heard the field hands complaining they'd run out of water, she volunteered to go up to the well to get more. She figured she would walk slowly, taking as much time as she could, to make the day go by faster.

Her thoughts turned to her two closest friends, Maddie and Rachel, who both lived in town. They had never been forced to pick cotton a day in their lives. She frowned as she pictured their reactions to her sunburned cheeks and then pulled her straw hat further down on her head.

She walked by a wild apple tree and bent down to pick one up. They were all green. Her mama had warned her against eating green apples, telling her she would get a stomachache. "Huh," she said aloud. She rubbed the apple against her dress and then examined it before taking a big bite. Instantly, she puckered as the tart, gritty flavor invaded her mouth. She took a couple more bites—just for spite—and then tossed it as far into the distance as she could.

The sun was shining brightly, and the sky looked like an endless sea of glass. She hummed a tune as she went along, her thoughts flittering between her rotten lot of having to pick cotton and the grand future she was going to create for herself.

*   *   *   *   *

Shelby was in such a state of frenzy when she left Ola Mae's place and was driving the horses so furiously she didn't see the other wagon until she was right up on it. As she jerked on the reins and slowed the horses, she instantly recognized the other driver.

"Harlan!" she exclaimed.

"Why in the devil were you going so fast?" he exploded.

"What? What are you doing all the way out here?"

He motioned toward the back of his wagon. "I came to deliver the drapery material you ordered."

She looked at him in surprise. "Oh? That's unusual. I didn't think you made special deliveries. I was going to come and pick it up."

His brow knitted in frustration. It annoyed him to have to explain himself. "I have a few other deliveries to make in addition to yours."

She let it go. "I'm sorry I almost ran you over."

He chuckled softly. "It wouldn't be the first time," he said under his breath.

"What?"

He shook his head.

Shelby waited for Harlan to retrieve her fabric from his wagon, but he remained seated. "Well," she began, "thanks for bringing the fabric. I'm in a hurry. I need to get home."

"I'll follow you up to the house."

"That won't be necessary," she interjected.

"I insist," he answered firmly.

Her eyes skimmed over his tight jaw, and she knew he'd made up his mind. "Okay," she huffed, "suit yourself."

They rode a few minutes, until they reached the spot on the road where the top of her house could be seen jutting up from the hillside. He pulled his wagon around beside hers and motioned for her to pull over.

She pulled her wagon to a halt. Her head jerked around sharply to look at him when he got out of his wagon and jumped in beside her. "What are you doing?" she demanded.

"I figure it's about time that you told me what's going on."

Her eyes widened. "What are you talking about?"

"Where were you going in such a hurry?"

She looked away from him and out at the nearby field.

"Would you please look at me?"

She turned to face him. The compassion and concern she saw in his golden eyes was enough to almost bring her to tears. She looked away.

It would've been so easy at that moment for her to confide in him. She knew he would help her any way he could. She could see it in his eyes. An image of the glamorous redhead she had seen in church flashed through her mind, and she knew she couldn't get him involved. It was not her place to ask him for help—he belonged to another.

With some effort, she plastered a smile on her face. "I'm fine," she assured him. "Really."

He scoffed. "What kind of a fool do you take me for?"

"It's none of your concern," she said defensively.

Harlan was growing tired of her charade. "How long have we known each other?"

"Don't—"

"Long enough for you to be honest with me."

This got under her skin. "What?" she spat. "How could you even suggest—?"

He cut her off before she could finish. "Can you honestly sit there with that wooden smile of yours and tell me that you don't need any help?"

His penetrating glare dared her to tell him anything but the truth. Her eyes began burn, and she feared that she would completely lose control. She blinked to hold back the tears. "No," she admitted. "I can't tell you that."

He studied her for a moment and then relaxed his shoulders. "Good, you can tell me all about it and then we'll go on up to the house."

* * * * *

Otis worked frantically as he snatched the tools off the side of the shed and threw them in the back of the wagon. His plan was to load up as many tools as he could and then hide them under an old tarp until he could get safely out of town. Then he would stop and pick up his cotton. He still didn't have enough cotton to make a full bale, but he would make do. His instinct told him that it was time to make a move.

He loaded up everything he could find in the shed and then made his way to the barn. His step slowed a little when he looked toward the house and saw that Miss Shelby's wagon was gone. He felt a surge of triumph. He'd known she'd be out in the field because he'd watched her out there picking right alongside the other field hands every day this week.

Yes, Mr. Jenkins was a little too curious about the cotton weight yesterday. He grinned wickedly. "It'll take more than those two birds to outfox me," he muttered. "By the time Miss Shelby realizes what's going on, me and my bunch'll have us some cotton of our own and be miles from this place."

He cursed under his breath as his hand slammed against a nail protruding from the side of the wagon.

"What do you think you're doing?" asked Sarah as she entered the barn with her water bucket.

Otis jumped guiltily. "Well, well," he said carefully with a grin, "what do we have here?"

Sarah's eyes narrowed, and her empty hand flew to her hip. "What are you doing with those tools? You're not supposed to be in here. Why aren't you in the fields?"

Rather than answering the question, Otis leaned over and spit out a plug of tobacco which narrowly missed Sarah's foot.

Her nose curled in disgust, and her green eyes began to blaze.

A sly smile stole across Otis' lean face. Running up on Miss Shelby's little sister was a bonus he hadn't counted on.

"You sure are a pretty little thang."

Sarah's eyes filled first with uncertainty and then with fear. She took a step backwards. "I'm going to get my sister."

He stepped forward and reached for her arm. She took the water bucket and hit him as hard as she could, then dropped it and began running through the barn. He caught hold of her dress and yanked her backwards, sending her toppling over a feeding trough.

"You stay away from me, you filthy pig," she screamed as she backed away from him.

"High and mighty, just like your sister, ain't ye?" Otis snarled as he reached for her again.

This time she was ready for him. She brought her hand up and scratched him across the face, causing blood to ooze from the marks. This gave her the precious seconds she needed to distance herself from him. She got up and ran out the front of the barn, screaming at the top of her lungs with Otis in close pursuit.

"Whoa," said Harlan as Sarah almost collided with him.

"What in the world..." Shelby let the sentence dangle in midair as her face paled.

Otis didn't know what to do. He just stood dumbfounded, looking back and forth between Shelby and Harlan. He winced when he saw Harlan clench his fists. Sarah was still screaming and hurling insults at Otis, and then she began to sob. Shelby took her in her arms and pushed her hair back from her face.

"Are you okay?" Shelby asked. "He didn't..?"

Sarah shook her head. "No, I got away from him. The vile animal," she hissed.

"Go in the house and clean yourself up." She then motioned toward Otis. "I'll take care of this."

Harlan stepped forward. "No, I'll take care of this," he said menacingly.

Otis cowered down as Harlan approached him and grabbed him by the shirt.

"I have a good mind to beat the livin' daylights out of you," Harlan muttered through clenched teeth. Shelby's presence beside him was the only thing that kept him from carrying out the threat. He let go of Otis and thrust him backwards.

"I suggest you get your family and get out of town." His eyes narrowed dangerously. "Fast!"

Otis backed away and glared at Shelby. "You owe me."

"Folks around here don't take too kindly to thieves and child molesters," continued Harlan. He glanced at Shelby and could tell she was visibly shaken. He reached in his pocket and pulled out a ten-dollar bill. "You don't deserve a cent, but just to make sure you don't go around tellin' everybody how Mrs. Carter cheated you, here." He thrust the bill at Otis.

Otis grabbed it and stormed off in a rage. He got a safe distance away from Harlan and then turned around and yelled, "You'll get what's comin' to ya! I'm just sorry I won't be here to see it!"

Shelby went over and sat down on the back of the steps. Harlan followed her. She shook her head and placed a shaky hand on her knee.

"To think what would've happened if we hadn't gotten here when we did."

"Don't do this to yourself," Harlan countered. "It's not your fault. You don't always have to take the blame."

"Don't you see?" she blurted. "It was a mistake to hire him from the very beginning. If only I'd listened to John. He tried to tell me."

"Why did you hire him?"

"What?" she asked. She shook her head and tried to clear her thoughts. She looked unseeingly over the yard, remembering the pitiful scene in front of the house. Finally, she looked back at Harlan. "I thought I could help his family."

Harlan nodded. He'd figured as much.

"I'm glad I won't have to see them leave."

"You can't solve the world's problems."

She lowered her head and began massaging her temples. "I know," she answered. "I just wish I could solve the problems in my own back yard."

"What will you do about the pickin'? Do you have enough help?"

She shook her head. "Even with Otis and his family, I was cutting it close. Now..." Her shoulders lifted and fell, and she smiled wanly. "Don't worry about me. I'll think of something."

Harlan was about to offer some advice when the sound of the screen door opening stopped him. He looked up as Rayford stepped out the door.

"What's that silly sister of yours squealing about now?" Rayford asked. "I heard her screaming in the yard earlier, and now she's in the house screaming." His scowl was instantly replaced with a cordial smile when he realized a visitor was present.

Shelby watched Harlan's face darken and felt hers go hot. She stood quickly, straightening her dress, and then shot Rayford a scathing glare. "You heard Sarah screaming in the yard, and you didn't even come out to see what was wrong? Sarah has every right to be upset," she continued coldly. "Otis tried to attack her."

Rayford was speechless. His eyes widened in surprise.

"We owe a great debt to Mr. Rhodes," she continued before he could speak. "He made Otis leave." She hoped her tone of voice would accurately convey the contempt she felt for her husband. "Were it not for him, I don't know what I would've done."

Rayford sprung into action. "Yes," he interjected, stepping down the stairs to shake Harlan's hand. "Thank you for what you did. You're the new store owner, aren't you?"

Harlan nodded coolly as he extended his hand. For a brief moment, he looked at Shelby and then back at Rayford. Shelby looked down at the ground.

"I've met your wife," Harlan continued dryly. "It's nice to finally meet you." He cleared his throat. "I just stopped by to make a delivery. I'm glad I could be of help."

"You're welcome to stop by anytime," offered Rayford.

Harlan looked at Shelby once more and held her eyes for a moment. "I'll keep that in mind," he said as he climbed in his wagon and grabbed the reins.

Rayford looked thoughtful as he watched Harlan drive away. "I guess it was lucky for you that he came by when he did."

"Yes. It's nice to know there are still some real men left in the world," she snapped as she walked inside, slamming the door behind her.

Chapter Twenty-Nine

The Bloody Bucket was unusually crowded as the stranger made his way over to the bar where he sat down. He turned and watched the people inside with a peculiar interest. It had been a stroke of luck that he learned about this place to begin with from one of the looser-tongued locals he'd struck up an acquaintance with. Most people in a small community were very suspicious of strangers—especially from the city.

Many of his contemporaries hadn't had the success he had simply because they weren't willing to get to know the people. Everyone knew there was a mountain of moonshine being run all over these parts. Finding it was the tricky part. There were so many pig trails and secret hiding places all over the hills. Enough for these country bumpkins to hide out in for weeks—even months—at a time.

"What'll ya have?" growled the bartender.

The man smiled slowly and put on his friendliest expression as he turned around to answer. "Whiskey."

The white liquid ran like fire down his throat, and the residue shot straight to his head. "That's some strong stuff," he murmured, hoping to strike up a conversation with the bartender.

To his disappointment, the bartender barely even acknowledged him.

The stranger downed the remainder of the liquid quickly. "Can I have another shot of that stuff?"

This earned him a nod and a grunt from the bartender. "Think you can hold it?" he grumbled.

The man chuckled. "I'm sure gonna try."

The bartender placed another glass of whiskey in front of the customer and remained standing in front of him. He raised a bushy eyebrow and eyed him curiously. "You must be visitin'. I ain't seen you around these parts."

The man nodded. "I travel all over."

"Looks like you need another shot," said the bartender, pointing toward the empty glass with his meaty finger.

Before the man could decline, he poured him another shot.

The stranger was beginning to feel light-headed, but he wanted to impress the bartender in the hopes that he would gain some information from him.

He swallowed the drink, trying hard not to wince in front of the burly man as the liquid scorched his throat. A few more minutes went by and then euphoria swept over the stranger like a tidal wave, and he began to open up to the bartender and talk about himself.

*　*　*　*　*

Bird went up to the partially opened door and peeked through the crack. "Would ya look at all them fancy ladies? The Bucket's really hoppin' tonight," he said as he scoped the room like a hungry wolf.

The sheriff chuckled and then tugged at the back of the younger man's shirt, pulling him back into Bobby Ray's office. "Yeah," he agreed, "there are some fancy women here tonight. Too bad we got a run to make."

Bird scowled.

"Just think about how much money you're gonna make," Rayford added.

This seemed to lighten Bird's mood a little. He smiled boyishly. "All right. I'll make the run and then I'll come back."

Rayford patted Bird on the back. No matter how much he tried, he just couldn't figure Bird out—it was as if he'd finally accepted Rayford into the group. That was the only way he could explain the boy's erratic behavior. For no apparent reason, Bird's animosity toward him had suddenly vanished. Then again, he'd never been able to figure out why the boy was so hateful toward him to begin with.

Rayford's thoughts turned to more important matters when Bobby Ray opened the back door and walked in.

"Y-you boys r-ready?"

"I believe so," the sheriff answered quickly.

Bobby Ray nodded in satisfaction and then proceeded to give a few last minute instructions.

The three men were getting ready to leave when J. D. burst into the room. "You'll never guess who I've been talkin' to." He motioned for the men to come and look out the door and then pointed over toward the bar. "Recognize him?" he asked with satisfaction.

"Well, I'll be!" exclaimed the sheriff.

Bird caught hold of the excitement. "It's him. That's the revenuer that stopped us."

Rayford stood on his toes to get a better look. "Yeah, it's him all right," he echoed.

Bobby Ray pushed the other men aside to see for himself. He then stepped away from the door and stroked his chin absently. "You sure it's h-him?"

The men nodded.

"That ain't the best part," said J. D. "The fool's been in there for the past half hour suckin' down whiskey like water. He's been shootin' off at the mouth saying how he's gonna get hisself a still."

Bobby Ray's soft cheek jiggled slightly as his jaw clenched, but his expression remained unreadable. He folded his arms and stood quietly for a moment as the other men watched him expectantly. He looked at J. D. "D-Don't give h-him anymore shots of whiskey. L-Let his head c-clear a little. I want him to remember this night."

*   *   *   *   *

They waited until the revenuer got into his car and then followed behind him with their lights turned off, using only the light of the moon to guide them. Bobby Ray had told them to let the man get a few miles away from the Bucket before stopping him. When they came to a secluded spot in the road, surrounded by dense foliage and tightly clustered trees, the sheriff accelerated so that the bumper of the truck was only a few feet behind the other car. Then he suddenly turned his lights on.

This startled the revenuer so much that he slammed on his brakes, forcing the sheriff to hit his brakes to keep from slamming into his back end. The sheriff swore.

The revenuer weaved first to the right and then to the left in an attempt to let the truck behind him pass.

"Look at 'im weavin' back and forth," cried Bird.

"The fool almost caused us to crash into the back of him," grumbled the sheriff, his animosity toward the revenuer mounting.

The sheriff pulled up beside the car, and Rayford stuck his arm out the window and motioned for the man to pull over to the side of the road.

The man shook his head and kept driving.

"He ain't stopping," exclaimed Bird.

"He'll stop," hissed the sheriff, turning his wheel slightly so that the truck went into the car.

The revenuer jerked hard on the wheel in the other direction to keep from hitting the truck but slid off on the side of the road. He tried to keep driving, but the sheriff kept inching him further off the road, leaving the revenuer no other choice but to pull over and stop.

The revenuer stumbled out of his car, hurling curses at the top of his lungs. He glared at the three men standing in front of him.

"Just what do you think you're doing?" he shouted indignantly, raising a clenched fist in the air. "I demand an apology."

The sheriff chuckled.

Something in the revenuer's demeanor suddenly changed, and he eyed the three men warily. He went for his gun, but the sheriff was faster.

"I wouldn't do that if I were you," warned the sheriff.

The man laughed nervously and put up his hands in defeat. "I don't want any trouble," he began.

The sheriff looked at Bird and Rayford in amusement. "Did you hear that boys? He don't want any trouble."

"That's right," echoed the man.

"You should've thought about that the other day when you pulled us over," said the sheriff, his eyes narrowing.

A vicious smile broke out across Bird's cratered face. "Why don't we give him another scar to match to one he already has," he said softly.

The man tried to bolt, but any effort on his part would've been futile.

Rayford hit him first, the force knocking him to his knees. Bird came up behind Rayford and kicked the man in the face. They each took a couple more turns assaulting him, and then Rayford backed away. Bird took one last jab and then stood and wiped his hands on his pants. The revenuer was lying face down on the ground, moaning.

Figuring the task was finished, Rayford headed for the truck. He took one step and then stopped dead in his tracks when he realized that the sheriff had gone over to stand beside the revenuer. The sheriff reached down and grabbed the man by the hair. "Have you learned your lesson?"

The man didn't answer, and so the sheriff hit him across the face. "I asked you a question," the sheriff hissed.

"Yes!" he man cried.

"I don't believe you have," said the sheriff and then kept pounding the pathetic wretch with a savagery that turned Rayford's stomach.

The man let out a high-pitched whimper that barely even sounded human as he writhed in pain under the repeated blows. "Stop! Please stop!"

Rayford averted his eyes; the little man being stripped of his last shred of dignity was too much for him.

Finally, the sheriff stopped. He lifted the man's bloody face. The raw terror in the man's eyes seemed to amuse him. He smiled. "Consider yourself lucky. If you'd a been a real man, we would've kilt you."

* * * * *

Mary Kate cocked her head and looked out the corner of her eye at Harlan who was studying his account ledger. "You'll never guess who came in earlier this morning."

Harlan's face was masked in concentration as he studied the figures. He looked up for a second and then back down at his ledger again. "Who?"

"Mrs. Drake."

"Oh?" The tone of his voice remained even enough, but she could tell she had his full attention.

"Yes, it's rather interesting," she said innocently. "She came in to pick up her drapery fabric."

His face colored.

"You know, the fabric you rushed out to deliver to her the other day."

*   *   *   *   *

The sky rolled with black clouds, and thunder rumbled softly in the distance. Even though the air felt eerily calm in contrast to the moving sky above, a charge of energy was building.

"It won't be long now," Shelby shouted as she looked up in exasperation. She raised her arm and wiped her hair away from her forehead and then bent down again and kept picking cotton as fast as she could. She said a silent prayer that they would be able to finish before the storm hit. The gloves she was wearing protected her hands, but the tops of her arms were scratched to pieces from the thistles. Her back ached and her muscles were stiff, but she barely even noticed. She'd been working as hard as she could for the past few hours, and so had all the other workers.

She glanced across the rows over toward Joe Johnson. He'd picked twice the amount of cotton anyone else had, including herself, and was still going strong. He smiled broadly at her. "I think we gonna make it, Miss Shelby."

"I sure do hope so!" she yelled back at him.

"I'm fixin' to be finished with this row. I'll help everyone else who needs finishin' up."

"That's sounds great," answered Shelby. Her mood lifted a little. Maybe they would make it after all. Thanks to the Johnsons. She shook her head in admiration as she thought about the family she'd hired to replace the Wilkersons. For the past three days, Mrs. Johnson and their three children had worked tirelessly right alongside Mr. Johnson. Most people in Alder Springs would never consider hiring a colored family to sharecrop the land; in fact, Shelby didn't know of one other person who'd ever done so. But she'd been in a tight spot, and this good family had needed the work. A picture of Miss Pearl chatting openly with Grover flashed in her mind, and she felt a warm rush come over her. She'd learned a long time ago that it was the character—not the color of the skin—that determines a person's worth.

She felt the first drops of rain and knew it wouldn't be much longer before the bottom fell out. The wind picked up. "Let's go!" she yelled over to Homer, dragging the heavy sack behind her. "Let's get everything loaded up on the wagon so we can get it to the barn before it gets soaked."

*   *   *   *   *

Rayford sat on the front porch and watched the steady drizzle of rain. He kept replaying the vicious attack on the revenuer over and over again in his mind. The incident had left him cold and empty inside. Afterwards, they'd gone back to the Bucket where he'd intended to drink away his self-loathing. Unfortunately, he didn't get the chance. Bobby Ray had pulled him aside. Even now, he cringed as he remembered the conversation.

Except for the time when Bobby Ray first hired him, he'd never had a one-on-one conversation with the man. So he knew something was going on when Bobby Ray wanted to speak to him alone. He'd begun the conversation by telling Rayford that he'd heard some troubling news.

"I-I just w-wanted to come straight to you about t-this."

Rayford's heart raced and he swallowed hard. "What's the trouble?"

"I-I h-heard that you've been hiring coloreds to w-work—live on your farm."

The news caught him completely off-guard. He hadn't known. Why would Shelby do such a thing?

Bobby Ray smiled benevolently, but his eyes hardened. "N-now y-you know I'm n-not trying to r-run your business. I-I don't r-really c-care w-what c-color you h-hire, b-but m-most p-people around h-here d-don't feel t-the same w-way. T-they feel l-l-like it's t-takin' food right o-out of white people's mouths." He shrugged. "T-that's j-just the w-way it is."

Rayford didn't know what to say. If he admitted that he didn't have any clue what his wife did with the farm then he would appear weak. He wanted to tell Bobby Ray that it was none of his or anybody else's business what he did on his own farm, but he knew better. So he smiled and shook his head.

"I'll take care of it," was all he said.

Bobby Ray gave him a swift pat on the back. "I-I knew I-I c-could c-count on y-you."

Rayford leaned back in the swing and watched as the drizzle turned into pouring rain. The conversation with Bobby Ray had been friendly enough on the surface, but the meaning had been clear.

He just had to figure out a way to convince Shelby.

Chapter Thirty

Shelby looked out the kitchen window. The rain had finally stopped, and the sun was trying to peek through the clouds. It had rained solidly for three days. She hated to think what the fields must look like because even the ground around the house was covered with mud puddles. At least they got the cotton in. She would get Mr. Johnson to take the last wagonload to the gin tomorrow.

Having the Johnsons' help had been a tremendous blessing. She'd tried to explain as much to Rayford, but her argument had fallen on deaf ears. Things were getting so nasty between them that she was contemplating taking Aaron and going to her mama's house for a while. He'd started in on her right after he saw Mr. Johnson helping her get the cotton into the barn before the storm. He'd even had the nerve to demand that she get rid of the Johnsons. When she refused, he got so angry she feared he was going to hit her. He might've done so if Aaron hadn't walked into the room. Things had cooled off, but they had not spoken a word to each other for two days.

Why was he so concerned about the Johnsons? He'd never cared before. In fact, his apathy toward her and the farm was the main source of their conflict.

She carefully placed the last bit of food into the basket and then placed a cloth over it, neatly tucking in the edges.

"Come on Aaron. It's getting late, and I want to get this food to the Johnsons and get back home before dark."

"I'm hungry. I wanna eat now. Why do we have to take those colored people something to eat anyway?" he whined.

She almost lectured him on the condescending tone of his voice but changed her mind. She knew he'd picked it up from Rayford.

He would change his way of thinking on his own when he got to know them. She tousled his hair.

"Grab a biscuit to take with you. We won't be gone long."

*   *   *   *   *

Mr. Johnson greeted Shelby and Aaron at the door. "Well, I'll be. What ya'll doin' out here?"

Shelby smiled and held up her basket. "I don't want to intrude, but I just wanted to bring you a token of appreciation for all of your hard work the other day."

"Well, that's mighty nice of ya. Come on in," he said in his rich, melodic voice.

"Maybe we shouldn't," Shelby replied, looking down at her feet. "Our shoes are covered in mud."

"Naw now. Don't you worry 'bout that. It's all right. Now come on in here."

She smiled and stepped inside. Joe Johnson reminded her of Joshua. He was big and strong but had a gentle way about him. In contrast, Mrs. Johnson was short and plump. As she came out of the kitchen carrying a plate of steaming, hot cornbread, the first thing that caught Shelby's eye was the colorful cloth that was wrapped around her plaited hair.

"Hello, ma'am," she said, her twinkling eyes radiating from her smooth skin.

Shelby placed the picnic basket filled with baked yams, fried chicken, and biscuits on the table beside the cornbread. "Aaron and I just wanted to bring this by to say how happy we are that you're here."

"Thank you, this will go just fine with our pinto beans and cornbread." Mrs. Johnson motioned at the table. "We're fixin' to eat a bite. Would you and your little young'un like to join us?"

Aaron eyed the food hungrily.

Shelby shook her head. "Thank you for asking, but we have to get back. It's getting dark. We'd better..."

Before she could finish her sentence, she was silenced by the sound of horse hoofs and angry shouts. A look of sheer terror filled

Mrs. Johnson's eyes, and her lower lip began to tremble. Mr. Johnson's eyes filled with fear as he reached behind the door and grabbed his rifle.

She was about to ask them to explain what was happening when the front window shattered, and a brick landed at her feet. The Johnsons' children started squealing, and Aaron crouched behind her skirt.

"Go take the children in the back room," Mr. Johnson ordered, "and hide under the bed."

Mrs. Johnson's dark eyes filled with tears. "No," she argued hoarsely, "I won't leave you."

He raised the rifle slightly. "Go! You've gotta keep them safe."

Their eyes locked for one pitiful moment, and she began to weep.

"Come on, Mama," urged her oldest son, tugging on her dress. Reluctantly, she nodded weakly and huddled her children into the back room.

Mr. Johnson looked at Shelby. "You'd best go too."

Shelby looked at his hands and saw they were shaking. She planted her feet firmly on the floor. "No, I'm staying right here."

She could tell that he was relieved. She walked over and reached for the doorknob, and he caught her by the arm.

"Us comin' here may've been a big mistake," he whispered hoarsely.

She turned to Aaron. "No matter what happens, you stay inside the house with Mr. Johnson." Aaron bit his lip and nodded as his eyes filled with tears.

Mr. Johnson looked at her in surprise. "You cain't go out there."

Before he could stop her, she grabbed the rifle from his hands and threw open the door.

She heard a collective gasp ripple through the group as she stepped outside. A shiver of fear ran up her spine as she looked at the dozen or so men on horses dressed in white robes, holding torches of fire. They had formed a half circle, facing the house, and a wooden cross was in the center. Never before had she felt such a chilling feeling of hatred.

Despite her instruction to Aaron, he was hiding behind her skirt, clutching her trembling legs.

She prayed that she could keep her voice steady. "What are you men doing here?" she shouted angrily. "You should be ashamed of yourselves."

One of the men was standing slightly in front. He appeared to be the leader. "This ain't no business of yours. Just give us what we come here fer." He looked past her. "Come on out here," he yelled.

This brought a cry from the mob.

"You come on out here and show your black face!" another man cursed.

Shelby couldn't pinpoint the voice, but she was sure that it was someone she knew.

She pointed the rifle toward the men. "Get off my land," she hollered.

"Folks 'round here don't take too kindly to you hiring coloreds. There's too many good, hard-workin' white folks a needin' work around here."

"This is my farm, and I'll hire who I please," she shouted, her anger giving her courage.

"Send him out," they began to chant, "or we'll burn this house to the ground."

Shelby heard Mr. Johnson take a step toward the door. "Get back in the house," she yelled over her shoulder and then raised the rifle and fired a shot in the air.

"You'll have to come through me first," she yelled.

They stood for a moment, and she could tell they were trying to decide what to do. The leader walked over to the cross and threw down his torch. The grass began to blaze, and then the angry flames licked their way up the cross until it was engulfed in fire.

"Woman," the voice pronounced in judgment, "you have been warned."

The leader got back on his horse, and then the riders rode off in a cloud of dust, yelling and cursing as they went.

Shelby's knees began to wobble, and she leaned against the door frame for support. Before she could speak to Mr. Johnson, Aaron pulled on her dress.

"Mama," he whined.

"It's okay," she said, hugging him near her, trying not to show her own fear.

She looked up at Mr. Johnson.

"Mama," Aaron interrupted again.

"Honey, I need to speak to Mr. Johnson now," she said in a soothing tone, raising her voice slightly.

But Aaron wouldn't be put off. "But Mama," he continued.

"Yes, Aaron," she exclaimed impatiently. "What is it?"

"One of those men had shoes just like Papa's."

*   *   *   *   *

A sick feeling of dread gnawed in the pit of Shelby's stomach as she opened Rayford's closet door. Aaron's comment about seeing his papa's shoes had been enough to sow the first seeds of doubt. She'd lain in her bed until after midnight, waiting and listening for the familiar sound of Rayford's footsteps to come shuffling down the wood floor, but the sound hadn't come. Around two o'clock she'd drifted off to an uneasy sleep.

This morning, she'd quietly opened his door and peeked into the room where he was sleeping. She'd hoped to catch a glimpse of his boots, but they were nowhere to be found. At breakfast, he acted perfectly normal—so normal, in fact, that she began to chide herself for suspecting anything so utterly ridiculous. Why would he burn a cross in his own field? It just didn't make any sense. There were probably dozens of men who wore the same type of boots, weren't there?

Rayford had eaten a hearty breakfast and then left early, telling her he had some errands to run in town. He didn't say what, and she didn't ask. As he was walking out the door, her throat caught when she looked down and realized that he was wearing his dress shoes instead of his boots.

With a trembling hand she pushed his clothes out of the way to get a good look at his shoes. She exhaled in relief when all she saw was an extra pair of old work shoes. For good measure she picked one up and turned it over, examining the sole. It was clean. She sighed and then put it back. Carefully, she arranged his clothes so they would look exactly the same way she found them. She frowned. Where were his boots? A pair of crumpled trousers shoved in the back corner caught her eye. She grabbed the pants and held them up to the light. The bottoms were stained with mud. Her heart began to pound, and a cold sweat broke out across her forehead as the cold, icy tentacles of fear encircled her heart and clutched it like a vice. She reached her hand back and pulled out the pair of black boots and then let them drop noisily to the floor. Rayford had hidden them under his trousers. She sat down and clasped her hands in an attempt to keep them from shaking as she stared at the boots in horror. They were caked in mud—the same mud she and Aaron had all over their shoes.

Chapter Thirty-One

"It's a shame that Alder Springs doesn't have more parties," Mary Kate mumbled under her breath as she expertly applied a hint or rouge slightly underneath her cheekbone. She then put on her lipstick and then took a step backwards from the mirror to admire herself. She had chosen a royal blue dress for the occasion. It was a tad too dressy for a harvest party, but she didn't care. She wanted to turn every head in the place, and she knew just how to do it.

At first she hadn't been very excited about the harvest party. After all, what was so exciting about having a party in the Walkers' old barn? The townsfolk didn't seem to share her opinion. The harvest party seemed to be on the lips of every customer who walked into the store, and as the event drew nearer, she began to get caught up in the excitement of it all. At least there would be music and dancing. In a bigger, more refined town, she would've had some competition from other women—but not here. She would be the belle of the party, and Harlan would have to vie with other suitors for her attention. Her green eyes shimmered with excitement at the thought.

A low whistle from behind gave her a start.

"Harlan, I didn't hear you come in," she said breathlessly, her face reddening slightly.

"Are you ready?"

"I am," she replied, reaching for her gloves. The look of admiration in his golden eyes filled her with pleasure.

"You look fantastic," he murmured.

"Thank you darling." She linked her arm through his. "Let's go show these country folks how it's done."

*   *   *   *   *

The lights from the Walker's place were like a welcome beacon on the lonely, country road. Mary Kate shivered and pulled her shawl tighter around her shoulders as a gust of wind whipped through the carriage. "It's nippy tonight."

Harlan nodded. "Sure is."

Mary Kate's eyebrows knitted in frustration. No matter how much she tried, she just couldn't figure out Harlan sometimes. He'd seemed fine when they'd left town but had grown quiet and moody during the drive out to the harvest party. Was it something she'd said? She'd been so excited about the party that she'd jabbered on and on for a good five miles before realizing that she was doing all the talking.

They pulled up to the farm just as other people were arriving. At least a dozen wagons and carriages lined the front of the house. The barn was located a short distance from the Walkers' house. Its massive doors were propped open, and people were pouring in.

"This is a stark contrast to the solitary stretch of road we just traveled on to get here," Mary Kate said as her eyes raked over the crowd. She plastered on her brightest smile and began nodding at the people around her as Harlan helped her from the carriage.

A fiddle was being played inside, and the notes floated cheerfully across the autumn air. A group of anxious children, some giggling and pushing, were huddled around a large, wooden washtub filled to the top with water and apples.

"Maybe I should join them," Harlan joked. "I haven't bobbed for apples since I was about ten."

Mary Kate laughed happily and tightened her grip on his arm, forgetting her earlier irritation toward him. "Oh, no you don't. You're gonna dance with me before you do anything else."

Hay covered the floor of the vast barn like a golden carpet, and a string of lanterns hung from the open beams. A few tables and chairs lined the walls, but most of the seating was made from bales of stacked hay. At the far end of the barn, a makeshift stage had been constructed out of crates and scrap wood. The fiddle player was standing in the center, his thin frame moving rapidly to the beat of the merry tune he was playing. A long table loaded with food had been placed along one wall, and people were gathered around it. Henrietta Potts and her sister, Ester Whitaker, were dipping apple cider from a large bowl into cups. Mary Kate turned her back on them quickly before one of them saw her. The last thing she wanted to do was to spend the evening serving food.

She squeezed Harlan's hand. "Let's dance."

They took two steps before Mildred Tucker caught them. "Well, looka here, Clayton. I told you they'd be here."

Mary Kate scowled inwardly. The very sound of the woman's voice trumped on her nerves. She glanced up at Harlan and stifled a smile when she saw the look of disgust on his face as he studied Mildred and the Reverend. Mildred was clasping her husband's arm tightly, almost as though she were afraid that if she let go for a second, he would disappear. And if the pinched expression on his face was any indication, he probably would.

"Mildred, Reverend Tucker. How are you doing?" Mary Kate asked.

"We can't complain," Mildred answered for them both. "This is quite a large turnout."

The Reverend looked at Harlan. "How's business at the store?"

Before Harlan could answer, Mildred cut in. "Now there'll be no talk of business tonight," she said in a loud voice.

"Thanks for asking. Business is steady, despite the drop in cotton prices," Harlan answered, his eyebrow raised. He looked directly at Mildred, daring her to say another word.

Her face flushed, and she became flustered. This won Harlan a look of appreciation from the Reverend.

Mildred took Mary Kate by the hand. "Come on, dear. Let's go over and see if the ladies need any help serving."

"We were just about to dance," protested Mary Kate, looking up at Harlan, her eyes pleading with him to back her up.

"It's okay," Harlan answered. "Go help Mrs. Tucker, and then we'll have our dance later."

Mary Kate's face grew a shade darker. "Okay," she said sweetly to Mildred, giving Harlan a hateful look.

*   *   *   *   *

Normally, Shelby looked forward to the annual harvest party. This year she almost didn't come at all. She had still not fully recovered from the incident at the Johnsons'. She chose a seat against the wall where she could sit and observe the people at the party. She despised what those men in white robes had done to her. They had robbed her of her peace of mind. Her eyes surveyed the room. Which friends and neighbors had been part of the hateful group? Her thoughts turned to Rayford. He had given her some flimsy excuse about why he couldn't come with her, and she'd been relieved. It had taken every amount of effort for her to act normal toward him. She'd felt many conflicting emotions toward him the past few years, but the fear she now felt was new. Her daily routine, as pitiful and empty as it was, was all she had to hold onto...and Aaron. A surge of emotion surfaced and expanded her chest. *Thank goodness for Aaron.*

"Excuse me. Is this seat taken?"

She looked up in surprise, the voice jolting her back to the party.

"No," she answered, and then looked up and realized it was Harlan who had spoken.

He sat down next to her.

Shelby had seen him earlier with his fiancée. She'd watched them for a moment until they became lost in the crowd.

"I hope I'm not interrupting anything."

She eyed him suspiciously before answering. "No, of course not. What could you possibly be interrupting?"

He chuckled. "You look preoccupied."

"No, I was just...no," she said finally. "I was just watching the dancing."

He pressed his lips together in doubt. "Hmmm."

"Where is your fiancée?"

The question caught him off-guard, and his face colored. She watched, even anticipated, the muscle in his jaw tighten and felt an ache as the warm feeling of familiarity swept over her.

"Who?"

"Your fiancée. The redhead. I saw you with her earlier."

He corrected her. "She's not my fiancée, and I don't know where she is at the moment. Anyway, I didn't come over here to talk about that."

"Oh? What did you come over here for?" she asked hotly and then instantly regretted her outburst. She had to put aside the past and remember that he was only trying to be her friend. She shook her head. "I'm sorry. You didn't deserve that."

He was looking at her quizzically. "It's okay," he said before changing the subject. "How are things at the farm?"

She wasn't expecting that, and her face dropped visibly before she could recover. "Things are fine."

"How did you make out with the harvest after all was said and done?"

Now she knew why he was talking to her. He wanted to know when she was going to settle up with him. She bristled. "I did all right," she answered and then added. "I'm planning on coming in next week to settle up with you."

He frowned and brushed the comment aside. "Whenever you want. I'm in no hurry. Are you sure you're okay?"

"Yes," she answered, a hit of exasperation coming out in her voice. "Why do you keep asking?"

"I deal with farmers every day—good farmers who don't know how they're gonna make ends meet if the price keeps dropping the way it has the past few years. What did you get? About five, six cents a pound?"

She looked down at her hands, and he knew that her silence was her answer.

"How are you gonna make it if the price keeps dropping?"

"Well I'll just economize...watch my spending..."

"Yeah, that's possible now, but what if the price drops even more next year? What then?"

She looked up at him, a pained expression in her dark eyes. "I'm not sure."

He studied her for a moment and then carefully chose his words. "There's something else I want to talk to you about."

"What?"

"I heard there was some trouble at your place a few nights ago."

Her jaw grew taut, and her eyes narrowed. "How did you know?"

"Word spreads like wildfire at the store."

"Do you know who they were?"

He shook his head. "No, but I wish I did, the blasted cowards." He looked into her eyes, and for a moment she felt as though they were the only two people there. "I wish I'd been there to help."

An involuntary shiver ran down her spine as she remembered the terrible event. "No, it was better that you weren't."

"You can't fight this alone. What happens when they come back? You know they won't let this lie."

"The Johnsons left this morning."

"Really?" he asked incredulously.

"They're moving up north. Mr. Johnson has a cousin who lives in Illinois. He thinks they'll have a better life there." She stared off in space for a moment, remembering his sorrowful expression as he had said goodbye. She'd been angry with herself over the relief she felt when she realized they were leaving.

Harlan placed his hand over hers, and she let hers remain under it for a second, enjoying the protectiveness of it. Then, she reluctantly pulled her hand away. She bit her lip. "Thank you," she whispered hoarsely.

He stood up to leave. His eyes caught hers and held them for a moment. "You look stunning. Red always has been your best color," he said, and then he was gone.

* * * * *

Mary Kate perked up a notch as the two men came toward her. She'd been stuck behind the stupid table serving apple cider for a half hour now. Mildred had expertly manipulated Mary Kate into helping serve before suddenly disappearing, leaving her stuck with the two sisters, or the two bickering old biddies as she liked to refer to them. Every time she'd tried to sneak away, one of them nabbed her. She hadn't seen any sign of Harlan anywhere. Where was he? She eyed the two approaching men with interest. If she could get one of them to ask her to dance, then Harlan would see her.

"I think most of our problems will be solved when we get that scalawag Hoover out of the White House next year and get us a good, hard-working democrat."

This brought a hearty chuckle from the other man. "I agree with you there, Henry."

"Excuse me," Mary Kate interjected. "Would either of you gentlemen like some cider?" she asked sweetly.

"Thank you," one of them answered as they both reached for a cup, barely even noticing her.

Before she could think of something witty to say, they'd turned their backs.

"I'm a putting my vote on Roosevelt," she heard one of them say as they walked away.

Her face grew as red as her hair. She dropped the ladle into the bowl, causing cider to splash out onto the white, tablecloth.

Henrietta was about to scold her but stopped short when she saw the glare in Mary Kate's eyes.

Mary Kate untied the apron from her waist and practically threw it at Henrietta. "I've done my share of serving tonight. I'm going to find my fiancé."

Mary Kate pushed her way through the dancing couples to the other side of the barn. She keenly searched over the crowd until she caught sight of Harlan's sandy hair. She'd give him a good tongue-lashing for leaving her. She walked toward him and then stopped dead in her tracks. He was not alone. Her mouth went dry, and she swallowed hard. It wasn't so much that he was talking to another woman; it was the expression on his face, as if he were hanging on her every word. A stab of jealously hit her so hard she could hardly breathe. She recognized the woman as Mrs. Carter, one of the farmers' wives. She'd been in the store several times, but Mary Kate had never paid her much attention. Until now. Her eyes flickered over the other woman, carefully sizing her up. Her heart began to pound wildly as she remembered the afternoon when Harlan had left the store in a mad rush. He'd rushed out to deliver drapery fabric to two people: Mrs. Drake and Mrs. Carter.

If her eyes had been daggers, they would have pierced through the wretched woman. She squared her shoulders and started toward the table, but Harlan was already standing up to leave. She stopped. Maybe a head-on confrontation wasn't the answer. No, there had to be a better way. She would find out more about this Mrs. Carter, and then she would decide what to do.

Mary Kate leaned over the counter with her chin propped up on the palm of her hand as she stared off in thought. Despite all of her calculated questions to Harlan, she hadn't learned much more about Mrs. Carter than she'd known to begin with. He'd seemed so totally uninterested in the subject that she was beginning to question her first assumption. Maybe he was just having a simple, polite conversation with another member of the community. She shook her head. She had to get this man to the altar soon, before she lost her mind.

"A penny for your thoughts."

Mary Kate jumped, and color crept into her cheeks as she turned toward Harlan.

"It must be good. You're grinnin' from ear to ear."

She laughed. "I was just thinking this might be a good day to close the store early."

He leaned back and folded his arms as he studied her. He finally shook his head and chuckled. "I guess I fell right into that one."

She shrugged. "You asked."

"We'll see," he answered. "It depends on how busy we get."

They both turned as the front door opened, and the object of Mary Kate's query walked into the store. She looked up at Harlan to see his reaction. His face remained impassive. Her gaze then flickered over Mrs. Carter. The blue, cotton dress she was wearing was simple, yet tasteful. Her dark curls were piled high on top of her head, making her look taller than she actually was.

Mary Kate smiled curtly. "May I help you?"

Shelby's eyes went first to Harlan and then to Mary Kate. Mary Kate stiffened. Was it her imagination or did some sort of exchange pass between Harlan and the woman in that brief moment?

"Yes," Shelby began. "I'd like to get ten pounds of sugar and a couple of sticks of peppermint."

"Will this be cash...." Or charge, she was about to ask, and then she realized that Harlan had already walked over to his ledger to record the charge.

"It'll be charge," Shelby responded.

A red flag went up in Mary Kate's head. She cocked her head.

"How did you know?"

He stopped writing and looked up. "Know what?"

"That she would charge it."

He shrugged and smiled apologetically at Mrs. Carter. "She usually does."

This really got Mary Kate's ire up.

"Is there a problem with my account?" Shelby asked, her face reddening. "I always settle all of my debts promptly."

"Of course you do," Harlan interjected and then shot Mary Kate a questioning look.

"There's no problem," Mary Kate answered, her voice loud. "I'll be right back with your sugar."

Mary Kate returned and dropped the sugar on the counter in front of Mrs. Carter. "Will there be anything else?" she demanded.

Shelby shook her head. "No, I think that'll be all."

Mary Kate looked Shelby squarely in the eyes. "Are you sure?" she repeated.

Shelby met her gaze. "Perfectly."

She reached to get the sugar, but Mary Kate put her hand over the top and then looked at Harlan and then back at Mrs. Carter. She knew it was risky, but she had to know for sure. And she'd be darned if she was gonna let some woman carry on with her man behind her back.

"Are you sure you don't want anything else?" she taunted.

Harlan walked over and stood beside Mary Kate. "What're you doin'?" he growled in her ear.

Mary Kate raised her chin and looked back at Shelby. "Are you sure you didn't come in here to talk to him? You two seemed pretty cozy at the harvest party."

Shelby's face grew crimson, and Harlan looked like he'd just been slapped. In that instant, Mary Kate knew her suspicions were correct.

Shelby turned on her heel and quickly fled the store. Harlan stood suspended for a moment and then gave Mary Kate a withering look. "You don't know what you've done," he said quietly, then grabbed the sugar and peppermint sticks and ran out to catch up with Shelby.

She was already in the wagon by the time he reached her. He

could tell from the look on her face that she was seething.

"I am so sorry," he began. "I don't know where that came from."

What alarmed him the most was not the anger in her dark eyes but the humiliation he detected.

"It's okay," she countered coolly. "We've just been foolin' ourselves to think we could have a friendship after what happened before." She grasped the reins. She wanted to leave before he saw the tears which were sure to follow.

He grabbed her hand to keep her from jerking the reins. "Nothing," he said firmly, looking into her eyes, "is as important to me as our friendship. Do you understand?"

Her eyes brimmed with tears, despite her best effort to hold them back.

"Don't take that away from me," he pleaded.

Their eyes met for one long moment.

"I have to go," she finally said.

He nodded and let go of her hand and then stepped back and watched her drive away.

Chapter Thirty-Two

The harvest of 1932 had been devastating to farmers, their cotton crop bringing in a meager five cents per pound on average, less than half what they had previously earned a few years prior. Nineteen thirty-three held little more hope for any better. Times were hard, but still they planted. They planted their cotton in the spring of '33 and waited. And prayed.

* * * * *

"Mama! Mama! Someone's comin' up the hill in an automobile!"

Shelby frowned and then quickly wiped her hands on her apron. Who could that be? She followed Aaron out the kitchen door.

A black truck was making its way up the drive. They waited for it to get closer so they could see who was driving it.

Aaron began jumping up and down. He ran down to the edge of the yard to get a better look.

"Don't get in the road," Shelby yelled after him.

"It's Papa! It's Papa!"

"What?" Shelby cried in disbelief.

As the truck rounded the last curve of the drive, Shelby could see that it was indeed Rayford driving. Aaron ran beside him as he pulled the truck up and stopped in front of the house.

"Papa, is it yours?" Aaron asked in wonderment.

"Sure is," he answered as he opened the door and got out.

He looked over at Shelby, his dark eyes shining with excitement. "Well, whadda ya think?"

What did she think? She wanted to tell him that she'd been in the kitchen all morning worrying about the farm and the drop in the price of cotton. And that she'd been trying to ration her sugar and cocoa to make it go as far as possible, but she didn't say any of these things. She knew it wouldn't do any good. She chose her words carefully.

"Is it yours?" she asked, echoing Aaron's earlier question.

"Yep," Rayford answered proudly. He ran his hand lovingly across the hood. "She's dusty right now, but with a little work, I'll have her shinin' like a new penny."

Worry clouded her expression. "Where did you get the money to buy it?"

Her question hung in the air as annoyance flicked over Rayford's face. Why did it always come down to the money? Why couldn't she just be happy for him just once? He ignored her question and turned his attention to Aaron.

"This here's a '29 Model A Ford. Do you know the difference between a Model A and Motel T?"

Aaron shook his head.

Rayford sat down behind the wheel. "Looka here," he said, pushing a button. The engine sputtered and then jumped to a steady purr.

Shelby watched her husband and son with mixed feelings. Aaron idolized his father. She was grateful Rayford was kind to Aaron but terrified that Aaron might one day grow up to be just like him. She walked over and stood next to them.

"The Model Ts have to be started in the front," Rayford explained. "You can't start one of them by just pushing a button. You have to get out and use a crank." He patted the steering wheel. "This is much better. And my truck has windows and windshield wipers. The Model T doesn't."

Aaron wrinkled his nose. "What's a win'shield wiper?"

Rayford chuckled in amusement. "It's a wiper on the front window that wipes away the rain so you can see while you're driving."

"Wow!" Aaron said.

Rayford looked at Shelby. "Won't we be a sight when I drive us all to church on Sunday? We'll be the finest-looking family in town."

Shelby's first thought was that he hadn't been to church with her in years. She remained silent and nodded her head.

Rayford looked at Aaron. "Let's take her for a drive."

Aaron let out a squeal of delight.

"Your mama can come too if she wants to," Rayford added casually, the hopeful expression in his eyes the only indicator of his true feelings.

Shelby didn't answer right away. She stood there staring at Rayford as if he were some strange creature that she'd never seen before. Was this the same man who less than two weeks ago had burnt a cross in his own field and been a part of the group that threatened his own wife and son? She was about to decline, but the longing expression on Aaron's face changed her mind. "All right," she finally said without enthusiasm. "Let me put my apron in the kitchen and get my pocketbook. I'll be right back."

*　*　*　*　*

Boy, was it his lucky day—and to think that he'd almost passed by this little hole-in-the-wall joint. The cigarette smoke and dim lighting had made it hard to see the faces of the other customers at first. But after his eyes adjusted to the darkness, there, as big as day, sitting at a table in the corner, were Rayford and Flora. His mind raced as he chose a booth out of their sight and watched them, gloating in his good fortune.

Yes, he could see how this would be a good place to meet. It was about fifty miles from home. No one would know them here. As they talked and laughed softly with their heads close together, it was impossible to tell what they were saying, but he could tell that they were about half shot.

Flora kept running her hand through her curled, bleached hair as she smoked her cigarette. Although her dress was pink silk, and her hair was caught up with a pink ribbon, her lips were painted bright red. *So typical of Flora*, he mused.

A half hour later, he moved back in the shadows as they staggered past his booth, arms encircling each others' waists. He chuckled to himself. He didn't know where they were going, but one thing he knew for sure: They sure weren't going to no church picnic.

*   *   *   *   *

"Liar! Liar! You're a liar!" screamed Sheriff Wendell, his knuckles turning white as his grip tightened around Bird's neck.

Bird let out a gurgle as he tried to breathe. "I seen 'um! I promise I did!" He managed to squeak.

The boy's face began to turn blue as the sheriff continued shaking him. Finally, he loosened his grip and threw Bird across the room like a discarded rag doll where Bird lay on the floor gasping for breath. Sheriff Wendell felt old as he staggered over to his desk and slumped down in a chair.

He'd suspected for some time that Flora was seeing someone else. His mind went back a couple of days to when Flora had come home late. He'd asked her where she'd been, and she'd given him some flimsy excuse about visiting a cousin. He'd known it was a lie but oh, how he'd wanted to believe it. He could still hear her laughter when he told her that he wished she wouldn't go around half-dressed. He remembered the pink, silk dress she'd been wearing, and his face darkened. Had she worn it for Rayford? Rage blacked across his eyes.

Bird got up off the floor and rubbed his neck. Red whelps marked his white skin. "That ain't all," he said. "Let me tell you what he did to me."

*   *   *   *   *

It had been a rough day for Harlan. After the blow-up with Mary Kate, she'd grown sullen and quiet. As the afternoon had worn on they'd settled into an uneasy truce. Normally they would've gone out for supper, but she'd feigned a headache. That was fine with him because he needed some time to himself to think. He stepped inside the Bucket and found a seat. As he looked around the dingy place, it took him all of five minutes to realize that he had no desire to be there. He was just about to leave when a familiar face caught his attention. He strained his eyes to get a better look, and his blood began to boil as he watched Rayford with his arm around another woman. Rayford whispered something in her ear, causing her to giggle and nod. He watched them for a few more minutes until he couldn't stand it any longer.

Rayford came stumbling out of the Bucket alone. He didn't notice the man standing off to the side until he heard his name being called out from the darkness. He swaggered toward the voice, trying to focus.

"Do I know you?" he called out.

Silence.

He took a step closer.

"You don't deserve her," the voice said menacingly.

Rayford stopped dead in his tracks. It was the sureness of the words that sent the shiver up his spine. "What? Who are you? What do you know about me?" he demanded, his voice tinged with fear.

He took another step toward the voice, but there was no one there.

*   *   *   *   *

Rayford almost jumped out of his skin when Sheriff Wendell slammed the envelope down on the table. "What's this for?" he asked with a puzzled expression on his face as he picked up the envelope and realized it was full of money.

"Why, it's your cut," the sheriff answered easily.

"Cut of what?" asked Rayford.

"Now, Rayford you know you need money to pay fer that fancy truck of yours." Before Rayford could answer, Sheriff Wendell continued. "And so do I. Keepin' Flora Mae up ain't cheap."

Rayford shook his head and put the money back on the table. "I dunno," he said, shaking his head, "if Bobby Ray finds out..."

"How's he gonna find out? We're only doin' it once." Sheriff Wendell looked meaningfully at Rayford. "He ain't gonna find out."

Rayford still wasn't convinced. The whole thing made him uneasy. "I don't think this is a good idea."

"Suit yourself."

The sheriff shrugged as he turned and walked away, leaving the envelope on the table.

Rayford looked at the envelope for a moment. Then he picked it up and shoved it into his pocket.

"There ain't no mistake. I double-checked the money twice just to make sure."

Bobby Ray sat behind his desk as he scrutinized the man standing in front of him.

"W-what makes y-you s-so sure it was Rayford?" he finally asked.

Sheriff Wendell's heart began to race. "I didn't want to believe it myself," he said. "You know how much I think of him, but he's really gone into debt lately with that fancy truck and all."

He watched anxiously for Bobby Ray to show some sign of emotion, but his pudgy face remained expressionless. The next few seconds seemed like hours for the Sheriff as he stood quietly waiting to hear what Bobby Ray would say. *He doesn't believe me*, his mind screamed. *He knows I'm lying.*

Bobby Ray leaned back in his chair and lit a cigar. "I-I sure do hate it," he said, exhaling a puff of smoke. "You know what has to be done."

The sheriff's heart leaped triumphantly, but he kept his face grim. "Yes, sir, I suppose I do."

"Do y-you t-think you can h-handle it?"

"Yes."

"The s-sooner the better."

Chapter Thirty-Three

"What're you doin' here?" Rayford hissed, looking back over his shoulder toward the house. "My wife is inside gettin' ready for the revival. She could come out any minute."

"It's about Wendell." Flora shuddered. "He knows, Rayford. Somehow he knows."

Rayford's blood chilled. He grabbed Flora by the arms and shook her. "What do you mean?" he demanded. "He couldn't possibly know."

She laughed loudly, her voice sounding unnaturally high-pitched, and then she began to whimper as her eyes rolled wildly back and forth, making Rayford wonder how much of a grasp she had on her sanity.

He took her in his arms and began stroking her back. "It's okay kitten," he purred. "It's gonna be..." He stopped suddenly and whirled around. "What was that?"

There stood Shelby, her face white. As their eyes met, Rayford's heart almost stopped, and a chill came over him. He'd never seen Shelby's eyes so cold, looking straight through him. He let go of Flora. "Now darling," he began, sobered by the realization of what she'd just seen.

"How could you?" she stormed.

Rayford took a step toward her.

"Stay away from me. How could you disgrace your family and yourself like this?"

He reached for her, but she escaped his grasp and ran out of the barn. She ran to her wagon and jumped in and took off down the driveway, going full speed.

Shelby's thoughts raced wildly from Aaron to Mama, to Harlan, and then to Rayford as she urged the horses on. Who else knew about Rayford and Flora? Did Mama and John know? Did Harlan know? She thought about Aaron. Thank goodness he had spent the afternoon with Mama.

The trees were a blur as she rode past them faster and faster. She wasn't sure what spooked the horses. It might've been a fox or a bobcat that darted out across the road. All she knew was that one minute she was racing down the road, and the next minute the horses were out of control. She yanked on the reins, but her effort had little effect. She heard a loud, cracking sound as the horses broke loose from the wagon. The wagon turned, and white lights exploded in her head as she was catapulted out.

* * * * *

Rayford's first impulse had been to go after Shelby to try to talk some sense into her, but he couldn't—not with Flora there. He stayed with Flora until he was able to get her calmed down enough to go home. Everything around him was unraveling fast. He would have to figure out a way to smooth things over with Wendell, but the first thing he had to do was find Shelby. He figured that she'd gone to the revival to pick up Aaron.

When he got to the church, the revival was just ending, and people were pouring out. He waited in his truck for a few minutes, hoping she would come out. Finally, he got out and walked up the front steps. He nodded politely as a couple of people spoke to him. He surveyed the crowd and spotted John and Ellen. He made his way toward them.

Aaron saw him. He broke free from Ellen's grasp and began running toward him. "Papa! Papa!" he exclaimed, grabbing Rayford's legs.

He tousled Aaron's hair and took his hand.

John and Ellen both looked surprised to see him. John shook his hand. "Rayford, it's good to see you. This is a surprise."

"I'm looking for Shelby. Have you seen her?"

Ellen regarded him coolly. Rayford looked away from her

accusatory stare. He knew how much Ellen detested him. He could see it in her eyes.

"You know that Shelby was supposed to meet us here," Ellen said. "You were going to drive her. What happened?"

He wasn't prepared for her direct line of questioning. "We had a fight," he stammered, "and I thought that she would come here."

"I see," Ellen answered.

Rayford cleared his throat. "Have you seen her?"

"No."

He waited to see if Ellen would offer him any more information, but she remained quiet.

Aaron tugged on his sleeve. "Is Mama okay?"

Instead of answering him, Rayford looked at Ellen. The two paused for a moment, a battle of wills dueling in the tense silence, the look on her face conveying all that she would never say.

"Well, if she goes to your place, tell her that I'll be waiting for her at home," Rayford lied. He had no intention of going home and sitting in an empty house.

"I'll keep Aaron with me until my daughter comes to get him," Ellen answered icily.

Rayford gave Aaron a quick kiss on the forehead and then turned and left the church. He got in his truck and pushed the start button. The engine turned over once and then died. He swore under his breath and then pounded the steering wheel with his fist. He tried pushing the button again, but nothing happened. He shook his head in frustration and stared off into the crowd as he tried to figure out what to do. *Why me?* he wondered.

*   *   *   *   *

"Miss, miss," said the concerned voice. "Are you all right?" Then he recognized her. "Mrs. Carter, can you hear me?" he asked, shaking her.

The words floated into Shelby's consciousness, and her eyelids fluttered. She shook her head in bewilderment.

"You took quite a spill," the voice continued.

She turned to the voice and then the speaker's face came into focus. "Mr. Walker," she said, still dazed. She looked around her and then sat up. The last thing she remembered was racing down the road. "What happened?" she asked, as much to herself as to him, as she tried to piece things together.

"I cain't say for sure, but it looks to me like the axle broke. I found your horses about a mile or so up the road."

"My horses?"

"Yeah, you were lucky," he said, his eyes surveying the wagon, now broken in pieces.

She rose to her feet and then toppled as her full weight came down on her right ankle. She winced in pain.

"Easy," the man urged. He reached down and examined her ankle. "It's not broken, just sprained, but you'll need to stay off it for a while."

Shelby nodded. "Thank you for your help."

"I'm just glad I saw the horses. That's what made me come lookin' for you." He motioned at the sky. "It's gettin' dark. Let's get you home."

*   *   *   *   *

Relief washed over Shelby when they got up the drive, and she saw that Rayford's truck was gone. She knew she would have to face him sooner or later, but she just couldn't handle it tonight.

Hugh Walker helped her inside and carefully placed her on the couch and then propped up her foot. "Can I get you a drink of water?" he asked.

She smiled politely. "No, thank you. I'm fine."

He hadn't inquired on the whereabouts of her husband or Aaron, and she was grateful, although she guessed that he was probably wondering.

"I'm gonna go and get Doc Larsen and your mother. The doc can tend to that ankle of yours."

"No," Shelby countered.

The man looked puzzled.

"They're probably still at the revival," she said in the way of an explanation. "And I don't want them to worry." She smiled thinly to reassure him. "I'll be fine."

He looked doubtful. "I cain't leave you here like this by yourself." He turned to go. "You rest, and I'll get Doc Larsen.

Panic seized her. She just couldn't face the humiliation of having to answer all of their questions. She needed time to compose herself first. "If you really want to be of help, you can go and get Mr. Rhodes."

"Harlan Rhodes, who runs the general store?" Mr. Walker's eyes widened in surprise, and Shelby realized how ridiculous her request must sound. She didn't even know why she'd asked such a thing. She'd said it without thinking, and the words had left her mouth before she could call them back.

"All right," she heard Hugh Walker say. "You just rest. I'll go and get Harlan."

She leaned her head back and closed her eyes. Harlan would know what to do.

*   *   *   *   *

Mary Kate hadn't wanted to get sick, but it sure had been nice having Harlan's full attention the past few days. He offered to come over to her place and make supper for her tonight. She chuckled as she watched him bungle his way around the kitchen. She knew what a sacrifice this was for him, since cooking was certainly not his favorite thing to do.

"Are you sure you don't need any help?" she called out playfully.

"No, I can handle it," came the reply.

She smiled. She knew the answer before she even asked.

The knock at the door put a damper on her mood. She didn't want any interruption to spoil their evening.

"I'll get it," Harlan yelled.

"Hugh, what brings you into town?" asked Harlan.

"I tried to find you at your house," he answered uneasily, looking at Mary Kate. "When you weren't there, I came here."

"What's going on?"

"It's Mrs. Carter."

Harlan's voice became anxious. "What happened?"

"She's had an accident."

Harlan's heart dropped as the color drained from his face.

"The axle on her wagon broke. She's okay, just a little banged up and has a sprained ankle, but she's asking for you to come."

As Harlan closed the door behind Hugh, he turned and realized that he had forgotten Mary Kate was even there. Her expression said it all. As they looked across the room at each other, they both knew that it was over. He stood frozen; she spoke first.

Mary Kate jumped to her feet. "To think," she scoffed, "of all the time I've wasted, waiting around on you!" Her voice grew louder, and her nostrils began to flair. "And all this time you've been pining away for some...some...some married woman who has a child already."

Harlan took a deep breath. "Would you please try to calm down?"

Mary Kate was anything but calm as she paced back and forth across the floor with her hands planted firmly on her hips and her red hair flying wildly as she turned sharply to change directions. She suddenly stopped and planted her feet firmly as she faced him.

"I've been a fool," she began shaking her head. Tears were welling in her eyes, and she angrily pushed them away. "I thought you wanted to move here so we could start fresh." A tickle began to form in her raw throat, and she fought off the urge to cough. She cleared her throat instead. "Now I know that you just wanted to be next to her," she sniffed and then laughed harshly. Her thick hair slung backwards as she lifted her head up sharply, giving Harlan the impression of a wild horse struggling to break free from the reins. He tried to concentrate on what she was saying.

"I've put up with so much because of you," she said, her eyes widening into green saucers. "I even put up with the likes of Mildred Tucker and her little followers."

"Mary Kate, I'm so sorry..."

"Don't even say it," she spat bitterly, throwing her hands in the air. She then turned her back on him and began to massage her throbbing temples. Her chest felt cold and heavy.

"Can we talk about this later? I don't have time for this right now."

Her shoulders were quivering. He figured she was crying, but when she turned back around to face him, her eyes were blazing.

"You wanna talk later? It's too late. You're a bigger fool than me. And so is she. I would've given anything, done anything to make you love me." She looked up at him, tears making a crooked path down her cheeks. "I would've given the world. But as it turns out, the only thing you've ever wanted is the one thing I'm not. Her!" she yelled.

"This conversation is futile," Harlan answered, feeling as though the time was furiously ticking away. "When you can calm down and I get back, we'll talk."

This flew all over Mary Kate, and she clenched her fists and growled through her teeth. "I will not calm down, and I will not wait! Harlan Rhodes, if you walk out that door, that's it! I will not be here when you get back."

"That's enough," he answered sharply, his eyes narrowing a fraction.

"No!" she retorted, her voice rising to a fevered pitch. "I've something to say, and you're gonna listen." She barely got the words out of her mouth before a spasm of coughs caused her to double over.

"You're not well. You need to sit down."

She shook her head in a refusal to sit. He'd hurt her, and now she wanted to hurt him. She smirked. "Do you really think she's going to leave her husband for you?"

Harlan's face turned a deep shade of red, and his jaw muscle tightened. "I said that's enough," he said, fighting to keep his voice steady.

The words dripped off her lips like syrupy venom as she put on an exaggerated southern drawl. "She'll stay married to that spineless weasel while she strings you along. You'll never know how she really feels about you because she's too much of a lady to ever let her true feelings show."

"You would do well to not talk about things which you don't understand," he said with a tone of warning in his voice.

"Oh, I understand," she replied. "I understand all too well."

Harlan ran his fingers through his hair. He looked at Mary Kate's tear-stained cheeks and the tears glistening in her bright green eyes, and his anger began to fade away. She put her hand to her mouth to muffle a cough, and her shoulders quivered. She looked so vulnerable and fragile. He opened up his arms to her. "Come here."

For a second, she almost did go to him. It would've been so easy to pretend. She had lied to herself over and over—had even convinced herself that anything would be enough. She straightened her shoulders and lifted her chin as she looked him squarely in the eyes.

"You don't love me," she said hoarsely. "You pity me. I can't live my life on pity, and I'll not play second fiddle to anybody."

"What are you saying?"

"I'm saying that I'm leaving you. I'm leaving you, and I'm leaving the South. I'm gonna go someplace where people say what they mean and mean what they say."

"That's ridiculous! Where would you go?"

She shrugged. "I'm not sure, but I'll figure it out when I get there."

He couldn't believe what he was hearing. "So this is it? You're just gonna leave when you don't even know where you're going?"

She smiled remorsefully. "Something like that."

Harlan sought for the right words. Mary Kate was right. He didn't love her, not the way she loved him. He cared just as much about her now as he ever had. But for Harlan, there would always be Shelby, and she needed him now. He had to get to her.

"I never meant to hurt you," he said.

"I know."

"I have to go," he finally said.

Her eyes met his. She held his gaze for a moment, and then she looked away.

"Don't worry about me, darling," he heard her say dramatically as he headed out the door. "I always land on my feet."

*   *   *   *   *

Harlan knocked once on the door and then went inside where he found Shelby lying on the couch with her eyes closed. He stopped in his tracks, feeling a mixture of compassion and anger, when he saw the state she was in. He moved to her side and gently brushed her cheek.

Shelby opened her eyes. "Thanks for coming," she said simply.

"What happened?" he said as he turned her head from side to side and looked at the bruise on her face. There were still blades of grass intertwined with the strands of her dark curls.

"It's my fault," she stammered. "I was angry with Rayford and made the horses go too fast."

"Shelby, I don't know what the fight was about this time, but it's high time you stopped trying to take the blame for everything." His voice became gentle. "Where else are you hurt?"

"I was afraid that I had broken my ankle, but Mr. Walker said it was just sprained."

Harlan carefully examined her ankle. "He right; it's not broken," he said as he placed a pillow under her ankle, all the while feeling the rage rising in his throat.

"Tell me what happened," he demanded.

Fear overwhelmed her as she attempted to articulate a response. What did Harlan know?

He seemed to read her thoughts. "It was another woman."

Her face confirmed the answer.

"Where is he, Shelby?"

"This is not your fight, Harlan. This is between Rayford and me."

"Are you blind? Have you really forgotten how I feel about you?"

Shelby laid her head back on the pillow, too exhausted to argue.

Harlan stood.

"Where are you going?"

"I'm going to do something I should have done a long time ago."

"What are you talking about?" she asked, her voice edged with fear.

"I'm going to take care of this once and for all."

She looked pleadingly at Harlan. "Please don't go."

"I have to."

Chapter Thirty-Four

Harlan eased closer. He had seen Rayford's truck at the church and had intended to confront him head on, then something—maybe instinct—made him leave his wagon down the road and he had walked until he heard voices. Shadows lurked like phantoms in the pale moonlight. Every movement, every sound sent Harlan's heart pounding. He leaned deeper into the bushes.

*   *   *   *   *

It was getting late, and Rayford had lost track of time. The church and grounds were empty. He had hoped that his engine might start when it cooled down, but no such luck. It just didn't make any sense; he had never had a minute's worth of trouble with his truck. He got out and slammed the door shut. A bead of perspiration trickled down his face. The humidity covered him like a wet blanket. He could hear katydids and an owl hooting in the distance. He chuckled humorlessly. A perfect ending to a perfect day. There was nothing like taking a late-night stroll with the rattlesnakes. He wrinkled his nose in disgust as he caught a whiff of old man Todd's hog pen.

He had gotten a couple of steps away from his truck when a noise caused him to turn. "That's strange," he uttered under his breath. "Who's there?"

He did not recognize the two figures until they stood directly in front of him.

Rayford laughed nervously. "Sheriff! Bird. Boy, am I glad to see ya'll," he began.

Silence.

"Something's wrong with my truck," Rayford offered. "It won't start."

He waited for the men to speak.

"What are ya'll doin' out here? Rayford asked, his uneasiness intensifying.

The cloud that had been covering the moon shifted, and a ray of moonlight shone down. A jolt of fear shot through Rayford when the moonlight reflected on Sheriff Wendell's pistol. When Rayford looked at the murderous expression on the older man's face, the full scale of his predicament hit him full force.

"You're not such a big shot now, are you?" the sheriff snarled.

"I don't know what you're talking about," lied Rayford.

"You know how I feel about her. I told you." The words were spoken softly, maliciously.

Rayford realized the futility of lying about himself and Flora. He had to somehow convince Wendell that it was her fault and not his.

"Let's calm down and talk about this," he said, using his most persuasive tone. "Now you know how Flora is, how she's always flauntin' around. She wouldn't leave me alone. If it hadn't been me, it would have been somebody else."

The sheriff's face contorted in fury. "I trusted you. I took you in like a brother, and you betrayed me like you've done everybody." The words hung in the air.

The sheriff handed his pistol to Bird. "Shoot 'im."

"You know you'll never get away with this," Rayford stated with more confidence than he felt. "What do you think Bobby Ray'll do when he finds out?"

The sheriff smiled slyly. "I don't think that'll be a problem." He shook his head. "Bobby Ray was real disappointed when he found out you'd been on the take."

Rayford's eyes narrowed. "I'm gonna put a stop to this right now. You just wait until I tell Bobby Ray what really happened."

"Go ahead, Bird," the sheriff barked. "Shoot 'im!"

Bird had been unusually quiet up until now. He took the gun from Wendell and aimed it at Rayford.

"Now, Bird," Rayford coaxed, "you know you don't wanna do this."

"Yes, I do!" he cried as his hand began to tremble.

"Do it now!" ordered the sheriff. "You have more reason to kill 'im than anybody. Think about what he did to your pa."

"What are you talkin' about?" demanded Rayford.

Instead of answering the Sheriff, Bird's hand began to shake uncontrollably and he began sobbing.

"Think about what he did that night at the Bucket. You told me yourself about the poker game. How he cheated your pa out of his farm. He didn't show him any mercy, did he?" taunted Wendell.

Rayford's eyes widened in disbelief and then filled with recognition as he remembered that cold, winter evening. The old man's redheaded son had come into the Bucket. He'd tried to get the old man to go home. "You're the boy who came in that night," he whispered hoarsely. He backed away in an attempt to run.

Wendell reached for the gun. "Give me that, you yella belly. I'll do it myself."

A gunshot pierced through the still evening, and Bird watched, mesmerized, as Rayford's surprised expression turned to terror when a bullet tore through his right side, knocking him to the ground.

Bird dropped to his knees and covered his face. "It was an accident," he whined in between sobs. "You jerked my arm, and I pulled the trigger by mistake."

The sheriff wrenched the pistol from Bird's hands and aimed it at Rayford.

"Please," Rayford begged, holding his hands over his side as the blood soaked his shirt, "you've already killed me. Please don't shoot me anymore."

Another shot sounded in the air. This time it was aimed at Rayford's heart.

In his dying moments, Rayford did something he should have been doing for years—he thought of Shelby.

* * * * *

"Let's get out of here," the sheriff demanded, tugging on Bird's sleeve in an attempt to heave him up. Bird was still sobbing.

Suddenly the sheriff stopped and strained his ears. "Shut up," he hissed. "What was that?"

Bird grew silent as he, too, strained to hear.

"Somebody's out there."

Panic overcame Bird, and he started laughing and crying hysterically. "Somebody's seen us! Somebody knows what we did!"

"Shut up."

*   *   *   *   *

Harlan's knees grew weak, and he fought the urge to wretch. He took a step backwards and cracked a twig. He looked through the bushes and realized with a sudden jolt that they were coming straight for him. He turned and broke into a dead sprint toward the cornfield.

"There he is," he heard one of them yell.

He felt a bullet whiz by his ear. If he could get to the cornfield, he just might make it. His heart was pounding wildly in his ears, and he heard two other shots as he reached the field. The husks were up to his chest as he madly threshed his way through the rows. They were gaining on him.

At the same time he heard the shot, a hot poker seared through Harlan and he fell headlong between the stalks of corn.

"We got 'im!" yelled Bird gleefully. "We got 'im!"

*   *   *   *   *

When John, Ellen, and Aaron arrived at Shelby's, they found her lying on the couch, her face pale.

"Mama, Mama," Aaron cried, throwing his arms around her neck. "Are you hurt?"

"I'm fine honey," she reassured him, hugging him tightly.

"What on earth happened to you?" cried Ellen as her hands flew to her mouth.

"The axle broke on the wagon, and I got thrown out," Shelby replied.

"How did you get home?" John asked.

Shelby explained how Hugh Walker had found her, leaving out the fight with Rayford and her conversation with Harlan.

"The first thing we need to do is to get you cleaned up and into some different clothes," Ellen said.

John stopped suddenly and looked around. "Is Rayford here?" asked John.

"No," Shelby answered.

"I heard a noise outside," John replied as he arose.

"Mama, it must be Papa," cried Aaron as he rushed in front of John and flung open the door.

The only sound heard in the still night was Shelby's scream as Harlan fell on the floor, his shirt covered with blood.

* * * * *

It seemed like an eternity to Shelby as she waited. Ellen had put Aaron to bed in Shelby's room, and John had taken Harlan into Aaron's room to care for him.

She looked up anxiously as John entered the living room.

"He's going to be fine," he replied as he dried his hands. "Luckily the bullet just grazed his shoulder." He shook his head in admiration. "He has lost a lot of blood, but he's a fighter."

She sighed in relief. Shelby looked back and forth between John and her mama. "What happened to him?" she asked, her voice cracking with emotion. She could tell by the look that passed between them that something was terribly wrong.

John sat down beside her and took her hand. "It's about Rayford," he began as he watched her dark eyes fill with fear.

Shelby waited, praying silently that her worst fear would not be confirmed. Yet, somehow she knew before he even spoke the words.

"Rayford was murdered tonight."

Moisture filled her eyes. "Was Harlan involved?" she barely managed to whisper.

"No," replied John. "They tried to kill him too, but he got away."

Another noise sounded outside the door, and they looked toward it expectantly. This time, they knew the news would be about Rayford.

"Well?" Bobby Ray demanded.

Sheriff Wendell stared at Bobby Ray's back as he watched the smoke from his cigar rise and swirl to the ceiling.

He cleared his throat. "It's done. Rayford's dead."

"Good," came the reply.

Wendell stood, fidgeting, watching Bobby Ray's back, trying to build up the nerve to tell him the rest. He swallowed hard. "We have a little problem."

Bobby Ray turned to face him. He studied Wendell's nervous expression. "W-where's Bird?

"He's in the truck," Wendell answered quickly. "He went crazy on me."

Color crept up Bobby Ray's face, starting at his neck until it filled his puffy face. Wendell had the uncanny impression that he was a giant turnip, ready to explode.

"What h-happened?" Bobby Ray asked.

"Someone saw us, and he freaked out."

Bobby Ray's beady eyes narrowed. "Who?"

Wendell's palms grew sweaty. "I dunno. After we shot Rayford, we heard a noise and then saw a man run. We went after 'im and shot 'im." He watched for a reaction, but Bobby Ray's face remained unreadable.

"D-Did you find the b-body?"

"No, it was too dark, and we were in the cornfield. And people starting coming when they heard the gunshots."

As Bobby Ray took a long draw on his cigar, he seemed to be absorbing all of the redness as his face returned to its normal color. He stubbed out his cigar and folded his meaty arms. "Do y-you think B-Bird'll keep his mouth s-shut?"

"I can control Bird," Wendell answered with conviction.

"Y-y'all sure made a m-mess of things," said Bobby Ray, shaking his head in disgust.

The sheriff looked down and stared at a spot on the floor, feeling foolish. What're we gonna do?" he asked, realizing that the rest of his life hinged on Bobby Ray's decision.

"I'll t-tell you what y-you're gonna do."

Wendell looked up for his instructions.

"Y-you and Bird are g-gonna march down to t-the Guntersville c-courthouse and t-turn yourselves over t-to Sheriff M-M-Martin."

Wendell's knees buckled, and a cold fear seized him. "What do you mean turn ourselves in?" he asked incredulously.

"D-do you have the p-pistol?"

Wendell nodded.

"T-take it with you and plead s-self-defense."

*   *   *   *   *

Judge White shifted uncomfortably in his chair, his plump stomach folding over the waistband of his pants. They don't make chairs as big as they used to, he thought. He shifted again, trying to find a comfortable spot. The judge looked up as Bobby Ray walked through the door. He then did something he seldom did when visitors entered the room.

He stood.

"What can I do for you Bobby Ray?"

"I see you've been going o-over t-the charges filed against Sheriff Myers and Bird Ragland," Bobby Ray said as he motioned toward the document on the judge's desk.

A few minutes later Bobby Ray left. The judge leaned back in his chair and peered over his spectacles as he studied the document in front of him. "Yesiree," he said under his breath. "This is clearly a case of self-defense."

Chapter Thirty-Five

"Has everyone left?"

"Yes," answered Ellen.

Shelby sighed in relief. "If you don't mind keeping an eye on Aaron, I think I'll go and lie down for a while."

Shelby's feet trudged heavily on the wooden floor as she made her way to her room. The past week had taken its toll; her nerves were raw. Aaron had stayed with her mother while Rayford's body lay in a casket on huge blocks of ice in the parlor for three, long days. The parade of family and so-called friends had been endless. She would've avoided even going into the parlor, or having his body in the house for that matter, but she knew how that would look to the family and neighbors. So she'd complied with tradition.

Even though she was exhausted, she didn't lie down, but sat down in a chair instead. Bits of whispered conversations and rumors she had heard concerning Rayford's death were still bouncing around in her mind.

The funeral had been short, and then they'd all walked the few short steps to the cemetery beside the church where they'd held a short graveside service. Afterwards, the funeral party moved to her house to eat dinner. In spite of Ellen's urging, Shelby had insisted on serving food to all of the guests. She had to do something to keep her mind off what had happened.

She stared unseeingly out the window. She barely heard her mother enter the room.

"Are you okay?" Ellen asked, concern filling her voice.

Shelby didn't answer at first. "During the funeral, I tried to feel something…anything. But I couldn't." She shook her head and looked at Ellen. Her voice trailed off as her mind drifted back to that morning so long ago when she had gone to the inn to try to find Harlan and tell him how she felt. The guilt that surfaced was so tangible that she could almost taste it.

"I just can't help but think," Shelby began again, "how different things might have been if I had loved him more."

Ellen came over and stood beside her. She shook her head in reproof, the corners of her mouth turned downwards. "Don't say that." she said sternly. "Don't even think such a thing. I don't know how you stood it as long as you did."

Shelby looked up, the vehemence in her mother's voice taking her by surprise. "Were it not for Aaron," Shelby said, "I couldn't have stood it. He loved Aaron."

"All these years I have kept my mouth shut," Ellen continued, "watching you give your heart and soul to a man who trampled all over you. You've tried every possible way to keep your marriage intact, always putting Rayford and Aaron before yourself. Well, I won't sit by quietly anymore, and I'll not have you blaming yourself for his death. You know as well as I do that he had it coming to him. If those men hadn't killed him, someone else would've."

Shelby sat stunned as the words pelted her like needles. If only Mama knew the half of it. An image of Rayford with Flora and her pursed, red lips flashed through her mind. Thankfully, her mama didn't know about that or the bills she'd just received from Albertville for the perfume Rayford had bought for Flora and no telling who else. She nodded. "You're probably right," she whispered.

But Ellen wasn't finished. She had held back too long, and now the dam had broken. "You once told me a long time ago that Rayford was throwing you a lifeline and that you were taking it."

The words were like salt on an open wound. Shelby winced. "I remember."

"The Lord is giving you a ray of sunshine, and I think you should take it. Now, I'm not saying that I'm glad about what happened to Rayford," she interjected quickly. "I'm just saying that you deserve to be happy." She paused as she looked at her daughter and noticed a tear trickling down her cheek.

"What are we going to do about those men?"

"John, Harlan, and I have already discussed this, and we agree that Harlan needs to keep quiet about what he saw. I won't have your life or his ruined over this."

"But what about justice?"

"Those men are the law around here. This is one time that we will have to leave justice to the Lord."

"What about Rayford's family? Mama, you know how mean and vengeful they are. You heard the things they were saying today about Rayford's death. They don't believe he was killed in self defense. They won't leave it alone."

"Oh, I wouldn't worry too much about that. It's mostly just talk. That will pass."

Ellen waited for Shelby to answer. When she didn't, Ellen pulled up a chair beside her. Shelby reached and clasped her mama's hand, and they both sat in silence, watching the last rays of sunlight fade across the sky and disappear into the evening.

* * * * *

"Howdy, Miss Shelby. Looks like there's gonna be a big turnout tonight."

"I believe you're right," Shelby answered, smiling warmly at Mr. Jenkins as she took her seat on the church pew.

"I was real sorry to hear about your husband."

"Thank you," she answered sincerely.

Although there were many familiar faces present, Mr. Jenkins had been the only one brave enough to speak to her. Everyone else looked at her with pity or with surprise that she would come to a farm meeting so soon after her husband's death.

The meeting wasn't due to start for at least another fifteen minutes or so, and all of the seats were nearly filled. She looked back toward the door. Farmers were still coming in. In a few more minutes, there would be standing room only. There had to be at least ninety people here already. They must've come from all over the county.

She craned her neck to get a better view of the front, and saw Harlan. She then caught sight of the Reverend and Mildred Tucker. She shook her head and wondered why they came. Everyone, it seemed, was interested in hearing about the New Deal.

She looked over at Mr. Jenkins. How would a reduction in cotton production affect his gin? The loud pounding of a wooden mallet interrupted her thoughts. She looked up at the pulpit and saw a man she didn't recognize standing behind it.

"Ladies and gentlemen," he began.

The roar of the crowd lowered a notch.

He pounded on the pulpit again. "May I have your attention?"

This time the room became silent as everyone directed their attention to the man.

"I want to welcome everyone out to tonight's meeting. My name is Callis Henderson, and I've come all the way from Montgomery to speak to you about the New Deal President Roosevelt is offering farmers."

This sent a few groans of protest rippling through the crowd.

The man held up his hands. "Ladies and gentlemen, if you will please listen to what I have to say..."

This calmed the crowd a little, but the tension in the air remained.

"As you know, the prices of cotton are lower this year than they've ever been, and unless we make some changes, there's no end in sight." He had everyone's attention now. He stopped speaking and looked out over the grim faces. Some were nodding their heads in agreement. He continued, his voice growing louder. "There's simply too much cotton, folks."

A somber mood settled over the farmers.

The speaker gripped the pulpit. "What I'm about to propose may seem unreasonable, but it will work. I can assure you of that." He leaned forward and peered over his captive audience. "Now is the time for the farmers to work together—to unite in a common purpose. Cotton prices are falling because there's too much of it. We're growing ourselves right out of business. We've got to plow some of it under."

There was a collective gasp from the crowd, followed by a deafening roar of protest as the farmers talked angrily among themselves. One man stood up and raised his fist.

"Is this your New Deal? Do you mean to tell me that I drove thirty miles to hear some city slicker get up and tell me to plow down my cotton? Who'd you say you're representin'? I thought Roosevelt was in office. This sounds like another Hoover speech to me." He jutted out his chest in an attempt to portray the former U. S. President. "Next, you'll be telling us that 'prosperity is just around the corner.'"

This brought some jeering whistles and mocking laughter.

Another man rose to his feet. "I've got the best crop this year that I've ever had, and I'm not about to plow it under."

Shelby saw a man leave his seat and walk up to the pulpit. It was Hugh Walker.

"Sit down!" he commanded in a thunderous voice. "Let's at least hear what the man has to say."

The speaker's face was beet red as he continued to explain the new deal. "Folks, please just listen to what I have to say. The government is not expecting us to plow under our crops without any compensation. Not only will the price of cotton rise to ten cents a pound, but they're also willing to pay us for every acre we plow under."

A hush fell over the crowd. The speaker had their attention.

* * * * *

Shades of lavender, blue, and pink filled the afternoon sky. Each purple cloud seemed to be poised on a fiery base. Harlan and Shelby walked side by side through the high stalks of cotton in companionable silence. The field was white, loaded with thick puffy bolls of cotton as far as the eye could see.

The crisp air felt good as Shelby breathed it in. "Have you ever seen anything so beautiful?"

Harlan smiled down at her. "Just once," he replied.

She acknowledged his compliment with a smile and then grew somber. "I never dreamed I'd see the day when I'd be plowing under perfectly good cotton." She shook her head. "Our way of life is changing."

He sensed her sadness. "Yep, things are changing," he agreed.

She reached down and grabbed a handful of soil. Harlan could tell by the look in her eyes that she was thinking of another place and time. "My uncle Joshua believed that the soil held some magical power, that he derived his strength from the rich, fertile earth." She opened her hand and let the dirt trickle through her fingers to the ground. "I think it's just the opposite. The soil receives its strength from us. We, through hard work and sheer determination, have willed it to produce."

He stopped walking. A wave of tenderness and concern flooded over Shelby when she saw him wince as he pulled something from his pocket.

"Is your shoulder hurting?"

"I'll be all right," he answered. She gasped when she saw what he was holding in his hand. "I believe these belong to you."

Her eyes brimmed with tears. "Oh, Harlan, the pearls," she uttered, too overwhelmed to say anything else.

"Here, let me help you put them on."

She lovingly touched the pearls on her neck, their significance even more priceless to her now than they had been when she'd first received them. She linked her arm through his, and they continued walking. "You know," she finally said. "I've been thinking a lot lately about Tobias, Mother Ramsey, and all of the others we left behind. I often wonder what happened to them." .

He nodded. "I think about them too. It seems like a lifetime ago."

She took a breath, ready to tell him something she'd harbored for many years. "I came looking for you."

"What?" he asked, his eyes widening.

"When you came to Alder Springs. Before I married Rayford. That night you left, I went to the inn the next morning, looking for you, but you had already gone."

His mind went back to that fateful night and the dark feelings that had almost torn him apart. He took a deep breath and let it out slowly. She watched as a flicker of surprise, tinged with regret, flashed in his eyes.

They stood still for a moment, watching the sunlight fade, and then he spoke. "If I lost the store tomorrow..." He motioned to the field. "And if you lost all of this, we'd still be okay. Look what we've overcome." He looked directly into her eyes. "We have each other." He let the words soak in and then continued. "This is not the end. This is the beginning. Look beyond the cotton," he urged. He took her hand in his. "I can't predict the future."

She sighed. "I know. Neither of us can. But we'll face it together."

He gave her the crooked grin that still had the power to melt her heart. "We're livin' in high cotton now."

"Yes," she answered resolutely, squeezing his hand. "This is our time—our time to live."

Epilogue

As Aaron Carter walked down the streets of Albertville on that cold, February afternoon there was a spring in his step— a weightlessness known only to those possessing a clear conscience with themselves and the world around them. He nodded cordially to an acquaintance he passed, and she nodded back, her affection and admiration for him showing in her warm smile.

Everyone knew Aaron, but occasionally there was some confusion surrounding his last name. For almost as long as he could remember, Rhodes had been his mother's last name, and it was the last name of his younger brother and baby sister. There was a time when Aaron had considered changing his name to Rhodes too, but he'd kept his original name. It was the only link he had to his real father. He couldn't really remember that much about him, just bits and pieces. Harlan Rhodes had been the only father he'd ever known.

The only thing Aaron knew about his real father was that he looked just like him. His mother had never told him this, but he'd heard it from relatives on his father's side—and then there was the one picture of him that he had. He'd kept it safely tucked under his bed all through his growing up years. He'd pulled it out and looked at it from time to time, and he had wondered...

*   *   *   *   *

Icy water seeped through the holes in the old man's shoes, causing sharp needles of pain to shoot through his feet with every step. He stumbled. *It's now or never,* he vowed. The old man had watched the young man walk down the street so many times before. He watched as the man's head turned, and he caught a glimpse of his face. That face. He shuddered. It took every shred of determination he could muster to keep from shrinking back. It was the face of his dreams. It had haunted him over and over. His feeble mind grew clouded, and he tried to focus. So many times before, he'd tried and failed. But his anguish kept pushing him, urging him on. He must catch him. He must catch him today. It was peace that he needed. Even the mere thought of the word was enough to make him quicken his step.

A gust of wind cut through his flimsy coat. He was a pitiful sight as he rushed down the sidewalk behind the well-dressed young man. He pulled the worn coat around his thin, twisted frame and held it tightly. The buttons had been lost many winters ago.

Just when he thought he was catching up to the man, it seemed that the man was walking faster, as he too wrapped his topcoat tighter around him.

"Sir!" he yelled in a hoarse voice, but the words floated up, getting lost in the wind. He tried to keep up with the man, but the gap was widening. In one last, desperate attempt, he plunged forward and reached for the man's coat, his fingers grasping wildly to catch hold. The man turned just in time to see him holding out a frail hand as he slumped to the ground.

Aaron didn't recognize the old man. He bent down and helped him to his feet. "Are you all right?" he asked.

The man didn't speak at first. He was shaking uncontrollably, and Aaron wasn't sure if it was from the cold or old age.

"Let's get you inside where it's warm," he said, taking the man by the arm and motioning toward a nearby store.

"No," the man protested weakly. "I need to talk to ya, make ya understand."

Aaron assumed the poor man was delirious. He ignored the plea. "Come on," he urged. "Let's go into the store."

"No," came the sharp cry. "Rayford, I need to talk...."

Stunned, Aaron let go of the old man's arm. "What did you call me?" he asked, his face white. "Who are you?"

"Bird, Ted Ragland. Don't ya remember me?"

Aaron felt the air leave his lungs. The old man's hair was white;

that's why he didn't recognize him at first, but he knew the name. There was no telling how many times over the years he'd read the worn, newspaper clipping recounting his father's death. The sheriff and his deputy had killed Rayford in self-defense; that was the official account. But there were other stories, people walking home from the revival who'd heard the shots. Some even swore they'd heard Rayford begging the men not to shoot him again. He'd vowed as a child that he would find the men who killed his father and would one day get even with them.

"Please," the old man begged, "please forgive me."

Aaron took a step back from the old man. Over the years, his hatred of the two men had faded. He'd dismissed any ideas of revenge, had thought that he'd come to terms with the whole ordeal. But now, as the man stood in front of him, the old hurt began to surface like an open sore that wouldn't ever heal.

"You have to understand," the man continued, "it weren't my fault. It was an accident."

Aaron shook his head. There was so much he ought to say to the man, so much he'd wanted to say over the years. But the man's sudden confession took him completely off-guard. Aaron couldn't get the words to come. He wondered how long the decrepit, old man had been tormented by his demons. It gave him brief satisfaction to think that the man was waiting year after year for his body to wither up and match his cankered soul.

The old man wanted forgiveness? From him? He'd never dreamed that either the Sheriff or this man would ask such a thing. The idea seemed preposterous.

Without really knowing why, Aaron thought of his mother. Aaron may have looked just like his father, but it was his mother's thoughts and values that pulsed through his veins. Images of his mother and Harlan flashed through Aaron's mind. How he'd loved them both.

Harlan had been the only father he'd really known. His memories of Rayford and Harlan were so intertwined that he hardly knew where the first one stopped and the second began. All he had of Rayford were vague impressions. He'd missed out on knowing his real father. This man had taken something away from him that he could never get back. "How can I forgive you for taking away my father?" he finally asked.

The old man reached for him, but Aaron pulled away. He couldn't deal with this. Not right now. He turned his back on the stricken man and continued walking down the street.

The walk to his car seemed long as he trudged his feet through the half-melted snow, now brown and dirty. He rounded a corner and instinctively ducked his chin into his chest as a blast of wind cut him to the bone. He shivered. Time meshed together, and the past became the present as echoes from before reverberated around him. Even as Aaron wrestled with the question placed before him, he knew in his heart that he would ultimately forgive. He pulled his coat tighter around himself and looked up. Just for a moment the clouds parted, and a ray of sunlight broke through the dismal sky and beamed down.

Heaven, it seemed, looked down from above and smiled at the prospect.

About the Authors

Jennifer Leigh Youngblood grew up in a rural town in Alabama where "everybody knows your life story and your brother's life story, your sister's life story, and so on." Growing up in such a small, close-knit community might seem confining to some, but not to Jennifer. She is proud of her southern heritage, believing that, "The oddities that make up the southern culture give it distinction."

Jennifer's love of writing began as a young teenager when she wrote stories for her high school English teacher to critique. She has written many poems and plays for personal and family use, but *Livin' in High Cotton* will be her first published work. Jennifer would have probably taken her writing more seriously at an early age were it not for her circumstance. She and her husband, Patrick, owned a monthly newspaper entitled *The Senior Times* where she worked as the editor. She remained the editor until 1994 when her first child was born, whereupon they sold their newspaper so that she could devote her full time to raising a family. In the midst of their hectic lives, the couple remodeled several homes as well.

In spring 2000, Patrick's job took the family to Fort Worth, Texas. It was there (with no house to remodel) that Jennifer grew serious about her writing and began working on *Livin' in High Cotton*. Set in rural Alabama during the 1920s and 1930s, the book required an extensive amount of research. This particular time was a turning point in southern history. The cotton industry, the livelihood that southerners had always depended on, was failing, and cotton was no longer king. *Livin' in High Cotton* explores how southerners faced and overcame these challenges. Jennifer says, "Writing *Livin' in High Cotton* gave me the opportunity to unearth and bring to life the legends of my childhood. I wanted to break down the ignorant, dejected, 'Hee Haw' stereotypes that are so commonly depicted. These were strong people who faced their challenges with courage and dignity. I have the highest admiration for these gritty, stubborn people who toiled their life away on a strip of land in a remote area of Alabama."

Jennifer's biggest challenge is balancing her writing with family life and church responsibilities. She does not have the liberty of secluding herself to a cabin in the woods for months on end. She, like the Victorian author Jane Austen, does most of her writing in the midst of her family. Some of her greatest inspiration has come while visiting museums with her children or running them to activities. For Jennifer, writing is a lot like putting together a puzzle. At the onset of every novel, she takes a while to get to know her characters, and then she lets them have free reign. "The characters I write about become real to me," she says. Jennifer and her mother, Sandra, write as a team. Jennifer loves working with her mother. She enjoys the feedback and appreciates the wealth of experience which Sandra has. The two are currently working on their second novel which is also set in Alabama but in the present.

Jennifer is from Alabama. She is a member of The Church of Jesus Christ of Latter-day Saints and attended Brigham Young University-Hawaii where she studied English. She also served as Miss BYU-Hawaii in 1989. She now lives in the mountains of Tennessee.

Sandra Poole has worked in the administrative field for over twenty-five years. She worked her way through college while her daughters were very young and completed a four-year degree in three years. Later, she earned a Masters in Business Administration. Her experience has ranged from being an executive secretary and human resource manager for Fortune 500 companies to being an assistant to one of the vice presidents at the university where she now works. She also taught writing classes to students studying for their general education equivalency exam.

She believes that every person you meet changes you in some way and makes you a better person. She and her daughter, Jennifer, are currently working on their second novel, *The Sawmill*. The idea for this novel germinated from Sandra's work experience as a Human Resource Manager in a hardwood sawmill in the early 1980s.

Sandra's family is the center of her life. She has four children and three step-children. Together, she and her husband have ten grandchildren. Sandra's oldest son recently returned from serving a mission for the Church of Jesus Christ of Latter-day Saints in Albuquerque, New Mexico, and her youngest son is currently serving a mission in Sao Paulo, Brazil.

For Sandra, writing is a continual journey of discovery. She has so many ideas for other books running through her mind that it's hard to focus on one at a time.

Easy Order From
CHECK YOUR LEADING BOOKSTORE
OR ORDER HERE

Item	Quantity	Price

Please include $1 shipping for each order.

Colorado residents add 7% sales tax.

_____ My check or money order for $_____ is enclosed.

_____ Please charge my credit card.

N a m e _____

Organization _____

Address _____

City/State/Zip _____

Phone _____ E-mail _____

_____ MasterCard _____ Visa _____ Discover

Card # _____

Exp. Date _____

Signature _____

Please make your check payable and return to:

Mapletree Publishing Company

6233 Harvard Lane

Highlands Ranch, CO 80130

Call your credit card order to: 800-537-0414

Fax: 303-791-9028

Secure online ordering: www.mapletreepublishing.com

Easy Order From
CHECK YOUR LEADING BOOKSTORE OR ORDER HERE

Item	Quantity	Price

Please include $1 shipping for each order.
Colorado residents add 7% sales tax.

____ My check or money order for $_____ is enclosed.
____ Please charge my credit card.

Name_____

Organization_____

Address_____

City/State/Zip_____

Phone_____E-mail_____

____ MasterCard ____ Visa ____ Discover

Card #_____

Exp. Date_____

Signature_____

Please make your check payable and return to:

Mapletree Publishing Company
6233 Harvard Lane
Highlands Ranch, CO 80130

Call your credit card order to: 800-537-0414
Fax: 303-791-9028
Secure online ordering: www.mapletreepublishing.com